T0401319

# Select Praise for Michelle Gable

"Fluffy and fun, Gable's novel takes readers on a whirlwind tour of the lives of Palm Beach jet-setters."
—*Washington Post*, **Best Books of April, on *The Beautiful People***

"A delight from start to finish, a literary feast any booklover will savor!"
—**Kate Quinn, *New York Times* bestselling author, on *The Bookseller's Secret***

"*The Book of Summer* is delightful . . . [A] charming, profane, funny, and touching read."
—*Shelf Awareness*

"Gable seamlessly weaves this modern love story with history . . . [C]ompassionate and intelligent."
—*Library Journal* **(starred review) on *The Summer I Met Jack***

"Gable has crafted another page-turner . . . This is the sort of fun, escapist read that is beloved by book clubs."
—*Fort Worth Star-Telegram* **on *I'll See You in Paris***

"This glittering novel shines as brightly as its heroine. A true delight."
—**Nicola Harrison, author of *Hotel Laguna*, on *The Beautiful People***

"Humorous and smartly written. [A] charming retreat."
—*Wall Street Journal* **on *The Book of Summer***

"A cracking good story, and a tribute to the courage and ingenuity of intelligence agents whose work has remained secret for so long."
—*Shelf Awareness* **on *The Lipstick Bureau***

"Filled with crisp dialogue and populated with delightful, intriguing characters, this novel sings with wit and wisdom."

**—Fiona Davis, *New York Times* bestselling author, on *The Bookseller's Secret***

"A brilliant, gripping historical novel . . . Well researched and smartly told, this novel is a must read."

**—*Library Journal* on *The Lipstick Bureau***

# DARLING BEASTS

**Also by Michelle Gable**

*A Paris Apartment*
*I'll See You in Paris*
*The Book of Summer*
*The Summer I Met Jack*
*The Bookseller's Secret*
*The Lipstick Bureau*
*The Beautiful People*

# DARLING
# BEASTS

**A Novel**

## MICHELLE GABLE

GRAYDON
HOUSE®

Recycling programs
for this product may
not exist in your area.

ISBN-13: 978-1-525-80504-2
ISBN-13: 978-1-525-80004-7 (Hardcover)

Darling Beasts

Graydon House
22 Adelaide St. West, 41st Floor
Toronto, Ontario M5H 4E3, Canada
www.GraydonHouseBooks.com

**Printed in U.S.A.**

For Lisa Wheatley—the original (and actual) "nice sister"

# AUGUST

# Prologue

## Water Mill, New York

On a hot, sticky day at the end of a hot, sticky summer, their stepmother summoned them to the Hamptons.

They didn't really call her this—their "stepmother." She was simply Ustenya, the mildly terrifying six-foot-tall Eastern European investment banker who'd married their father five years before. Even after half a decade, she remained an enigma, a mystery for which all three Gunn siblings were still gathering clues. She didn't wear gloves while skiing, for instance, and escaped her country as a teenager, in a truck full of goats. What country, they did not know, other than her culture involved a lot of sour cream and spitting over one's shoulder for good luck. Regardless, their dad seemed happy, and Ustenya was over forty and came with her own money. It was the best-case scenario for a rich man's second wife.

On the appointed day at the appointed time, the three Gunns made their separate journeys to Water Mill, and the 12,000-square-foot house on Mecox Bay. That they still owned the Hamptons spread was something of a miracle, but maybe they were finally climbing out of the wreckage.

Talia arrived first, and fifteen minutes early, as eldest daughters and corporate labor attorneys were wont to do. She wore a navy blue logo-less baseball cap and clogs. The woman loved big, clunky shoes.

Ozzie, the youngest, came next, and with great flair. In tight gray pants and a white dress shirt unbuttoned to his navel, he leapt out of his helicopter, landing perfectly on a pair of shiny black loafers as his assistant filmed. It was another peek into the life of @DegenerateOz, rich douchebag influencer and the black sheep of a formerly storied family.

Middle child Gabby swept into the house twenty minutes late, making excuses about the drive while Talia dramatically consulted her Cartier Tank watch. It was Gabby's choice to start a "Cultural Collective" in the Hudson Valley so she couldn't complain that it took longer to get everywhere. On that day, Gabby was dressed in cargo pants and a tank top probably, though it could've been literally anything else as she wasn't one for fashion or caring how she looked. She was almost twenty-five, a fact that would be important later.

Ustenya stood in front of the massive dark gray marble fireplace in the library, looking flinty in a metallic leopard print. As their father yammered on the phone, on the other side of the black-framed French doors, the three Gunns all wondered if they were about to be hit with more bad news.

*TOP BRASS AT F.D. GUNN UNDER INVESTIGATION FOR FRAUD* read the initial headline. Uncle Doug had done the fraud, but as the CEO of a media conglomerate that'd been in the family for generations, the light shone directly on their dad, even as he claimed to be in the dark. The courts agreed, but articles detailing *THE WILLFUL IGNORANCE OF MARSTON GUNN* stung. He'd trusted his brother, same as the old ladies his brother had bilked.

Eventually, Uncle Doug pleaded down, but Dad had to cobble together cash for fines and restitution. One year ago, he was chairman and CEO of a $15 billion market cap company that owned ninety newspapers, fifty local television stations, and a wildly successful reality network. Now he was unemployed, and F.D. Gunn had been sold for parts. The private jets were gone and vacation homes, too. Adult children could no longer ask for money to purchase penthouses on the Upper East Side.

Now the Gunns sat staring at the marble fireplace in various states of concern and angst. Whatever the news, Ozzie didn't think it'd be *that* awful. Dad couldn't get any broker. Talia understood there was more than one way a person could go down in flames and she'd been racking her brain for answers, replaying every conversation over the past three months, searching for hints. Gabby smiled and hoped for the best.

"So, when ya gonna coax the big guy inside?" Ozzie asked. His sunglasses were still on. "Some of us are on a tight schedule."

Talia whipped her head in his direction. "You're not staying for dinner?"

"I've got shit to do." Ozzie never stayed for dinner, not when their stepmother was involved. You might not think a wealthy middle-aged woman would enjoy cooking, but you'd be wrong. Almost every meal began with a "salad," an unholy slop of cod, mayonnaise, vinegar, mustard, and onions, not a speck of green to be found.

"It would be nice to move this along," Talia said. "We're all on the edge of our seats."

Frustrated—by them or her husband, who really knew?—Ustenya tromped over to the windows and banged on them with both hands. Marston startled. He fumbled his phone, catching it before it hit the ground. After saying goodbye to the person on the other end, he dropped the phone into the front pocket of his shirt and swung open the door.

"Hello, all!" he said as his smile swept the room, covering everything but landing on no one. "My gorgeous family, all in one place." He sidled up beside his wife. With Ustenya in her heels, they made for an imposing couple, together topping out at six-foot-five. "I can't wait to hear what everyone's been up to this summer, but first things first. We can't waste a second." He flashed another grin. "We're already behind in the game."

"Oh, God, what game?" Ozzie looked at their dad, probably, but it was impossible to know what was going on behind the aviators. "You're not planning to do more criming?"

Marston ignored this, though they could see his ears redden. "Since my great-great-great-grandfather founded the F.D. Gunn Company in 1871," he began, "the Gunn name has stood for determination and integrity. For building something out of nothing and being great while doing good."

Talia made a face. "It has?"

"LOL." Ozzie snickered. "Get wrecked."

Gabby kept smiling pleasantly, trying to seem neutral, her signature move.

"It's been a tough time for the family," their dad continued, "but I sincerely believe that when one door closes, another one opens."

Collectively, the kids sighed. Typical Marston Gunn. Their father was a real "clean slate" kinda guy, a "glass half-full" denier of bad things. Uncle Doug embezzled money from old ladies, and Marston still viewed his brother not as a criminal but someone with "historically bad judgment." Although, notably, they were no longer speaking, so Marston had that going for him in the morals department.

"F.D. Gunn might be a relic of the past, but the Gunn family is not finished. We have an exciting opportunity ahead. A chance to build something new." He smiled again, though in a slightly pained way, like he was passing gas. "And we can do it together."

All three kids cocked their heads, curious about this "together" stuff. None of them had ever worked at F.D. Gunn. None of them wanted to, proving that maybe they were smarter than they appeared.

"A new business. Nice. I'm gonna call into this bullet point." Ozzie tossed his phone aside and leaned forward, resting both elbows on his knees. "What's the industry?" he said as his aviators slid to the end of his nose. "What kind of capital are we working with? I knew you were smart enough to hide your money from the Feds."

"I didn't hide anything from the Feds."

"Gotcha, Dad. EVERYTHING IS VERY ABOVEBOARD," Ozzie said with an exaggerated wink. He was, of course, thinking they might be under surveillance.

"This is not business-related. It's something completely different." Their father beamed, and many hearts in the room kerplunked. "I'm running for the United States Senate, and you're all going to be part of the campaign."

# Chapter One

## Gabby

Dad really knew how to kill a vibe, and the vibes weren't great to start. I'd driven four hours for this nonsense? Talk about things that could've been said in an email.

"What huge news!" I chirped, after we all sat around dumbfounded for a minute or two. Somebody had to chime in. "I think I can speak for everyone when I say we wish you all the best."

"Are you for real right now?" Ozzie said, yanking off his sunglasses. *"Politics?"*

"This is crazy," Talia agreed, and it was nice to see them on the same page for once. "You have zero experience."

"And no money!" Ozzie pointed out. "You lost ninety-nine percent of your fortune, and now you're looking to spend the leftovers on ads about some asshole's bad policies?" He made a gagging sound. "Of all the things to do with your few remaining years on earth—"

"He has more than a few years," I said, and smiled encouragingly in Dad's direction. Meanwhile, he'd backed up against the fireplace, and his face had gone pale. "Dad's in his prime. He's going to outlive us all."

*Prime* was an overstatement, but with his full head of hair and straight white teeth, Dad looked younger than most sixty-one-year-olds, not that I knew many to compare him to. But he did work out every morning at five and kept a personal physician on staff, though not for the usual reasons a rich guy might, like to procure medicinal cocaine.

"I guess you could sell out to the gun lobby or whatever," Ozzie offered. "That'd be one way to fund it."

"No one's taking money from the NRA," Talia said.

Through it all, Ustenya remained uncharacteristically silent, not an admonishment or "Ust-ism" to be heard. *Come on,* I pleaded in my brain. *Tell us we're acting like we've been drinking gas, or vaginas don't want fairy tales. Anything to make the conversation less awkward.*

"Why, Dad?" Talia pressed. "Why are you doing this?"

"You're gonna lose," Ozzie said. "You know that, right?"

"You guys . . ." I tried. Obviously, it was a wretched plan, but my siblings didn't have to be so *mean.* He wasn't the greatest dad, but he'd been through some tough times, and we didn't need the greatest because we had Diane, who sat next to me in her pearl-button sweater and prim bob. Technically, Diane was our nanny, which was an admittedly weird thing to say when the baby of the family was twenty-three, but she'd swooped in when I was nine, filling a mom-sized hole and changing our lives for the better.

"I'm a tad taken aback by this reaction," Dad said. "I thought you all might be excited about the prospect of joining the campaign."

Ozzie burst out laughing. "Come on, man. We don't know jack shit about politics. We'd just fuck it up."

"Speak for yourself," Talia said.

"You are all being extremely difficult," Ustenya chimed in at last. "Who are you to reject his request? He could win, if you put in some effort. Many geese defeat a pig."

Ozzie asked who the pig was in this scenario and Ustenya took to cursing him in her native tongue, whatever that was. It lacked a future tense, that's all we knew.

"It'd probably make more sense if we understood the thought

process," I said. It was getting heated around here and everyone needed to take a step back. "Maybe you could explain what's driving the decision?" Diane squeezed my knee as if to say, *good girl*. Or, perhaps, *nice try*.

"Oh, for fuck's sake," Ozzie grumbled.

"Gabby's right," Talia said. "Please." She swept a hand. "Explain."

Dad bit down on his lip. He took a minute to gather his words, the front pocket of his shirt repeatedly flashing blue with incoming texts. "There are many reasons," he said. "One, the opportunity to restore our name."

"By running for political office?" Ozzie balked, and fair enough.

Dad sighed. "I need to do *something* with the rest of my life. Despite your assumptions . . ." He passed Ozzie a look. "I still have a few decades left in me."

"God willing." Ustenya crossed her chest.

"The idea of starting over with some new business doesn't appeal to me at all. Busting my hump just to grow my own personal net worth? No thanks. It'll never be what it was, and do I even care?"

"Yes! You care!" Ozzie said. "We all do!"

"It's kind of admirable . . ." I said.

"I asked myself, why not completely switch gears? Do something that might change lives, on a large scale?"

"Oh, God." Ozzie threw back his head and groaned. "Not *making a difference*."

"I want the name Gunn to be associated with something good. And I want to achieve this with my children."

"Okay . . ." Talia said, pulling her ponytail over her left shoulder. "If restoring the family name is your goal, is this the best way to do it? There's a ton of risk involved, and I can't recall a single documented case of someone *improving* their social capital after running for office."

Dad chuckled nervously. "Geez, folks. If I were paranoid, I'd worry you don't see me as a good candidate."

"You'd make a great candidate," I jumped in, scratching my arm, which was suddenly very itchy. Could this be . . . ? I shook my head, pushing away the thought. "But I think the hesitation you're sensing is about us working on the campaign?"

"No actually, it's the candidate part," Ozzie said.

"F.D. Gunn was supposed to be a family affair," Dad said, "but by the time it got to my generation, it was only me and Uncle Doug. Is the concept of a family business so outlandish?"

It was outlandish, especially since he'd never asked any of us to work at FDG. None of us ever wanted to, but that was neither here nor there. "It's a generous offer," I said, "but we already have jobs?"

Ustenya snorted, because she and also likely Dad believed only Talia qualified. In their minds, neither running an experimental theater company (me) nor influencing (@DegenerateOz) was a legitimate form of work, even though Ozzie probably made three to four times what Talia and I did combined.

"Bags has a point," Ozzie said. "I'm not upending my life for something that will burn out in flames by next week. Can a Republican even win in the state of New York?"

"It's not about winning per se," Ustenya said. "Also, he's not—"

"It's a little about winning . . ." Dad mumbled.

"There was the one Republican," Talia said, "who claimed to have played volleyball in college, and his mom died in 9/11? But he didn't last long."

"I'm not a Republican!" Dad said, and we gasped. *Not all billionaires*, I thought, then remembered Dad wasn't a billionaire anymore, if he ever was in the first place. "I've been voting Democrat since Mondale."

A second gasp rippled through the crowd.

"What, was Jimmy Carter a bridge too far?" Ozzie joked, and I cranked my head toward him, shocked my brother was familiar with presidential candidates from the 1900s. He wasn't exactly the brains of the family—no offense. "You're not a storm-the-capitol type, but your whole aesthetic. It's giving . . ." He swirled a hand. "Deep Reagan."

I opened my mouth. A protest. A defense of Dad. Something to take this down a notch. But before I could spit out a single word, a burning scent filled my nose and hives began to crawl up my arms. *Oh, God.* It was happening again.

Diane leaned into me. "Are you okay?" she whispered. "You look . . . unwell."

Ignoring Diane, I hopped to my feet. The timing was atrocious, but I had to leave *now*, if it wasn't already too late. Muttering excuses about not feeling well, I rushed out of the room.

"Gabby!" Talia barked. "We aren't done."

I froze in the doorway. Stay or go—these were my two very bad options. If I left, Talia might never speak to me again. If I stayed . . . God only knew. Perhaps if I stood in this spot, just outside the room, everything would be fine. I swiveled back to the group and Talia offered me an icy blue glare before returning to Dad.

"Anyway." She let out a puff of air and flicked her ponytail behind her again. "Have you weighed this from a social capital perspective? Aren't you friends with at least one sitting senator from New York?"

Talia paused to check my location. Like a good girl, I remained in the doorway, even as I grew increasingly itchy, like I'd been rubbed down with poison ivy. Also, the stench. God, I hated the smell.

"Wouldn't competing against one of your friends be deemed poor form?" Talia said.

"That's the best part." Dad threw on a grin, and my stomach turned over. *Oh.* This was going to be worse than I thought. "I'm running for the open seat in California. The Gunns are moving to the West Coast."

# Chapter Two

## Talia

*California?* The idea was so preposterous even the perennially people-pleasing Gabby couldn't pretend to be on board. She stood half in, half out of the room, unable to dredge up a single nice thing to say.

"Dad. Seriously. Why California?" Talia asked. She honestly could not believe this. "Are you allowed to pick a random state to run in?"

"For real," Ozzie said, shaking his head as he typed something into his phone. Talia hoped he wasn't posting this somewhere. *POV: your family is going insane.*

"There are several benefits to California," Dad said, extracting his phone from his front pocket. He scanned the incoming texts. "Not the least of which is the fact there's an empty seat because what's-her-name croaked."

"Jesus, Dad," Gabby said, as she inexplicably scratched around under her shirt.

"Our family has a long history in the state," Dad continued, dropping his phone back into his pocket. Meanwhile, Talia unlocked hers, curious about this woman who "croaked." *Dead senator California.* Oh. Right. Well. She'd been ninety years old. "Need I remind everyone that F.D. Gunn began in San Diego?"

He didn't need to remind anyone because the lore had been drilled into them. Shortly after the Civil War, Frederick Gunn relocated from the Midwest to San Diego for health reasons and bought the local paper. One newspaper became hundreds more, and Gunn moved the whole deal back to his home state of Ohio to get the rest of the family involved. The next two generations added radio, local television, and cable assets, and by the 1980s, F.D. Gunn had morphed into a New York–based media empire. Their dad assumed the helm in 1990, at the age of twenty-eight.

"I don't think you can call something a long history," Ozzie pointed out, "when it involved one dude briefly living in San Diego a hundred and fifty years ago to clear up his gouty arthritis or whatever."

"His wife gave birth to children there!"

"Good for her, I guess."

Dad slumped his shoulders. Sighing, Talia heaved her tote onto her lap and scrabbled around for a pen. Somebody needed to take notes and bring a speck of logic to the conversation, and Talia considered herself the one for the job. She was a note-taker, a researcher, a liner-up of facts. She debated, she stewed, she checked Reddit forums and sketchy Google search links, all of which would make her feel better until she felt worse.

"Do you appreciate how ubiquitous our name is in Southern California?" Dad said. "Our philanthropic efforts are *vast*."

"Okay, calm down," Ozzie said.

"Dad's right," Talia said, placing her tote back onto the floor. She'd been to San Diego more than any of them and was familiar with the hospitals and museums and marine biological institute. Now that Talia thought about it, their name *did* still mean something in California. Maybe this scheme wasn't so harebrained, after all.

"California sounds great!" Diane chimed in. "The beaches, the weather. I hear they don't really have bugs."

Talia let out a small huff. What was Diane even doing there? Well, technically, she'd driven Talia from the city, but, like, what was the existential reason? Diane was a nanny, and the "kids" were now legal adults. Shouldn't everyone move on with their lives?

"Let's talk logistics," Talia said, tapping her pen. "If you proceed with the campaign—" She wrote *CALIFORNIA?* at the top of page one.

"Oh, we're proceeding," Ustenya said, though sounded kind of pissed about it.

"What roles would you see us in?" Talia asked.

It was weird. He'd never pressured any of them to join FDG and maybe she should take his request to work together now as a compliment. Then again, he also wanted Gabby and Ozzie. Don't get her wrong. Talia loved her siblings, but what did they bring to the table? Neither had a college degree, and while Ozzie was a good guy deep down, he was also clueless and could come across as an ass. Plus, his teenage years were spotty, a possible liability for someone running for office. As for Gabby, she was *the nicest person in the world* according to everyone, but her professional experience involved owning an experimental theater. It was a real Island of Misfit Toys out there.

On the other hand, Ozzie was quite deft at social media, and one might describe Gabby as a "community builder," and suddenly Talia wondered what was so useful about *her*. A law degree could be helpful, but only sometimes, and in very specific ways.

"Your roles are something my campaign manager will work out," Dad said. "Rest assured, he's seen your CVs."

"The fuck?" Ozzie said, pulling his chin into his neck. "I've never had a damned CV."

"What city will you run the campaign from?" Talia asked. She wrote and underlined *Los Angeles?* It wouldn't be her first pick. LA was too spread out, too charmless and trafficky. San Francisco probably made the most sense—close to Silicon Valley and all that—but it seemed like the city was going through it right now.

"We'll be based out of San Diego, obviously."

Talia's head jerked up. "San Diego?" she repeated, her heart in her throat. "*Where* in San Diego?" There was only one answer, an impossible answer, yet he was about to say it. Talia braced for the words.

"The Ranch," Dad said, exactly as she expected and feared he would.

Talia felt suddenly dizzy and ungrounded, like she was about to float off into space. The Ranch was where her mother had lived after her parents separated, and the place she'd died.

Didn't Dad remember what he'd said after the small, private memorial service they'd held beside the lake? *Let's take comfort in the fact your mother loved this property, and it sustained her as long as it could. Now that Daphne's gone, it's time to board up the Ranch for the season.* Because there were no seasons in San Diego, Talia took this as a metaphor about closing the book on the wild, colorful season of Daphne Carter Gunn, and thus their family's association with the Ranch. No one had mentioned it in the eleven years since.

"But . . . Dad . . . why? How?" Talia stammered. "I thought you sold it."

Dad first screwed up his face, then laughed. He laughed! Talia burned with rage. "The Ranch has been in the family for a hundred and fifty years. I'd never sell it. And good thing, too. It'll make perfect campaign headquarters."

Talia would never, not in a million years, consider the Ranch *his* home. He saw it as an asset, something handed down, part of a portfolio like a stock certificate or his great-grandfather's collection of pipes.

"But it's Mom's house," Talia said. Diane scooted closer, and Talia wiggled away. "She lived there. It was her home!"

"I let your mother stay there," Dad said, "but it's always belonged to me."

"It's a beautiful property," Ustenya mused, sounding wistful for the first time in her life. "Reminds me of the old country."

Now Talia was reeling. Dad and Ustenya had . . . *visited the Ranch?* Like, on vacation? This felt like a violation, along the lines of trespassing. "You've been actively going to the Ranch? What the actual fuck?"

"Oh, shit," Ozzie said, chortling.

Talia looked toward the doorway, hoping for backup. Surely even Gabby could drum up some outrage, but—whaddya know—she was gone. What was the point of a sister if not for times like these? Talia didn't expect them to be besties or anything, but would've loved a confidant, a partner, a pal on the inside. Someone to turn to and say, *Can you fucking believe this?* It's the reason Talia occasionally thought of herself as an only child.

Jiggling her head, Talia returned her attentions to the group. "Why do you still own it?" she asked, though this was the least of her problems with all this. "You kept seventy acres of prime real estate less than ten miles from the ocean while you were going broke?"

"Valid," Ozzie said. "But, like, good for you, man." He fist-bumped the air.

"I don't owe either of you an explanation of my property holdings," Dad grumbled, "but since you're so interested, we've taken cost-cutting measures at the Ranch." He went on to describe boarded-up buildings, the shuttered recreation pavilion, and how they watered only some lawns. "We also made a very handsome profit selling this house."

Ozzie leapt to his feet. "WHAT?" he yelped. "*This* house? The one we are currently sitting in?"

"And we're going to Airbnb the apartment," Ustenya added cheerfully.

Ozzie's face flamed. "Let me get this straight," he said. "You got rid of the sickest crib in Water Mill, and now you're turning an Upper East Side penthouse into a short-term *vacation rental?* You've got to be shitting me." Ozzie slipped on his sunglasses. "Good Lord. I'm a celebrity. Get me out of here. Best wishes on your little campaign, but I gots to go." He peered over his sunglasses at Diane. "Tell Ballsack to get the heli ready."

Diane tucked her neat brown bob behind her ears, frowning as Ozzie explained that Ballsack was his assistant. "How nice," she said, smoothing her hair again. "But I'm not your assistant, or Ballsack's for that matter. Therefore, the answer is no."

"We're spicy today. I see you," Ozzie said, pointing two fingers first at his eyes and then Diane's. "Goodbye, everyone." After adjusting his comically large gold watch, Ozzie pivoted on a heel and marched off, waving overhead as he went.

"And then there was one," Dad said, and Talia truly thought she might throw up. "Listen." He put his hands together in a kind of suction-y clap. "We've thrown a lot at you, but it all boils down to one thing. I want you with me, on this campaign. Can you find it in your heart to help your old dad? I know that together we can do something great."

# Chapter Three

## Ozzie

Ozzie felt lost. Not, like, literally. The helicopter was going in the right direction. But mentally he was messed up and feeling sorry for his dad in a way he hadn't before. It was crazy that it'd taken Ozzie this long to understand the gravity of the situation. Running for office, selling the Hamptons house, Airbnbing the apartment. The man was falling apart. *Poor bastard*, he thought, shaking his head.

"Ballsack," Ozzie shouted over the whirr of the helicopter blades. "Dad's selling Water Mill, and your boy can't be caught lacking. We need a place in the Hamptons. Where should we look?"

Ballsack donned his pondering face. "It's a pretty big area. Are you thinking Southampton or East Hampton?"

"I don't know! That's why I'm asking!" Ozzie took a breath. "Sorry. Didn't mean to yell. It's been a long night."

"We chill," Ballsack said.

"Thanks, bro." He pounded his chest. "I appreciate you."

Times like these, Ozzie wished he could remember the kid's name. Ballsack was a friend of a friend who'd needed a job and to be paid in cash "for security reasons." Ozzie never learned his real name, or maybe he forgot. Either way, after three months, it was too late to ask, and Ozzie felt pretty shitty about the whole thing. Like, maybe focus for a minute or two, you absolute douche.

"I don't care where in the Hamptons," Ozzie said. "Something up-and-coming would be fire. A pre-hip location, if you will."

"Um. Okay. I'm not sure there are any pre-hip areas in the Hamptons, but I'll look into it?"

"Sick."

Ozzie picked up his phone. The auction for the art piece *The Bestiary of Chaos* would be over before they landed. He was edging out the other bidder but now harbored second thoughts. However badly he wanted it, the price currently sat at $1.3 mil, and that'd fund some nice upgrades to his future Hamptons spread.

Two minutes left.

Ozzie peered out the window. It was dusk, the city lights just beginning to flicker below. The buildings had a glowy, orangish cast, and it somehow *looked* every bit as muggy and hot as it was.

One minute left.

He was going to win this auction, and the realization made Ozzie start to sweat. *It's an important piece*, he assured himself. At the end of the day, how much was $1.3—Ozzie checked his phone again—$1.345 million? His collection was undefeated, and to go undefeated, you had to take risks.

Unlike his dad, he wasn't *broke*. Granted, his bank balance was on the low side these days, but no worries. Thanks to Gramps Gunn (RIP), Ozzie received the mildly embarrassing (for a trust fund) but not insubstantial $50K per month, and his collab game was strong. He was the king of brand deals. Or, he had been. He needed to get back on the grind.

Ozzie already felt better, and he wasn't even factoring in the definitely probably seven-figure payday he'd receive in a year and a half when he turned twenty-five, also courtesy of Gramps. The plus-twenty-five Gunn progeny weren't permitted to reveal the amount, though Talia had called it "not insignificant," while their cousin Tug described it as "fine," and Ozzie guessed this pointed to somewhere between \$1 and \$5 million. Luckily, Gabby's birthday was December 1, and she'd spill, no problem.

Anyway. His bid was in, and Ozzie could work out the math later. Or not. That's what business managers were for, and he should find one, at some point. Aside from the fact he was about to be minus one Hamptons pad, nothing had really changed for Ozzie since F.D. Gunn went down. He wouldn't get a massive windfall when Pops became one with the earth, but how much did a person need? Ozzie was against billionaires, as a rule.

Suddenly, his and Ballsack's phones dinged in unison. Dread washed over Ozzie, which was not a great sign.

"Hey! You won *Bestiary*," Ballsack said, waving his phone.

"Yep," Ozzie answered between gritted teeth. "Pretty cool stuff."

"I like the juxtaposition of the piece," he said, trying his best. "How, on the surface, it represents the containment of danger, yet the danger can spread infinitely."

"Period," Ozzie said.

If worse came to worst, he'd sell it. Or other pieces of art. His collection was sick as hell.

As they approached the heliport, Ozzie began to relax. @DegenerateOz was a brand, and *Bestiary* fit right in. He thought of the other people in his family, who were out here running for office and starting experimental theaters and working in office buildings for the love of Christ. It was nice to be the only one who had it all figured out.

# Chapter Four

## Gabby

I drove the one hundred eighty miles home, hunched over the steering wheel, my skin itching the whole way. Ozzie once offered to let me borrow his helicopter—anytime—and I'd laughed. If only I'd had the tiniest bit of imagination, because a helicopter would have been pretty useful right then.

I turned down my quiet country road. Up ahead was the entrance to my property. A twenty-four-year-old probably didn't need a thirty-acre farm on the Hudson River or indeed an 1820s farmhouse with original beamed ceilings, but I ran my entire business from the place. Also, I liked the peace and quiet.

Engine still running, I popped out of the car and slid open the gate. The sign on it read:

Welcome to the
### Spooky Hollow Cultural Collective
### OUR VISION

To draw people together so we can bear witness to
and celebrate our similarities and differences and
share in our humanity.

### OUR MISSION

To create performative art that fosters open
communication, nonhierarchical collaboration, and

community engagement. At SHCC, every voice will be heard, and every story honored.

*\*\*\*The Spooky Hollow Cultural Collective acknowledges and recognizes the Wappinger and other members of the Algonquin Federation, who lived on the east bank of the Mahikannituck (Hudson River) in peace for centuries until 1609, when Henry Hudson sailed in and laid claim to their land on behalf of the Dutch Crown.*

My best friend and business partner, Sydney, came up with most of it.

Standing in the car's headlights, I checked my arms. The rash raged on, and the noxious scent continued to fill my nose. Two years. I'd been symptom-free for two years. I really thought I'd outgrown this.

I jumped back in the car and barreled up the road toward my house. When I rolled to a stop, it took several minutes to drum up the nerve to get out. Who knew what I might find? It could be literally anything. Finally, and with a deep breath, I flung open the door and stepped onto the gravel drive.

The night was silent, the only sound the buzzing of late summer bugs. Floodlights illuminated the front of the house, the driveway, fields on both sides. I saw nothing amiss. Cautiously, I tiptoed around the house. After slipping through the side gate, I unlocked the kitchen door, tossed my mini backpack onto the counter, and began opening the cabinets, one by one.

I tackled the ground floor first, checking closets and built-in bookcases, peering behind radiators and furniture, lifting up window seats. All three bathrooms appeared free and clear, likewise the rarely used guest room. As I finished one last sweep, my phone buzzed in the back of my pants.

"Is it a flare?" Diane said, straight from the jump. "Is that why you left so suddenly? Your skin looked pretty red."

"I have all the symptoms, but nothing so far," I said, winding my way back to the living room. I flopped onto the white slip-covered couch and kicked off my Birks. "Nothing over there?"

"Nothing," Diane confirmed, and I breathed a literal sigh of relief.

"Were people mad I left?" I asked, wincing, fingers crossed. Talia was usually good for a comment or two, some salty observation muttered under her breath.

"Nobody mentioned a thing," Diane said, and I was instantly annoyed with myself for assuming they'd care either way. "That is not a personal indictment!" she added, knowing how my brain worked. "Ozzie left right after you did. Talia was very busy with her questions and lists."

I chuckled. "God love her for trying to make sense of it," I said. "Running for office. It's so bizarre. He can't really want to 'do good' or whatever."

Diane took a second to weigh this. "No, probably not. I think he just wants to create something new. He inherited FDG and lost it, and likely feels guilty, even though it's not his fault."

Was it his fault? I'd wondered more than once. He wasn't in jail, which was a pretty strong sign, and Uncle Doug had carried out his misdeeds from a company not directly linked to FDG. But Dad did own one third of Doug's so-called "special purpose vehicle" and while I couldn't imagine him intentionally breaking any laws, it was possible he'd looked the other way.

"I hope he gets something worthwhile out of it. The guy needs a win." I glanced down, startling at the sight of my pale, regular, nonrashy skin. When I inhaled, the only smell was the old, woody scent of my home. "Oh my God," I said, sitting straight up. "I think the symptoms just . . . stopped?"

"Really? Oh, Gabby, that's terrific news!" Diane said, and I could feel her smile through the phone. She sounded relieved, and why not? My problems always became her problems, too.

"I can't believe it," I said, marveling at my beautiful, beautiful arm. "Maybe I am finished with this bullshit. There are worse diseases—I get it—but it's a pain in the ass. And they say it's not deadly, but do we really know—" Something moved in my periphery and my rambling screeched to a halt.

"Gabby?" Diane said. "You still there?"

"Still here."

It moved again and I rose to my feet, eyes narrowing in on the fireplace mantel. On the mantel sat the model ship my father gave me as a housewarming gift despite the fact Gunns weren't into boats. In the ship, poking out from between two sails, was a pink beak. Attached to the beak was a fluffy white bird. I screamed and dropped the phone. My PBS had returned.

---

The symptoms began on the second day of my very first period, a few weeks shy of my fourteenth birthday. As I stood in front of the linen cabinet, pondering the definition of "flow" and checking boxes for expiration dates, my skin began to itch. Badly. An odd scent filled the room. I'd never heard of menstrual symptoms that involved rashes or the smell of burnt hair, but what the hell did I know?

After selecting a "medium flow" pad and getting it into place, I returned to my bedroom. The itching had ratcheted up and, *good Lord, that smell was legit rancid.* I opened my closet door, half expecting to encounter a small fire. What I found instead was a bald eagle, sitting atop a nest of school uniforms.

I slammed the door. "Help! Anyone!" I shouted, my voice echoing through the empty apartment. The only other sound was the rain pelting the windows.

My heart rate spiked. Was there such thing as period-induced hallucinations? Why would I hallucinate a bald eagle? I didn't even like America that much. I briefly contemplated whether Ozzie might be playing a prank, but just as quickly shot it down. My brother wouldn't *not* put a bald eagle in someone's closet, if the urge struck, but he never messed with me. We were friends. He said I was like a big brother, but better. I'd never given him a wedgie or punched him in the face. Also, I was the only person who laughed at all his dumb shit and, trust, there was a lot of it.

After collecting what remained of my wits, I peeked inside the closet again. The eagle locked his beady black eyes on mine, then sighed dramatically and rotated his head toward the wall.

I stumbled out of the room.

"Dad?" I called out hopelessly. "Dad? Are you still here?" He didn't hang around much in the morning, didn't hang around much at all, but it was earlier than usual, and maybe he hadn't left for the office yet. "DAD!" I said, my voice reverberating off the walls.

I picked up the hallway phone. Who was I going to call, exactly? What would I say? *Hello, police, I'd like to report a large bird.* The police. Harboring a bald eagle had to be some kind of felony.

As the busy signal bleated in my ear, the elevator dinged. I practically flew out of my skin. "Hello?" I warbled. "Who's there?"

"Gabby, is everything okay?" came the calm, reassuring voice of Diane. *Thank you, Jesus*, I whispered. But who needed religion when you had a Diane?

I dropped the phone and sprinted to where she stood in the entryway, shaking the rain from her umbrella. "You won't believe what happened—" Panting, I stopped. It took a beat for my brain to catch up with the scene. I'd found a bald eagle in my closet, but the present conundrum was Diane, who always, always, *always* arrived when Ozzie and I were back from school. But here she was, before eight o'clock in the a.m. Dread plopped like a stone into my stomach. "What are you doing here so early?"

Diane slid off her trench coat. "Your father had to go out of town," she said. "He asked me to stay with you guys."

I scowled. A little heads-up would've been nice, but we didn't have that kind of dad. *Just doing the best he can*, I reminded myself. Diane said that all the time. "Where'd he go?" I asked.

"California, I think?" Diane cleared her throat. "It was last-minute, and he didn't give me any details, but swore he'd call tonight—"

"First time for everything," I mumbled.

"Anyway! Lucky me!" Diane threw on a smile but missed, landing on a clenched grimace instead. "We get to have a slumber party. That will brighten this dreary, rainy week." She considered me for a minute, head cocked. "Is everything okay? You seem a bit . . . frantic. Is that a rash on your face?"

"Ummm . . ." My eyes darted toward my bedroom. "Will you do me a favor? Can you . . . look in my closet? Let me know if you see anything strange?"

Diane let out a hiccup of alarm. "Oh, God! Don't tell me it's a rat or mouse!"

I sat for a moment in my shock, bewildered that Grand Diane could be felled by something as ordinary as a rodent. There were millions of them in New York, though likely none in my closet, if the bird was still in there. "No rats," I said. "But, please, go see for yourself."

---

"What a way to start the week!" Diane kept saying, both before and after the man from the fish and wildlife department confiscated the bird. He seemed thoroughly unfazed, even as he confirmed that, no, this was not common at all. "We're lucky the warden was able to get here in this weather. The subway is flooded!"

"Oh," I said, rubbing my face. I doubted he'd take the subway with a bald eagle, but it was probably beside the point. "Well. That's solved. Can you call the attendance office and let them know I'll be late to school? I guess Ozzie won't be going." My eyes slid in the general direction of his bedroom.

"Didn't you hear?" Diane asked. "School has been canceled."

I scrunched my nose. "Because of a little rain?"

"It's more than a little rain. It's a mess out there! An absolute mess!" Hurricane Sandy was scheduled to make landfall that day, and they'd closed the stock market, which was a pretty ominous sign. If people weren't up for making money, anything was possible.

"Oh," I said again, and looked around. Two major problems in one morning—eagle, hurricane—yet it felt anticlimactic somehow. A funny thought, in hindsight.

It was hard to remember what happened next. Maybe Diane and I sat around watching *The Price Is Right*. Maybe I did some homework or maybe I put off my homework and screwed around on the computer instead. The details were hazy, but not what happened when Dad called sometime around five o'clock.

"Yes, they're here," Diane said in a very bad whisper. "Gabby's right next to me. I'll put you on speaker."

"NO!" I mouthed, frantically waving my hands, feeling betrayed. I'd expected Diane to soften the blow about the eagle, as she did with most things, and now it seemed I was supposed to break the news.

"Get your brother," she said, and I glared. We were not a "group phone call" family, and why did Ozzie need to be involved? But I did as asked, because I was that sort of kid.

As we gathered around the phone, I snuck a glimpse of Diane, who had tears bubbling in her eyes. *This isn't about any closet eagles*, I realized, my suspicions confirmed ten seconds later when Dad confessed he wasn't in California for work. He'd gone because his estranged wife—our mother—was dead.

Nobody cared about eagles after that.

# Chapter Five

## Talia

Talia had been expecting this call since last night, since the moment she'd been driven off in Diane's Volkswagen Passat.

"Hello, Ustenya," she said. "What's up? I'm on my way to work—"

Talia heard the door close, and the sound of Spencer's footsteps as he circled back. *Shit.* She didn't want him listening or chiming in with his two cents. He found the very notion of a family-run campaign nothing short of outrageous. It was another example of how Marston Gunn thought about no one but himself.

"I only have a minute," Talia said to Ustenya as Spencer materialized in front of her, backpack affixed to his shoulders. "This will need to be quick." She looked at him defiantly, proud of her rock-solid boundaries. Despite her boyfriend's views on the matter, Talia didn't always let Ustenya and Dad walk all over her.

"What is your decision?" Ustenya barked. "Tell me now."

"Wow. Okay. I highly doubt you need to know *now*," Talia said. "And I'm still ruminating. You've given us a lot to consider."

"All you must consider is that he is your father, and he asked, and you will go."

Talia glanced up and caught eyes with Spencer. He made a slicing motion across his neck. She turned and walked into the dining room.

"There are logistics involved," she said. "My job, for example. I've only been at Schaefer for a year." Crossing one arm over her waist, Talia stared out through the floor-to-ceiling casement windows, past the treetops and redbrick buildings, fixing her gaze on the wood water tank in the distance.

"Quit your job," Ustenya said. "You do this often, no?"

Talia winced. Yes, she did change jobs more than the average person, but it wasn't her fault that they never lived up to their promises. She'd gone into employment law to help people receive fair treatment in the workplace, not advise corporations on how to tastefully settle sexual harassment and EEOC claims.

"I wouldn't say I change jobs *often*. What's with the pressure, anyway?" Talia studied her reflection in the glass as she spoke, wondering when she'd developed the two lines between her brows. She relaxed her face, which somehow made her look harder, even more intense. "It's been less than twenty-four hours."

"Your father and I leave on Thursday. There is no time to waste."

Talia's breath caught. Wait. Dad was actually doing this? She was surprised by her own shock. Some part of her must've believed he was merely testing the waters, throwing a few pitches, whatever analogy meant he'd eventually return to his senses.

"Let me ask you something," Talia said, spinning around. Spencer stood in front of her, scowling, hissing at her to hang up. "Do you really think a political campaign is the best use of Dad's time and energy?"

"Not at all," Ustenya said, and Talia almost laughed at how readily she admitted it. "He does not need to rebuild his name, for example. His name is fine. Of course, I tend to take a relaxed stance on things."

"Ha!" Talia squawked.

"For me, if there is no horse, a donkey is good enough."

"Sure, sure," Talia said, trying to recall whether she'd heard this one before. Something about being thankful for what you had.

"Alas, this is very much what Marston wants. The campaign. Working with his children. So I've decided perhaps a change will be nice?"

"I understand wanting a fresh start," Talia said. "But launching a campaign feels like a lot of work? Has he considered other options?" Visiting a spa, for example, or Dubai, or trekking to see the gorillas in Rwanda. Surely he had enough money left for normal old rich people stuff, especially if he'd sold the Hamptons house.

"I'm worried about your father," Ustenya said, and the words hit Talia like a jolt to the spine. She didn't know her stepmother had access to this feeling. "Marston spent so many months on the lawsuits, and moving money from one bucket to the next. But it kept him *busy*, and focused. Without work, rest is not sweet, and now he is lost."

"I don't think he's lost?" Talia said. On second thought, he did seem unusually tired, though it probably was quite exhausting to lose a billion dollars and your life's purpose in one calendar year.

"I fear if he doesn't have something important to work on," Ustenya added, "he'll be off to see the forefathers before his time."

"Ustenya!" Talia said. "Don't talk like that!" She suspected this wasn't a literal fear, just one of those Ustenya things, but Talia already had one dead parent and wasn't looking to be a full orphan.

"It's the Ranch," Ustenya said. "That's why you're resisting, why you're acting like a cat staring at a calendar."

"What? No." Or was it yes? Maybe? Talia didn't grasp the cat expression and was dizzy from the quick turn this conversation had taken.

*"Hang up,"* Spencer said, and Talia jumped. She'd forgotten he was there.

"You're afraid of it," Ustenya said. "The Ranch."

"According to who?" Okay, Talia was a *little* afraid and wished Ustenya would cut her some slack, given what had happened there.

"It is so obvious, Talia. Why not confront these fears now? Anyway, you'll need to come out to California eventually to deal with your mom's old, cluttered barn."

"Barn?" Talia repeated, and every muscle in her body tensed. "Do you mean my mom's art studio?" Spencer dropped an f-bomb somewhere behind her.

"Whatever you want to call it. I'm weary of the dusty, rotting shrine. I've spent years promising your father I wouldn't touch it, but enough's enough. If you need anything from it, now's your chance."

Talia blinked, her thoughts all tangled up. The idea of Mom's art studio existing like a time capsule was beyond comprehension, and she tried to picture the space as it'd been—flooded with sunshine, reeking of paint, cluttered with canvases and drop cloths. Despite the return of her cancer, Mom had been so prolific her last summer. She worked morning and night, pushing past the pain. No one would have guessed she'd be gone in a few short months. Her death took everyone, even Talia, by surprise.

"Why are you suddenly doing something about it *now*?" Talia managed to ask.

"We need the space. Volunteer housing is one of our campaign's main selling points."

Talia opened her mouth, but no words came out. The Ranch had multiple freestanding apartments in addition to the six-thousand-square-foot main house. How many people were they bringing on?

"Tell us what you plan to do ASAP," Ustenya said. "This is important to your father. You don't want to regret anything, so please weigh your decision carefully."

"I always do."

"Marston is asking for your help."

"I'm thinking about it."

"And we're relying on you to convince the others. Remember, Talia. Of all the children, your dad needs you the most."

With that, the line went dead.

―――――

"You're considering it," Spencer said, his penny-colored eyes boring into her.

"I didn't say that."

"Last night you acted like the campaign was the most absurd idea in the world—"

"I was being a tad overdramatic. You know me!" Talia tried for a smile, but Spencer's face was hard as stone.

"And now you're telling Ustenya you'll think about it?"

Talia exhaled. Well, the gig was up. Yesterday she *did* think it was absurd but already her mind was changing. Talia had spent the past year in a state of mild desperation, anxious to help her dad in some small way but his problems were always too massive, too far out of reach. Maybe now was her chance to do something.

Spencer crossed his arms over his performance fleece vest. "Why would you upend your life to work on some pointless campaign?"

"Who said I'd upend my life?"

"You'd leave your job. You'd leave *me* for an indeterminate length of time. Do you even remember we're supposed to go to Italy in October?"

"We can reschedule. Why are you making this so difficult?" Talia rubbed the space between her eyes. No wonder she was developing early-onset wrinkles, what with always having to be around such difficult people. "Do I think running for office is the best plan?" she said, brushing past him as she marched toward the kitchen. "I do not. But it's been a hard year, and he needs us." She opened a cabinet and reached for a water glass, only to be confronted by stemware anarchy. Perhaps putting Spencer in charge of unloading the dishwasher didn't actually make her life easier. "Dad asked for our help, and he's never asked anything of us before. Shouldn't a family support each other?"

"Some families, yes," Spencer said, and Talia glowered.

Her boyfriend wasn't a big fan of the Gunns, specifically Marston, who he thought treated Talia like a girl he was stringing along. Talia appreciated his protectiveness, but Spencer was raised by uncomplicated parents in a large, early-aughts Northern Virginia tract home. He went on a fishing trip with his two brothers *every year* and would therefore never understand her family dynamics. Talia *did* tend to expect more from her dad—from all the Gunns—than any were willing to give, but she loved them, and people could change.

"Look, I won't insist we're super functional—"

"Ha," Spencer said with a snort.

Talia shut the cabinet. Why was a soiled dish towel, just sitting there, on the counter? "But we love each other?" she said, her tone more a question than a statement of fact. "And it's a chance for us all to come together. That's *specifically* what Dad wants. You're always saying it's weird I'm not closer with my siblings."

"They aren't going," Spencer said. "You told me yourself."

"I said I wasn't *sure*." Ozzie did come out as staunchly against the campaign, and who the hell knew what Gabby was thinking, though she'd get a free pass from all involved. Everyone loved Gabby. Thought she was so damned sweet. And while she did have heart, and empathy, and all that, being quiet and sneaky was not the same as nice. This was a girl so averse to confrontation she'd conjure actual wild animals to weasel out of it.

"I get that your dad quote-unquote 'asked for help,'" Spencer said, "which you *believe* is some kind of anomaly."

"Believe?" Talia repeated, choking on the word. "It's a fact."

"And I know you've been worried, but you can't fix him, or his problems. If Ustenya implied you could, it proves how manipulative she is."

"She's not manipulative. It just seems that way. Cultural differences."

"What'd she threaten to do to the art barn?" he asked. Talia froze. Her shoulders hiked up to her ears. "You said something about your mom's studio."

"Just wants me to clean it out or whatever. No big." She rolled the dirty dish towel into a ball and spun around.

Ustenya had said the art studio was filled with her mother's things, but *what* things? The art she'd been working on but never finished? So, yes, the barn was one reason she felt herself starting to turn, but it was also Ustenya's parting words. Your dad needs you *the most*. Talia had ignored this call before and was sure—absolutely positive—everyone secretly blamed her for the disaster that followed.

"You're going to do it," Spencer said. "I can tell. Ozzie and Gabby will wisely opt out, and you'll hightail it to California to gobble up whatever scraps Marston Gunn throws your way."

"Spencer . . ."

"You do what you want. But if you're the only one who goes . . ." He sucked in a breath. "I might not be here when you get back."

# Chapter Six

## Gabby

The baby flamingo—*flaminglet*—from the mantel multiplied overnight, and now a dozen grown flamingos frolicked in my pond. A flock was called a *flamboyance*, which might've been fun if they were in someone else's yard. But alas. My clean streak had ended. It was my nineteenth flare.

On account of Mom's unexpected death, the eagle was pretty ignorable, a secret between me and Diane. Ditto the pair of ocelot kittens curled up on my pillow six months later. But when the mongoose hit the book bag, Diane leapt into action. Over the course of two weeks, she took me to see a bizarre cast of characters, including her personal internist, a paranormal doctor, a pet psychic, and several vets. One doctor locked me in a room with a tabby cat and told me to jot down its innermost thoughts. I guessed he was hungry, but that was as far as I got.

At first, I didn't mind. It was nice to have something to focus on other than Mom. In the year following her death, Talia transferred schools and moved home. Dad grew increasingly distant and short-tempered, his demeanor not enhanced by Ozzie's new hobby of casual fire experimentation. Meanwhile, I wandered around half-dazed, worried I wasn't feeling the right things.

I was seven and a half when Mom was diagnosed with thyroid cancer, nine when she moved to the Ranch and Dad hired

Diane. Mom was supposed to be in California temporarily, to recuperate, and work on her art, but one year turned into two, and soon the arrangement became the accepted state of things. Honestly, I didn't feel too awful about it. Mom treated Talia like a best friend, but regarded Ozzie and me with a detached curiosity, as though we were somebody else's pet she'd been assigned to watch, usually while accompanied by an assistant or housecleaner or some other person who hung around for three months and disappeared.

When Mom died, I hadn't seen her in many months. It would have been many more until I'd see her again, and because of that, I wasn't as sad as I knew I should be. A dead mom was canonically Very Tragic, and I kept waiting to experience something deeper. The animals gave me a new reason to feel ashamed.

"We'll solve this," Diane vowed. "If I have to go to the ends of the earth."

Finally, after weeks of interviews and blood tests and consultations, Diane's internist called us into his office and delivered the news. I had Portum Bestiae Syndrome, a condition that resulted in the manifestation of live animals.

"Exactly what I thought!" Diane said, and this was news to me. Apparently, she'd read about it online.

"So, I'm a port for beasts?" I said, my voice trembling. "That's my disease?" The doctor explained that technically it was a syndrome not a disease because it involved a group of symptoms with no clear cause or treatment path, which I didn't find helpful at all. Mostly I wanted to know whether I was going to die.

"I guess it depends what animal shows up," the doctor said, then proceeded to briefly laugh his head off.

The prevailing theory—to the extent there was one—linked PBS to weather disturbances. A storm hit a part of the globe, and an animal from that region appeared somewhere else, alongside a PBSer. The ocelot kittens could be tied to flooding in Mexico. The mongoose arrived during India's monsoon season. But what was a "weather disturbance" in this day and age, I wondered? Wasn't some part of the planet always burning or flooding? The real question was, why was it happening to me, and how could I stop it?

"I'm sorry. I have no idea," the doctor said as he looped his Snoopy tie through his fingers. "I'd never heard of PBS until Diane brought it up. It seems the medical community hasn't quite gotten its arms around it yet." There were only about one hundred documented cases worldwide, and no known cures. It was a treat-the-symptoms kind of situation, and I'd been treating the symptoms ever since.

---

"What if I kept them?" I said to Diane, about the flamingos, over the phone.

"You are not keeping anything," she said, firmly. "That never ends well. Your good intentions always spiral out of control."

"Hey!"

"Plus, I doubt they'd survive the winter. You wouldn't want anything bad to happen to them," she said ominously. I silently fumed.

Usually Diane acted like my care for the animals was a bad trait. *You're the only person in the world who keeps worrying about a problem after it's gone*, she liked to tease, because I checked on my vanquished animals from time to time. Maybe this meant I coddled my symptoms, but they were living creatures, so what else was I supposed to do? I no longer trusted most governmental agencies, not after what happened with the Tasmanian devil, and rescue organizations were almost impossible to vet (lol).

"What's the plan?" Diane pressed. "Have you tried googling 'flamingo rescue New York'?"

"Yes, Diane," I said, sighing, rolling my eyes. Unfortunately, the only results were news stories about a flamingo found in the Hamptons and several warnings not to dye pigeons pink. When I expanded the parameters to include the entire Eastern Sea-board, the few operations I unlocked looked very fly-by-night, so to speak. Petting zoos. Crusty guys with inflatable pools in their backyards.

"I'll help you search," Diane said. "Do you know what to feed them in the meantime?"

"Flamingos eat shrimp. *Obviously*. It's why they're pink. Get it together, Diane!"

She chuckled. "Just checking. Don't want another jerboa incident."

"We can drop the jerboa thing." Jerboas—my most recent flare—subsisted on a diet of windblown seeds, which explained why Diane walked in on me standing over three tiny rodents, holding a hairdryer and bag of quinoa. She laughed until she cried. "Oh, Diane," I moaned, rubbing my face, turning away from the pond. "I'm so sick of this shit. It's been eleven years. Why hasn't science made any progress?"

"Progress *is* being made," she said. "If you bothered to visit the message boards, you'd be aware of this."

"Thanks for the tip," I grumbled. Diane understood perfectly well that I found the online PBS support group neither helpful nor supportive. Did I really need to know that one guy ported a *Gorilla gorilla gorilla*—a critically endangered subspecies of the *Gorilla gorilla*—and ended up with two broken arms? No, I did not. The man was lucky he hadn't been torn to shreds, and I saw no reason to torture myself with worst-case scenarios.

"Dr. dos Santos has some interesting research underway," Diane said. "You might consider him a charlatan, but he's the world's foremost expert on your condition."

"Why do you keep gassing him up? He's a wildlife vet-erinarian." In fairness, dos Santos specialized in fragmented

populations, and flamingos in the Hudson Valley certainly qualified, but from what I'd seen, his chief contributions were poop-
based or about obscure animal diseases. Also, he worked at a
zoo, which was not very encouraging, as a human.

"He's at the end of a five-year study out of Brazil," Diane
continued, and it dawned on me that if she'd been lurking
around the support group, I was the only one who believed
my PBS was in remission. "He's also conducting a smaller study
in the US, from his office. Funny coincidence . . ." She let out
a wobbly laugh, and I groaned inside. Diane was about to say
something awful. I could feel it. "He's the new chief conservation expert at the San Diego Zoo, and—what luck!—last night,
you were given a reason to be in town."

It took me a beat to catch on. "Dad's campaign?" I couldn't
believe my ears. "You're suggesting I move to California? And
get involved in *politics*? I'm not even registered to vote!"

"Oh, dear. I don't like that at all."

"I thought you agreed the whole plan was stupid?"

"I never said *stupid*. But maybe it's worth a shot? You could
work for your dad's campaign—it would make him *so* happy—
and be near the only PBS expert in the world."

I gasped, loudly, to drive the point home. Why would I care
about making my dad *happy*? I mean, yes, I wanted him to
thrive, live it up, et cetera, but not at the expense of my own
mental health. How could my greatest champion suggest aban-
doning my life to work on Dad's vanity project? What policies
did he even have? They couldn't be anything good.

Also, if I was symptomatic, the last place I should be was
"around family." When it came to PBS, they literally knew the
half of it. I'd shielded them as best I could, coming clean only
when it was unavoidable, like if a cop showed up at the door.
Dad and Ustenya found the condition thoroughly vexing (on
the days they deemed it legit), and Talia hated it, too. *Just stop*,
she'd said once. *Try not to think about it.*

In fairness, it *was* irritating to suddenly be faced with a screaming hairy armadillo or an infestation of capybaras, the world's largest rodent, so I held space for their aggravation. Staying out of their way was half the reason I moved out to the farm, and I wasn't looking to take my circus on the road. Not to mention, Dad wanted us to move to California right *now*, and I had a whole flamboyance to deal with.

Also, I understood something dos Santos did not. A medium-to-major disaster followed each flare, and I didn't need some vet to tell me that PBS made me a harbinger of doom. Life had been good—*normal*—these past two years, but with the arrival of the flamingos, one thing was clear. This campaign would be a disaster, and I refused to get near it.

# Chapter Seven

## Ozzie

*The Bestiary of Chaos* was glorious.

A courier brought it over late Monday afternoon, and now it sat on the entryway table as Ozzie contemplated how best to show it off to his seven million followers. Pictures? A video? Maybe Freja would pose next to it, in a bikini. Ozzie shook his head. Nah. He loved the girl but didn't trust her to handle it properly. Like lots of models, she was gangly and awkward. It was part of her charm.

His phone buzzed from . . . somewhere. Ozzie glanced around before spotting it on the recently purchased $70,000 Hermès bench. Talia's name flashed across the screen. She was downstairs. Could he let her up?

Ozzie's first thought was, *Did somebody die?* Talia wasn't the type to show up unannounced, especially not to see him. All the years gone by, and she'd never stopped thinking of him as a pesky toddler who left handprints on all her shiny things.

"Hey, girl," Ozzie said when he opened the door two minutes later. "Nice fit." He wasn't used to seeing her in, like, business slacks or whatever. His sister loved a baseball hat and clogs, always with a full beat on, inexplicably. Why spend so much time on makeup but half-ass it with clothes? It couldn't take that much extra effort to get a look off.

"They're basic black pants," Talia said, pushing past him into the apartment. "Honestly, I'm not in the mood to be heckled right now."

Ozzie twisted up his face. "Who's heckling?" he said, and Talia flipped around.

"Can I borrow a car?"

That explained it. Talia needed something. It was nice to know she found him useful every once in a while. Ozzie was happy to help. "Sure. You bet," he said. "What do you need it for? Is everything okay? You seem kinda . . . anxious."

Then again, frazzled and high-strung was Talia's general vibe. Freja called her "the hummingbird" because she flapped from one place to the next at a million miles per hour. *Probably takes speed*, Freja opined (neutral), *to keep her weight down*. Ozzie assumed she simply didn't eat.

"I'm running some errands outside the city tomorrow," she said, "and forgot to reserve a car. Figured I'd check with you on my way home from work."

"Not a problem." There was obviously more going on, not that she'd ever tell him. "Which car? Any preference?"

Talia rolled her eyes. "It doesn't matter. Something with four wheels and an engine."

"Got it, got it," Ozzie said, nodding. "I have the perfect sled in mind."

"Awesome. Thanks." Talia exhaled. Her body visibly loosened, and she stood there for a second as if debating what to do next.

"Do you want to stick around?" Ozzie said, the idea popping into his brain. It'd be fun to chill, hang out, shoot the shit, all that. "Fray and I are staying in tonight. Gonna get a pizza and rot. You down?"

Talia chuckled, and Ozzie felt himself tense. "Thanks for the offer. Rotting sounds great, but I have work to do, especially since I'm taking tomorrow morning—" Talia froze. She blinked once, slowly, and peered around him, toward the hall table. "What is *that*?"

Her eyes locked onto *The Bestiary of Chaos*, and Ozzie's heart did an excited little hop. He knew *Bestiary* would be a statement piece.

"What. On earth," she said, squinting as she stalked closer. "Did you buy another Theranos miniLab?"

"Of course not," Ozzie scoffed, wondering how anyone could mistake *Bestiary* for an inoperable blood processing unit. "The miniLab is part of a *collection*. A compendium of failed startup projects. One is perfect. Two would be unnecessary."

"Indeed," Talia said. "So, what is it? Looks like a laptop."

"A 2008 Samsung."

Talia reached for it, but Ozzie slapped her hand away.

"It's art!" he said. "No touching!"

"That piece of junk is *art*?"

"It's a laptop infected with six pieces of the most damaging malware known to man. It represents the physical manifestation of online threats that might otherwise seem abstract. It's called *The Bestiary of Chaos*. Put some respect on the name."

"How much did you pay for it?" Talia asked, and Ozzie felt sorry for his sister for being so pedestrian and not understanding culture. Gabby's plays were wacky as fuck—Ozzie couldn't fathom why anyone would pay to watch a dude silently peel an orange onstage—but at least the people at the Collective were attempting to make sense of the world.

"I didn't *pay* for it," Ozzie said. "That's so gauche. I *won* it. For one-point-three-four-five."

"As in, million *dollars*?" Talia let her mouth fall open dramatically.

"Pretty insignificant given the malware caused financial damages in excess of $95 billion. Also, it came with a power cord."

"Ozzie, you do realize things have changed. You can't—"

"Talia!" someone called out. "I thought I heard a voice."

Suddenly Freja appeared, padding across the black-and-white inlay marble flooring in a sports bra and tiny shorts. Sometimes

Ozzie couldn't believe she was his. Not that he viewed her in those terms. *His*. Give him some credit. He wasn't a misogynist.

The two women exchanged hugs.

"So you've met the latest purchase," Freja said with a quick toss of the eyes. "He swears it's a wise investment, but I have to question the sanity of bringing several viruses into a home almost entirely controlled by computers."

"It's firewalled," Ozzie said. "And you're just mad because you still haven't figured out how to flush the toilet." He gave her a squeeze, and she playfully batted him away.

"Oz told me about your dad's big plans," Freja said, hopping up onto the hallway table, crossing her legs. Ozzie eyed her for a second. She was sitting awfully close to *Bestiary* . . . "You're not doing it, are you? Moving to California? Obviously not. That would be ridiculous."

"Totally," Talia agreed, eyes darting away.

"What'd Gabby have to say about it? Oz wasn't any help." She lightly kicked his leg, and the table jiggled. "He couldn't remember her reaction!"

"I'm going to move this," Ozzie said. As he returned *Bestiary* to the Hermès bench, Talia confessed she didn't know Gabby's reaction, either, because she'd vanished mid-conversation.

Freja snorted. "Figures," she said, and Ozzie gave her a look. His girlfriend's opinion of Gabby bothered him, especially since Freja liked Talia, who was objectively the worse sister. Also, had she forgotten? Gabby was how they'd gotten together.

Freja and Gabby were roommates years ago, until Gabby started up with one of her . . . What did she call them? *Flares.* One morning there was a chicken turtle in the living room and, several months later, a grackle in the Frosted Flakes. It was a harmless little bird, but no matter. Freja moved out the next day because she "didn't fuck with wildlife."

Four years later, Ozzie ran into Freja at a house party in the Hamptons. After they worked out how they knew each other,

Ozzie invited her to dinner. To his shock (but, actually? not really), Freja declined. He was very cute and charming, but his sister was a freak.

"Clearly you don't know my sister very well," he'd said. "She's great. Everybody loves her." Gabby was far from perfect—obviously—but *come on*. "Freak" was taking it too far.

No, sorry, Freja insisted, this Port-Beast-Whatever was *weird*. Like Munchausen, but with animals, and Freja refused to let go of this take no matter how many times Ozzie swore it was a real condition. He eventually got her to agree to a date, and in the year they'd been together, he'd done a decent job of keeping these two parts of his life separate. Maybe the old Ozzie wouldn't have put up with the bashing of his sister, but she wasn't the best friend he'd grown up with.

"Okay, Tal, I'm dropping you a pin with my garage's location," Ozzie said, now eager to speed up the conversation. "I'll text the garage, tell them to pull up the car. Feel free to hang on to it as long as you need."

"Thanks . . ." Frowning, Talia looked back at the laptop. "Listen, I don't pretend to 'get' that type of art, but I hope you know what you're doing."

"Don't worry, sis," Ozzie said, pushing her toward the door. "I always do."

# Chapter Eight

## Gabby

By Tuesday, the flamingo deportation plan was in place.

A sanctuary in Miami agreed to take them—would *love* to take them—and Diane was at present checking one of the aviation companies she'd previously used to see about renting a cargo plane. It was not lost on me that we were paying to *fly birds* somewhere. PBS had a way of jacking with one's shit in unnecessarily complicated ways.

After solidifying the details with Diane, I biked over to the Collective's administrative yurt, which sat on the opposite end of the property from my house. Beyond the yurt were two performance spaces—a converted barn and a black box theater—and an amphitheater cut into a hill. There was a meadow, and a few cabins, which we rented out to performers, directors, and writers.

As I lowered my bike onto the ground, I peered through the yurt's open door to see a woman in a pinkish-maroon full-body leotard standing at Sydney's desk. There was almost always someone around completing paperwork, or discussing schedules, or very occasionally receiving a check. Often, they wanted Sydney's advice, or to complain about whoever they were beefing with that week. The feelings at SHCC ran strong.

The actress whipped around when I walked in. Beneath her

arm she held a long, curved hat topped with a white ball of fluff. It took a second to piece together that this woman was a uterus, holding her own fallopian tube. "Oh! Hi, Gabby," she said, and for the life of me I could not remember her name. *All uteruses look the same*, I joked to myself. "Anyway." She flipped back to Sydney. "Sorry for complaining but—*gah!*—it's so hard to play the role when the script never mentions how bad hormonal birth control is for women. Maybe we can hand out DIVA Cups during the performance?"

"I'll talk to Ginny about it," she said.

"I'd appreciate it!" With that, the actress bounded out of the yurt, ovary bouncing as she went.

"Perfect timing," Sydney said, tying her wavy brown hair into a knot on top of her head. "We need to nail down the fall calendar. We've never had this many performances happening at the same time." She hauled a paper calendar onto the desk. "The playback group is settled, but the climate change people need more dates." She gnawed on the unicorn horn capping the end of her pencil. "Maybe we can move the bullying folks? We also have the Plant Cabaret, but need a few weeks of downtime to repair the roof of the theater barn." Sydney glanced up, and I was glad for the break because I was already exhausted from all this *work*. "I got an estimate. It's not going to be cheap, but more economical than the lawsuits when it inevitably caves in."

"Fine. Whatever it takes," I said and sat at my official desk, though I only came to the headquarters once, maybe twice per week. The Collective didn't *need* me, because as the front of house manager, Sydney was brilliant, and organized, and, unlike some people (me), would never double-book *Sex Worker Monologues* and a children's Christmas play in the same space. She was also strict about our published facility rental rates, whereas I tended to waive any fee if the person asked nicely enough.

*If we don't try to make money, then this is just a hobby,* Sydney said more than I thought was necessary or even polite.

"Sooo . . . we didn't really have a chance to chat yesterday," I began.

"Yeah, you were dodging my texts," Sydney said, smirking as she reached for her MALE TEARS mug. "I heard your voice memo, but it was kind of crackly. Something about your dad getting a new office?"

"*Running* for office," I said. "As a Democrat. In California."

Sydney wrinkled her freckled nose. "A Democrat? I assumed—"

"Same. And he wants *us* to work for him. As in, me, Talia, and Ozzie." I checked my phone. No message yet from Diane confirming Project Flamboyance was a go. "Obviously, none of us agreed. He might be able to trick Talia into it, but it's a no for me. What the hell would I even do? I refuse to be, like, the campaign's quirky sidekick."

"For what it's worth, you *do* have management experience. You run this place."

"Sort of." We both knew Sydney ran the show, and our "employees" were basically an assemblage of our oddest but most dedicated friends. Some might have called them outcasts, but not wanting to waste your twenties working eighty hours a week on Wall Street seemed normal to me. "Plus it's going to be a catastrophe. How do I know this? One word." I paused for effect. *"Flamingos."*

Sydney's eyes flew up. "No! Shit, Gabs. I'm sorry. How many are there?" She reached again for her mug, her middle finger covering the *T* as she drank. I wondered whether MALE EARS was the funnier slogan.

I shrugged. "A thousand?" Sydney's brows popped. "I mean, not literally. It's like a dozen, but they have the spiritual energy of a thousand."

"Totally," Sydney said, nodding earnestly. She was the only person aside from Diane who'd known about every flare.

Sydney was like a sister to me. Better than a sister because she didn't judge, and we had something in common. "Have you told anyone else? Your family?"

I shook my head. "Only Diane. The rest are so weird about the PBS and my dad will just chalk it up to changing migration patterns or whatever," I said, checking my phone again. "I'm so tired of this. I know what you're thinking. Hasn't it been a while? It's happened eighteen previous times, so what's the big deal?"

"I wasn't thinking that at all."

"There's something about *this* one . . ." In the past twenty-six months while I'd been symptom-free, I'd bought this farm, started the Collective, and acted like a grown-up for the very first time. Part of me believed we were different people, city and farm Gabby, and PBS wouldn't follow me into this new world.

"So, what do you think this flare is warning you against?" Sydney asked.

"Dad's campaign is for sure doomed. Another reason to stay far away."

A look passed over Sydney's face, as though she'd been waiting to say something and I'd granted her permission to spit it out. "Have you ever considered . . ." She sucked in her breath. "That if a fiasco is imminent, maybe you shouldn't run and hide. Perhaps the animals are a sign to do the opposite of whatever your natural instincts are telling you?"

"Fun theory, but it could also make the situation worse. Imagine more animals. Animals upon animals. What if they started eating each other?" My phone vibrated with a text. I would like to go on record as saying I hate this idea, Diane wrote. But the plan is a go. "Thank you, Jesus," I said, looking up into the rafters, or whatever you'd call the top of a yurt. "Once again, the Big D came through." I glanced at Sydney, but she wasn't listening, too occupied by something on her computer, which was strange, because she was a real analog girl. "Hello? You alive over there?"

"I'm looking at the Ring feed." She offered a weak smile. "You should go back to the house. A new creature is waiting on your front porch."

# Chapter Nine

## Talia

Talia was five seconds from leaving Gabby's when a bike came flying around the corner. She startled, nearly dropping her tray of coffee.

"Talia!" Gabby said, skidding to a halt. "This is a surprise!"

"Thought I'd swing by," Talia said, heart thrumming, head pounding from the cackling flamingos. *Flamingos.* What was going on around here? "I brought coffee. And bagels." She lifted the sack. "I hope it isn't a bad time. Are you in the middle of something?"

Gabby shoved her bike into a bush. "No, I was just up at the yurt," she said as they stalked up the grassy hill toward the house. "Catching up on things. What about you? Aren't you supposed to be at work?"

"Took the morning off so we could discuss Dad's big plans."

"You came all this way for *that*?"

Talia shrugged. "Why not. It's important." She figured she'd get a better read on Gabby face-to-face versus over the phone, and also the trip would give her a chance to check out the Collective in person. Talia hadn't visited since Gabby moved in and was curious to see what she was up to since her sister was so evasive about things. Apparently, she was up to flamingos. "You left so quickly the other night, we didn't get a chance to debrief," she said.

"What's to debrief?" Gabby unlocked the door. "It's pretty straightforward. No thanks and good luck."

They walked into the kitchen, and Talia set the coffee on the center island. "The conversation's a bit more complicated than 'no thanks,'" she said, passing Gabby the bagel bag. "The fact he's running the campaign from the Ranch blew my mind. It's like, why does he even still own the place?"

"Yeah, no." Gabby scooted up onto a stool. "That surprised me, too."

"Spencer's theory is that he feels he *has* to keep it, since he lost everything else. Makes sense, I guess," Talia said, using a napkin to clean what she mistook for coffee drips, until realizing they were flecks of amber glass embedded in the countertop. "You have to admit, it's quite groundbreaking he asked us to join him."

"Eh," Gabby said and took a chomp of bagel. "Groundbreaking or not—who cares? I'm an ally to the cause, but leave me out of it."

Talia blotted the dry countertop again. "I'm doing it," she said, just spitting it out. "I'm joining Dad's campaign."

Gabby's eyes bugged. "No. Talia. Don't get sucked in."

"But he asked. And he's survived the worst year of his life. We couldn't help him then, but we can help him now."

Answering Dad's call was the right thing to do regardless but Talia did need to get at least one sibling involved to avoid being dumped. She doubted Spencer would make good on his threat but wasn't looking to roll the dice. Ozzie was a lost cause, but Gabby was smart, and people were oddly drawn to her, and Talia liked the idea of teaming up. Maybe the campaign would bring them closer, and she'd finally get to the bottom of whether Gabby secretly blamed her for what happened all those years ago.

"It just seems to make sense," Talia said. "And . . . And . . ." She swallowed. "I want you to go with me."

Gabby laughed. She laughed! Talia's face burned all the way to her scalp. "Yeah, no. And don't fall for the guilt trip. There's a reason none of us ever worked at FDG."

"We were never asked," Talia said. "Please, Gabby? Nobody's claiming the job would be easy or fun, but we could actually help him. Don't you want Dad to be happy?"

"Friends will be friends but still cheese costs money," Gabby said, performing a pretty solid Ustenya impression. It meant *I can't go around helping other people when I need to take care of myself.* Half of their stepmother's idioms, she'd noticed, involved refusing to do a favor for someone else. "I'm not looking to turn my life upside down on the off chance it might make Dad feel good about himself. The question is, why are *you* doing it? You're the one with a boyfriend and a real job. Who'd fight the man without you around?"

"My job is not that important," Talia said, gaze sliding away. "I'll take a leave of absence or something." The partners would think it was exciting, right? One of their own working on a senatorial campaign? Worst case, she'd find a new job once it was over. People like her had options. It wasn't fair, but facts were facts.

"And Spencer? What's his take on all this?"

Talia sighed. "He's not thrilled. But it's a finite period of time. The primary is in March, and he can travel back and forth in between. Plus, we've been so busy lately, he'll hardly register my absence. If anything, we'll speak *more* often, since we won't both be in the office until ten o'clock every night!" These were valid points, and Talia made a mental note to remind him later.

"Hmm." Gabby sipped her coffee. It had to be cold by now—Talia's was—and it was so very Gabby to feign drinkability. "I don't suppose you're giving Ozzie this hard sell."

"God, no," Talia said, and Gabby narrowed her eyes. "Don't get me wrong. I love Oz, but he'd do something dumb, like use campaign funds to purchase Mussolini's Alfa Romeo, and we'd all end up in jail."

"Okay, that's unfair—"

"Come on, Bags."

"Don't call me that."

"This is a man who buys infected laptops for over a million dollars—" Talia stopped to clock Gabby's expression. Her eyebrows inched ever so slightly higher. "Are you familiar with *The Bestiary of Chaos*?"

"Um, I'm not sure?" Gabby said, her voice cracking. "We haven't seen much of each other lately."

"It's 'art.' Apparently."

"Huh. Fun." Gabby polished off the rest of her coffee, which must've tasted like sludge. "I should get back to the yurt. Busy day ahead."

Talia studied her sister. She'd struck a nerve with the Ozzie thing, but there was no point in pressing for more because Gabby rarely let anyone scratch below the surface. Maybe Ozzie on occasion, but never Talia.

Sighing, Talia slid off her stool. "Well, that was a bust." She forced a laugh. On the drive up, she'd convinced herself that she could use Gabby's people-pleasing nature against her. *Don't you want Dad to be happy?* But Gabby was too clever to fall for it.

"I really thought I'd be able to coax you into taking a sabbatical or something," Talia said, trying one last time. "A reset. A chance to get your ducks in a row."

"I don't need to get any *ducks* in a row," Gabby said mysteriously. She grabbed her phone from the counter, and they proceeded to the front of the house. "Sorry you drove all this way for nothing. You're welcome to stick around. We have some new plays debuting this weekend. One of them is practicing in the barn."

"Thanks, but I'm allegedly working from home today and should bill a few hours." Talia reached for the door. "And I didn't mind the drive at all. It was oddly liberating. I felt like a suburban kid who just got her license. Windows down, stereo blasting the whole way. Driving is fun. Who knew." She smiled, pivoted on a heel, and stepped outside.

A small pause.

"What the fuck!" Talia screamed, jumping back.

Gabby peered around her. "Oh. No worries. It's only a flamingo." The bird honked.

"I *know* it's a flamingo," Talia said, a hand on her chest, heart thundering beneath it. "But it scared the shit out of me. Why is it here, anyway?"

"Oh, um, for a play."

"Wild," Talia said. Well, flamingos sounded better than one of last month's shows, which billed itself to newsletter subscribers as a "true story of fetal cannibalism and male feasting, set to music." Talia flushed, recalling how she'd somewhat meanly shared the link in a group text with law school friends. Craaaazy . . . one person wrote after an hour or two of silence. The others did not respond.

"The flamingos don't attack, do they?" Talia asked. "Like geese?"

"I don't think so? But you should get on the road in case one of them goes rogue," Gabby said, pushing Talia toward the driveway. "Where'd you park? Geez, whose car is that? Someone's grandmother is probably wandering the property again." She lifted onto her toes, craning as if this was an effective way for a five-foot-nothing person to scan dozens of acres.

Talia walked around to the driver's side of the silver touring sedan. "The car is mine," she said. "Well, technically it's Ozzie's. When I asked to borrow one, he offered the most expensive car in his fleet, which is how I ended up driving Betty White's Cadillac Seville, circa 2000."

Gabby gaped.

"It's a nice ride. Comes fully equipped with a six-disc CD

changer." Talia started to get in and then hesitated, squinting against the sun. "Will you think about the California thing?"

"I don't—" Gabby began, then immediately stopped as the phone lit up in her hand. "Fuck. Why is Ustenya calling me?"

"Probably the same reason she called me. Please tell her I was here and already tried." Talia slid into the car. "Good luck," she said, and slammed the door. She pressed Play and threw the car into Drive. *I don't want no scrub* blared from the speaker as she drove off.

# Chapter Ten

## Gabby

Despite my better judgment, I answered Ustenya's call. You didn't mess around with someone who, at eleven years old, tried to sell her little brother to a local gang. She claimed it all turned out fine, and everyone found it hilarious, but this story remained the first and last we'd heard of any siblings, so who really knew.

"Hi, Ustenya!" I said, my heart skittering up into my throat. "What a coincidence! Talia just left. She says hello." A flurry of expletives greeted me, but I caught very little, other than a line about a knife reaching the bone. Plastic surgery gone wrong was my guess, but I wasn't going to put my life in jeopardy by saying it out loud. "What happened? Did Ozzie do something?"

I hated that Ozzie trouble was the first thing that came to mind, but it was Talia's fault, because she'd put it there with talks of million-dollar laptops. *Talia.* It was bizarre she'd shown up on my doorstep, stranger still that she'd known about Ozzie's new art piece and I hadn't. A petty quibble, but they were never alone, the two of them, without me.

"This has nothing to do with Oscar!" Ustenya shouted. "You used your father's credit card to charter a plane. What my dick were you doing?"

I blinked, racking my brain, until one of the flamingos

squawked, giving me a hint. Right. Operation Flamboyance. The Pink Feather Sanctuary. "Oh, yeah, sorry," I said. "It was an emergency." Although I didn't love getting berated in multiple languages, it was heartening to learn Dad was paying closer attention to his finances. Maybe he'd grown from the Uncle Doug debacle, after all. I felt proud of him.

"You tell us you're too busy to work on the campaign, and now you're flying down to South Beach to party?" Ustenya said.

"I never said I was too busy. Also, the plane isn't for me." I rotated away from the pond and walked toward the house. "It's a long story, but rest assured I'll pay you back." Naturally, I wouldn't mention the flare, lest I be treated to a lecture about migration patterns again. Plus, the look on Talia's face when she encountered a single flamingo on my front walk told me everything I needed to know. My condition was some freaky shit, and it was best to keep normal people out of it.

"Cancel the flight," Ustenya said.

"I can't really undo it at this point?" I probably could have, but wasn't going to, because we had no plan B. "I said I'd pay you back."

"How would you even do that? By moving funds from one of our accounts to another of our accounts?"

"I do have my own bank account." I sniffed. "And I run a whole business."

Granted, the theater didn't exactly throw off a ton of cash. Sydney always said the Collective could generate a profit if we tried, but I wasn't going to jack up my prices. There weren't many places for theater troupes to put on plays about reproductive cycles or showcase the brilliance of Team Peppa, in which characters from the *Peppa Pig* cartoon worked together to accomplish something, like navigate a muddy puddle or cover up a homicide. Fans loved it, and I refused to price anyone out, and we covered any shortfall with a monthly $50K disbursement courtesy of my dead grandfather. Granted, I never had much left at the end of the month, especially when you factored in property taxes and flamingo sanctuary donations and roof repairs, and damn, I'd really wedged myself into a tricky spot.

"I'll pay you back," I repeated, beginning to sweat. It was crazy how a person could feel fine, financially speaking, one minute, and then a bunch of small and medium things snowballed into an avalanche. "But it might take a while."

I stopped. A realization washed over me, followed by a warm rush of relief. The twenty-five-year gift. My birthday was soon, and although I didn't know the amount, it had to be enough to charter a cargo plane. *Phew.* Really dodged a bullet there.

"It is astounding," Ustenya said, "how you and Oscar take, take, take. Eating like bears, working like bugs. Then your father asks one little thing—and you refuse! Talia is the only one who gives a damn."

*She is the favorite child*, I thought as I resumed my trudge up to the house.

"This ends now. You and Ozzie. You will be chopped."

"Chopped?" One of my Birks caught on a stone step. I stumbled, regaining my balance seconds before I face-planted on the slate. "What do you mean *chopped*?" For all our jokes about Ustenya being a former assassin, I didn't think she'd *actually* murder us. Not with Dad running for office, at least.

"What is it they say in America? *We're cutting off your monthly disbursement.*"

I took a beat to process the information. "Forgive me for sounding crass," I said, feeling my cheeks flame. "But are you allowed to cut us off? That money is from our grandfather."

"There's a very flexible carve-out for any descendant the trustee determines is not living up to family expectations. Your father is the trustee."

"Oh. Great . . ."

"He can slice and dice at his discretion. This applies to both your monthly distribution and whatever you expect to receive in . . ." She paused to check a calendar or something. "In December?"

My mouth opened, but no words came out. I might've lost consciousness for a second. Was I being . . . blackmailed? I'd never known Ustenya to bluff, which meant I was screwed. Last month's production had it right. *Capitalism Prison*, for real.

"I'll figure something out, but you can't punish Ozzie, too."

"It isn't punitive," Ustenya said, and I didn't see how this could be true. "We simply cannot afford to keep you children on the payroll if you're not contributing to the campaign. We need to free up the cash and make room for bodies. You and Ozzie are replaceable."

"Ouch . . ."

"But it is not too late," Ustenya said, and I could hear her smiling the smug smile of a person who held all the cards. "Everything stays intact if you agree to your father's request."

*Maybe you should go*, a dark, sick part of my brain whispered. *Sydney has the Collective under control.* But no. Absolutely not. I'd finally put some distance between me and my family and refused to reverse course. My PBS was back, and I was hardly going to flamingo at the Ranch, in full view of Dad and Talia and everyone else.

"Let me think on it," I said, feeling myself waver. I'd always considered myself different, better than other trust fund babies, even the ones in my own family. I wasn't flashy and never bought top-of-the-line. I lived on a farm and thrifted my clothes. People called me "unassuming" and "down-to-earth," but that was all surface stuff. It was easy to play the artsy girl in the country who didn't care about money when you had enough to go around two or three times.

"The offer expires tomorrow," Ustenya said.

"I need to crunch some numbers, talk to Diane." My stomach

turned over. Diane had already told me to go, and she'd do it again, probably because it was the right call.

Ustenya cackled, chilling me to the core. "Sure. Yes. Fine. Call Diane. But she might not pick up. I cannot believe you roped her into the plane gambit."

"Don't be mad at Diane! She thought it was a horrible idea, but I made her."

"That's the problem. You're twenty-four years old and still have a nanny to boss around. I've let this linger too long. Diane has been fired."

"What?"

"And if you don't come to California, you'll be off the payroll, too."

# Chapter Eleven

## Ozzie

Yeah, so, this was not great news. Getting cut off. But Ozzie wasn't giving up his whole life for a measly $50K.

According to Talia, Gabby didn't bite, either, and honestly, Ozzie was surprised. He wouldn't expect his sister to jump at the chance or anything, but people were turning the screws, and Gabby tended to avoid conflict no matter the cost. Talia drove all the way out to the Collective to talk her into it, but still, *no*. Notably, she did not try with him. Ozzie understood he wasn't the world's most together or reliable guy, but sometimes he wished his family liked him half as much as his followers did. Don't get it twisted. He knew they loved him, no question. But liking was a different beast.

Fortunately, Ozzie saw himself as an optimist. He had to be, in this family, and he'd already taken steps to secure his lifestyle. Yesterday he reached out to an auction house to sell the pieces he didn't give a shit about. If Ozzie got really desperate, he'd let *Bestiary* go, even though it looked damn good in the gallery beside his best piece, the original Hundred Acre Wood map from *Winnie the Pooh*. The map was fictional and full of whimsy, whereas *Bestiary* represented the stark realities of everyday life. Contrast. Juxtaposition. Yin and yang.

Dozens if not hundreds of works had come into and out of the collection, but Ozzie's first and forever love would remain Pooh's map. *Think, think, think. Oh, bother!* Man, he loved that chubby little bear, and leaving the map to him was the only decent thing Grandma Yvonne ever did. This was a woman so awful not even Dad was upset when she died. Apparently she didn't believe in hugging children or touching them at all except with a wooden spoon.

Regardless. Ozzie was ready to stand on business, and he was therefore sitting in a viewless, charmless conference room, preparing for his new, more responsible life. He was glad Freja's manager didn't ball out for premium space, but Ozzie was dizzied by the blandness, and the scent of synthetic carpet.

Spinning his phone on the table, Ozzie tried to envision what vibe this Barclay character might bring. Probably some real "disappointed dad" energy, if he were to guess. Yes, Ozzie had made mistakes, and a few of his investments weren't "sure bets" after all. He'd jumped into crypto at its descent but, give him a break, he was only nineteen when Superstonk/GME came down from its peak. Also nineteen when he purchased a midtown office building two months before everyone started working from home.

The money sitch was a little snug, but no worries. Once Ozzie sold some things, and signed a few more brand deals, he'd be fine. The $50K per month draw was awkwardly low for a proper trust fund, and he wasn't going to debase himself to hang on to it.

*You're doing the right thing*, his Aunt Kathy had said when he told her about Barclay. *Stopping a problem before it begins.* Unlike her husband, she didn't have to say. Ozzie adored Aunt Kathy. She was funny, and chill, and would never judge him since she stayed with Uncle Doug against literally everyone's advice.

At last the conference room door opened. Ozzie rose to his feet.

"Ah, Oscar," Barclay said, brandishing a very sharp smile. "I'm glad you could make it. I hope you've cleared your calendar. We have a lot to discuss."

From: Gabby Gunn <shccgabby@gmail.com>
Sent: Monday, August 28 2:15 PM
To: Eli dos Santos <Eli_dosSantos@sdzwa.org>
Subject: PBS study

Dear Dr. dos Santos,
I've had PBS for the past eleven years. Congratulations on wrapping up your Brazilian study! I saw on the message boards that you're launching a smaller study in San Diego and, as luck would have it, I'll be in the area starting after Labor Day. I'm not sure about participating in any experiments but would love to meet up and discuss your findings. I have my own theory and am curious whether it might align with yours.

Thank you in advance for considering a meetup. I look forward to hearing from you!
Gabby Gunn

---

From: Eli dos Santos <Eli_dosSantos@sdzwa.org>
Sent: Monday, August 28 2:47 PM
To: Gabby Gunn <shccgabby@gmail.com>
Subject: Re: PBS study

Dear Gabby,
It was wonderful to receive your email. I would love to discuss PBS, though will not be sharing my findings at this juncture. Please reach out when you arrive in San Diego. Things are busy at the SDZWA, but I will find a way to fit you in.

Best,
Dr. Eli dos Santos, D.V.M., Dipl. ACZM, Dipl. ECZM (ZHM)
Chief Conservation and Wildlife Expert
San Diego Zoo Wildlife Alliance
619-555-0251

# SEPTEMBER

# Long-shot media mogul enters crowded Democratic field in US Senate race

BY MICAH BETZ, *The San Diego Union-Tribune*

SAN DIEGO—Former media mogul Marston Gunn announced Friday that he has entered the U.S. Senate contest in California, adding another Democrat to a large field of candidates that includes three sitting members of Congress. Gunn is a long-shot who has never run for or held office, yet he's taking on the nation's most populous state, which is home to 22 million voters. Although Gunn's last known address was in New York, he will operate his campaign out of a family compound in Rancho Santa Fe.

Gunn is the former Chairman and CEO of F.D. Gunn Company, a media conglomerate that, as of the end of last calendar year, included 90 newspapers, 50 local television stations, a home improvement network and the reality television network For Real TV. Although he is from the family that founded the Frederick D. Gunn Hospital system, Gunn Gallery of Art, Gunn Marine Biological Institute, and Gunn College, Marston Gunn has little to no name recognition in California, therefore entering the race without a base of support in a field already splintered by candidates, including Democratic U.S. Reps. Angie Parker, David Slimp and Sandra Grant.

"Does anyone truly think Congress is knocking it out of the park?" Gunn says in an online video launching his campaign. "From my point of view, not a single one of these candidates has done anything to improve California or this country. That's why I'm stepping in."

In Gunn's opinion, when it comes to national politics, the largest state in the union is pushed aside. "All the attention is given to the other states," he says, "when California makes up 12% of the population and contributes 15% of the GDP. People expect us to shut up and keep doing our thing. It's time for California to make some noise."

Despite his ties to New York, Gunn claims his San Diego roots run deep. The F.D. Gunn Company began in 1871 after Frederick D. Gunn moved from the Midwest to San Diego and happened upon a village of a few hundred people living on the bay front. He purchased a plot of land at K Street and Seventh Avenue and took a job at the *San Diego Union*, which he eventually acquired.

Over time, Frederick Gunn snatched up other dailies across the West before expanding nationally. By the 1980s, the F.D. Gunn Company owned dozens of television and radio stations, and in the '90s, it created a lifestyle-oriented cable network. The Company went public in 1996 and continued its acquisition spree. At its height, F.D. Gunn had a market cap of $20 billion.

During the past twelve months, Gunn was forced to liquidate the majority of his holdings to address the legal issues of his brother, Douglas Gunn. As part of the divestiture, the newspapers were sold to a Chinese billionaire for an estimated $500 million, and the two television networks were spun off and taken public under the name Chaos Live, Inc. (NYSE: GURL), in which Gunn holds a minority stake.

Gunn filed a statement of candidacy with federal election regulators on August 16 and designated a committee to raise funds. He says he'll spend personal funds on the campaign, though it remains unclear the extent to which he'll be able to, especially in a state that includes several of the nation's most expensive media markets. It typically takes tens of millions of dollars to wage a successful statewide campaign in California.

As for why he's running for office now, Gunn, 61, says, "I've always been interested in politics, but am increasingly concerned about what's happening in the country, and California specifically. It's time to bring a new voice into Senate. I can't wait to get started."

# Chapter Twelve

## Talia

After passing through a set of gates, they drove along a quiet, meandering road, beneath a canopy of eucalyptus trees. The white stucco, red-tiled roof of the main house loomed in the distance, the tip of the bell tower just beyond. Talia closed her eyes and pictured all she couldn't see—the hiking and horse trails, the tennis courts, the pools. Mom's art studio with its view of the lake.

They pulled into the motor court. Tony the driver barked something into his walkie-talkie and opened the liftgate. Inhaling, Talia kicked open the door. She jumped out and looked around. Eleven years was a long time and suddenly, her entire past was a blur, and she couldn't distinguish between actual memories and residual feelings lodged deep in the pit of her being.

"Ivan is on his way," Tony said, swiftly flinging each piece of Talia's luggage onto a cart. "Might take a minute to walk over from HQ."

Talia blinked. "I'm sorry. Ivan?"

Tony flicked a bead of sweat from his forehead. "Campaign manager," he said.

Talia blinked again. "Are my dad and Ustenya . . . ?"

"In San Francisco. They took off . . ." Tony bit his lip, trying to remember. "Yesterday? It was a fundraising trip. They should be back soon."

"Oh, right! Dad mentioned that." He definitely had not, and Talia felt herself deflate, floored that no one could be bothered to greet her. Though this did explain why Dad hadn't responded to any of her texts. She'd sent one as she left New York, another when her plane touched down in San Diego, and a third after getting into Tony's SUV. See you in thirty! Nothing but crickets.

"You'll be staying in the main house," Tony said. "Second bedroom at the top of the stairs. Your luggage will be up soon."

Tony offered a small bottle of water, but Talia was already several yards ahead, striding past a burbling fountain and between the two leopards now flanking the front door. She stopped in the entryway, beneath an enormous wrought-iron lighting fixture. Around her, sun filtered through the skylights, spilling across the terra-cotta floors and hand-painted Mexican tiles.

"Talia?" A pale man with dark hair poked his head around an arched doorway. "I'm Ivan, your dad's campaign manager."

"Oh! Hi!" she said, trying to appear happy and normal and not like she was crumbling inside. "Nice to meet you!"

They shook hands, and Ivan immediately began prattling about schedules, and lanyards, and who to go to for this or that. Talia studied him as he spoke, noting the faint purple circles beneath his eyes. She hoped it wasn't a sign of things to come.

"Campaign headquarters are that way," he said, pointing to somewhere behind the house. "The main barn has been converted into offices."

Talia nodded blindly, too exhausted to register more than an instruction or two. She wasn't ready to do this. Whatever *this* was. She felt so overwhelmed she almost couldn't breathe. "I'm sorry to interrupt," she said at last. "But it's been a long trip. Do you mind if I go upstairs and, um, lie down?" It wasn't like Talia to shirk her duties right from the jump, but she felt like death, and Dad wasn't there, so actually, fuck him.

"Great idea. Rest up for the work ahead." Ivan took Talia's

phone. "I'll type in my number. Text as soon as you're ready, and I'll tell you everything you need to know about being a field organizer."

"Oh. Okay. Cool." The possibility of a legitimate title hadn't occurred to Talia. Mostly she'd envisioned attending fundraising events and editing speeches, occasionally serving as a reliable sounding board. What even was a field organizer? She'd google it later.

"I'm throwing a lot at you," Ivan said, "but if you'd rather wait until your sister arrives to go over everything, that totally works."

"My sister?" Talia said, squinting. "Yeah, no. Gabby's not coming. Neither is my brother. They both opted not to participate." She shrugged, as in, *What are you gonna do?*

"Huh." Ivan checked his phone. "According to the information I was given, her flight gets in tomorrow afternoon. Ustenya's assistant just forwarded me her itinerary." He waggled his phone.

"What the fuck!" Talia swiped the phone and scanned the words on the screen. There she was, in all caps: GUNN/GABRIELLA. Talia's heart sunk. If Gabby couldn't even bother to tell her she'd changed her mind, "develop closer relationship with sister" was probably one thing to strike from the list of what Talia wanted to accomplish in San Diego.

Smiling sheepishly, Talia returned the phone. "Sorry about that. I didn't mean to be all grabby. I'm. Um. Extremely surprised?"

Ivan frowned and scratched the back of his lily-white neck. "You and Gabby are supposed to share an office, but if you don't get along, I can figure out a temporary solution? We're not fully staffed yet, so there should be plenty of room."

"No, no," Talia said, waving a hand. "It's fine. We get along *great*. It's just . . . the last time we spoke, she wasn't coming."

Talia told herself this was good news. It's why she'd driven all the way out to bumfuck nowhere. The arrival of Gabby would also help with Spencer. Her leaving wouldn't feel so personal, and he couldn't be mad. Well, he could be mad, but it'd have to be for a different reason.

"If it's any consolation," Ivan said, "she was a last-minute add."

Talia nodded. It did make her feel better, actually.

"To be perfectly candid . . ." Ivan looked to the left, and to the right. He leaned forward, and she caught a strong whiff of breath mints. "I got the impression something happened. Like maybe she had to come, because she found herself in a bit of hot water?"

Talia's gut clenched.

"There were birds involved. And a cargo plane? Honestly, I didn't really follow." Ivan pulled back. "But one day it was just you, and the next, her one-way ticket was booked."

—————

Talia woke up early the next morning, before six o'clock, starving, like her stomach was eating itself from the inside out. She didn't mind the sensation. Sometimes, hunger felt like fuel. She'd never be able to explain it.

She slipped into a pair of shorts, a sports bra, and running shoes, and snuck downstairs and out the doors near the pool. After jogging through a grove of sycamore trees, she crossed a road and cut across a meadow. The morning was quiet save the occasional whoosh from a hot-air balloon overhead.

Despite the lack of sleep and hunger pangs, Talia held a steady pace, until the pickleball pavilion came into sight and her breath knotted up. All this time, she'd assumed the Ranch was, if not sold, at least shuttered. Meanwhile, Dad had visited with enough frequency he'd needed to accommodate a very mild pickleball habit.

Talia kept going. Up ahead stood a pair of two-story town-homes. Both had living quarters upstairs—one bedroom, one bath, a full-sized kitchen, and living room—and a garage on the ground floor. Mom's apartment was on the right, but somebody else probably lived there now.

Talia scooted between the apartments. With each step she took, Dad's money problems became increasingly obvious. Carefully tended rosebushes gave way to unpruned trees. Sprinklers were crusty and dry, building facades were faded and chipped. A discarded Doritos bag lay in the middle of her path.

When she reached Mom's art studio, Talia stopped. Her eyes swept the lake, the boathouse, the acres of dry brush beyond. As a lizard skittered past, Talia heard a tapping sound. She looked up to see a shutter hanging on by a single rusty hinge.

Standing on her toes, Talia peered through the transom window, but the milky glass offered no hint of what might be inside. She landed with a thud back onto the dirt, the memories hitting her all at once. The paint fumes. The opera blaring. Mom in a paint-smeared black apron, crouching and stretching, debating which part of the canvas to attack next.

Daphne worked furiously that last summer, high off the accolades from a show featuring the first half of her *MOTHER/NATURE* series. Talia still remembered the headline from *The Escondido Daily Times-Advocate*. She'd framed the review and given it to her mom as a gift.

## DAPHNE CARTER RECKONS WITH MOTHERHOOD

Daphne's goal was to complete the collection before the holidays, and Talia wondered how far she'd gotten, and if any pieces were still in the barn. Uncharacteristically, Mom hadn't shown her anything along the way. Maybe Talia should've read more into this or asked to see a piece or two. Of course, she'd been apprehensive about a whole new group of paintings that "reckoned with motherhood," considering most people didn't think Daphne reckoned with it very well. The shown pieces had nothing to which Talia could take any particular offense, but Daphne promised to go "deeper and darker" in part two.

A hot-air balloon's burner flared, and Talia startled. Tourists called out, waving from their basket. Talia waved back. After checking her watch, she assessed the barn again. The door was probably unlocked, but now was not the time to dredge up the past. She had work to do.

# Chapter Thirteen

## Gabby

"Welcome to the Ranch!" said Dad's campaign manager as we stepped into the entryway, the heavy walnut door clomping shut behind us. "You'll be staying on the second floor."

I smiled thinly and glanced around, wondering where everybody was. No Dad, no Talia, not even a smug-faced Ustenya.

So. It happened. I was working for my dad, the one thing my siblings and I swore we'd never do. This was different than what we'd imagined, but by different it was also worse, and I wouldn't have Diane at my side.

*Diane.* I was still reeling from the news. I felt horrible for getting her fired, but honestly, she didn't seem too shaken up. *These things usually work out for the best,* she said. Also, the timing was terrific with Bill having retired in May.

"Oh. How nice," I'd answered through my teeth, having forgotten about Bill's retirement because I was an awful person who thought of Diane's husband so infrequently, he could've been a fictional character from a book I neglected to read in high school.

Diane assured me that her firing changed absolutely nothing. We had a fifteen-year history, and she was there for me, night or day, but already I knew I'd leave her alone. Who wanted some old employer calling on the reg?

"Can you believe a Gunn has only one bag?" Tony the driver said to Ivan. "I don't even need a luggage cart."

"A light traveler," Ivan said. "I love it." Dad's campaign manager reminded me of a vampire—white skin, black hair, an extremely pronounced widow's peak. He might've been thirty or a hundred years old. It was impossible to know.

As I started to explain the light luggage (total lack of personal style), a prickly sensation washed over me. Something, somewhere, went *click, click, clickity, click*, nails on terra-cotta tiles. My vision clouded for a second and then cleared to reveal a white creature with pointed ears and a curled tail.

I staggered backward, sending a six-foot-tall candelabra crashing to the floor. Tony grabbed me before I went down, too. "Hey, hey, I've got ya," he said.

"Are you alright?" Ivan said, and I was shocked to see his skin could turn an even more translucent shade of white. "I'm so sorry! I should've locked him up. Nobody warned me you were scared of dogs."

"You know this creature?" I asked, attempting to regain my composure.

Ivan chuckled nervously. "Yeah, I mean, we're not friends or anything," he said. "But we are acquainted. It's a Jindo."

I made some kind of face because what the hell was a Jindo? It sounded like something my PBS might dredge up.

"Korea's Fifty-Third National Treasure," Ivan said. "I believe they're in the spitz category?"

I snuck a glimpse of the Jindo. While it gave off dog-*like* vibes, it also seemed wilder, more feral, like some cross between a coyote and a white fox. "So it's a dog," I said to confirm.

The men exchanged concerned looks.

"Don't worry," Ivan said. "He's friendly. Well. Not *friendly*. He's actually pretty aloof, but I haven't seen him attack anyone."

"Oh. Okay." I pushed back my bangs. "Does he have a name?"

"Good question." Ivan checked with Tony, who shrugged.

"Doesn't it say Frosted Faces on the collar?" he asked.

"That's the name of the rescue organization." Ivan looked at me. "It's your dad's dog, so you'll have to ask him."

I stared at Ivan, unsure where exactly this conversation had derailed. "I think you might be confused?" I said. "My dad is extremely anti-pet. He doesn't believe animals belong indoors. Maybe someone's missing him? Should we put up signs?"

"It's definitely your Dad's," Ivan said, and I contemplated whether I'd just lost my mind. "I thought a pet would be good for his image. They make great running mates. Get it?" He cackled, sounding exactly like Count von Count from *Sesame Street*. "Remember how Raphael Warnock borrowed a beagle when he ran for Senate?"

"Sure," I lied.

"A lot of people credit the dog with his win. Long story short, we got this guy a few days ago from a place that rescues senior dogs."

"A senior dog for a senior person," Tony said, chortling to himself.

"He's not that old," Ivan said, and I wasn't sure who he was talking about—the dog or my dad. "Somewhere between eight and ten, and he's quite spry. The rescue folks were wary about your dad's lack of experience—"

*A sentiment soon shared by voters across California*, I mused.

"But they were having trouble getting rid of him, so I think they saw their chance and took it. Anyhoo." He smacked his hands together. "Now that we've cleared that up, how about a tour?"

———

Ivan led me out of the house, through the back, by the pool.

"You just missed lunch," he said, consulting his bright blue-banded Apple watch. Every day, between twelve and two o'clock, I could head over to the meditation loggia to grab a salad, or a sandwich, or a salad and a sandwich, plus a drink, and corn on the cob, for some reason. "It's a great perk."

I peered back at the loggia, where a couple of workers were gathering up uneaten cobs.

"There's a lap pool by the tennis courts," Ivan said, dog leash wrapped tightly around his hand. "The property manager will drain it soon, so get your laps in while you can. Speaking of Mindy, there she goes." He pointed at a little blonde lady in pastel athleisure wear hopping into a golf cart.

"Why is she carrying a stick?" I asked.

He paused. "To scare away rattlesnakes?" Ivan's tone told me he didn't believe this, and neither should I. "There's a yoga studio by the lap pool," he went on. "That's new. And a pickleball pavilion beyond the family barn."

This place was chock-full of pavilions, and I thought about how strange it was Mom lived here. Daphne Carter had been wealthy thanks to her marriage, but she was an artist, a bohemian, always walking around with paint in her hair. Then again, the Ranch offered solitude, like your own private gated community. Mom never seemed to like other people much. Aside from Talia.

"What about the recreation pavilion?" I asked as we walked beneath a canopy of sycamore trees. "Dad mentioned something about closing it down?"

"Boarded up and out of use," Ivan said. We crossed a small, lonely road—or maybe more driveway?—and turned left. "It was pretty expensive to keep running."

I frowned, suddenly touched by homesickness for the only building on the Ranch I felt any attachment to. Unlike Talia, Ozzie and I didn't have the patience to sit around and watch Mom paint for twelve hours a day, and so we entertained ourselves in the recreation pavilion—bowling, and singing karaoke, and beating each other's high scores on six different arcade games. I'd give anything to return to those days, even if for a short time. We used to be so close. Frick and Frack, they called us. I supposed it was natural to drift apart in adulthood, but that didn't mean I had to like it.

"Campaign HQ is in the main barn," Ivan said as we passed a sand arena and grand prix field. "There are a few horses in the family barn if you want to ride. That's something else Mindy can help you with. It's Mindy for most things, as you've probably deduced. Your father has really pared back."

There'd been a huge staff back in the day, I recalled, thinking of the pool boy, two tennis pros, and *gauchos*, for the love of God. I wished Ozzie was with me so I could turn to him and joke, *No wonder Mom loved the Ranch.*

"Here we are," Ivan said as we entered the expansive, light-filled main barn, with its washed brick floors, white stucco walls, and open wood-beamed ceilings. "HQ. Where we'll make magic happen."

The horse stalls had been converted into offices, Ivan explained, and each had its own skylight and Dutch door to the outside. His office was in the former farrier and grooming space, near the gourmet kitchen and conference room. I snickered, picturing a pack of thoroughbreds hanging around, making coffee, talking shit.

Ivan stopped in front of a stall. "This is where you'll be working," he said. "You're sharing an office with your sister. I hope you don't mind."

I didn't have a chance to mind because here sat Talia behind a large oak table, brows pushed together as she studied something on a computer. Sensing our presence, she peered up. A look passed over her face. The opposite of thrilled to see me.

"I'll let you two get situated," Ivan said, and promptly vanished. I stood in the doorway, smiling blandly like a dope.

"Let the games begin!" I sang.

Talia appraised me, as if deciding whether to make the effort to stand. But she wasn't a hugger, so instead she swept a hand, gesturing to the chair across from her.

"Well, this is fun," I said, lowering into my seat. "A bona fide j-o-b. Get me the Roan Report. Stat." I lightly banged my fist on the desk.

"What an unexpected turn of events," Talia said, and clattered out a few sentences on her laptop. "Last we spoke, you were dead set against California."

"Game-time decision," I said, realizing I should've texted her in advance. My sister did not relish surprises. "Sorry for not giving you the heads-up. In the rush of everything, I totally forgot. I'm here now!" I eyed the laptop in front of me, a clunky thing probably old enough to get a learner's permit. "Is this mine? Or does it belong to Ozzie's art collection?"

"Can we not talk about that? It stresses me out."

I bobbed my head. Talia was not countenancing any levity today. *Noted.* The girl was mad about something, but I would tread with caution. Talia was a hothead. Anything might set her off. Her mood always blew over, but waiting for the storm to pass could be rough. When I first moved to the Hudson Valley, she took it as a personal affront and ghosted me for three months.

"Oh, geez," I said, noticing a sticker affixed to the computer. On a light blue background, a navy blue megaphone screamed GUNN! in bright yellow. "What's with the yelling?"

"I guess he mentioned 'making noise' in an interview."

"We're gonna wind up in Dad merch eventually, aren't we? Lord help us." I grinned widely, but the gesture fell flat. I was really working to smooth Talia's prickles, break the ice, get us to the other side of whatever was going on around here.

"Why?" Talia blurted, locking her eyes onto my face. Her eyebrows seemed stronger than usual, like she'd purposefully darkened them to increase the intensity of her scowl. "Why are you here?"

"Because I was asked? Multiple times. Including by you." I still didn't understand why Talia asked me in person, especially when she had to go to the effort of borrowing a car. A better sister might've given her the benefit of the doubt, but I couldn't shake the notion that she wanted to snoop or spy or otherwise check things out. Talia was a nosy gal, forever suspicious about what the rest of us were doing, but too afraid to ask outright.

"You told me no," Talia reminded me. "I'm asking, what changed?"

I shrugged, unwilling to admit I'd done it for the money, because I refused to let money be the whole deal. I'd convinced myself I'd come to work, and "help Dad," and perhaps get even more out of it. Credit for time served with family, or a missing piece of the PBS puzzle, if dos Santos stopped smelling his own farts for a second. Either way, I'd stay for a month or two to build a cushion and secure my twenty-five-year gift. In the meantime, Sydney would come up with a plan to make SHCC profitable.

"I thought about it," I told Talia, and this was true enough. "You made several good points, and Ustenya . . ." I flicked my eyes away. "She also presented a compelling argument."

"Oh. I'll bet," Talia said.

"In the end, I didn't have a good reason to say no."

"Interesting. Where's Diane?"

I cocked my head, debating whether this was a trick or some kind of power play. She must've already known about Diane. Due to her snooping and status as number one kid, Talia was always in on the tea. But, in that moment, her face remained blank.

"Ustenya fired her," I spit out, and Talia gasped.

"Oh, Gabs. I had no idea," she said, sincerely. "I mean, it makes sense, obviously."

"Obviously." My eyes started to water.

"Don't cry. It's not like she's dead!"

"Definitely not," I agreed, though it sort of felt that way. "Anyway. You're right. Who cares." I flapped a hand. "Bound to happen. And so on. Okay, moving on! What am I supposed to do now?"

Talia hesitated, as if wanting to say something more. Finally, she exhaled. "Here," she said, plucking a neon-pink sticky note from the wall behind her. "Your log-in credentials."

I grabbed the paper, mildly annoyed she had my password because *ugh, that was so Talia.* But then I remembered I could change it, and there wasn't even anything to see yet.

Username: GABBY@MarstonGunn4CA.org

Password: Gunn100%

My problems were really piling up, and now I had a whole new inbox to check, and an email address that used Dad's government name. This job was getting very serious, very quickly, and I began to swirl in a storm of inner despair.

"This is also for you." Talia passed me a badge affixed to a bright yellow lanyard. On it was a picture of me I'd never seen before. My eyes were downcast, and I suspected it was taken by one of the security cameras at Water Mill. Beneath the incredibly sketchy photo were two words. Reading them, I pulled back. "What is a *Comms Director*?"

"It's *you*," Talia said. "This is not a vacay, Gabby. You're not here to sun yourself by the pool."

I snorted. "Have you met me?" I lifted a very pale arm. "I haven't 'sunned' myself a day in my life. I assumed my title would be a little more . . . plebeian. Like 'errand girl.' Who decided this?" Surely not Dad. He wouldn't place anything so important in my small, shaky hands.

Talia returned her attentions to her computer. "Beats me. You're way overthinking this," she said, which was super freaking rich, coming from her. "It's a job, and you'll do it. What's the worst that could happen?"

"Do you want a list, or . . . ?"

"Not to worry. You'll catch on eventually. In the meantime, if you're looking for something to do, can you figure out why Ivan deposited a live dog by our door?"

# Chapter Fourteen

## Ozzie

It was his third meeting with Barclay in one week. A lot more money was going out than coming in, and Ozzie needed a *plan*. He'd already agreed to sell the plane. It almost made him puke thinking about it, but Barclay wasn't satisfied.

"You have to stop spending money on nonessentials," he said.

"I have!" Ozzie protested. "I've been so good. I gave you access to all my accounts. You can see for yourself!"

"That's the problem." Barclay pushed a piece of paper toward him. "Explain the highlighted purchases, all made since we started working together. They appear auction-related?"

Ozzie's stomach dropped. Okay, so they weren't essential, not in the traditional sense of the word, but for important pieces of Americana, they were quite reasonably priced.

"Let's begin with this purchase," Barclay said, pointing to an item, and this guy was really going to make him go through it. "A microscopic Louis Vuitton handbag?"

"Yeah. It's dope." Or it seemed that way, from the listing. In hindsight, he'd probably need a microscope to fully appreciate it. He wondered how much one might cost.

"Also, why did you pay $5,000 for a font?"

"Okay, but not just any font. Times Newer Roman. Iconic. And come on, five K? Is that even worth fretting about?"

"Right now, every K counts," Barclay said, furrowing his brow. "Do I even want to hear a description of 'Jesus Shoes'?"

"Sneakers," Ozzie mumbled. "Air Maxes. Filled with holy water." Barclay groaned. "It's an investment! It'll pay off in the long run. The short run, probably!"

Barclay used his knuckles to aggressively rub his face.

These purchases weren't critical—Ozzie got that—but were minor in the grand scheme of things, and Barclay didn't know him well enough to be so dramatically annoyed. Plus, now that Ozzie understood the parameters of his new lifestyle, he could do better, spending-wise.

"Your sponsorship income is another trouble spot," Barclay said. "It's declined meaningfully."

Ozzie was starting to feel ill. He'd sensed things were a little off, the vagaries of the market and such, but *meaningfully*? "By how much?"

"Let's see." Barclay opened his laptop and clicked around for a minute. "Last quarter, it declined twelve percent sequentially and was down twenty-five percent from the prior year quarter."

Ozzie made a face. The prior year quarter? What kind of word salad was that? "That's cheeks," he said, and Barclay looked at him, puzzled. "As in butt cheeks? As in ass?" He sighed. "I'm saying it sucks."

"Ah. Indeed. Also, you're losing quite a lot of followers."

This was getting worse by the second. Ozzie had noticed less engagement but neglected to really pull back the covers. Damn, just when you thought you had the algorithm on lock, the tech mercenaries fucked it up. He *hoped* it was the algorithm, in any case. Ozzie didn't want to consider other explanations.

"What does your pipeline for brand deals and sponsored content look like?" Barclay asked. "Are you in talks with any companies? Maybe you can revive some partnerships you've lost?"

"Bro. I have to believe in the product I'm selling. For example. Busta Nutz wanted to work together. The T-shirt company? But their shirts—which they sell for two hundred bucks, by the way—are made by unpaid labor in Myanmar. I'm not down with that."

"Admirable," Barclay said, but smirking, so Ozzie didn't know how to read him. "Do you have a list of current clients, and anyone you're in discussions with?"

"Sure, sure, I'll get it to you ASAP." He made a note in his phone. There was a list, sort of, but it resided in Ozzie's head and was only half-baked.

"Going forward, I'll need to review all contracts before you sign them." Barclay shoved his computer aside. "Regarding the monthly disbursement. I did speak to your stepmother's advisor, and she wasn't bluffing. The money has been pulled."

He'd figured as much when the cash failed to land in his account on the first of the month. Ozzie had been holding out hope it was a power trip orchestrated by Ustenya and she'd eventually back down. Dad was a lot of things, but he wasn't cruel, and Ozzie couldn't imagine he'd permanently cut him off. Admittedly, it was a lot of faith to put in the dude given their history.

"The good news," Barclay began, and Ozzie's chest lifted, "is the deal isn't off the table. Ustenya's people made it clear the monthly stipend would be reinstated if you complied with your family's wishes."

"Terrific," Ozzie said glumly. On some level, it was nice to be wanted, especially by this crew, when normally it was like, *Please, Ozzie, stay ten feet away and don't touch anything.* Gabby tried to fake tolerance of him, but that was an act. Case in point: she'd told him she was "no" on California, but went to San Diego anyway, without ever mentioning it. If they were such besties, why hadn't she said anything? Why didn't she ask him to go, too?

"I must say," Barclay went on, "you're the most interesting

client I've personally dealt with, and one guy introduced ec-
stasy into the US."

Ozzie nodded. "Nice."

"I've never encountered an arrangement like this and, frankly,
I'm mystified. Why is your involvement in the campaign so
critical?"

Ozzie shrugged. He was pretty mystified himself. Talia was
smart and Gabby was pleasant as hell, so those two made sense.
But him? It didn't add up.

"I suppose where I'm struggling is . . . Why not agree?"
Barclay pressed. "It's a very beneficial arrangement without a
lot of risk."

Fifty thousand dollars per month wasn't *that* much, but Ozzie
probably shouldn't point this out to the man who had such a
shit fit about the Times Newer Roman font. He'd need to find
another way to explain it, and bless, there were many reasons
not to relent.

"I know it *seems* attractive," Ozzie said, "but relocating to
San Diego would hurt me in the long run." @DegenerateOz
was all about jets (RIP) and yachts and exotic beaches and being *seen*. There was absolutely no one and nowhere important
in San Diego, and its beaches were hardly Seychelles or Nusa
Dua or Côte d'Azur. They weren't even Florida's Gulf Coast.
"How will I secure the best collabs if I'm hanging out in some
sad-sack loser campaign office?"

Barclay sighed. "Maybe it's a lever to push in the future."

"Right on," Ozzie said, grateful Barclay wasn't giving him
the hard sell. "Listen, Barc, it's not as bad as you think. We only
need to make the numbers work for the next eighteen months.
We're golden after that."

Barclay narrowed his eyes, confused.

"When I turn twenty-five, I'll receive a lump sum from my
grandfather. I don't suppose Ustenya's people clued you in on
the amount? They're so fucking cagey. Drives me up a wall. But
it's a mil, at least."

Barclay opened his mouth and stopped, leaving a little mouse hole in the center of his face. Ozzie had probably blown his mind with how easy this was turning out to be.

"I'm sorry?" Barclay said at last. "I thought . . . They told me . . . I'm sorry if they didn't make it clear to you, but if you don't go to California, the twenty-five-year gift is off the table, too."

# Chapter Fifteen

## Talia

Talia poked her head out of the office to make sure the coast was clear. Dad never let them have pets growing up, and she had no concept of how long it'd take a person—in particular a Gabby-type person—to walk a dog. Talia had suggested letting it roam, but Jindos were "runners," apparently, and capable of jumping six-foot fences.

Heart racing, Talia darted back inside and glanced at her sister's phone, left face up on the desk. Why was Gabby here? Was she *really* threatened, and why? Talia found herself almost lost in the possibilities. We need you, she imagined her dad texting Gabby. Talia overthinks everything. She can't handle this alone.

Paranoia? Perhaps. But yesterday she'd googled "duties field organizer senatorial candidate" and stumbled across a post for her own job.

Exciting up-and-coming candidate needs a Field Organizer, based out of Rancho Santa Fe. Supporter housing available! Work to promote progressive issues while living on a luxurious property designed in the style of an Argentinian estancia.

The luxurious part was mortifying, and who even knew about estancias, but what did it *mean*? Talia forced herself to believe someone had posted it weeks ago and forgot to take it down.

Her eyes skipped over to Gabby's phone, and she snatched it, striking quick as a snake. The thing didn't have a passcode or use face recognition, which was so trusting and so Gabby Gunn she could barely stand it. Yes, Talia understood this was a violation, but her sister did leave it open, and she swore she'd only read things pertaining to her.

Sweat beading on her hairline, Talia scrolled through Gabby's texts, stopping when she saw her name in a preview. The text was from Sydney, and it said, Have fun in SD tell Talia hello.

Talia let her arm drop. She felt her body wither in shame. Whenever friends talked about sisterly bonds, Talia wondered why it'd never been like that with them. Was it their age difference, or Gabby's quirkiness? Maybe it was Talia's . . . however her personality could be described (please, don't tell her). She wanted to be closer to Gabby, and had the chance to do this without Ozzie around, so did it matter why she'd come?

Talia tossed the phone back onto the desk and slumped in her chair. Five minutes later, Gabby returned with the Jindo, otherwise known as Korea's Fifty-Third National Treasure.

"Sorry I took so long," Gabby said, tying the dog's leash to the table. "I met some of the other campaign workers. The TikTok influencers. Bea and Montana? They're super prominent in the AAPI activist community."

Talia tried not to scowl. This was par for the course. Her sister had a knack for drawing people in, for collecting new friends within five minutes of arriving somewhere. This unrelenting likeability stung because of how hard Gabby worked to avoid the rest of them. Moving to the country. Leaving get-togethers early. Attending Thanksgiving "dinner" only for the dessert. She did the bare minimum, and everyone accepted it because a little Gabby was better than no Gabby at all.

*She's here now*, Talia reminded herself. Things could still change.

"Quick question," Gabby said as she fired up her computer. "How would one leave the property?"

Talia startled, taken aback. "You just got here. You're already going to bail?" Typical. So typical.

"I don't mean right now. Eventually," Gabby said, squinting as she typed.

"But why? The Ranch has everything you could possibly need. Anything it doesn't, just ask Mindy to pick it up."

"Mindy seems to have a lot on her plate," Gabby said, "and I don't want to bother her just because I need tampons or whatever. Is there an old beater around, or maybe some sort of shuttle system that ferries people to the Real World?"

"Real World?" Talia blinked.

"Unless this is a cult or something, and we're not allowed to leave. It'd explain all the linen. Lol."

Talia could not reply. She was, quite literally, speechless. They had a long way to go to get on the same page.

From: Gabby Gunn <shccgabby@gmail.com>
Sent: Wednesday, September 6 4:13 PM
To: Eli dos Santos <Eli_dosSantos@sdzwa.org>
Subject: Re: PBS study

Hello,
It's Gabby Gunn, the PBSer. I'm officially in San Diego for the next month (? or two?) and would love to meet whenever is convenient for you. I'll just need some advance notice because I don't have my own car.

Thanks,
Gabby

---

From: Eli dos Santos <Eli_dosSantos@sdzwa.org>
Sent: Wednesday, September 6 4:45 PM
To: Gabby Gunn <shccgabby@gmail.com>
Subject: Re: PBS study

Nice to hear from you. I'm a little surprised, to be honest. PBSers tend to be secretive and insular. They like to deal with things on their own.

Would four o'clock on Friday work? I'll be meeting with another PBSer at that time, and it'd be a nice opportunity to chat, put our heads together for a bit.

Best,
Dr. Eli dos Santos, D.V.M., Dipl. ACZM, Dipl. ECZM (ZHM)
Chief Conservation and Wildlife Expert
San Diego Zoo Wildlife Alliance
619-555-0251

---

From: Gabby Gunn <shccgabby@gmail.com>
Sent: Wednesday, September 6 4:47 PM

To: Eli dos Santos <Eli_dosSantos@sdzwa.org>
Subject: Re: PBS study

I wouldn't call myself secretive but Friday at four is on the books. I'm not sure how I'll get there, but I'll make it happen, come hell or high water!

---

From: Eli dos Santos <Eli_dosSantos@sdzwa.org>
Sent: Thursday, September 7 7:59 AM
To: Gabby Gunn <shccgabby@gmail.com>
Subject: Re: PBS study

High water won't be much of a concern. We are currently in a drought.
    See you on Friday.

Best,
Dr. Eli dos Santos, D.V.M., Dipl. ACZM, Dipl. ECZM (ZHM)
Chief Conservation and Wildlife Expert
San Diego Zoo Wildlife Alliance
619-555-0251

---

From: Gabby Gunn <shccgabby@gmail.com>
Sent: Friday, September 8 9:15 AM
To: Eli dos Santos <Eli_dosSantos@sdzwa.org>
Subject: Re: PBS study

Hi,
I'm having some trouble securing a ride. Any chance we could catch up over the phone?

Thanks,
Gabby

---

From: Eli dos Santos <Eli_dosSantos@sdzwa.org>
Sent: Friday, September 8 9:26 AM

To: Gabby Gunn <shccgabby@gmail.com>
Subject: Re: PBS study

It would be more helpful to meet in person.

Best,
Dr. Eli dos Santos, D.V.M., Dipl. ACZM, Dipl. ECZM (ZHM)
Chief Conservation and Wildlife Expert
San Diego Zoo Wildlife Alliance
619-555-0251

---

From: Gabby Gunn <shccgabby@gmail.com>
Sent: Friday, September 8 9:28 AM
To: Eli dos Santos <Eli_dosSantos@sdzwa.org>
Subject: Re: PBS study

While I appreciate that meeting in person is preferable, I don't have a car, and I'm not very close to the zoo. Also, I'm brand new at my job, and I can't go screwing up yet. LOL!

A quick call would be great, if you can swing it. I'd love to chat and hear why you're being so mysterious about your research!

---

From: Eli dos Santos <Eli_dosSantos@sdzwa.org>
Sent: Friday, September 8 10:31 AM
To: Gabby Gunn <shccgabby@gmail.com>
Subject: Re: PBS study

I'm not being mysterious. It is irresponsible to publish data before it is ready.

Best,
Dr. Eli dos Santos, D.V.M., Dipl. ACZM, Dipl. ECZM (ZHM)
Chief Conservation and Wildlife Expert
San Diego Zoo Wildlife Alliance
619-555-0251

# Chapter Sixteen

## Gabby

I buried my face in my hands. The cost of the theater roof would be twice the initial estimate. Whatever fantasies I'd entertained of staying only a month vanished like smoke.

"We have options," Sydney insisted, but these "options" weren't exactly firing me up. A home equity loan—hard pass. Charging "normal prices" for shows—who could afford those? Sydney then lectured me about how most people had to balance the life they wanted with what was practical and, honestly, she could get bent.

"Everything okay?" Talia asked, picking up on my mood.

"Yeah. Sure," I lied, reaching down to pet the dog. His name was Frosty now, after the Frosted Faces on his name tag. "It's been a long week." I checked the time on my laptop. I wouldn't make it to the zoo by four o'clock, not in Friday traffic.

It was probably for the best, I reasoned. For one, dos Santos seemed quite difficult. He'd made the weird drought comment, and I didn't enjoy getting bullied by a large animal veterinarian. What was so bad about being "secretive" anyway? Trust, no one wanted to deal with swamp rabbits or weasels or cancer-ridden Tasmanian devils. I involved Diane with my flamingos and look where it got me. Directing comms for a shitty candidate. No offense.

Diane's voice rang in my head: *You'll use any excuse to avoid dealing with your PBS.*

*I tried!* I mentally spit back. *Why do you care?* She'd success-fully extricated herself from the sad, strange world of Gabrielle Gunn and awesome! I loved that for her! I hoped she and Bill were living it up Down the ShoreTM.

"Hey, ladies." Ivan popped his head through the door, nearly scaring me out of my skin. "Making sure you saw the calendar invite. Your dad and Ustenya are on their way home from the airport. They want to meet in the tasting room at five fifteen for a glass of wine, followed by dinner."

"About time they made an appearance," Talia grumbled.

"I have a calendar?" I said.

"Oh, Gabby, you crack me up," Ivan said, chuckling. "In advance of the meeting, I figured I'd check in to see how ev-eryone did with their week one goals."

I groaned internally, as Talia gleefully reported that not only had she installed supporter management software, but she'd also signed up one hundred new volunteers and several exciting meet-the-candidate events were in the works. Then it was my turn. I'd never had a real job, but was pretty sure you weren't paid if you failed, which meant I was thoroughly screwed.

"Just working through the list you sent!" I chirped, weigh-ing whether I should take the blame or tactfully explain that it was quite difficult to direct the comms of a person absolutely nobody wished to hear from. Even *The Union-Tribune* blew me off, unmoved by the fact my quadruple-great grandfather owned the paper in 1875.

"What does Marston Gunn even stand for?" asked the only reporter who picked up the phone and, girl, *same*, because when I went through the briefing book, the "key issues" section was empty. Dad didn't have any of those, apparently, not a single hot or cold take. The reporter told me to call back if he ever man-aged to do anything interesting, and good luck with that.

"Okay, but what specifically have you ticked off the list?" Ivan asked. "We entered this race super late, and it's important his name starts getting hits."

"Um, a lot of people seem to be out of office? Or OOO. I just learned that fun acronym!"

Ivan's eyes turned to glass.

"I'm genuinely doing my best," I added. Or at least my eighty-five percent—the roof was a real distraction.

"Yep, yep," Ivan clucked, bobbing his head. "It's a toughie. Listen. You're new to this and it's okay to admit you're struggling. Do you want me to put you in contact with a friend of mine who's done this before? She might be a great resource."

"Oh, thanks, that's so nice." I wiped the sweat from my brow. "But I'll figure it out on my own—"

"Classic Gabby," Talia piped in. "Squirrelly." I whipped in her direction. "Doesn't let other people behind the curtain. But we'll fix her." She passed me a wink. "You and I are going to be besties by the end of this, and that's a promise."

*Besties?* What was she talking about? Was the room spinning right now?

"Er. Cool," Ivan said. "I'll just call my friend—"

"Wait! I did chat with . . ." I checked my notes. "Kyle Sperber at *The North County Intelligencer*? She might be interested in covering him at some point." I didn't mention the "if he does anything interesting" part, or that the overall tone was "eat shit and die."

*"The Intelligencer?"* Ivan grinned, showing his pointy incisors to maximum effect. "That's awesome!"

"She didn't make any guarantees," I added quickly, my stomach plummeting to the ground. "What even is *The North County Intelligencer*? Sounds lame."

"Oh, they're terrific," Ivan said. "Their under-forty audience is huge." It wasn't the mainstay but still a perfectly legitimate news source, he explained. They had millions of social media followers and multiple media properties, including a YouTube channel and podcast about San Diego–based true crimes.

"Wow. So great," I said, pulling my sweatshirt away from my body.

Ivan blathered on about how they often appeared on the nightly news to report on local scams, but I only heard every third or fourth word because I was too focused on my skin, which was starting to burn.

"Gabby?" Squinting, Ivan walked all the way into the room. "Are you okay?"

"Yes. Of course." Now my throat was scratchy. "Why wouldn't I be?"

An acrid scent filled the room and Frosty hopped to his feet. He stood at attention beside me, staring up with his soupy brown eyes. *Shit*, I thought as my mind whirred with an inventory of animals that might show up. Grackles or flamingos or wolverines, it was anyone's guess.

"Gabby?" Talia said, craning.

"I have to go. I'm not feeling well. Ivan, can you watch Frosty?" I shoved the leash into his hand. "Be careful. I read online that Jindos are runners."

"Where the fuck are you going?" Talia demanded. "Did you not hear what Ivan said about the dinner?"

"Sorry," I said, grabbing my phone, my ChapStick, what else did I need? "I'll try to be back in time but I'm sure you can handle it on your own."

# Chapter Seventeen

## Talia

"Gabby!" Talia yelled, jogging out of her office. "We're not done!" But it was too late. Her sister was gone. *You can handle it on your own.* Exactly what Talia had been doing since forever.

"Huh," said a voice. "What's this?" Talia looked to her left, to where Ivan lingered outside her door, hands on hips, peering at a pile of something on the ground. As Talia walked closer, he announced, "It's poop. Fresh, from the looks of it."

"IVAN!" Talia screeched, jumping back. "Why are you standing so close to it? That's disgusting. God. Is the Jindo even potty-trained?"

"It's not Frosty's," Ivan said. "This has berries in it. Believe me when I say the dog eschews anything healthy. I'm very familiar with the consistency and makeup of his poop."

"I wouldn't go around bragging about that." Talia glanced over to where the dog stood in the open doorway, an utterly blank expression on its face. Gabby disappeared and left a pile of shit in her wake. There was probably a metaphor in there somewhere, but Talia refused to look.

"I'm serious," Ivan said. "He'll spit out the smallest speck of carrot." He pulled out his phone. For a brief and horrific moment, Talia thought he was about to snap a picture.

"WHAT ARE YOU DOING?"

"Sheesh. Calm down. I'm texting Mindy to send someone to clean it up."

Talia sighed. The meeting with Dad was already going to be a disaster. She'd managed to check a few items off her list, but they were piddly, inconsequential things. Highlighting these "accomplishments" might kill five minutes, perhaps seven, but Gabby's absence would be hard to explain.

"I'm on it!" Mindy shouted, rushing into the barn, a plastic shield covering her face. She held paper towels and trash bags in one hand, a shovel and some sort of spray in the other. "Everyone stand back!"

Talia bent down to retrieve Frosty's leash.

"Looks like monkey shit," Mindy observed.

Talia looped the leash around Ivan's neck. "You'd better hang on to that," she said. "Jindos are runners." She pivoted and walked out into the late afternoon sun.

The bell tower rang, which was weird, because it was not on the hour. Talia stopped and gazed in the direction of the art studio, not that she could see it from here. She'd need to deal with it at some point, despite not fully comprehending what "deal with it" meant. At the end of the day, it was a barn, and Talia had to prepare herself for the possibility she wasn't going to find any answers inside.

Sighing, Talia turned toward the house. She'd taken two, maybe three steps when the sound of growling erupted overhead. She quickened her pace, but the growls intensified, sounding strangely like Gregorian chants. Going against every instinct and all better judgment, Talia looked up and locked eyes with a monkey perched in a tree. "Are you fucking kidding me right now?" she said, laughing, even crying a tiny bit.

The monkey howled again.

"Fine, fine, I hear you," she said, more annoyed than scared. She hustled back to the barn to let Mindy know the culprit had been found. Yes, ma'am, it was a monkey. The property manager literally knew her shit.

# Chapter Eighteen

## Ozzie

Spencer shook Ozzie's hand. "Hey, brother, how's it going?" he said. "Thanks for inviting me. I brought my coworker, Paul. The pad looks great."

"Thanks, man." Ozzie shut the door behind them. He wasn't sure about the presence of this Paul character but since he hadn't expected Spencer to show up at all, he'd take the win. *Art show at my place Fri nite*, he'd written. *Lets hang w/o the ladies.* Freja was in Milan. Or Rome, maybe. It was hard to keep up.

Ozzie invited other people, too, and was optimistic about the prospect of making some bank. The money situation was tighter than he'd thought, and boy oh boy was Barclay throwing a fit over the back taxes, which Ozzie forgot to mention the first few times they met. Yes, half a million was a lot to owe, but an election year was coming up, so Ozzie was kind of counting on getting his slate wiped clean?

"That's not how it works," Barclay said, sighing with his whole body. "Tax breaks are not retroactive." Also, Ozzie probably didn't make enough to benefit from any tax cuts for the truly wealthy, which, like, *ouch*. Barclay then warned him that unless he came up with the money in the next ninety days, he might find himself playing handball with Uncle Doug at Otisville.

Dad didn't have the money to lend him anymore, and he wasn't about to sell the crib, and thus Ozzie would focus on selling art. There were tax implications for this, too, depending on cost basis and whatnot, but it sounded like a problem for future Ozzie. Step one was getting people in the door.

"Let me show you the goods," Ozzie said, leading the way. When they stepped inside the gallery, Ballsack approached carrying a tray of champagne.

"Veuve, anyone?" he said, and Paul gave him a sideways look—probably on account of the shorts and tank top—but accepted a glass nonetheless. The men began to peruse the collection.

"That's Sharon Tate's face steamer," Ozzie said, trailing behind them. "Burt Reynolds's Rolodex." An AMA award Kenny Rogers received for "The Gambler." A Ted Williams game used bat. Part of the Eiffel Tower's spiral staircase. And so on.

Finally, Paul stopped at the Hundred Acre Wood map from *Winnie the Pooh*, the most famous map in all of children's literature. It was the last thing Ozzie wanted to give up. He'd only left it in the gallery because it elevated everything else.

"Big *Pooh* fan?" Ozzie said. "Fun fact, Winnie's government name was Edward."

"That's right, I forgot about your *Winnie the Pooh* deal," Spencer said, and Ozzie wondered what the hell he meant. "Isn't that why you painted your front door green?"

"No. The green door represents money," Ozzie said, glowering, even though yes, of course Christopher Robin *lived behind a green door in another part of the forest*. How had Spencer known? It wasn't the sort of thing Ozzie would admit to Talia. Maybe Gabby said something. She was quite the sneak.

"Huh," Paul said, moving closer, inspecting each place on the map, from Kanga's House to the Sandy Pit Where Roo Plays. "My wife would love this. Pooh Bear is my nickname for her."

"Gross," Ozzie muttered.

"And she's expecting. It'd be perfect for the nursery."

Ozzie pulled a face. The guy had long cleared sixty. It must've been a second or third wife.

Spencer squinted at the map. "I don't get it," he said. "'Nice for Piknicks'? 'Big Stones and Rox'?" He glanced over his shoulder. "Why are so many things spelled wrong?"

"It's meant to be *cheeky*," Ozzie said. "It's supposed to have been drawn by a *child*."

"Okay, but 'Eeyore's Gloomy Place, Rather Boggy and Sad'? Seems kind of depressing for a nursery."

"We all need a gloomy place, Spencer," Ozzie said. Little did the guy know that "rather boggy and sad" was how he thought of Spencer and Talia's relationship. "If you're in the market for something cheerier, I have several Bob Ross paintings. Who wouldn't want to look at happy little trees all day?"

Paul wasn't listening. Instead, he took a picture of the map, probably to show his wife. "How much?" he asked and flipped around.

"Seven hundred fifty thousand," Ozzie said, shooting for the moon. It'd last been appraised for $500K but Paul nodded, unfazed.

If the guy was willing to pay it, Ozzie couldn't say no, but, God, he could puke just imagining this masterpiece in the clutches of some dumb baby. "Maybe she'd be interested in some smaller Pooh memorabilia instead?" he tried. "I have an ink drawing of Pooh, Piglet, and Christopher Robin peering over a bridge, and another of Eeyore laying tits up in his bog . . ."

"The map is perfect," Paul said, sliding his phone back into his pocket. "I'll check with her tonight. Hopefully by the end of the weekend, we'll close the deal, and this adorable scene will be up in the nursery."

# Chapter Nineteen

## Gabby

We pulled up to the entrance. "Thanks, Tony," I said as I leapt out of the car. "I really appreciate everything." By everything I meant the drive, his discretion, and most of all the way he'd maintained a scary calm when I sprinted up to him in the motor court, demanding to be taken to the zoo. Now it was one full hour past my scheduled meeting with dos Santos, and I didn't know whether he'd still be at work, but my symptoms were raging, and I needed to act.

I tried the administration building first, but the doors were locked. The park itself was open, so I made a beeline for the nearest obvious employee. "Hello! Hi! Excuse me!" I said, panting, practically foaming at the mouth. "I'm looking for Dr. Eli dos Santos. Any idea where he is?"

The girl—a teenage ticket taker—tilted her head, confused.

"HE'S THE CHIEF CONSERVATION OFFICER," I shouted. "Sorry. I didn't mean to yell. He's expecting me."

"He left ten minutes ago," said a voice. I whirled around to find a tall man, in his early thirties, best guess, dressed in a plaid button-down, khaki pants, and scuffed-up Vans. "You must be Gabby," the man said as the ticket taker shuffled away. He extended a hand and smiled with a set of impressively white teeth. "I'm Raj. From the message boards? *Mydaus javanensis.* The Sunda stink badger."

"Raj! The San Diego PBSer," I said, at once consumed by such a profound sense of relief I honestly could've wept. "It's so nice to meet you," I gushed, shaking and shaking and shaking his hand. "Someone who gets it. Wow. Sorry I missed the meeting. How was dos Santos? Is he such a turd IRL?"

"Beg pardon?"

"He's just . . ." Biting my lip, I scratched my left arm. "His tendency to withhold information is extremely aggravating. Does he want to help or not? Anyway." My eyes darted around. "I have a problem." I pushed up a sleeve to reveal my bumpy, mottled arm. "I'm flaring and don't know what the hell I'm supposed to do."

Raj nodded, smiling with his lips closed. "Let's take a stroll." He gestured toward the entrance. "If you're flaring, a zoo's the perfect place to be. No one will notice an extra creature or two."

"Brilliant," I said, wondering if they'd let me move in.

---

A flamboyance of flamingos greeted us as we entered the zoo. I hadn't considered this "stroll" might become a memory lane of horrors, but it seemed too late to back out. We swapped PBS origin stories as we ventured down Treetops Way.

Raj's symptoms began five years ago, when a volcanic island collapsed into the sea, causing a tsunami in the Sunda strait, after which Raj was visited upon by a trio of baby stink badgers. Our early warning signs were similar, though Raj described the scent as "burnt tires."

I told Raj about my bald eagle, the ocelots, "and a bunch more after that," not wanting to get into it. Also, I was distracted by the intense itchiness and the buzzing of my phone with a barrage of incoming texts from my sister. There'd been a monkey. And poop in the barn. Talia was demonstrably irritated, but thank God it wasn't some vicious carnivore that would've ripped everyone to shreds.

Urgent situation, I wrote.

Friend in need.
Planning to make it to dinner!

I had no desire to attend the tasting room summit but hated to leave Talia in a lurch. Flying under the radar was key with my sister, and bailing on dinner was the kind of thing she'd never let me forget. But, right now, I had bigger issues to tackle. The monkey showed up but I was still scratching like crazy. Would something else appear?

"I can't decide which is worse," Raj mused as we passed the orangutan enclosure. "A different animal every time would be stressful, but nonstop stink badgers suck. They're basically skunks, but worse."

I noodled on this, checking my arms, which were red but calming down. "Yeah," I said. "You'd almost rather have a skunk, because baby skunks are pretty cute?"

"That's what I'm saying," Raj agreed.

"I've had some badger-adjacent creatures," I said, mentally ticking through the list. On my left rib cage, eighteen dime-sized tattoos ran in two lines. An eagle head. An ocelot spot. A mongoose foot and so on. One tattoo for each flare, minus the flamingos. And monkey, I supposed. I hadn't gotten around to them yet.

"Two otters," I said. "I also had a 'least weasel.' The wolverine. He didn't smell so great, either. Like stinky cheese." A wolverine's anal gland secretions were "complex," said the guy who picked him up, and while there was nothing creepy about his reporting of this, it was not something a sixteen-year-old girl cared to hear from a wildlife rescue man.

We rounded the corner and saw the gorillas. Or *Gorilla gorilla gorillas*, who really knew. Raj and I exchanged looks. We were thinking the same thing.

"I don't envy your stink badgers," I said. "But at least you can create a plan of attack? I always have to come up with a new solution. And let me tell you, there aren't a plethora of screaming hairy armadillo rescues around, much less one you can trust."

"I never thought about that . . ." Raj said with a frown.

"And maybe I shouldn't care? About finding the 'best' place for them? Diane says I'm too picky, and I coddle my symptoms. But what am I going to do? Just let these animals suffer? They didn't ask to show up in my bedroom."

"Who's Diane? Your sister? A therapist?"

A smile snuck out. "Therapist is pretty accurate, but actually Diane's, uh, a family friend. She was the first one to bring up PBS. If not for her, I don't know what I would've done . . ." I sniffed. My emotions were getting all backed up, and I was now both rashy and hot. I yanked off my hoodie and tied it around my waist.

"For my first few flares," I went on, "everyone thought I was making it up. When they were forced to acknowledge I wasn't in a position to acquire multiple exotic animals, they went into full gaslighting mode. *The wolverine is a coincidence, Gabby. They are capable of traveling up to twenty miles per day.*" My Dad impression was pretty good, and I was sad Raj couldn't appreciate it. "That's when I started getting these." I lifted the side of my shirt. "A tattoo for each flare."

Raj stopped. He leaned down to study the symbols. "Those are so cool," he said, running his finger along them without touching me.

"The wolverine was what prompted it." I dropped my shirt. "He was my seventh flare, so I had to backdate a few, but it suddenly seemed necessary to establish proof. It's become a ritual. Makes me feel like I'm paying homage to the animals. Diane thinks it's ridiculous. Back to the coddling thing again."

Raj flashed his brilliant white smile. "It makes all the sense in the world."

We stopped in front of the aviary. I peered up at the sign. GUNN AVIARY. What was the price of putting one's name on an oversized birdcage, I wondered?

"You coming?" Raj said, holding open the door.

"Oh, yeah, sorry." I scrambled inside, and the door clapped shut behind us. "I'm envious yours came on as an adult. No one to accuse you of being an attention whore."

"My parents are great about it," Raj said, and I felt a pang of envy. "They help me as much as they can, but they don't have a ton of money and live in a condo themselves. Family is not my problem—"

"Must be nice . . ."

"Unfortunately, thanks to PBS, I'm currently unemployed."

Until recently, Raj had been a lawyer with the transit authority. Long story short, his department was invited to a ribbon-cutting ceremony to celebrate the opening of a new trolley station. All the San Diego bigwigs were there—the mayor, city council members, the tribal chairman of the Sycuan Band of the Kumeyaay Nation—but before anyone had a chance to wield the prop scissors, the station was overrun by "skunks."

People were concerned about terrorism, and maybe they should close the entire transit system? The other lawyers agreed that yes, absolutely, they had to shut it all down. Folks would have a hard time getting to work and school, but the risk wasn't worth it. Raj knew then he had to confess it was him, not animal terrorism, and was fired on the spot. They got rid of one lawyer but had to hire six more, and a crisis PR team, to deal with the onslaught of lawsuits from attendees and animal rights groups.

"Are they even allowed to fire you, legally?" I asked as we exited the aviary. "PBS isn't your fault." Talia would be all over that. She'd send menacing letters to his employer, telling them she'd see them in court.

"I could've probably filed something under the ADA. But I felt weird about adding another lawsuit to the ones I'd already created. At least no one was hurt." Raj exhaled, and I sensed him doing the it-could-be-worse mental gymnastics. I'd been there. "But it wasn't just the firing. PBS tends to result in a cascade of problems."

"Oh, I'm familiar with the cascade." A flare derailed a day, a week, a whole life. You might be interested in someone romantically, until your roommate is disgusted by a mere grackle—one of the better animals, honestly—and your family is like, *God, not again*, and you remember you are a complete freak, and it's not worth involving anyone else. Perhaps later, you're symptomless for a year or two, and wonder, am I finally free of this? Then you find a flaminglet on the mantel and, next thing you know, are living in California under duress.

"I'm looking for a new job," Raj said, "but can't ask for a recommendation, and if I don't find something in the next two or three months, I'll have to move. What then? Who would rent to an unemployed guy who's known to harbor pet skunks? Wherever I go has to be affordable *and* capable of accommodating up to ten stink badgers at one time."

"Jesus," I muttered, counting my lucky stars that I'd always had money and space (and Diane) to handle my flares. But for how much longer would this be true? Dad could fire me. More roofs might fall. My safety net felt thin, and I hated myself for assuming it would hold forever.

"I'm white-knuckling it until everything collapses, I guess." Raj forced a laugh, and I shriveled into myself. "And that's the logistical stuff. Do you ever worry about . . . ?" He swallowed. "Finding a romantic relationship?"

"No. Never," I lied.

"I haven't dated anyone long-term since I was diagnosed. I seriously need to follow the Stuart model."

I glanced over, understanding I was supposed to recognize

the name from the message boards. Diane used my log-in, so Raj probably assumed I was on there all the time.

"Come on, you know Stu. He has nonspecific PBS, like yours? He married someone with trimethylaminuria—fish odor disease?"

"Oh, right." It sounded vaguely familiar. "Well. Good for them," I said, wondering what he expected me to take from this.

"He's got it all figured out. Find a woman who gets the complexities of a bizarre condition."

I wanted to tell Raj to aim a little higher than fish odor, but it wasn't my place. Anyway, I knew what he meant.

"That's why the discussion forum is such a godsend," he added. "It gives me a sense of community and reminds me I'm not alone. Plus, it's how I met Dr. dos Santos."

"Oh, yeah. He's heaven-sent. Love the guy."

"Right? I've been working with him for nine months and haven't flared in all that time. Fingers crossed it holds out."

I threw him a look. Now, this was a surprise. "What does he have you doing?" I asked.

"Relaxation techniques. Meditation. Talk therapy. Stuff like that."

"Cool," I said, narrowing my eyes. This was awfully close to it's-all-in-your-head territory, but I didn't want to burst Raj's balloon.

"I should head out," he said as we circled back to the flamingos.

"Yeah. Same."

"How are you feeling? Still itchy?"

"Yeah, I guess . . ." I began, but . . . actually . . . I examined my arm. My *skin*. It was smooth, not a hint of red. I sniffed, and the air smelled fine. Well, not *fine*, but like a zoo. "Oh my God," I said, looking around. All animals appeared to be in their proper enclosures and, when I checked my phone, Talia had texted that Mindy captured the monkey but when they went to feed it, the creature had—poof!—vanished. Craziest thing.

"Everything okay?" Raj asked, furrowing his brow.

"My rash disappeared," I marveled. "So did the monkey, apparently. That's never happened before. I'm always the one who has to rehome it." My brain was spinning. "Did I stop the symptoms? Is it even possible?"

"Anything's possible," Raj said with yet another of his grins. "That's what I tell myself, anyway. Some days, it's the only way to survive."

# Chapter Twenty

## Talia

Talia tried three times, but Spencer wasn't answering. As she made her way to the tasting room, she checked his location and saw he wasn't in their apartment. He seemed to be walking around near Ozzie's building.

As Talia debated what to do next, her dad's voice reverberated through the house, coming from the opposite direction of the tasting room. She pulled a one-eighty and followed the sound, winding past the library and craft room until she spotted him through a window, sitting on one of the verandas, across from Ustenya, in a red-and-gold-striped chair. After checking her reflection in an antique mirror, Talia inhaled, threw her hair behind her shoulders, and stepped outside.

"Angie Parker can go fuck herself," Dad was saying. He glanced up. "Oh. Hi, sweetheart."

"Hi, guys," Talia said, unsure where to sit—across from Dad but beside Ustenya, or vice versa? As always, Dad wasn't helping. It was the first they'd seen each other in California, and a hug or handshake would've been nice.

"I'm glad you two made it back safely," Talia said, picking the seat beside Ustenya as Dad continued his bitching. Apparently, Representative Parker told *The O.C. Register* that the "relentless mansplainer Marston Gunn" tossed her his keys as they were walking into a Democratic fundraising dinner.

"But this did happen, yes?" Ustenya said, pouring Talia a glass of Pinot Grigio.

"It was her fault for dressing like a goddamn valet."

"Ah. Yes. Well. She can go walk a bear. Anyhow, other candidates badmouthing you is a good sign," Ustenya said. "It means they see you as a threat."

"Valid point," Talia said and took a gulp of wine.

"Speaking of other candidates, who do I need to suck off to stop hearing about Dave fucking Slimp and his goddamn $32 million in the bank?"

"Jesus, Dad," Talia said, setting her glass back on the table with a wobbly hand. The fundraising trip, it seemed, had not gone well.

"I apologize for your father's boorish behavior," Ustenya said. "He is very grouchy from all the wretched traveling. There is an airline in this country that doesn't even assign seats. Have you heard of this? It's for a fart." She flubbered her lips. "I say, you can quit! You can quit this campaign right now. I would be happy for it!"

"You're a very supportive wife," Dad grumbled.

"I'm sorry," Ustenya said, "but this is very tiring, and you look like death. He looks terrible, doesn't he? It's okay. You can tell the truth."

Talia, of course, wasn't about to get in the middle. She made a bland comment about Dad's vigor and how he appeared quite trim.

"Yes, yes, you are handsome as ever," Ustenya said, flapping a hand, "but what do you need with all this stress? Always having a bitch jumping in your ass?" Someone else might've assumed she was invoking Angie Parker again, but Talia had heard this one before. A bitch jumping in your ass meant you were under pressure.

"You know why I'm doing this," Dad responded, and then launched a new rant. Everyone was calling him a "former media mogul," and where was the damned justice?

Talia studied him as he spoke, and maybe Ustenya was onto something, because he did suddenly seem like a much older man than the one she'd seen two weeks ago in New York. His skin was sallow, and his scalp was now visible beneath his salt-and-pepper hair.

"What about you?" Dad said, turning his attentions to Talia. "What have you been up to? Hopefully you have some good news."

Talia cleared her throat, then took a sip of wine to give herself a moment to think. "Well, let's see. I installed the new supporter management software." God, she was really milking that one. "I've also spent some time poking around in the database to get a sense of demographics."

They'd started phone-banking—the team had very high daily targets!—and now that he was back in town, Talia was aiming for three to five meet-the-candidate events. Maybe he could do some canvassing with them next weekend? Door-knocking sounded inefficient, but it was still the best way to get people to the polls. According to Google, anyway.

"You're doing a great job," Ustenya said. She winked, gave a thumbs-up.

"Oh. Thanks." Talia flushed. It was the second, maybe third compliment she'd ever received from Ustenya.

"You see?" Ustenya said to Dad. "I told you she could do it."

"Someone thought I couldn't?"

"Come on." Ustenya popped to her feet. "Dinner should be ready."

Dad stood with a groan, and Talia followed, still stung by the comment and wondering when somebody was going to mention Gabby. An *emergency situation*. With a *friend*. How did she already have a friend in San Diego? Where was she always getting these people?

"What was Mindy saying earlier?" Dad said as they walked into the house. "About poop in the HQ?"

Every feature on Ustenya's face pinched together. "It's the damned jippo. Why did I let you talk me into that thing?"

"It wasn't the Jindo," Talia said. "Mindy captured a monkey, but we're not sure where it went."

Dad peered over his shoulder. "You lost a *monkey*?"

"I didn't lose it. I was barely involved."

"That sounds like an issue."

Talia's face burned. "It probably belongs to a neighbor," she said. "Everyone around here is sitting on multiple acres. Some-one must have an exotic pet or two."

A thought struck Talia. Was this a Gabby thing? God, she hoped not. They had enough problems without a bunch of birds or reptiles showing up. Maybe it was good Gabby was off with her friend. She wasn't Ozzie. She wasn't blowing things up or burning them down. But Gabby had a knack for creat-ing a special brand of chaos, the kind that made you question yourself and everything you'd just seen.

# Chapter Twenty-One

## Gabby

It was past ten o'clock, but I could see the light peeking out from beneath Talia's door. I knocked lightly and asked if she had a minute.

"Sure. Come in," she said, and I walked in to find her on the bed, sitting with one leg bent, the other draped over the side. A laptop was open in front of her.

"Ustenya has such interesting taste," I said, taking in the room. Talia's looked like mine: same ornate dark wood furniture, same white comforter, same seven pillows on the bed. "What would you call that style of headboard? It's very torture-chamber. Very world-without-joy."

Talia let a smirk slip out, and I was glad for the crack in the tension between us. I'd made it to dinner, but arrived late, leaving her to hold things down for an hour when the vibes were demonstrably terrible. Dad was cranky as hell, and Ustenya was dialed up to eleven, as if doing an impression of herself.

"Italian Renaissance Revival," Talia said, about the furniture. "Bulky. Dark. Architectural appeal trumps domestic utility."

"Totally," I said. "Anyway. Again. I'm sorry for my tardiness."

"You made it. That's what counts," she said unconvincingly as she typed something into her computer. "How's your friend? Will she survive whatever catastrophe you pulled her from the brink of?"

"Oh. Yeah. He lost his job. Tough break." I winced, realizing how dickish it was to use Raj's problems to cover my own ass. "But he'll be fine, eventually . . ."

"He?" Talia straightened all the way up. "Is this a boyfriend?"

"God, no. Just a friend," I said.

"Oh. Okay." She laughed to herself. "Mystery solved. Yeah, I didn't think you'd be into men."

"Um, what now?" I pulled my chin into my neck.

"I was confused. Since you're gay. Or I assumed so, anyway." Talia stopped to contemplate this. "Although I guess it's not so straightforward these days." She shrugged merrily and returned to computing.

I stared, flummoxed. I wasn't gay. Then again, I wasn't *not* gay, either. I'd hooked up with three girls—a rugby player, the homecoming queen, an apprentice at the New York City Ballet—and two different guys from my dorm at NYU. There were other boys kissed, other women flirted with and eyed from afar, but sex was so daunting, and way too intimate, which, yes, I understood was the point. Also, I had PBS, and Freja's reaction when she was my roommate told the whole story. I was weird. Disgusting. Too much to take. Suddenly, Raj's find-someone-with-fish-odor plan didn't seem so wild.

"I don't mean to be rude," Talia said, "but I need to work. I sold Dad on the importance of meet-the-candidate events, and he wants a list of options by tomorrow morning. Never mind it's Friday night."

"Can I help?"

"Ha," she said, scowling.

"Um. Okay." I backed up. "I'll leave you to—"

"Why are you here?" Talia looked up. "In California? You've barely done any work—"

"That's not my fault!"

"And when Dad is finally around to meet, you run off to see a 'friend.' Have you gotten him one interview?" she asked.

"Not sure if you've noticed, but he's a pretty shitty candidate."

"Why. Are. You. Here."

"Ustenya blackmailed me," I blurted, and Talia's eyes flew open. "I used Dad's credit card for some, um, personal expenses, and Ustenya threatened to cut me off if I didn't join the campaign. The monthly disbursement, the twenty-five-year gift, all of it." I paused to catch up with my own breath as Talia remained speechless, donning an expression I couldn't read.

"You're probably wondering why they deemed it so important to have me here and SAME!" I threw up my hands. "But I'm not merely collecting a paycheck. I want the money, but not for free." *The irony*, I thought, when I'd been getting it for free all these years. "It's why I spend all damned day cold-calling every newspaper on the West Coast. It's demoralizing. But I keep doing it, because I'm trying to hold up my end of the bargain."

Sighing, Talia pushed her computer aside. "I appreciate you telling me that," she said. "And it *is* demoralizing, but it won't last forever."

"Yeah. He'll totally have to quit soon."

"No. I mean." Talia shook her head. "I've spent all week combing through our database, and I see an opening for Dad." According to Talia, California's primary system benefited lesser-known candidates, because the top two vote-getters moved on to the general, regardless of party. It was the rare case in which a crowded field and splitting the vote were advantages, for no-names, anyway. "I know he doesn't seem very compelling right now."

I snorted. "That's one way to put it—"

"But he's not the worst candidate," she said, and this was also true. Based on what I'd read in the briefing book, the docket was full of immigrant bashers, climate deniers, anti-vaxxers, and moms of "unfairly maligned" January 6 insurrectionists. There was a convicted sex offender who promised to fight against "poor people who hate rich people, black people who hate white people, gay people who hate straight people, feminists who hate men, and bratty college kids who hate their parents" and a guy running on a "fake toxic masculinity" platform, though he didn't say whether he was for or against it. On the other hand, at least these folks had some "key issues."

"We have a real opportunity here," Talia continued. "Dad is a blank slate as far as the public's concerned. He's not controversial. He's never been accused of anything questionable in the workplace."

"I guess . . ." I said, though honestly, this felt like a close call.

"Here. Check this out," Talia said, turning the computer toward me. I lowered—cautiously—onto the bed. "San Diego's coastal communities are deeply blue, but turnout can vary wildly. In Cardiff, for example, only twenty-seven percent of registered voters show up for the primary. But there's no reason it can't be similar to Carlsbad, where turnout is as high as eighty percent in some precincts. It's a statewide election, but the trick for Dad will be to build local enthusiasm first."

"Wow," I said, dizzy with the numbers and jargon. "Maybe you should've been in politics this whole time."

Talia wielded one of her face-stretching grins, not even bothering to cover it up like she usually did. No matter how many people complimented her wide, dazzling smile, she was self-conscious about her "jack-o'-lantern face," probably because in ninth grade, some boy asked if she was related to Terrance and Phillip from the cartoon *South Park*. At first she assumed they thought she was gassy, or possibly Canadian, when actually they were trying to imply her mouth resembled a line cutting her head in two. Talia was devastated, even after Diane insisted that if a person went to such lengths to explain a joke, it was objectively not funny. Unlike when Keith Biglia told me I looked like Lucy from *Peanuts*. Everyone understood precisely what he meant.

"I'm happy you're here," Talia said, and it was one of the nicest compliments she'd ever paid me. "I know you were forced to come, but I'm glad you want to help. I was depressed during dinner, thinking Dad seems so old—"

"He's not young."

"And now I'm downright invigorated. I'm telling you, it's that Ranch magic."

I smiled, as in, *sure, okay*.

"How 'bout it?" Talia put up a hand for a high-five. "Up top for Team Gunn."

I rolled my eyes. "You're a dork," I said, nudging her in the thigh instead. It was nice to feel things were okay between us, for a little while at least.

# Chapter Twenty-Two

## Ozzie

Ballsack was in the guest room, rolling calls. The art show hadn't gone as expected.

Only a few people came—valid, since it was Friday night—but Ozzie's bank account didn't care about days of the week. He had someone on the hook for Fidel Castro's toilet, so fingers crossed, but *Winnie the Pooh*'s map was off the table, and honestly, it was for the best. That one sale would've changed everything, but it was like selling a family member. To a baby.

Ballsack stumbled into the kitchen to provide an update, which wasn't much. He'd tried contacting the backup bidder on *Bestiary*, but the guy was now focused on a partially shredded Banksy print.

"It's tough stuff," Ballsack said, rubbing his face. The kid looked like he'd just woken up from a three-day bender. "Your art is very specific. I'll keeping trying, though! Until I fall over dead. Any luck with the brand deals?"

Ozzie shook his head. They were losing followers on the daily. Ten thousand here, fifty thousand there. It felt like an active conspiracy, though Ozzie suspected something simpler, but also worse. He was too old and too poor to be interesting.

"Um, I have to ask?" Ballsack said, scratching his scalp. "What's the plan if we don't sell anything? Can you borrow money? From a bank or your dad?"

"A bank?" Ozzie screwed up his face. "Do people even use those anymore? And, not sure if you've kept up with the news, but Pops is broke."

"What about your sisters?"

"I can't ask my sisters! Get it together, Ballsack!"

But wait.

Maybe a sister *was* his ticket out. They probably had tons of cash, what with their boring lives. Plus, Talia earned a real-life salary and had already locked in the twenty-five-year gift. He doubted Gabby's theater made jack, but she didn't own property in the city or invest in art. Ozzie could see her squirreling away money in a cookie jar or some shit.

"Break over," Ballsack said as he grabbed a kiwi guava Celsius from the fridge. "Gotta get back on that grind."

As he wandered off, Ozzie pondered the sisters some more. Logistically speaking, Talia was the better choice, though she'd obviously make him do something depraved, like adhere to a budget. Gabby would be easier to convince. Either way, both already considered him a raging loser, so why not double down?

Ozzie unlocked his phone and scrolled. He had to go back pretty far to find the number. Hesitating, he hovered a finger over the name. Finally, he inhaled and pressed down. Somewhere in California, a phone rang.

# Chapter Twenty-Three

## Talia

When they arrived at Cardiff State Beach, the white tents were set up, likewise the tables, chairs, and extra trash bins. Four all-terrain wheelchairs waited at the edge of the parking lot and two dozen volunteers in blue T-shirts milled around, chatting, and filling canisters with pens. It was their first meet-the-candidate event.

"Should you pick him up or something?" Talia said, literally tapping her foot, her body full of nerves. Gabby was taking a thousand years to coax the damned Jindo out of the car.

"Jindos are very stubborn. Give us a second." Gabby yanked the leash, and Frosty finally relented, spilling out of the SUV like a sack of lazy dog. "How is this going to work?" she asked as they walked toward the sand. The ocean and skies were gray, the air thick with salt and the vague scent of fish. "It's a 'beach cleanup and surf lesson,' but are people supposed to do one or both or what?"

"Whatever they want," Talia snapped, like it was the most obvious thing in the world even as she began to panic that she'd not made the format clear enough. First they'd pick up trash. Afterward, an optional (free) surf lesson with one of the pros, accompanied by Dad.

"Well, I'm sure it'll be a huge success," Gabby said.

Talia eyed her sister, wondering if she was fucking with her. "Yeah . . ." she said, warily.

Talia scanned the crowd and saw only volunteers. She'd advertised. Her team had texted hundreds of voters, and Gabby had called all the reporters who'd previously blown her off. They'd put in the effort, but what if it was still a bust?

"I guess the only question is . . ." Gabby said. They stopped to let a red lifeguard truck drive by. "Will anyone *want* to surf with Dad?"

"Geez! How about some positive energy?" Talia said, but her sister was really over here reading her mind. "Either way, I'm happy to jump in. I could use a refresh. It's been a while."

Gabby smirked. "Oh yeah? Are the waves rad on the Upper East Side? Didn't know you were such a surfer."

"Um, I've been surfing since forever?" Talia said. "I spent every summer in San Diego and went out most days."

"That's right," Gabby said as she guided Frosty onto the wood planks they'd set down to accommodate anyone who might struggle to negotiate sand. "Sometimes I forget you got all the California perks, whereas Ozzie and I spent our time rotting in the rec pavilion."

Talia narrowed her eyes. Was that pointed? It sounded pointed. It wasn't Talia's fault she visited Mom whenever she could, while Gabby and Ozzie only did to comply with what Talia presumed was a legal decree. Granted, they were young, and not as close to Daphne, but they'd so easily accepted the "absentee parent" narrative, happily letting Diane step into her place.

"You and Ozzie attended surf camp," Talia said, suddenly remembering. *These two*, she thought, *always with their revisionist history.*

Gabby chuckled. "You're thinking of when we did Junior Lifeguards," she said. "And we didn't touch the water after the first day. We spent the week laying out on the beach. Ozzie called it tanning camp."

"I'm sure the people in charge were thrilled."

"Oh, they loved it. Two fewer jerk kids to keep track of."

They walked beneath the main canopy, where the volunteers stood at attention. Now that Talia saw the new merch on human bodies, she realized it kind of sucked. Dad dreamt up the slogan—*GUNNING FOR YOU!*—which Talia found both aggressive and confusing, and she suspected that more than one person would mistake Gunning for his last name. Meanwhile, beyond the tent waved a pair of flags. *Rip currents*, they advertised. *Do not swim between these two spots.* Literal red flags. Terrific. Talia was making everyone sign liability waivers, but didn't want to actually have to use them.

"It sucks he's not here," Gabby said.

Talia startled, almost having forgotten where she was. "Who? Dad? He's over there."

"No." Gabby laughed. "Ozzie."

Talia snorted. "San Diego is the last place he needs to be, given his life is such a mess right now."

"A mess?" Gabby repeated, brows pinched. "In what way?"

Talia paused to collect her thoughts. He called—what was it?—a week ago? He needed a favor, and this favor was to borrow several hundred thousand dollars. The ask was so outrageous Talia made him repeat it two or three times. But, no, she'd heard correctly, and *maybe* she could've cobbled it together in a life-or-death scenario, but not to "clear up a tax oversight," whatever that meant.

"Thanks for considering it," Ozzie had mumbled, before quickly hanging up.

"Talia . . . ?" Gabby prodded.

Talia shook her head. "Oh. Yeah. I guess he's having financial issues," she said, surprised he hadn't asked Gabby for the money. He probably respected her too much. Just like that, any lingering regrets Talia had about denying him flew away.

"You must've misunderstood," Gabby said with some authority, because she was the only expert on the subject of Oscar M. Gunn. It was so tiresome, their little gang of two. "He paid over a million bucks for a broken computer."

"You see the problem, then."

"You're always assuming the worst of him," Gabby said, squatting to retrieve a fresh pile of Frosty poop. "Don't take this the wrong way, but you tend to read into things."

Talia clenched her jaw. Even when the problem was Ozzie, she somehow got painted as the bad guy. Enough was enough. "He invited Spencer to his apartment for an *art show*," she said, "and apparently the whole affair had quite the whiff of desperation. He's already trying to sell the damn computer."

Gabby gave the slightest jump—a twitch, really—but just as soon regained her composure. Of course. She'd never let herself think poorly of sweet little Oscar. "He probably realized purchasing it was a mistake," she said, "or thinks he can flip it for a profit. Anyway, if he were so desperate, wouldn't he be here, same as me?"

Talia sighed. It was a fair point. Maybe the situation wasn't dire, and he'd simply seen Talia as an easy target.

"You're right. I am overthinking it," Talia said, slightly hating herself for copping to this reputation of hers. "Forget I brought it up. You two are so close. If he were in any kind of trouble, you'd know."

# Chapter Twenty-Four

## Gabby

I was thinking about Ozzie, and trying to recall the last time we spoke, when Talia marched up and shoved a stack of fliers into my hand. "I need to check on the sign language interpreter," she said. "And then it's time to get this show on the road."

I jiggled my head, hoping to clear out the Ozzie-related fog. My sister had rattled me, but also, I'd made an excellent point. Desperate people bent to Ustenya's wishes. I knew firsthand.

"Let's review the marching orders," Talia said.

"I think I got it . . ."

"When you mingle," Talia said, "hit the points we discussed." She gestured to her list of very normal conversational topics.

Who are you voting for in the primary?
Do you need help filling out a voter registration form?
What's your plan for getting to the polls?

Anything a voter said, even and especially if they complained, I was supposed to work Dad's name into it. *Marston Gunn would agree with a lot of that. It sounds like you and Marston Gunn share a lot of the same values.*

"Got it, got it," I said. My eyes drifted toward Dad and—jump scare. He was standing around with his wetsuit open and unzipped to the waist, his saggy old-man pecs on display for all to see. Normally I wouldn't have cared—live and let live and all that—but the stakes felt higher than usual. Dad was running for political office, and I'd invited my professional contacts to the event. Granted, this included one hundred news outlets who'd ghosted me plus Raj and Dr. dos Santos, but Dad was not presenting himself as a serious candidate, and for some reason, I was taking it personally.

"As soon as he finishes his opening remarks," Talia said, "grab a trash-picker-upper and a bag and mingle. It's good you brought the Jindo." Her eyes skipped over to Frosty. "Dogs are great ice breakers. Even if yours is a bit mangy."

"Hey!"

"And don't forget to ask for contact information," Talia said. "We're establishing relationships so we can help people across the finish line in March."

"March. Right. Because we'll still be here then."

Talia glowered. "Anyway. If you don't mind, check on Dad every once in a while. Make sure he has enough water and breath mints."

With that, Talia marched off, kicking up sand as she went. She wasn't wearing clogs today, but even her sneakers were suspiciously thick-soled. Why was she always doing a *thing* with her shoes? I never would've guessed someone who was five-foot-six could have such hang-ups about her height.

Eventually people filtered down from the parking lot. After sending Sydney a selfie, I scrolled through my text messages, alarmed by how far I had to go to reach Ozzie's name. Admittedly, I'd had to text a lot of random people lately, and he should've been pinned, but I'd never needed to do that before.

He had to be fine, right? Ozzie made gobs of money with his sponcon and loved to brag about having invested in the

Duolingo IPO. Also, he had something Talia and I did not—his settlement cash. The whole thing was terrible, and he deserved the money, but windfalls were windfalls, however you got them.

Talia's voice crackled from the speakers. "Hello, everyone!" she said. "Thank you for coming to the first Meet Marston event. If you can gather over here, he'd like to say a few words before we start the cleanup."

I sighed and returned the phone to my back pocket.

---

Forty minutes later, Frosty and I meandered along the shoreline, on the search for constituents to bother and trash to retrieve but not finding much of either. Talia's awkward questions weren't the conversation starters she'd promised and Frosty hated eye contact and being petted and was so afraid of water that he kept running into people to escape the gently encroaching tide.

We ventured all the way down the beach, turning back once we hit the river mouth. Kids were in school, and the morning fog hadn't burned off, so it was quiet, with only our volunteers, some surfers, and a contingent of walkers and dogs. This felt like a failure, and I worried Talia would take it too much to heart.

As we approached the tent, I spotted the TikTok girls hanging around by the sign-in sheets. We were the same age, but something about them made me feel old and uncool like a boomer, or worse, a millennial. When Montana waved, I blushed through every layer of skin. I was over here in my *GUNNING FOR YOU!* shirt and frog socks while those two looked ready to shoot content. Today, Montana's hair was long and loose, reaching all the way to her waist. Bea's was scooped up into a ponytail and dyed blond underneath. Bea wore a maxi skirt and Montaña had on shorts, which showed off the thick bands of triangles and other shapes encircling her left thigh. The tattoos seemed important, like they could be a family story handed down, and I suddenly felt quite silly about my animals.

I returned a feeble, bashful smile and began to walk toward them. Then someone tapped me on the shoulder. I spun around. Behind me stood a fortyish woman in high-waisted leggings and a cropped shirt. "Hello!" I said brightly. "My name is Gabby. Thanks for coming."

"I didn't *mean* to come," she said. "I was here to jog."

"Oh. Nice. Well. Looks like you've picked up one of our fliers," I said, gesturing to the crumpled piece of paper in her hand. "Do you know your polling location?"

She scrunched her face. "Polling location? Your candidate ruined my whole routine. Marston Gunn will make some noise? What does that even mean?"

"I'm glad you asked," I said. "Marston Gunn feels like Californians are ignored. We have the good laws—"

"I'm sorry, *the good laws*?" The woman let her mouth hang.

Sensing danger, Frosty tried to drag me away. He might've been old, but Jindos were strong and very stubborn, and I used every bit of my admittedly lacking core strength just to keep us in place.

"We have the fifth largest economy in the world," I continued, "but it's like, people focus on Pennsylvania or whatever and assume we've got it handled over here."

The woman snorted. "Has Marston Gunn met our governor?"

"I don't know. Probably?" The woman blinked. I smiled. Frosty jerked again. I scanned the list of talking points but didn't feel I could make the case for *Marston Gunn sharing a lot of your values!*

"Here's a question." The woman re-crumpled the paper and tossed it onto the sand. At least I had a piece of trash to pick up.

"What is Mr. Gunn going to do about all the homeless people? Cardiff is *teeming* with them."

"Um, really?" I scratched the back of my neck. "Seems like a nice place, but I'm happy to find out the names of your city council members. May I jot down your phone number?" I was a little proud of myself for this one.

"The jackoffs at the Encinitas city council aren't going to do anything unless it's related to outdoor dining or ADUs. Meanwhile, drug addicts are ruining our city. If you pay several million dollars for a house, you shouldn't have to worry about tripping over junkies on the way to the mailbox. The cops take forever to arrest them and it's like, do a countywide sweep and be done with it."

"These are people," I said. The green light to debate constituents was not in my packet, but this lady was working my nerves. "They can't just dissolve into the ether."

"Fortune favors those who help themselves," she said.

"I mean, not really," I said. *Leave, Gabby. You're in over your head.*

"Wouldn't you be upset if you were spending a day at the park and there was a drifter sleeping in a tent nearby?"

"Um, yeah, because a human had to sleep in a tent." I took a deep breath and counted to three. When I looked up, I saw what appeared to be Raj creeping across the parking lot. I wasn't sure why I'd invited him, other than he seemed lonely and sad and maybe he could network and get a lead on a job? Could a transit attorney even network at a beach? Who really knew. But I was glad he'd come. Now I had an excuse to detach.

"There are a million services available," the woman said as I watched Talia approach Raj. This would never do. My sister couldn't help but pry and she'd mistake him for my boyfriend again. Then they might start talking about PBS, and she'd find out the monkey was mine, and cans of worms would spill everywhere.

"It's been wonderful speaking to you," I said to the terrible lady. "I'll leave you to review the materials."

With that, I turned and hustled toward the tent, calling Raj's name, but he was too busy looking at my sister, head tilted, as though she had something fascinating to say.

# Chapter Twenty-Five

## Talia

The man laughed. He had a nice set of teeth. "I don't know who I'm voting for in the primary. But I'm here to meet a friend." He looked around. "She told me this was a community get-together, but it appears to be some kind of political rally?"

"Not a rally," Talia said. "A beach cleanup. A chance to brighten the community alongside the candidate."

"Who's the candidate?" he asked, craning over the very modest crowd.

"My father. Marston Gunn. He's running for the United States Senate." Talia studied the man, racking her brain. He was her age, maybe a little older, and therefore too old to be friends with most of the volunteers. Maybe he knew Ivan. "You said somebody invited you?"

"I'm here to see Gabby. Gabby . . . I'm not sure of her last name?" He laughed again. "Wow, that's embarrassing."

Talia stared, incredulous. "That Gabby?" She pointed. "Talking to the scowling blonde lady?" The woman seemed less than thrilled to be in Gabby's company, but at least her sister was actively engaging someone instead of taking what appeared to be a long and solitary walk.

"Yes, that's her!" the man said, and Talia rolled her eyes. Of course. Who else would describe the event in such a squirrelly, half-assed manner? A "community get-together." For the love of God.

"That's my sister. Gabby Gunn." Gabby was making her way over, a look of sheer terror on her face. "I'm sorry." She swiveled back to the man. "What did you say your name was?"

He introduced himself as Raj, and it took a beat for the name to ring a bell. It was him—the supposed *friend*—and Talia had to restrain herself from inquiring whether they were hooking up. It was weird she didn't know what her sister was up to, and whether or not she was gay. Ozzie must've. Maybe even their dad. Did Gabby assume Talia wouldn't be supportive? Talia loved gay people! She was an ally!

Suddenly a fresh idea began to take shape. Gabby was extremely cagey about this Raj character. Was she . . . *having an affair*? Talia didn't think Gabby would intentionally seek out a married man but could imagine a scenario where, through a series of polite misunderstandings, Gabby ended up in a relationship with one, unable to find her way out.

"I'm going to say hello," Raj said, and started to step away. "Thanks for pointing me in the right direction."

Talia grabbed his sleeve. "My name's Talia, by the way," she said, extending a hand. He eyed it for a second before returning the gesture. "I hope you don't mind me asking, but are you registered to vote?"

He said he was, and Gabby was now jogging toward them, looking quite silly plodding clumsily through the sand. The Jindo had a much swifter time of it.

"What about your wife?" Talia pressed. "Is she also registered to vote?"

"I'm not married," Raj said a little glumly.

"Hey! Hey! Hey!" Gabby said, stumbling up. She had a thick sheen of sweat on her forehead though the weather was cool. "What's going on over here? Discussing corporate law? You're both lawyers. Isn't that funny?"

"Wait," Raj said, looking back and forth between the sisters as he pieced things together. "Gabby. You never mentioned you were a Gunn. What the heck?"

"It didn't come up," she said, eyes darting away.

"We were in the Gunn Aviary!"

"I'm sorry," Talia said. "The Gunn Aviary?"

"At the zoo," Gabby said, and this cleared up nothing. "Anyway! Welcome to Team Gunn! Not that you're on the team. God forbid. I don't even know your politics. Don't know my father's either, to be honest."

"Gabby!" Talia snapped. "Somebody might hear you!"

Raj chuckled. "I appreciate a person who's open to new concepts."

"I wouldn't call our dad open-minded. But if you're looking for a lack of conviction, you've come to the right place." Gabby exhaled and repeatedly pushed back her bangs, like she was trying and failing to tuck them behind her ears. "Talia. We need some talking points about Dad's policies. If he has them. It'd help when we're cornered by batty old crones." She cranked a finger in the blonde woman's direction.

"You can't talk about voters like that," Talia hissed. Also, old crone? That woman was in her forties, early fifties at most. And a San Diego fifty, which was a whole other thing.

"You should've heard what *she* was saying," Gabby huffed. "Don't get her wrong, the exorbitant cost of living is *fine*, but sometimes she must see poor people in the wild, and, *gross*. She's a round-up-the-unhoused type. Meanwhile, she's definitely voted no on every ballot measure to build affordable housing in her zip code. It's like, don't complain about the unhoused when you actively don't want them to have a place to live."

"Wow. Okay," Talia said, going a little cross-eyed.

Gabby let out a puff of air. "Sorry," she said, mostly to Raj. "I hate that shit."

"The housing prices *are* out of control," he said. "Even professionals with advanced degrees are being priced out of the market." He gave Gabby a meaningful look, and now Talia wondered what the hell was going on. "Something needs to be done at a structural level."

"Huh." Talia crossed her arms. "It sounds like you might have some interesting thoughts. Anything concrete and easy to understand we could bring to our dad?"

"It must be *very* easy," Gabby added. "He's a real dope."

"Gabby!"

"Er, at the risk of oversimplifying the problem," Raj said, "a good start would be to get private equity out of the real estate market so regular people can win in competitive bidding situations. And we need to unravel the excessive single-family zoning in California. It's obliterated the housing supply."

"Totally," Gabby said.

He rambled off a few more things—about Section 8, and housing vouchers, and waitlists that ran for years. He volunteered at Legal Aid San Diego, and a person tended to develop a lot of opinions after spending so much time helping people navigate a very fucked-up system.

"I think we're onto something," Talia said, hardly able to believe this guy was friends with Gabby. He seemed normal. Not "theatrical" at all. "If Dad took up the mantle on this, he might actually help people, which was his whole reason for running for office." Goose bumps prickled her arms.

"That was not his whole reason," Gabby said. "It wasn't even reason two or three."

"Let me be clear," Raj added. "The problem is extremely complex. Nobody—not your dad or anyone else—could just step into office and solve it."

"Period," Gabby said, and Talia backhanded her shoulder.

"What is it we're trying to solve?" said a voice.

The three flipped around to find a woman in cargo pants and old, scratched-up sunglasses. She was kind of lumpy in the middle, and Talia hated herself for noticing.

"I apologize for eavesdropping," the woman said, "but you all seemed to be having a very rousing conversation."

"Indeed! We were speaking about some of the issues that matter most to Marston Gunn." Talia grinned, proud of herself for snapping so quickly into sell-the-candidate mode. "Specifically, California's housing crisis. Marston puts a priority on listening to voters, and Raj here was sharing his viewpoints. I'm Talia, by the way." She squinted at her name tag. *KYLE SPERBER*. Why did that sound familiar?

"Oh my God!" Gabby said, rushing forward, hand outstretched. "Kyle Sperber! From *The North County Intelligencer*. I can't believe you—" She stopped and cleared her throat. "Er. Um. Thank you for taking the time to come out. It's wonderful to meet you in person!"

"You left enough messages," Kyle Sperber said, smirking with great intensity. Talia briefly wanted to die. "I live nearby and thought I'd check out the event. I'll admit, Marston Gunn is starting to intrigue me as a candidate. I'd love to do a quick interview. If you have the time."

"Yes, of course!" Gabby said. "Should we sit over there?"

"Sounds perfect," Kyle said, and Talia nodded approvingly. Ivan had given her such shit about being *the sort of lunatic who brings folding chairs to the beach*. Who was the lunatic now?

"Have a nice chat, you two," Talia said, giving her sister a nudge. "Raj and I will continue our brainstorming."

"Oh, I wasn't trying to brainstorm—"

Gabby hesitated. She looked back and forth between Talia and Raj, a flintiness in her eyes. Finally, after issuing Raj a stern glare, she shortened Frosty's leash and led the Jindo, and Kyle Sperber, away.

Talia felt her entire body smile. There was something in the air, and it wasn't just the beach's briny scent. It was hope and excitement and the realization this campaign was about to find its footing. She couldn't wait to tell Dad.

# Will anyone in California take Marston Gunn seriously?

BY KYLE SPERBER, *The North County Intelligencer*

SAN DIEGO—Marston Gunn fancies himself a San Diego native. His triple-great grandfather founded F.D. Gunn Company (FDG) in America's Finest City way back in 1871, which separates Gunn from San Diego by more than a century and a half. While his name is all over California—the college, the hospitals, the marine biological institute—he's lived most of his life in New York.

If you're familiar with Mr. Gunn, you probably know him as the former CEO of FDG, a media conglomerate that once included 90 newspapers, 50 local television stations, a home improvement network, and the reality television channel For Real TV. Earlier this year, he was forced to liquidate the majority of his holdings after his brother was busted for perpetrating a series of financial schemes through which he enriched himself by an estimated $250 million. Douglas Gunn is currently serving 10 to 15 years at Federal Correctional Institution, Otisville. Marston Gunn's name is on the founding documents of his brother's shady enterprise, but when pressed, he's vague about how this could've occurred under his watch, which begs the question, was he complicit or simply clueless?

Either way, with this ignominy behind him, Marston Gunn is tackling a new industry as one of twelve Democratic candidates vying for the open U.S. Senate seat in California. Priscilla Pham was appointed to fill the interim position but is not running for reelection.

We hadn't planned to cover Gunn here at the *Intelligencer*. His story was too banal, his chances too long-shot, but thanks to the efforts of one very dogged communications director, I decided to dig around and ask, who is Marston Gunn?

The failed mogul is father to three charming but dysfunctional adult children. "The smart one, the nice one, the rich idiot," as a source close to the family summarized it. The middle child—the "nice one"—is twenty-four-year-old Gabrielle "Gabby" Gunn, the campaign's communications director. When not leaving panicky voicemails on behalf of her father, Gabby runs an experimental theater in upstate New York.

The oldest Gunn is thirty-one-year-old Talia, who serves as the campaign's field organizer. She's widely considered the most competent, though is known to be "a little self-conscious" and "prone to gentle paranoia." Talia is currently on leave from one of the top law firms in Manhattan. When asked why her sister would absent herself from such a prestigious position, Gabby Gunn was evasive, but ultimately implied Gunn is paying his kids handsomely.

The youngest Gunn is twenty-three-year-old influencer @DegenerateOz. Oscar, or "Ozzie" as he's called, resembles a thousand others of his type—tight clothes, sunglasses, hair slicked into a mini pompadour. With all the swagger he displays online, I was surprised to hear friends describe the founder and sole employee of "Rizz Holdings LLC" in a host of unflattering terms, such as "not conventionally attractive," "overly styled," and "on the brink of chubby." He's also "very strange, but in an entertaining way," a comment that likely refers to his unusual eye for art. Rumors abound that he's overspent on his collection and is scrambling to sell it off. Young Ozzie is not part of the campaign, and one wonders if he's been purposefully excluded.

Despite growing up in luxury, with private planes and multiple homes, the Gunns have not had it easy. Their mother, Marston Gunn's first wife, the artist Daphne Carter, ended her life at age forty-three. She died from hanging, in a barn, on the very piece of land from which her former husband is currently running his campaign. When asked about it, Gabby Gunn said they were separated, living on opposite coasts. Daphne was suffering a recurrence of thyroid cancer, but one senses this is not the full story. Gunn has since remarried, to a woman named Ustenya described by a family member as a cross between Elvira and Tony Soprano. A close family friend recalls a time when Ustenya made sprat sandwiches and in the process hacked off a chunk of her thumb. After spurting copious amounts of blood, "she then applied stitches to her own self."

With each new conversation, my interest rose, and I was delighted to discover the campaign was holding a meet-the-candidate event less than a mile from my home. I missed Gunn's opening remarks, but the literature handed out was thin, focused on "making noise" and "standing up for California." The smattering of would-be voters were baffled about his policies, and Gabby Gunn seemed similarly in the dark. During our interview, she hemmed and hawed and danced around the softball question of "what does your father believe in?" before finally spitting out that he is keen to address the unhoused. Goodness! Fixing homelessness! Perhaps I'd misjudged his ambition. As for specifics, Ms. Gunn promised to "circle back."

I'll confess. The Gunn family amuses me, but I still have more questions than answers about Marston Gunn, the chief one being, why, exactly, is he running? The race is wide open, but the top three candidates (all sitting U.S. Congresspeople) are polling in the double digits, while Marston's support hovers around three percent. In a recent poll, ten percent of people viewed him favorably, ten percent unfavorably, and the remaining eighty percent had "no opinion." He's also woefully behind in terms of fundraising, with a scant $1 million in the bank. The leading candidate, David Slimp, is sitting on a $32 million war chest. If Gunn can't draw from his own coffers, will he ever catch up?

Does Marston Gunn genuinely think he can pull this off, or is he in it to play spoiler on behalf of someone else? His candidacy might seem innocuous ("local" man makes undetectable splash), but his very presence could shake up the election. With California's top-two primary system, only Democrats have advanced to the general election the past few cycles. But the more Democrats who enter the race, the more the votes will be split, leaving room for a Republican to sneak in.

"For the past several senatorial election cycles, Californians have had the chance to vote *for* someone based on their platform and policies instead of *against* things like book banning, racism, and the downfall of democracy," says independent Democratic strategist Theo Lemke, who has worked for several senatorial campaigns in California. "Marston Gunn has no chance to win, but his involvement will undoubtedly tip the scales. One or two percentage points could make all the difference in this race, and his doomed campaign dramatically increases the chances of a Democrat-Republican general election in November."

How much longer Marston Gunn will last remains to be seen, but his campaign looks to be an entertaining follow. We will keep readers apprised of developments. Thank you to Gabby Gunn for ensuring we stay on top of the news.

# Chapter Twenty-Six

## Gabby

The article came out on Sunday morning, and the news whipped through the Ranch, California wildfire fast. Dad and Ustenya were fundraising in Santa Barbara, so I spent a full twenty-four hours worrying myself sick, waiting for my bill to come due.

"What did you say to this woman?" Talia asked first thing on Monday, clutching a newspaper as we hurried toward the conference room. The article was readable on a phone, but my sister went the extra step of picking up a few copies so we could relive my ignominy in print. "Dad is going to *solve homelessness?*"

"I didn't say that exactly."

"You really fucked up, Gabby," Ivan said, speaking between chomps of his protein bar. "Your father is losing his mind."

"I don't know how this happened. Half of it doesn't make sense. How can Dad be hapless *and* a threat? Pick a lane, lady!" The worst part was, I thought the interview *went well.* Of course, I'd also been out of my depth, not to mention distracted by Talia and Raj, who stood nearby, deep in conversation. I had to keep PBS away from my family, and this was a clash of my worlds.

"Whoever her sources were . . ." Ivan began. *Chomp chomp chomp.* His teeth clicked together as he ate. "They did you guys dirty. Especially your brother."

Ozzie. *God, Ozzie.* Being called chubby, unattractive, the whole deal. He played a confident game, but inside, my brother was mush. I'd texted him five times, called him once, but he'd gone dark. I didn't blame him. I wanted to jump off a bridge.

"A slap in the face," Talia muttered. "I'm not sure I'll get over it, honestly."

Talia wasn't sure *she'd* get over it? Out of everyone, she came across the best.

We filed into the conference room. I sat down, and Talia picked a seat on the opposite side of the table, beside Ustenya. Ivan entered the room next, followed by Mindy, the TikTokers, and a couple of staffers whose names I didn't know. My anxiety spiked upon realizing I'd screwed up so badly we needed a whole meeting about it.

"Well, Bags." Dad swung his head in my direction. My gaze was fixed on my lap, so I didn't see him do this, but felt it, all the way to my core. "What do you have to say for yourself?"

"At least you're getting noticed?" I said, spitting out the first thing that came to mind. "There's no such thing as bad press, right?" Was that still something people said?

"You threw every member of our family under the bus."

"Technically, anonymous sources did."

"Meanwhile, I'm killing myself, flying all over this god-damned state—*commercial*, no less—and for what? To have my kids shit on me behind my back?"

"Why are you blaming Gabby?" Bea the TikToker piped in. My dad rotated toward her as she took a hit of her vape. "The *Intelligencer* loves to stir shit up. And Gabby looks pretty bad in the piece." She glanced at me. "No offense," she said, and I put up a hand. "I don't think she's the source of the negative comments."

"I'm sorry. Who are you?" Dad said, lifting a brow.

"One of our social media managers," Ivan said. "And TikTok is the part of the campaign that's firing on all cylinders, so kudos to Bea and Montana." He offered a short round of applause. I was the only one who joined in.

"It's not just the article," Dad said. "Our messaging is garbage. Explain to me why I'm repeatedly called an 'unknown' when I've run a multibillion-dollar company and my name is on dozens of buildings in this city."

"Darling." Ustenya placed a hand on his forearm, her pointy red nails like slashes of blood against his white button-down shirt. "There's no need for the bluster. It's not good for you."

It was a shame she'd never had children, I thought. She loved to mother the man.

"The bluster is not the problem," Dad said. "It's the incompetence of the people on the team." He bit down on his lip and scanned the room. "Where the hell is Ozzie, anyway? I made it clear I wanted all three kids here, and you were supposed to make it happen." His eyes zeroed in on Talia, and she jumped.

"Me?" she said. "Gabby's the one he's closest to."

"We all tried," Ustenya said wearily. "That boy is stubborn as a donkey on a bridge. But it's probably for the best, no?"

Dad jerked his arm out of Ustenya's hold. "What about endorsements?" he asked. "Why don't we have one yet? Not even from Bobby! What the fuck is up with that?" Dad shifted his eyes from Ivan to me to Talia and back, and it took us all a minute to puzzle out "Bobby" was Robert Quinonez, the mayor of San Diego.

"We're trying," Ivan said. "But he has some concerns. Mainly about how you differentiate yourself from the other candidates. I told him you brought a fresh voice, but he was looking for more."

"Well, fuck that guy."

"Sadly, we can't fuck him," Ivan said, blushing. Meanwhile, Bea snorted. "His endorsement is key to moving on to the general. Also, I suspect his concerns are widely shared, so it's best to address them now and eliminate the problem."

"What do you suggest?" Dad asked. He reached into his sport coat and pulled out a pen and a piece of paper—a boarding pass, from the looks of it.

"We need to nail down your platform, and—good news—Gabby got the ball rolling," Ivan said.

Dad's eyebrows went wonky. "How'd she do that?"

"By promising you'd solve homelessness," Talia said.

"Enough!" I hissed.

"What?" Talia returned a big, dramatic shrug. "It's a starting point. People in California *are* upset about the proliferation of tent cities, and housing affordability, and it's all connected. Gabby's . . . friend?" Her eyes flickered toward me. "Had some interesting thoughts about zoning."

"Is that possible?" Bea mused. "Interesting thoughts about zoning?"

"Sounds like a local problem," Dad said, and I continued eyeing my sister. What was her deal? I couldn't figure out whether we were working together or in some kind of fight. "Ivan. I gave you a list of key issues. Let's review it."

Ivan pretended to check something on his phone, but his screen was dark. He babbled and stammered for several seconds before admitting, "I'm thinking the issues we discussed aren't the right ones for this moment in time?"

"Just remind me what they are," Dad said wearily as he rubbed his temples.

Ivan cleared his throat. "You mentioned border security, parental rights, and getting trans kids out of girls' sports."

"Dad!" I gasped.

"I am literally screaming." Bea hit her vape pen again.

"What?" Dad said, and Ivan launched into a whole thing about how these ideas were already used, by the other side. Yes, even immigration.

"We should go back to housing," Talia said. "Some fixes could be tackled at the federal level. For example, private equity firms are a huge reason for escalating home prices. Banning hedge funds from owning residential real estate could be done through Congress."

"I don't want to cool off the housing market," Dad said. "And I absolutely cannot piss off Wall Street. Okay, we're done."

Dad began to pack up his things. That was it? We were ending the meeting without a plan? I should've been relieved to exit the hot seat but somehow was not. The article felt like something that would come back later to bite me in the ass.

"Thanks for your time, everyone," Dad said. "I'm certain you'll find out a way to get this campaign back on track. And if you could be more careful around the media . . ." He shot me a look. "I sure would appreciate it."

# Chapter Twenty-Seven

## Talia

Talia found Gabby on the basketball court, practicing free throws. The Jindo snoozed on the ground nearby.

"There she is," Talia said as a ball clattered through the hoop. "Standing strong at five-foot-one, two-time all-conference point guard Gabby Gunn!"

"I was *second* team all-conference," Gabby said, shooting again. "I did make first team for volleyball, though. Tore up the small private school league." She fetched the ball and pivoted toward Talia. Her eyes were red. "Am I about to be fired?"

Talia shook her head. Although she remained thoroughly bewildered that Gabby could screw up so badly in such a short period of time, she also knew her sister didn't mean to make anyone sound like jerks. "It wasn't your fault," she said.

"It was a little my fault. I was just trying to get Dad some press. I promise I didn't say any of those awful things."

"The Elvira–Tony Soprano thing was pretty funny," Talia allowed. "I know you didn't want this to happen, and Dad's not blameless. Maybe if he was around more, or contemplated stuff in advance, you wouldn't have been forced to wing it. Sometimes I worry he's not totally locked in."

Gabby snorted. "Ya think?"

"Like, big surprise, someone is calling you on your shit. You can no longer get by on a smile and good name."

"*Formerly* good name," Gabby corrected her.

"Also, his rant about Ozzie not being here?" Talia took the ball from Gabby's hands. "Old news. And what's he even complaining about? That's called dodging a bullet."

Gabby glowered. "Kind of a low blow," she said. "After what was written about him."

"The insults were uncalled for, but that doesn't mean I'm wrong. Shit's always going on with the kid." To wit, Ozzie was at the moment attempting to weasel Spencer into buying some or all of his watch collection. Talia knew she was right about their brother's money problems, even if Gabby refused to acknowledge it.

"Anyway . . ." Talia began to dribble, quite terribly. "Don't make fun of me. I'm more of a tennis girlie." Lips pressed together, Talia lifted onto her toes and released the ball. It made a perfect arc, landing cleanly through the net. "Yes!" She pumped her fist.

"Typical Talia," Gabby said. "That's why you're LMP. Little Miss Perfect."

Talia spun around, grinning, her ponytail swishing across her back. "Beginner's luck," she said. Talia enjoyed being good at things, even things that didn't matter, and although she was far from LMP, she liked when other people saw her that way.

"Thanks for saving me at the end of the meeting," Gabby said as Talia passed the ball.

"Yeah. Well. Dad *does* need to stand for something. And I like the housing angle. Raj has been incredibly helpful. I'm jealous he's managed to use his law degree in a meaningful way."

"Raj is great," Gabby said, rushing the words. "Anyhow. I'd better get back to HQ. Before the campaign goes to hell without my careful oversight." She tossed the ball into a gray plastic storage bin. "Thanks for being so chill. Let's never speak of it again."

"There is something bothering me," Talia blurted. "About

the article." Gabby froze. "I'm sorry, but I have to bring it up. It's the Mom stuff. Saying it was suicide when she had cancer. Why did Kyle Sperber get that impression?"

Gabby opened her mouth but stopped, dropping a pause so heavy it practically made a sound. "But . . ." Her voice got very, very small. "That *was* how she died?"

"Yeah, no, technically. But only because she had cancer and didn't want to fight it anymore, and . . ." Talia said a bunch more words as Gabby stared. "It's the emphasis." She was shaking now. "Like, why did it need to be in there? I guess I'm wondering . . . what you told her? I know you and Ozzie . . . you guys haven't ever really forgiven Mom for taking her own life." Talia cringed as she said this, but there was no stopping her now. "Why wouldn't you talk to *me* about it, instead of confessing to some reporter?"

"Talia." Gabby's face was in full shell shock.

"You can admit it," Talia pressed. "You've always been angry."

"How could I be *angry*? If anything, I'm sad. Sad for her—for *anyone*—who sees it as their only option. God, Talia. It's fucked up you'd think that."

Talia swiped the tears from her eyes. "It's the logical conclusion. You never mention her. When I bring her up, you become all tense and immediately change subjects."

Gabby blinked, letting the silence hang as she worked through something. "So, it's true?" she said at last. "The cancer actually came back?"

Talia's stomach tumbled. She ran through ten to twelve emotions—surprise and outrage and all the rest, even though part of her had waited years for this question. "You think Dad would lie about that?"

"I didn't think he'd specifically lie," Gabby said evenly. "But people are weird about mental illness, and Dad didn't utter the word 'cancer' until *after* she died."

"They were separated," Talia said. She could feel the thrum

of her heart in her ears. "*God.* I've always suspected that you and Ozzie somehow blamed me, or assumed I was lying or—"

"Tal." Gabby placed a hand on Talia's shoulder. "You were the closest to Mom, and here the entire summer, so if you tell me she was sick, it's all I need."

"Oh. Okay. But—"

"Wow." Gabby released Talia's arm. "I can't believe how relieved I am right now." She shook her head, astonished. "Apparently I *was* skeptical about Mom's death. Hello! Light bulb moment! We probably should've had a bit more therapy, huh? Wild stuff." She started to walk away.

"Mom loved you so much," Talia said, and Gabby froze. "I witnessed it firsthand. She was over the moon when you were born. You were such a happy baby, which she bragged about all the time. *Sweet Gabby. She never complains!*"

"That does sound like me," Gabby said, her voice raspy and choked.

"For the record, she wanted you around more often. I swear! But Dad always got in the way."

Gabby went to protest, but Talia refused to allow it. "I wish you'd known her better. When Mom was healthy, she was the best. Loving and creative and fun. And she lacked that . . ." Talia chewed on this. "That motherly self-consciousness. She rarely cared what other people thought, and always gave the most bizarre yet oddly helpful advice. Stand tall, walk loudly, make an impression."

"*Walk loudly?*" Gabby repeated. She turned to face her again, a smile spilling across her cheeks. "Is that why you wear such heavy shoes?"

"No, I—" Talia reconsidered. "I guess it is!" She laughed, and Gabby joined in, and life was sweet for a second, until they were stopped by the sound of someone screeching their names.

"*Basketball?*" Mindy said, stomping in their direction, rattlesnake stick in hand. "You people will do anything aside from work. Oh, man." She cackled. "It's been quite a week, huh?"

"It's Monday morning," Gabby said.

"I know, right?"

"What's going on?" Talia said as panic fluttered in her chest.

Mindy laughed again, and a look passed over her face. A barely concealed smirk, or maybe indigestion. "I could tell you, but it's more fun if you see for yourself."

# Chapter Twenty-Eight

## Ozzie

His sisters, they were not stoked. They stood there on the other side of the pool like they'd been knocked on the head. Ozzie hadn't expected a celebration or anything, but they could've faked some enthusiasm. Hadn't Gabby majored in theater during her illustrious two to three months of college?

As always, it was up to him to break the ice. "Ladies. What's with all the gawping? It's like you've seen a celebrity." Ozzie chuckled. "I guess you have. Come on." He spread his arms. "Get over here and give your baby brother a hug."

Gabby moved first, bolting to his side and collapsing into his arms in what could only be described as a slump. "Are you mad?" she asked as she pulled back.

"It was pretty shady . . ."

"Ugh!" Gabby covered her face. "I know. You must've flown out here the second you saw the article."

Ozzie smile-grimaced. He'd meant *she* was shady about coming to California and not warning him they were getting cut off. Ozzie hoped she'd own up to it eventually. He knew it was a lot to ask.

"I don't give two shits about the article," he said. "Nobody reads newspapers, and haters gonna hate." Ozzie glanced at Talia, who remained frozen beneath a tree, its teensy pink flowers falling softly onto her head. "You can't be that shocked to see me," he called out.

Truth be told, Ozzie was a tad shocked to be here himself, but times were tough. He hadn't inked any collabs or sold much art or many watches and Talia declined the opportunity to "invest in the business of @DegenerateOz." He'd really been starting to sweat it when, yesterday, a Google alert pinged with his name, and a new course was set.

Did the article bother him? Mostly no. Ozzie never considered himself conventionally attractive, and he knew he was "on the brink of chubby." He had eyeballs and a scale, okay? Ozzie said much worse things to himself, every day, so welcome to the club. He was feeling pretty neutral about it all until he reached the sentence where *Gunn is paying his kids handsomely*, and yeah, that was quite fucking true. As Barclay said, $50K per month wasn't nothing. More importantly, if Ozzie went to California, the twenty-five-year gift was back in play.

Suddenly Ozzie's reasons for not wanting to work on the campaign didn't seem important anymore. Staying in New York hadn't done much for his image, and there were no longer jets or yachts in his life, which meant nothing to miss. San Diego would be something different, and the Ranch was freakin' lit. He'd also have a whole new pool of buyers for his art and Californians were more open and freethinking, which he understood thanks to Mom, RIP.

"Ah, here she comes," Ozzie said as Talia finally made her way over. "Don't worry. Just because I flew commercial doesn't mean I have a communicable disease. Then again." He pretended to contemplate this, fake-scratching his chin. "Who really knows?"

"Are you here for a visit, or . . . ?" Talia sounded out of breath, though she literally could not have moved any slower.

"No, silly goose!" Ozzie said, rumpling her hair. "I'm joining the campaign. The more I thought about it—"

"You *thought* about it?" Talia said, and Ozzie reminded himself to play it cool. He was the good-time guy, the loveable bear, and he wasn't looking to provoke Talia, even though it was so easy and often fun to do.

"Yeah. I was *ruminating*. My entire business is optics, and my shtick is I'm the golden boy and black sheep of a dynasty."

Talia made a face. "You can't be both. Those are opposites."

"You're so pedantic," Ozzie said, mildly blowing his sister's mind with his use of the word. "The lore is I get into scrapes, but things always work out. My business manager thinks the campaign will open up new sponsorship opportunities and make for good content."

"But you're not going to actually do anything, right?" Talia said, and Gabby nudged her in the ribs. "Like, you're here for the vibes or the location or whatever. We have enough people getting into *scrapes* around here." She narrowed her gaze on Gabby.

"Of course I'm going to do something."

Talia audibly sighed, and Ozzie was sure she was about to fling herself into the pool. He knew he wasn't her favorite person but wished she'd give him some credit. He'd survived this long, after all.

"Also, you guys are here," Ozzie added, slinging an arm around each sister. "And I can't miss out on the fun. Look at us." He gave them each a squeeze—first Gabby, then Talia. "Los tres amigos, the three musketeers, back in action."

"We were never that," Talia said, wiggling out of his grasp.

"Three musketeers . . ." Ozzie cocked his head. "And a dog, it seems?" Beside Gabby was a white dog with very pointy ears. It stared at him with great skepticism.

"Yes. A Jindo. I inherited it from Dad," Gabby said, though he must've heard wrong. Meanwhile, Talia was walking away, telling them to have fun catching up, but *some of us have work to do.*

"God, she's fun." Ozzie threw himself onto a lounger. He

dropped his aviators over his eyes and folded his hands atop his stomach. "You're quiet."

"I'm just surprised?"

"*You're* surprised? I seem to recall *you* insisting you'd never come here. What's the deal, sis? I thought we were a team."

"We are!" Gabby said, and he laughed.

Ozzie hadn't bought the "team" garbage for ages—obviously—but Gabby still clung to the old tale. He loved his sister, but she needed to get a clue. "Be for real, Gabs," he said. "You didn't tell me for a reason."

"There's not some big conspiracy, Oz. It must've slipped my mind. You don't sound like yourself. Where is this coming from?" she said, and wasn't that fucking rich. *I dunno, sis, maybe it's your hobby of not mentioning things, letting them slip your mind. Like when your kid brother is sent away for nine whole months, and you pretend it was no longer than a night.*

"Wanna know my theory," Ozzie said. "You were worried if you brought it up, I'd want to come, too, and *quelle catastrophe!* Degenerate Oz will only screw everything up."

"Ozzie!" she yelped. "That's not true! In case you haven't noticed, *I'm* the one screwing up around here. Your sudden appearance is practically a lifeline. Best thing that could've happened."

Ozzie chuckled again. "Okay, sis."

Gabby started to yap about how she couldn't be happier, and he was the smartest person she knew, and they were all better off with him on the scene. Midway through this pile of absolute bullshit, she stopped abruptly.

"Do you smell that?" she asked, sniffing, violently scratching her arms.

"I smell nothing," he said.

"Fuck. Shit." A few more f-bombs besides. "Can you watch the dog for me?" she said, tying its leash to his chair.

Ozzie yanked the sunglasses off his face. "You've got to be

kidding." He'd been in San Diego all of thirty seconds and Gabby was already bailing and leaving him with a random-ass dog.

"His name is Frosty. Please, can you watch him for me? I'll explain later, but I have to deal with something *right now*, and I don't know how long it will take."

# Chapter Twenty-Nine

## Gabby

"You're welcome to go see him," the woman at the front desk said—probably. I'd already bolted down the hall before the first word was out of her mouth.

I found dos Santos two doors from the end. He was instantly recognizable from his photo on the website—close-cropped, bristly black hair, unstylish glasses, a lime-green polo shirt with the zoo's logo embroidered on the chest.

"Hello," I said, knocking on the doorframe. "Gabby Gunn."

"Miss Gunn," he said, cautiously rising to his feet. On the wall behind him were photographs of a younger, tanner, less bookish dos Santos as he tended to a variety of tigers and black-footed cats. The man had done some cool things, and I wondered why he bothered with a bunch of sad-sack PBSers. "It's nice to finally meet you."

"Likewise." I shut the door behind me and plopped down into a chair. "Sorry for busting in on you like this, but I'm currently mid-flare. My brother showed up out of nowhere, which is a problem I can't get into right now." I stopped to aggressively rub my forearm on my jeans. "I had nowhere else to go. I figured, this is a zoo, right? And I was symptomatic the last time I came here, and it stopped. Have you ever seen that before? Symptoms start and just go away?"

"I have, yes, as part of the Brazilian study."

"Excellent." I dug my nails into my scalp. "How were they able to stave it off? I know you love to be all mysterious about your results, but—"

"I prefer to think of it as careful," he said, and smiled like a son of a bitch.

"Okay. Yes. Ha. So careful. But this isn't an academic exercise for me, okay? I am flaring. An animal could materialize at any time, and I have family and friends and a freaking *dog* to worry about."

My stomach turned over. I'd never forgive myself if some animal mauled Frosty, or my sister, or Ozzie, or even Ivan or Mindy. This was why I shouldn't have pets or a love interest or anything precious in my life. A wolverine could show up and ruin everything.

"Please. Dr. dos Santos. I need your help," I begged. Tears were building, forming a knot in my throat. "I'm desperate."

"I have a few thoughts I can share." He leaned back in his cracked leather rolling chair and mulled things over before continuing. "You're no doubt aware of the leading theory, that atmospheric disturbances trigger PBS. A storm in Florida sends an alligator to someone's bathtub. But the question I've been grappling with is, why this alligator? Why that bathtub?"

"Are you doing philosophy or . . . ?" I said, scratching my scalp again.

"With the Brazilian study, I've spent five years documenting the Campos sisters' flares to discern a pattern. The climate piece is undeniable, but internal disturbances also seem to come into play. The intersection of stress on the planet and stress in one's personal life creates a flare. It makes sense if you think about it. Humans and animals can *both* be affected by the weather."

"Are you implying I'm, like, histrionic or something?" I said. "That I'm overly affected by the *weather* and basically throw a fit and manifest a bunch of animals?"

"No, no, that's not—"

"For the record, I'm *famously* laid-back and go-with-the-flow. It's, like, my calling card. I'm the family peacekeeper."

"Or are you the family secret keeper?" he asked, wryly.

"Um. What the hell? PS, I don't love the implication this is some kind of mental disorder."

"I'm not implying it's a mental disorder," dos Santos said, but then hedged. "Although the mental and physical do go hand in hand."

"These all seem like excuses to me." Suddenly the lone PBS expert on the planet sounded like my family. Seeing one thing but calling it another. They'd done it with Mom. Or maybe not, based on my conversation with Talia, though some part of me remained skeptical, because these were the same people who chalked up PBS to migration. The people who insisted Mom was so excited when I was born, or that she tolerated children at all.

"I'm sorry," dos Santos said, rubbing his eyes. "I'm not getting my point across. As you may have gleaned, my conversational skills are . . . subpar. The cause of most problems in my life. Or so I've been told. You can see why I've chosen to work with animals and not humans."

Dos Santos laughed without any humor, and my anger evaporated. I imagined some wife or partner haranguing him about his awkward personality, and my heart went out to the guy. "I'm the one who's sorry," I said. "Talking about PBS gets me heated, and not knowing when the symptoms will appear or what animal will show up is hard. And, like, I care about the animals? So it's not a matter of simply getting rid of them."

He exhaled. "I want to solve this. For you, and for everyone else dealing with it. I understand how dramatically it can affect a person's life. Let me ask, have *you* noticed any patterns in the presentation of your symptoms?"

"Yes. Definitely. I flare before something bad happens. Like today. As I mentioned, my brother is in town, which may sound innocuous, but trust me, it's not. I could go through each of my flares and point to a very specific disaster occurring shortly thereafter. My skill is foretelling doom, which is not as cool as it sounds."

"Hmm," dos Santos mused, spinning his black wedding band around his finger. "Maybe it's your *reaction* to the 'doom' that's causing the disturbance."

"My reactions are incredibly normal! Today, for instance. My brother showed up out of nowhere, and it was like, *yikes*, because we're supposed to be . . . We have this new family business." I wasn't sure why I felt compelled to lie, but I was still embarrassed about the whole thing. "Ozzie tends to get into 'scrapes,' by his own admission! Things with the, um, business are precarious, so when I saw him . . ." I grimaced. "I wasn't thrilled."

"Interesting." Dos Santos clasped his hands together. "Did you confess your feelings?"

"Of course not! But honestly, those feelings were very short-lived. I'm glad he's here. I love my brother. We're super close, and his 'scrapes,' well, we can live with them." At the end of the day, Ozzie wasn't a bad kid. Every boy I'd ever met had a list of childhood shenanigans that included at least one to three misdemeanors. Ozzie wasn't any worse than the rest. He just tended to be the one who got caught.

"It sounds like you were conflicted?" dos Santos said, looking almost joyful about it. "Bad with humans" indeed.

"For a second, maybe? But then I remembered this was Ozzie." My brother was about more than screwing up. I made a mental note to remind Talia of this since she came into every interaction with him already hot.

"I'd like to offer an observation," dos Santos started, only to be interrupted by a loud, blaring tone.

"Dr. dos Santos?" said a woman's disembodied voice. Where was it coming from? His phone? A hidden speaker? The fake ficus tree? "There's a Mr. Khan here to see you. He says it's an emergency."

"You can send him in, Jane."

Before I could remind the doctor that I wasn't a black-footed cat and humans deserved medical privacy, the door flew open. In walked Raj, wearing his customary plaid button-down shirt.

"What's going on?" dos Santos said as he stood.

Raj shook his head. He looked rumpled, and red-eyed, and notably worse for wear. "It's Stuart's wife. She's been injured. They *think* she'll pull through. But . . . But . . . it was a grizzly bear."

"Oh my God," I said, a hand clapped over my mouth as Raj told us that Stuart from the discussion group flared a grizzly bear and it tried to devour his wife, likely because it mistook her for a giant fish. The poor woman. And poor Stuart. Fish odor disease wouldn't solve his problems, after all.

Raj sank into a chair. He chucked his glasses onto dos Santos's desk and buried his face in his hands. "What hope do any of us have?" he asked quietly.

"I'll reach out to Stuart when we're done," dos Santos said, walking around to our side of the desk. He sat on the corner, like a teacher getting real with his class. "This is horrible news, but you can't extrapolate. Especially not with something as unpredictable as PBS."

"Are stink badgers even dangerous?" I asked, realizing how unhelpful this was a beat too late. I suspected Raj was worried about Stuart's wife, yes, but also his own romantic prospects.

"The unpredictability," dos Santos continued, "is one of the most aggravating things about the disease."

"Syndrome," I reminded everyone.

Raj lifted his tear-mottled face. "I saw your texts," he said to me. "You're flaring? With what?" He glanced around. *Shit.* I'd been so fixated on Frosty and my siblings and the others at the Ranch, I'd forgotten I was putting everyone else in danger, too.

"I should go," I said, leaping to my feet. "I'll wait this out . . . in the middle of a field or something." I strode toward the door but froze short of it. My heart skipped a beat as I lifted one arm.

My skin was cool.

My rash had disappeared.

The air smelled like bad coffee instead of burnt hair.

"It *stopped*," I said to myself. "I was flaring, and it stopped. *Again*." I whipped around, my pulse racing triple-time. "It's you," I said to Raj, locking eyes. "You're my cure."

# Chapter Thirty

## Talia

Talia hopped into Mindy's golf cart. It was a real "ask forgiveness, not permission" situation, but what's the worst that could happen? She wasn't afraid of a rattlesnake stick.

*Ozzie.* Talia couldn't believe he was here. The campaign had enough problems without her brother strutting around, making "content," landing his "heli" on the lawn. Plus he had a penchant for distracting Gabby. Fair or not, Talia felt like he'd come to ruin things with the campaign, with everyone.

Talia parked the golf cart and jumped out. In front of her stood Mom's art studio and she took a minute to soak it in, heart thwapping wildly in her chest. Gabby had some questions about Mom, and apparently Talia did, too.

The door opened easily, and Talia stepped inside, her eyes sweeping the familiar space. Sketches tacked to the walls, canvases shoved into racks, countless discarded brushes and twisted, flattened tubes of paint. On the worktable sat half a dozen crusty Mason jars, a coffee mug, and a bottle of moisturizer.

Holding her breath, Talia turned toward Mom's easel, and immediately wondered, *That's it?* When she died, Mom was (supposedly) down to the final piece in her collection, but all Talia saw on the canvas were a few swipes of dark brown and some splashes of tan and blue.

*What the fuck?*

Daphne kept saying she was in a groove, on a wave, almost done, and Talia had therefore anticipated more. Way more. Maybe not a masterpiece—though, okay, she was a little bit expecting that—but, at a minimum, one or more completed works of art. Was she missing something? Talia checked the drying racks and found more of the same. A stranger might mistake these for abstract paintings, but they weren't Daphne Carter's style at all.

Talia rooted around near the easel. Her mom always started with a photograph or sketch of a person, usually some stranger she'd met at the beach, or in yoga class, or at a wedding she'd crashed. *I'm an artist working on a series about brides and you're the perfect muse*, she'd say in one long breath. If and when the person agreed, they'd find themselves intensely befriended by Daphne, who'd paint them over a series of months. After the work inevitably took a dark turn, the relationship would go up in flames.

But Talia saw no inspiration here, other than sketches for already finished pieces. What had Mom been doing all those weeks and months? *I'm almost there! I'll be finished any day!*

Deep down, Talia must've known her "almost there" was a lie, because she never asked to see anything when they chatted over Skype. Of course, there'd been some distance between them those last few months, distance created by Talia, who'd left the Ranch feeling cranky and smothered, while her mom metaphorically clung to her leg, begging her not to go.

"We didn't get enough time together," she'd said. "Why don't you spend the upcoming term at the Ranch?"

Talia scoffed, deciding the *MOTHER/NATURE* of it all must've been getting to her. "I can't skip an entire term," she'd said.

"Doesn't Dartmouth have a flexible schedule?" her mom asked, nearly causing Talia to faint dead away. Daphne Carter was not one to pay attention to those kinds of details, but she was right, and it wouldn't have been too difficult to shift stuff around. Under different circumstances, Talia might've, but Mom was more erratic than usual, more up and down, and . . . okay, she could admit it . . . more annoying.

Plus, Talia had been reeling from the Padres internship that ended in humiliation. Her dating history wasn't the longest, and it never occurred to her she wasn't the only person hooking up with the backup first baseman. All that to say, Talia was itching to leave town. Now it all seemed so stupid in hindsight. She should've stayed.

Talia rotated away from the easel to face the faded green velvet armchair, now covered in dust. It's where Talia sat on the rare occasion Daphne invited her in. Next to the chair, on Daphne's desk, something caught Talia's eye. She stepped closer and recognized the gift she'd sent that final September, a framed copy of the review from *The Escondido Daily Times-Advocate*.

## DAPHNE CARTER RECKONS WITH MOTHERHOOD

Even though Talia was the one who sent it, the starkness of the headline made her stomach drop. That and the fact the present had been sitting there atop the rose gold wrapping paper, barely opened, for eleven years. Her mom just . . . left it there? Why?

Talia picked up the frame and skimmed the first two paragraphs.

> "As my children grow older, and are starting to pass me by, I've been interested in exploring the trippy, surreal experience of motherhood," Daphne Carter explains in the catalog for her new show.

Talia shook her head. Children passing her by? Gabby was, what, thirteen?

"In this collection I'm feeling for the line, the barrier between where the mother ends and her child begins."

For the mother, is there a line? This is one of the questions explored in *MOTHER/NATURE*, Carter's exhibition at the Distinction Gallery in Escondido, which features ten paintings, mostly of herself and a child she calls "Circe." Carter is a mother of three but is quick to point out that Circe is a "symbolic child."

Circe might've been symbolic, but the basis of every piece in *MOTHER/NATURE* part one was a photograph or sketch of *Talia*, ages two through twenty years old. Being likened to the goddess of magic was flattering and all, but the whole thing made her uncomfortable, then and now.

"If it upsets you, I can go in a different direction," Mom had said when Talia expressed her misgivings.

She said no, it was fine, which was the only right answer.

Part self-portrait, part cautionary tale, *MOTHER/NATURE* explores the tensions between motherhood and personhood, and it highlights Carter's ability to combine abstraction and figuration. The people in her paintings are burnt-out and consumed, yet still beautiful. The collection itself is a testament to the expansive nature of a mother's love and an acknowledgment there is a dark side to even the best parts of life.

"Motherhood is stunning. It's treacherous," Carter says. "It's life-affirming and life-giving, but in the end, it shatters your heart. Because eventually, the family unit becomes extinct, one by one. Children go on with their lives, and the mother is left clinging to the husks of what was."

*But you're the one who left*, Talia thought, then pushed the notion away. She'd obviously been spending too much time with Gabby. Sighing, she set down the frame.

A whistling sound made Talia jump. Something banged against the side of the barn, and her heart crawled all the way up into her throat. She scanned the room for a weapon, a hiding place, some means of escape. Another bang and Talia got a grip. It was nothing. Just the dry California winds running through this creaky old place.

*It's a barn, only a barn*, she reminded herself, as the hair stood on her arms. She peered up, and in the rafters saw only cobwebs. Talia didn't believe in ghosts, or in hauntings, even though this barn was where her mother spent the last four years of her life. Even though it's where she died. Talia had to get out of there.

After swiping the article from the desk and a sketch of her five-year-old self from the wall, Talia walked back out of the barn. The campaign meant a lot to her father, and she had to focus on him, not unanswerable questions and her long list of regrets. Maybe Talia could've helped Mom if she'd stayed, but it was too late now. One parent still needed her, and she refused to fuck it up twice.

# Chapter Thirty-One

## Gabby

"I am not moving in with you," Raj said. "That is absurd." We were standing outside the administration building because dos Santos kicked us out. He had a meeting, allegedly, at 11:43 a.m.

"Don't you see?" I said. "It's the perfect solution. I'd have a remedy for my symptoms—a victory for PBSers everywhere." At this, Raj rolled his eyes. "And you'd have a free place to live. You could work on the campaign!"

Raj pulled a face. "Why would I want to do that?"

"It'd give you something to do and look good on your résumé?" I didn't know from résumés, but people were always saying crap like that. "Plus, you did wow my sister with your insights about the housing crisis. This is the best idea. I can't believe I came up with it."

"Gabby. We met a month ago."

"Yeah, yeah." I flapped a hand. "Listen. I hate flexing like this, but it's not an ordinary house. You wouldn't be staying in some dank guest room that hasn't been dusted in ten years. It's a full-on estate. There's a property manager and everything." I flashed a smile, hoping he didn't think I was a complete jerk. "I'm not proud of this, to be clear."

Raj stared, dumbfounded.

"Do you like pickleball?"

*"Pickleball?"*

"We have a pavilion! And tennis. Clay and hardcourt. Swimming and bowling and horseback riding." I blathered on about the property's outbuildings, its apartments and cottages, the bass-filled lake. "You'd have your own space, with plenty of room for any future stink badgers. You could even sublet your apartment in the meantime and make some extra cash."

I stopped to regain my bearings. Yes, this was a good plan, but also, I slightly hated myself. I'd never had to worry about housing, and it felt gross to play on his fear, but times were tough out here.

"What if I agreed to this?" Raj said, and my body rocked with a confusing mixture of excitement and dread. "What's the long-term plan? We live together until death do us part?"

"Ew. Gross. No. I'm not going to be in San Diego for more than a few months. It'd be a temporary arrangement, long enough to see whether you're the antidote. Maybe, if it works, you could give me a lock of hair or a toenail clipping or something."

I was sixty percent joking, but Raj was one hundred percent horrified. His lips were hiked up and curled back.

"What about a piece of clothing?" I tried. "It'd have to be dirty, of course."

"Are you some kind of pervert?"

"Get over yourself," I said, glad I hadn't mentioned a skin shaving, which was another possibility that'd popped into my head. "For the record, girls are asked for their underwear all the time."

"And they absolutely shouldn't hand it over to any weirdo who asks," Raj said.

"Men are so dramatic," I muttered, picturing Sydney's mug. MALE TEARS. Was that a possible avenue, vis-à-vis Raj? Probably best to ask later, given the trajectory of this conversation.

Raj sighed. "Listen, Gabby. You seem like a nice girl, and I understand how PBS messes with your shit, but I can't abandon my entire life, however pathetic it may appear to you."

"Not pathetic at all," I said, but Raj wasn't done.

"I rent my apartment. I lease my car. My bank account has about two months of runway, and I pray to God that any potential employers don't find out about the trolley incident. If I don't hang on to what little I have, what does it say about my life? I have to believe there's some point to me. And it's not going to help if I'm living as someone else's talisman. If there's one thing my clients at Legal Aid have taught me, it's humans need to feel valued."

"I'll pay you a million dollars." The words shot out of me, unexpected and mortifying, like a fart. Raj's eyes bulged out of his skull. "I wouldn't be able to pay you for a few months," I added. "But in December, I'm supposed to come into an inheritance." It had to be at least a million dollars, right? Probably more. Even if I gave Raj most of it, I'd have enough left over to get the Collective into the black.

"How could it possibly be worth that much to you?" Raj said. "Especially since we don't know it will work. What if I moved in and you flared?"

"You'd still get the money," I said, wondering what the hell I was doing. Then again, I didn't have a million dollars now, so what did it matter if I gave away a million dollars in December? I needed to think of this like a clinical study for a new drug. Trials were expensive. Most did not pan out, but when one did, it could change lives. And if I cured PBS, it'd save me money in the long run. Maybe the math mathed after all.

"A million dollars." Raj studied me for a thousand years. "How would that work for tax purposes?"

"Are you really over here asking about tax planning? Please consider it? Even if you don't mean it, can you pretend you'll sleep on it or something?"

Raj exhaled. "Sure, Gabby, I'll think about it."

I grinned. *Off to the races*, I thought.

# OCTOBER

# Chapter Thirty-Two

## Talia

She began with a text. Hey, it's Talia Gunn. From the Gunn campaign?

It'd been two weeks since they met, and Raj would likely think she was overreaching, but Dad's campaign needed direction. While Gabby popped off to reporters and Ozzie did Lord only knew what (working with the TikTokers, supposedly), Talia was determined to get shit done.

> Could I join you the next time you volunteer at LASD? I have a law degree, so I promise to be somewhat useful!

Useful was debatable, but Talia had to come up with something.

Absolutely! Raj texted back right away. Can you meet me downtown at 9 o'clock Tuesday morning?

Talia could and she did, and after forty-five minutes at LASD, she still struggled to digest all she'd heard. Qualifying for housing assistance was merely the first step in a very long and convoluted process. More than 70,000 people sat on San Diego's waitlist, and it took decades to get off it.

One woman—Nina was her name—was approved for Section 8 twelve years ago as a mother of two. Now she had four children, and the whole family was still couch surfing and occasionally sleeping in their car. When Nina said a person was notified they'd made it off the waitlist by *United States post*, Talia almost screamed. I'm sorry, but actual mail? To reach someone who didn't have a permanent address?

The waitlist only grew, and funds and units shrank, and because vouchers were so hard to come by people who needed them ignored illegal rent hikes and other treachery. The situation felt dire, borderline hopeless. By the time Raj and Talia said goodbye to everyone and stepped outside, Talia had sweated through her suit.

"Are you okay?" Raj asked, handing her a napkin.

Talia nodded and dabbed her forehead. "I knew there was a problem, but not that it was this bad. The rent hikes are criminal." One man's rent jumped from $1,000 per month to $1,950 in *a single year*, and a family's current $1,400 was about to more than double to $3,200. "Why aren't there rules against this kind of thing?"

"There are, but the rules aren't always followed," Raj said, passing her another napkin. "I'm working with a group on a lawsuit against the San Diego Housing Commission right now." California had a ten percent rent cap, Raj explained, but the local Commission claimed Section 8 was a federal program, and thus the rent cap didn't apply. The logic made no sense and was unbearably cruel.

"How can it continue without society collapsing into itself?" Talia said as they stood on the noisy street, cars whipping past, an unhoused man pushing a shopping cart on the other side of the road. "I *have* to make my dad care about this. Despite the gruff exterior, he does have a heart. Maybe you can go with me to the Ranch and tell him everything you know?"

Raj replied with a grim chuckle. "That'd be a brief conversation." He placed a hand on her shoulder. It was oddly comforting considering they'd just met, and he was Gabby's (random, mysterious) friend. "It's an incredibly overwhelming situation, and I sympathize with the urge to act. It's why I do this." He gestured to the building behind them. "You can't change the system, but you can help the person in front of you. The trick is taking small bites."

"But it needs to be more! With your knowledge and my dad's platform, we could do something on a larger scale. He wouldn't even need to win to wake people up." Her mind was spinning, but Raj appeared skeptical, already checked out.

"What?" she said. "What is that look? You think I'm naive."

"I love the ambition," he said. "By all means, encourage your dad to discuss the problem. The more people who understand it, the better. But you can't expect him to fix everything."

"Come work on the campaign." The words came out so quickly and with such force it nearly knocked the wind out of her.

Raj made a face as he digested the offer. Weirdly, he seemed a little pissed?

"I'm sorry, did I say something offensive?"

"You and your sister really see the world as a pool of potential employees."

"Huh?" Talia jiggled her head. "I literally have no idea what you're talking about, and whatever Gabby's done . . . trust that we rarely see *anything* the same way. From my point of view, your insight is invaluable, and my dad would listen to you *much* more readily than he'd listen to me. Instead of helping in small ways, you could take bigger bites. That's what I'm suggesting. You can even stay at the Ranch."

Raj's brow darkened again.

"I could probably get you a salary," Talia added hastily, unsure how she kept veering off course. "And that's good, right? My sister mentioned you weren't working now?"

"FYI, people usually don't like to be reminded of that sort of thing."

"Oh. I didn't realize it . . ." Talia swallowed. When Gabby said Raj was "between jobs," it hadn't occurred to her he might've been fired. She didn't know this guy and, maybe, somewhere in San Diego, the West Coast version of Talia Gunn was settling his harassment suit. She started to panic. "Okay, well, never mind . . ."

"I take it your sister didn't tell you why I left my job?" Raj said.

"She doesn't tell me anything."

Raj sighed, and all prior tension slid from his face. "I wasn't fired, if that's what you're thinking. I mean, it was inevitable, but I quit before they could do it."

"Why were you assuming you'd be fired?" Talia asked, somehow managing to stop herself from pointing out he probably should've *let* himself be fired in order to collect unemployment.

"I guess you could say there are some things about me that put others off. Stuff I can't change and or hide. I was tired of worrying when the hammer was going to fall, so I left on my own."

Talia bobbed her head. *Racism*, she thought. "Look. I get that you're not excited about the prospect of joining a losing political campaign, but I think you'd help, and the Ranch is sweet. It has two pools."

"Not really a swimmer, but I might be interested if there was pickleball."

"Oh my God!" She grabbed his arm. "There is!"

Raj laughed. "That was a joke. It's a very compelling offer, but it seems like one of those situations where I could end up in over my head. Anyway, it was nice to see you." He reached out a hand.

Befuddled, Talia shook it. "You too. Remember, you could help people!" she called out as he began to walk away.

He grinned over his shoulder. "That's what people keep telling me," he said.

# Chapter Thirty-Three

## Ozzie

Despite what everyone thought, Ozzie wasn't an idiot. He knew he was being sidelined, but the joke was on them. They'd pawned him off on the TikTok baddies, which was one million times better than getting seethed at by Talia or listening to Gabby eat shit whenever she attempted to speak to another human on the phone.

Thanks to Montana and Bea, he understood TikTok was the best social media platform for campaigning. It had a "high contactability score," and users were less politically engaged, which sounded bad but made for a huge audience of *potential* voters. Plus, Gen Z actually gave a shit and were easy to mobilize.

Montana initially went viral for a "red flag/beige flag" thing she did with public figures and now Ozzie was on the case. He'd spent the morning wandering the Ranch, looking for randoms to quiz about Dad's opponents. *Angie Parker calls herself "your average minivan mom" but doesn't own a minivan. Red or beige flag?* After filming every person willing to answer, Ozzie wrapped for lunch.

As he made his way to the main house, Ozzie scanned the property, really taking it in for the first time since he arrived ten days before. Had there always been two tennis courts? A yoga studio? The recreation pavilion he remembered, mostly because of all the hours spent fucking around in there with

Gabby. Overall, the Ranch felt *almost* familiar, like trying to put a name to the face.

Ozzie entered the meditation loggia. He snagged a box marked "ham," tucked it beneath his arm, and walked back out, munching on a cob as he went. Hooking right, he spotted someone on the far side of the pool. *Well, well, well, look what the cat dragged in.* Marston Gunn, lounging on a cabana bed.

"Hey, Pops," he said, sidling up.

"Hello, son," Dad said, and Ozzie bristled. He always called him that. *Son.* Gabby was Bags and Talia was Tal and *son* felt pointed, like an expectation he wasn't living up to.

"So . . ." Ozzie said and discarded his cob in a nearby trash can. "How's it going?"

"Oh, you know . . ." Dad said, and Ozzie nodded although he didn't know, which was why he'd asked. "Soaking in a little sunshine, I guess."

"Perfect day for it." Ozzie lowered onto the cabana bed. God. This was weird. Dad outside, by the pool. They'd taken whole-ass trips to Maui where he never stepped foot on the beach or changed out of his slacks.

Ozzie sensed something was up with the big guy, but nobody else seemed to notice, not even Talia who was usually wigging out about someone being mad at her. Ozzie wished Gabby were around so they could talk it through. Well, she was around physically, but mentally was another matter. She'd done the classic Gabby move. When things got tough, she detached.

"So, what's up with you?" Dad asked, using a hand to shield his eyes. "Are you having fun?"

"Oh, yeah, it's great. Ya know, I was skeptical about San Diego. Small town. No swag. But the weather is ideal, and the Ranch is fire. I'd kind of forgotten." Ozzie smiled, pleased he'd ferreted out a nugget of truth.

"Agreed. I regret not spending more time in San Diego," Dad said. "Have I ever told you that I lived here for two years in high school?"

Ozzie looked at him. "You lived at the Ranch?"

Dad shook his head. "No. Not here. My parents sent me to live with an aunt near Sunset Cliffs."

"Oh yeah? You got expelled, too?" Ozzie said with a smirk. He'd never been able to relate to his dad, and how ironic if getting booted from their own families was how it finally went down.

"No. Nothing like that," Marston said, glancing away, and didn't it fucking figure. "Long story short, my grades weren't very strong, and they were worried about my chances of getting into Yale." A stint in a public high school might boost his GPA and make him seem more interesting, his parents reasoned, so they shipped him off to live with his aunt. After spending his sophomore and junior years at Point Loma High, he returned to New York and eventually enrolled at Brown.

"Wow, Dad, I had no idea," Ozzie said, trying to digest the information. They were both sent away, but his dad's parents were attempting to create an easier path for their son as opposed to whatever the fuck Dad was doing with him. Ozzie never asked because it wasn't worth bringing up.

"I loved it," Dad said, staring out across the pool. "I made great friends and played on the baseball team and in general had the time of my life. That all feels so distant now. I wish I'd appreciated it more." Dad exhaled, and Ozzie swore he saw tears glistening in his blue eyes. "Time goes fast, and you get so wrapped up in the day-to-day bullshit, it's hard to see the big picture. Then suddenly you blink, and you're on the downhill slide to the grave."

"Yeah. Time flies. And it sucks. Anyhow." Ozzie patted his dad's leg and pushed himself to standing. "I'll let you continue your daydreaming." He started to walk away.

Then he stopped. A feeling latched on to him, a very familiar feeling, one Freja said accounted for his tendency to "hire every down-and-out douchebag" he came across. Ozzie hated the thought of leaving someone sad and alone.

"Hey, Dad," Ozzie said, turning around, even though he didn't want to, not really. "You don't seem to be doing much right now. No offense."

Dad snorted. "None taken."

"What do you say we get out of here? I'm in the mood for a field trip and have the perfect idea."

# Chapter Thirty-Four

## Gabby

Raj walked into the main house, openly gawping as he looked around. "Holy shit, you weren't kidding about the *estate*," he said, brushing a finger along a carved walnut chair.

"Yeah, it's a showpiece," I said. My belly was full of nerves, even though this was exactly what I'd wanted. Unfortunately, Sydney hated the arrangement, and now her doubts were lodged in my brain.

"This seems . . . problematic?" she'd said when we'd chatted earlier. "Forcing someone to move in so you can steal their 'essence'?"

"First of all, nobody's being forced," I'd insisted, though it did sound sketchy when she put it like that. "Raj needs a place to live, and a job, and I will pay him handsomely." Admittedly, my hypothesis was half-baked and premature—Ustenya might say I was *making a whip out of shit*—but I preferred to call it positivity and at least I was trying to solve the PBS puzzle. The universe threw Raj into my path for a reason, I assured Sydney. Everything would be fine.

"Can't wait to hear what happens next," my "best friend" said before we hung up, and it sounded kind of like a threat.

As Raj and I exited the back of the house, he commented on the pool. Funny how it didn't have a waterfall or slide or anything, he mused, and I wondered whether he'd always been such a princess. Suddenly his apartment felt twelve miles away and it began to hit home how unhinged it was to ask (pay!) a stranger to move in.

"Talia was excited when I told her you were joining the campaign," I said as we crossed the road. Raj's luggage sped past us on Mindy's golf cart. "She's sorry she couldn't be here to greet you, but she had a meeting downtown. With the mayor, I think? It's a big deal. She's been trying to get on his calendar basically since we arrived."

"Yeah, she told me," Raj said, and I cranked my head in his direction.

"You've been talking to Talia?" This felt like a betrayal, but by who and why I could not articulate.

"You guys really don't talk much, do you?"

"Huh?"

Raj laughed to himself, and I narrowed my eyes. "We met at the beach cleanup?" he reminded me. "And now that you've gone on the record about your dad wanting to single-handedly solve homelessness . . ."

"You read the *Intelligencer*. Terrific."

Raj snickered through his nose. "Talia reached out about volunteering at LASD to get her arms around the problem," he said. "She's also assisting with a lawsuit we're filing against the San Diego Housing Commission."

"Gosh! So many hobbies," I warbled. Well, this explained why she'd been rolling into the office at noon, often yammering about zoning laws. Irritation began to creep in though I had no valid reason to be mad. Talia was actively helping Dad—he'd added "limit private equity investment in residential housing" to his platform and those words got her the Quinonez meeting—yet, I still felt weird about her working with Raj. If my worlds were going to collide, I'd prefer it didn't happen behind my back.

"Let's cut through here," I said, opening the door to the

pickleball pavilion. "They razed the property's umpteenth horse ring to make room for pickleball but left two trainers' apartments. You'll be staying in one of them."

Once back outside, we made our way down a winding dirt path. Ahead stood a pair of freestanding white stucco apartments with red tile roofs. Between the two buildings, Mom's art studio was visible, and beyond that, a glimpse of the lake.

"Yours is on the left," I said. After grabbing one of the duffels Mindy deposited at the bottom step, I trudged upstairs. "For the record, Talia doesn't know why you're here."

"She doesn't know about the campaign?" he teased.

"Ha ha," I said, dryly. "Also, I don't really discuss PBS with my family. So if you can keep it on the DL, I'd be most grateful."

"Noted," Raj said.

"And you're not obligated to actually *work*. Bare minimum is totally fine. Feel free to fake it while enjoying the Ranch's amenities."

"I'm quite looking forward to getting involved."

"Fantastic." I dropped the duffel on the landing and opened the door. The apartment appeared clean but smelled . . . unused. *Dusty* was maybe a better word. I heaved the duffel back onto my shoulder and went inside. My Birks slapped on the terracotta tiles as I marched across the room. "Just . . . don't get too invested," I said.

"We'll see."

"Let's not."

"We'll see," Raj said again.

"Suddenly you're all sorts of trouble," I said and threw open a window.

"*Me?* Gabby! The insult! I'm always on my best behavior . . ."

"Yes. And thirty people from a trolley opening would definitely agree."

# Chapter Thirty-Five

## Talia

Talia slid the piece of paper across the table. Dad cupped a hand around it to block out the sun. They sat on the patio outside his bedroom, beneath a bougainvillea-covered pergola. "What am I looking at?" he asked. On the paper were four cartoons: a list, a guy holding a bag of money, an apartment building, a map.

"It's supposed to represent the main problems in the California housing market," Talia said, gesturing to each picture with the tip of her pen.

An impossibly long waiting list, private equity (Dad already knew about that), a lack of multifamily dwellings, and exclusionary zoning laws. Was he aware? Most cities in the US were seventy-five percent or more zoned for single-family only, which was quite outrageous.

Dad bit into his sandwich. "And you're telling me this with cartoons?" he said, his mouth half-full of chicken salad. "Were you concerned I wouldn't grasp words?"

Talia flushed. "No, I was just keeping it simple."

Raj had created the document, and she'd neglected to think it through. The cartoon was perhaps a misstep, but it was nice to have someone around who understood the concept of real problems and actually wanted to fix them, especially given how dismissive Spencer had been lately. *Get a grip, Tal. Your dad is not going to fix homelessness*. The comment rankled. What was *he* doing to improve anyone's life, aside from turning one pile of money into two? Such-and-such company should trade at ten times EBITDA, but why? Says who? They were all passing dollars around. Not actual cash. The concept of it. That man needed to get out of New York.

"Forget the cartoons," Talia said to her father. "Flip to the next page. The details are there. Complete sentences and everything."

Dad scanned the paper, his face devoid of expression.

"Admittedly, many of these suggestions are hyper-local," Talia went on, "but we need to shore up local support before we go wider." She paused, waiting for him to remind her that his name was on buildings and hospitals and marine biological institutes and why not rest his laurels on that. Name recognition was probably his platform all along, and he likely never stopped to consider whether people would make the connection, or if they'd care.

"Mayor Quinonez ran on fixing housing in San Diego," Talia said and dipped her fork into a pot of vinaigrette. She stabbed a piece of lettuce. "An endorsement from him would be a game changer. San Diego is *super* messed up . . . They're not adhering to state rent caps."

"Sounds bad. Someone should do something."

*Is this supposed to be funny?* Talia wondered as she finished crunching her lettuce. She took a sip of Diet Coke before continuing. "Well, someone is," she said. "There's a whole lawsuit underway against the housing commission." She told him about Raj, and his work with Black Men and Women United San Diego, the group preparing the lawsuit. They were filing it any day, and she'd contributed her well-honed research skills. "The commission keeps insisting they don't need to comply with laws but—"

"I was joking," Dad snapped, and Talia felt literally put in her place. "Why are we even talking about this? I added the private equity thing on my website. End of discussion."

Talia sighed and pushed her salad aside. "Dad. I'm just trying to help."

"I know." He leaned back, his chair squeaking beneath him. "How's it going, Talia?" he asked, out of damned nowhere. "Are you happy, being here in California?"

Was Talia *happy*? What kind of question was that? "Um. Sure," she said, suddenly dizzy. "Are you?"

Her father chuckled dryly. "Sure," he said, parroting her answer. "I am thrilled Ozzie finally made it. He brings a certain lightness, don't you think?"

"He definitely brings something . . ."

"His presence reminds you to enjoy the good things in life. Did I tell you he took me to my old stomping grounds the other day?" he said, and launched into a convoluted tale about a high school he'd attended for two years, and how he and Ozzie went to visit and watch a women's volleyball game. As he spoke, Talia prayed that no one cottoned to the fact a sixty-one-year-old man was watching teenage girls he didn't know jump around in small shorts.

"Sounds like a memorable experience," Talia grumbled. Volleyball. Meanwhile, some of them were trying to get this campaign out of the basement.

"One kid recognized Ozzie," Dad went on. He stopped to wipe his lips, but a dollop of mayonnaise lingered. "The guy filmed us for his social media."

"Oh, God," Talia groaned. Someone *did* cotton to it after all and she could only imagine how that looked. According to Ivan, it played well online and while Talia seriously doubted this, Dad hadn't been immediately canceled, which was tremendous news.

"Alright. Lunch meeting over." Dad closed up his sandwich box. It still had half a sandwich left, and Talia felt a flicker of worry. In a video of his speech at the Del Mar Rotary Club, he'd come across as exhausted, very low blood sugar. Campaigns were grueling, and a person needed to lock in their nutrition.

"Did you eat enough?" Talia asked. Granted, she'd only finished about a third of her salad, but she was different. She'd been getting by on practically nothing her whole life. "Do you want a salad? Some chips? A cob of corn?"

"Nah. I'm fine. You're working hard, Tal. And I appreciate it. But you should take a page out of Ozzie's playbook. Get out more. The Ranch is expansive but can feel claustrophobic at times."

"Oh. Well. I do get out when I volunteer at LASD or work on the lawsuit. Otherwise, I'm pretty busy with the campaign. How lucky for Ozzie, though, he has the free time!" Talia wished she hadn't been so quick to discard the salad. She could've used a way to occupy her mouth right now.

"Free time begets free time," Dad said, chortling to himself. "Someone told me that recently."

No doubt that someone was Ozzie. Dad really lit up when he talked about him so maybe Marston Gunn didn't need more food or sleep, but simply more Ozzie. No matter what happened, no matter how many bridges he literally or figuratively burned, her little brother held the top position in most hearts. If Gabby was universally beloved, and Ozzie specifically adored, where did that leave Talia? The one person who'd loved and known her the best was long gone.

"Before you declare our lunch meeting over," Talia began, widening her eyes, trying to create a dam against the emotions building behind them. "Can we come to a resolution on these ideas?" She tapped the stapled sheets of paper in front of her, the top one flapping in the breeze.

"What do you mean *resolution*?"

"Can we officially add the other three issues to your platform?"

Dad pondered this for a beat. "Sure. Why not," he said, shrugging, slowly rising to his feet. "As long as you don't piss off Wall Street, it's good for me." He excused himself, leaving Talia alone at the table, feeling inexplicably defeated even though she'd just won.

# Gunn sees unlikely uptick in support

BY KYLE SPERBER, *The North County Intelligencer*

SAN DIEGO—The race to fill California's vacated U.S. Senate seat remains wide open. Democratic Congressional representatives David Slimp and Angie Parker are leading the field, but a large portion of the state's likely voters (32%) are undecided. Parker stands atop the heap, with 18%, a figure that has not changed since July, while support for Slimp has declined to 17% from a high of 20% in August. U.S. Representative Sandra Grant has held steady at 10%.

In a shift no one anticipated, former reality television executive Marston Gunn has seen a surge in support. Until recently, Gunn's campaign was widely considered dead on arrival, but either his message is starting to resonate, or the campaign is in the throes of terminal lucidity—the jolt of energy prior to death. Gunn's communications director, who happens to be his youngest daughter, Gabrielle Gunn, believes voters are reacting to his "concrete measures to tackle America's housing crisis."

Gunn's newly released plans include, among other things, funding and expanding the voucher system, replete with annual cost-of-living adjustments, increasing the number of affordable housing units nationwide, banning hedge funds from buying residential units, and creating more restrictions around flipping homes. On the purchaser side, he favors federal down payment and mortgage insurance assistance for low- to moderate-income and minority homebuyers.

"Our goal is to significantly reduce the length of time a qualified individual or family must wait for housing relief," says Gunn's field organizer, Talia Gunn. "We also want to ensure voucher amounts are in line with rents. While these are very local problems, Section 8 is a federal program, which means Congress should get involved."

These are high aspirations for a campaign that's barely chugging along. Gunn's poll numbers are improving, but with a mere million in the bank as of the end of the third quarter, he still lags significantly behind the other candidates. He hasn't secured any notable endorsements, but Team Gunn is eyeing a nod from San Diego's chief, who they feel shares similar policy positions and goals.

"Our mayor is laser-focused on implementing practical solutions to address San Diego's housing crisis," says Talia Gunn. "And he's made tremendous progress since stepping into office two years ago. Not only has Mr. Quinonez expanded shelters and implemented a safe sleeping program, but he's also successfully enacted legislation to create more middle-class housing and a faster permitting track for low-income units. His policies are closely aligned with ours, and we look forward to working with him to move important programs forward."

When reached for comment, Mayor Robert Quinonez told *The Intelligencer* that he has not yet formally endorsed anyone. "We are fortunate to have many excellent Democratic candidates to choose from," he says.

One thing Gunn does have on his side is a seemingly unified campaign. While there are talks of an exodus of unhappy staffers from Parker's office (untenable hours, yelling, the throwing of staplers at heads), Gunn's small staff is growing. His son, Oscar, has recently entered the fold and is by all accounts making a positive contribution. He was the brains behind a TikTok video that, as of this writing, has had half a million views.

"Dad spent two years as a Point Loma Pointer," says Oscar Gunn. "We were wandering the campus for nostalgia's sake and stopped to watch a volleyball match. While in the bleachers, Dad got the chance to connect with parents and students about their greatest concerns."

In the video (*Homie out here watching girls volleyball* is linked here), Marston Gunn, wearing jeans, a navy blue sweatshirt, and a matching blue baseball cap with a horse head logo embroidered in teal, answers a series of questions about the state of the world. He responds to each, even the more complicated ones, calmly, assuredly, and with great empathy. He doesn't make any promises, but mostly listens and shares what he would hope to do. This video makes him come across as genuine, and more than a little appealing.

"I don't know whether to have a crush on him or wish he was my dad," reads one of the comments.

A mildly viral TikTok video might not seem like a huge advantage, but it is a boon for a fledgling campaign.

"This is a prime example of user-generated content, or UGC," says independent Democratic strategist Theo Lemke. "Spending millions on advertisements is great, if you have the money, but campaigns can also benefit from regular people amplifying a message to their various small communities. No one is going to vote for a guy because he turns up in a high school gym for an hour, but if friends tell friends who tell friends, that's when things can snowball."

The final question asked in the video was why Gunn was at a volleyball game in the first place.

"My happiest memories involve watching my kids play sports," Gunn answers, eyes visibly welling. "One of the saddest days of my life was my daughter Gabby's senior night, walking out of the gym with her for the very last time."

If you'd like to see dad/crush Marston Gunn in person, a meet-the-candidate event is scheduled for next Tuesday. Check the campaign website for details or reach out to OZZIE@Marston-Gunn4CA.org, who is organizing the event.

# Chapter Thirty-Six

## Gabby

I spotted Talia just outside the recreation pavilion, standing near a lemon tree, phone tucked between her shoulder and ear. She gave me a "hold on" gesture before hanging up with a, "'K love you, bye."

"How's Spencer?" I asked, tightening Frosty's leash around my hand.

"Fine, I guess," Talia said and tiptoed over to me while navigating the dozens of lemons in various stages of rot on the ground. "He's sick of hearing about Dad's campaign."

"Relatable. Any clue why we've been summoned here?" I turned toward the building, my eyes sweeping the mess of cracked stucco, rotting wood, and spiderwebs. The place was in a serious state of disrepair.

"It's Ozzie, so who knows."

As we approached the door, I peered up to where bright pink bougainvillea appeared to be eating the roof. "What if it collapses?" I pondered aloud. Roofs were on my mind, and I felt iffy about the structural integrity of this one.

"It hasn't been *that* long," Talia said and pushed open the door.

We crept inside to find three dust-caked televisions hanging from the rafters, and drop cloths covering the arcade games, air hockey, and pool tables. Stacked chairs lined the bowling alleys and, between them, a karaoke machine waited for a singer who would never return.

"Yikes," I said. "It's very 'documentary about a family murder' in here."

"Guess we're not bowling," Talia said.

"Welcome, ladies!" Ozzie popped up from behind the bar and plunked a large bottle of something amber-colored onto the counter. "It's Friday evening, and we need to celebrate. Finally, some good news for Dad." He pivoted and began rooting around in the cabinet behind him.

"Pretty sad that an article declaring us 'not dead yet' is good news," Talia said. She picked up the bottle and made a face. "*Scotch?* In a recreation pavilion? Only Dad."

"As if Dad's ever stepped foot in here." Ozzie flipped back around and wiped the insides of three shot glasses with his shirt. "Everybody down for a shot?"

"Sure, why not," I said, freeing Frosty from his leash. He darted off to sniff, nails clacking on the floors. "Though I'm not much of a drinker—"

"She likes the herb," Ozzie said, using one hand to perform the universal sign for smoking a blunt, while he poured out shots with the other.

"Not as much as some people," I said and reached for one of the glasses.

"To Team Gunn!" Ozzie said, raising his overhead.

"Gunning for you!" I said. We clinked and threw back our shots. I grimaced, the alcohol burning on the way down. "That is disgusting."

"Totally," Talia agreed and asked for another.

"Look at us," Ozzie said. "Three charming but dysfunctional children, getting it done. Talia using her competence to make Dad stand for something."

"It was easy. Almost too easy." She frowned. "He told me to do . . . whatever. I don't trust it."

"Don't overthink," Ozzie said. "Meanwhile, Gabby secured not one but two labor endorsements with her legendary niceness."

"Yep." I bobbed my head. My tally so far: the Sailors' Union of the Pacific and the local branch of the International Alliance of Theatrical Stage Employees. I'd like to think my theater background brought the second one over the finish line.

"Even the resident dipshit can contribute," Ozzie said, hopping up onto the bar.

"Please," Talia scoffed. "If you become any more adored, they're going to ask *you* to run instead." She took another shot and made her way to the opposite side of the room.

"Aw," Ozzie said, tilting his head. "That's the sweetest thing you've ever said to me."

"No one's accused me of being the nice one." Talia opened the door to the gym and peeked inside. "Everything's unplugged," she said. "It doesn't look like anyone's been in here for years. Isn't Dad a gym every day at five a.m. guy?"

"I've seen him jogging the property," I said. "And Ustenya mentioned having an elliptical in their bedroom?"

"He's also pretty into pickleball," Ozzie offered.

Talia shut the door and whirled back around.

"Man. It's a trip being here now," Ozzie said as he cast his gaze about the place. "We spent *so* much time here as kids."

"Not me," Talia said. She went behind the bar and squatted to check the inventory. "I only came for the gym."

Ozzie and I raised eyebrows at each other, as in, *of course*.

Talia reappeared with a bottle of vodka and removed a tumbler from the shelf. "Though Mom did hold a birthday party here for me once, but it was just her friends' kids."

"Wow, Mom throwing a birthday party," I said. "What must it have been like?"

"I was seventeen, by the way," Talia said, and I snort-laughed.

Vodka in hand, Talia wandered over and flicked on one of

the arcade games. I heard the telltale start-up music, followed by *chomp chomp chomp chomp*. As Talia maneuvered Ms. Pac-Man through her maze, I craned forward, zeroing in on the dozens of little holes dotting the machine.

"Oh my God!" I said, pointing as a memory clicked into place. Ozzie was nine and absolutely fixated on the idea of a BB gun.

"If you can figure out a way to get one," Mom had said, "go for it. But don't involve me."

Cut to us biking eight miles to the fairgrounds, where a gun show was being held, and from which Ozzie purchased a Daisy Red Ryder. We biked home triumphant, narrowly avoiding three separate accidents along the way, but our giddiness was short-lived. A BB gun sounded cool—our friends in New York didn't have anything like that—but Ozzie wasn't looking to kill innocent animals, so what were we supposed to do with it? Shoot up the recreation pavilion, it turned out.

"The infamous BB gun," Ozzie said now. "I'll never forget Dad screaming at me on the phone. *Why? Whyyyyyy? What was going through your head?*"

"He loved when you answered, 'I dunno, seemed fun?'"

My brother laughed, and it was the first time I'd seen the real Ozzie since he arrived. This was the kid I knew. Cool. Funny. Mind operating on a different, better plane. These past two weeks he didn't seem uptight per se, but definitely like he was holding something back.

"We had some good times here," he said. "It's sad it ended so abruptly."

"Yes, *that's* what's sad," Talia said to the sound of Ms. Pac-Man dying. Literally giving up the ghost. "The loss of the opportunity to shoot BBs at arcade games."

"Yeah, cuz it was the fucking bomb."

"You two." Talia took a swig of vodka straight from the bottle. "The way you act about Mom, it's not . . ." She fished around for the word. "You're mad she left, and I get it. But the leaving doesn't define her. We used to have fun together, all of us."

"Okay . . ." I said. Mostly I recalled nannies and babysitters, but wasn't about to pipe up and risk my life.

"Believe it or not, we had fun back in New York," Talia said, sensing my skepticism. "We were a normal family, doing normal family stuff. Like how practically every other day Gabby made us trek over to Hippo Playground in Riverside Park."

"I totally remember that!" Ozzie said, and funny enough, I remembered it, too. Hippos were for sure one animal I was glad to have never manifested and KNOCK ON WOOD.

"There was a real relationship," Talia said, "and it's not right how you pretend nothing changed after she was gone."

"But nothing did change," I said.

"Our mom died!"

"I'm talking about logistically, one day to the next. Think about it, Tal. I kept getting up and going to school, and practicing for whatever sport was in season. Diane came every afternoon, and each night I studied in the kitchen where she cooked the same meals. Always chicken cacciatore on Tuesdays."

"Thirty Ways to Cook a Chicken: the Diane Randolph Story," Ozzie joked.

"Stop pretending Diane could be a replacement for Mom."

"You're not listening," Ozzie said. "What Bags is saying is that Mom's death was tragic, on an intellectual level, but she left us long before she died."

"She didn't leave you. She went to California. *Temporarily*. Because she was ill."

"Was she, though? Was she ill the whole time?" Ozzie said.

Talia balked. She looked between him and me and back again. "Gabby and I talked about this—"

"And what's 'temporary'?" Ozzie said. "It doesn't feel very temporary when you're eight years old. When she misses your ninth birthday. And your tenth, eleventh, twelfth, et cetera."

Talia gaped, suddenly made speechless from these truths, from counting the missed birthdays. Talia was a Fourth of July baby. She was with Mom for every one of hers, ages zero through twenty. For us, it was a different tale.

"She missed your birthdays?" Talia managed to spit out. "I never knew—"

"Yeah. But, hey, it's chill," Ozzie said, jumping down from the bar. "We had Dad, and Diane, and Daphne was obviously going through some stuff. You remember her as the greatest woman in the world or whatever, and I'm glad you have that. But, like, other peoples' experiences are different?"

Talia remained bug-eyed as his words worked their way through her brain. "I hope you didn't think I was . . . Jesus." She swallowed. "No wonder everyone thinks I'm a bitch."

Ozzie laughed. "Hey, that's not true." He slung an arm around her, and she melted into his hold. "I'm not trying to rock your world or anything. You keep your narrative, and we'll keep ours."

He winked at me and I smiled back, grateful to be part of Bags and Oz again.

"We all have our stories," he said. "Sometimes it's what we need to get by. Anyway." He released Talia and spun around. "Who's up for some air hockey? Gabby, swear to God, I'm not going to let you cheat this time."

# Chapter Thirty-Seven

## Ozzie

Ozzie was starting to sweat it. No one had RSVP'd, and he was the only one here aside from the balloonist, the crew, and two sad, deflated hot-air balloons laid out across the ground.

"Not sure what's happening," Ozzie said, checking his phone. Gabby and Talia *had* to show up. And Dad. It was a meet-the-candidate event, for the love of God. Ozzie had finally won everyone over—his greatest and now confirmed only skill—but ruined it in one fell swoop. Talia would never shut up about this.

"We need begin lift-off prep in the next ten minutes," one of the guys said. "Or we won't be able to take off at all."

"Yes, I know!" Ozzie winced. He hadn't meant to snap, but he was on edge—because of this impending piece-of-shit event but also the call he'd received from Barclay on the way over. Ozzie had to come up with $400K for the IRS in thirty days or . . . what? Barclay hadn't said, and he was too afraid to ask.

"Sorry, buddy," he said to the balloonist. "I'm a smidge stressed. I appreciate you." They exchanged a fist bump.

The dude's name was Brody, and he was a real crusty, sunburnt type. The kind of guy who lived life at the beach, surfing a million waves and purchasing zero bottles of sunscreen. It was upsetting how little respect he had for his complexion.

Suddenly, a black SUV screeched around the corner. Ozzie exhaled in relief as Tony pulled onto the lot, kicking up dirt and rocks. One of the back doors opened. Out hopped his sisters and that Indian fella. Raj something. Ozzie didn't know where he'd come from.

Ozzie waited. He looked around. "You're it?" he said. "Where's Dad?"

"Driving separately. Where are the voters?" Talia said, looking around.

"Uh. They'll be here any second," Ozzie lied.

Gabby twisted up her face, visibly straining to conceal her judgment. Sometimes Ozzie wished she'd take a hint from Talia and be more open with her feelings. It'd save everyone a lot of hassle.

"Hey, guys?" Tony said, leaning out of the car. "I received a text from the chief. Apparently he's just learned this was a hot-air balloon excursion and has opted out. He gets motion sickness and is afraid of heights."

"Since *when*?" Talia said.

Tony swung his gaze toward Gabby. "Your dad wants you to text him if anyone shows up. He'll come by at the end, say hello to everyone."

"Why am I in charge?" Gabby squawked. "This is very specifically Ozzie's thing!"

Ozzie glowered. Gabby was on one lately, and he'd tried to be nice. Organizing an impromptu happy hour, for example. Forgiving her for all the tiny slights. But it was like every time Ozzie turned around, she did some new thing to undermine him. Then she'd smile and tell everyone they were BFFs.

"How did you advertise this?" Talia asked. "Not on social media, I hope."

"Uhhhhh . . ."

"Do you even have any followers in San Diego?" Talia tossed up her hands. "This is insane!" And in this way Ozzie learned that neither sister followed him on the socials. Millions of fans online, but none IRL.

"Are we still a go?" Brody called out. The crew was packing up the second balloon.

"Might as well," Ozzie said. "It's paid for and we're here."

Raj, whose face was almost green, said he'd stay behind. Talia wanted to join him, but Gabby gave her a look, and now the three Gunns were stamping across weeds and rocks, toward a rainbow-striped balloon. Honestly, Ozzie had expected something less basic, like a whale or a dolphin, or Mickey Mouse at the very least. That's what an online coupon got you, he supposed. Welcome to life as a discount shopper.

"Why, Ozzie?" Talia said. "Why hot-air ballooning?"

"It's very Southern California! I was attempting to be creative."

Brody flicked on an incredibly loud machine. It was the cold inflation part of the process, he explained, which got things started.

"This is our balloonist," Ozzie said over the thrum of the machine. "Brody."

"Pilot," Brody corrected him, and then went literally inside the balloon to check on things.

"This is wild," Gabby said, unlocking her phone. "How does hot-air ballooning even work?"

As Grabby scrolled, Brody walked back out. He switched to hot inflation, which involved shooting fire directly into the balloon. Crew members held the basket on the ground as the balloon began to rise.

"Oh, God," Gabby said, swiping down her screen. "Yikes. Did not need to know that." She slid the phone back into her jeans.

"Hold on." Talia's eyes landed on Ozzie. "Something occurred to me. There's a balloon in *Winnie the Pooh*, isn't there? I can picture him holding it. Oh my God. You're really out here making us reenact *Winnie the Pooh*."

"That balloon was for *honey*," Ozzie said.

"Did he use it for transportation, yes or no?"

"Yes. Until Christopher Robin shot it with a gun."

"He had a gun?" Gabby said. "Wow. Dark."

Ozzie rolled his eyes. There were much darker aspects to Christopher Robin, like the fact he was based on A. A. Milne's son, who notoriously hated it. *My father had got where he was by climbing on my infant shoulders*, he told a reporter. The *author filched his good name* and left him *nothing but empty fame*. Empty fame. Relatable.

"Christopher Robin always carried a gun," Ozzie informed his sisters. "You should understand the lore before relating it to things."

Talia shook her head. "Hope no one shoots ours."

"There wasn't a basket involved, okay? He was holding on to the balloon. Like this." Ozzie stretched his arms overhead. "Then he got stuck like that for a week."

"Oh my God." Talia barked out a laugh. She waved a hand in front of her face like she was wafting away a bad smell. "I just . . . I can't."

"Okay, guys," one of the crew members said. "Time to jump in."

The Gunns froze. They all traded looks, each one silently daring someone else to move.

"We don't have all day." Brody hopped in.

Gabby went next, leaping deftly over the side of the basket. A crew member assisted Talia, and finally it was Ozzie's turn. He attempted a one-handed sideways deal, something a skateboarder might do, but didn't clear the rim.

"Not a great sign," Talia said, peeking over the basket to where Ozzie lay splayed on the ground.

"I'm not the one steering it," Ozzie said and tried again, the crew helping him this time.

"You don't steer a hot-air balloon," Brody pointed out. "You go with the wind. It's more of an art than a science."

"Terrific!" Talia sang. "Love that for us!"

"What an adventure," Gabby said.

*Ugh*, Ozzie thought, shooting daggers. He really wished she'd stop pretending to be on his side when obviously she hadn't wanted him here, same as Talia.

"Don't worry, everyone," Brody said. "The ground crew will follow along. Wherever we land, they'll pick us up."

"We don't know where we're going to land?" Gabby said. Talia went to say something, too, but Brody blasted the propane, drowning them both out.

At last, the crew stepped away from the basket, waving as the balloon lifted them up, up, up and away. Ozzie closed his eyes and took several deep breaths. Well, if they went down in literal flames, at least he wouldn't have to listen to his sisters bitch about this for the next three to five years.

"Raj is recording us," Gabby said, craning over the basket. "Or taking pictures. Maybe Montana and Bea can do something with it."

"That'll get Dad some eyeballs," Talia said. The fire roared again. "The last known photograph of Marston Gunn's three children. All presumed dead."

# Chapter Thirty-Eight

## Gabby

The mood in the balloon had gone from very tense to . . . whatever this was. Probably on account of Talia pounding champagne. The lines between her brows had all but disappeared, and now she stood on the other side of the balloon, marveling at the views, whooping it up. Meanwhile I smiled blandly into the void, wishing I hadn't googled "how fire hot air balloon" back when we were still on the ground. The search results offered no explanations, just a bunch of videos of balloons catching on actual fire and news stories counting the number of people dead.

*If Talia can enjoy this, you certainly can*, I told myself. Peering down, my eyes swept the land beneath us, from the hills to the golf courses to the racetrack. With the Pacific Ocean glittering ten miles in the distance, I felt a semblance of peace. Until Brody hocked a big one over the side.

"Ew!" I yelped. "Gross!"

"My bad," he said. "Should've given you a heads-up. It's how I measure which way we're goin'. The wind changes speed and direction based on altitude, and my job is to figure out how to ride each stream. Some people use wood shavings, but why shell out for supplies when I have everything I need inside?" He patted his belly.

"How resourceful!" I chirped, and tried not to think too hard about the fact our pilot considered wood chips a luxury. Also, he undeniably reeked of pot. Maybe it calmed him. Maybe it was medicinal.

Brody fired the propane like a very large bong. Talia continued to take swigs of her champagne, and I avoided looking at my brother because I couldn't bear it. *Dammit, Ozzie.* He'd been doing so well, and this was going to end up as another black mark. Why did he have to make everything so hard on himself?

"Look at us!" Talia said, as Brody juiced the burner again. "A real family bonding session. Three thousand feet in the air. Let's all go around and say one thing we love about California."

Oh, God, she was doing this now? When she was drunk, and we were sober (aside from Brody, possibly), and a small stroke of bad luck away from catching on fire? But this was Talia, and she hated to let something go.

"Fresh corn on the cob," I said, and Ozzie snorted.

"The weather is sick," he said.

"I'm glad we're all together," Talia said. "Truly." She looked at Ozzie, pointedly, and my gut constricted. Like, maybe don't directly address the fact you never wanted him here? "I know you think I'm prone to false nostalgia."

"Facts," Ozzie said, squatting to pour himself a glass of champagne.

"I loved being together the other night, in the recreation pavilion, even though, if I'm being honest, it made me sad." She paused, staring wistfully out toward the horizon as she sipped her champagne. "It was a reminder of how you guys were always together, engaging in your shenanigans, and I was always left out. Not that I was interested in biking around Southampton to egg people's tennis courts—"

"RIP Mrs. Merchin's newly coiffed hair," Ozzie said as he rose to standing.

"For the record," I said. "I never really had a choice with the 'shenanigans.' He didn't warn me in advance."

"Oh, poor Gabby," Ozzie grumbled.

"But you went along for the ride," Talia said. "It would've been nice to be included every once in a while."

Suddenly, Brody let out a yelp. We all cranked in his direction.

"It's all good!" he said, voice cracking. "We're a wee bit off course. Just need to change elevations and catch the wind moving west."

Grimacing, I reminded myself this was very normal. It's why we had to "ride the streams" while the crew followed along in a truck. This would be fine, right? I checked my skin and found it rash-free. The air smelled crisp and clean. My PBS sensors detected no imminent danger.

"Oh my God," Talia said when Brody whoa-nellied again. "Can we land this damned thing?"

"Yeah, deadass, bro," Ozzie said. "It's feeling kinda sketchy."

"I'm trying," Brody said, a bead of sweat rolling down his temple. "But we missed another landing spot."

*"Another?"* I squawked.

"Try, try again. That's the name of the game." Brody said something else, but the surge of propane drowned out his words. "Missing landing spots is very common," he went on. "Happens all the time. Well, not *all* the time. But often enough. It's why they're closing down this corridor. Too many homeowner complaints and, you know, the fire danger. Totally valid. It's that time of year."

"Terrific!" I sang. "This is all such helpful information!"

Talia tensed her jaw. She squeezed her champagne flute. For a second, I worried it might shatter in her hand. "Jesus fucking Christ!" she shouted into the sky, then jerked her whole self toward Ozzie. "I knew having you on the campaign would be a mistake, but I didn't think it'd get us killed."

"No one is getting killed," Brody promised as we began to make what I hoped was a planned descent.

"Let's all stay calm," I said half-heartedly, and looked down to gauge our elevation. A family picnicked below. They were waving, or screaming, or something.

"You're a fucking idiot, Oscar," Talia said.

"Hey. Back off," I said and snuck a glance at Brody, who was now sweating bullets. "Everyone's over here doing their best."

"You're so fake, Gabby," Ozzie said.

My heart thumped. *"Me?"*

"Yes. You." Ozzie yanked off his aviators. "I'm so sick of your goddamn act. I respect Talia for being so straightforward in her disdain."

"What disdain?"

"But you? You pretend you want me here, but you're full of shit. I don't know why everyone thinks you're so nice. You're not that nice!"

"Yes. Thank you," Talia said. "I've been saying this forever."

"You play the protective older sister, but you're never up to the job when things count. Maybe you *were* the source for all the bad things said about me in that stupid paper."

"What? That's not true! I'm always on your side," I said, eyes growing hot. "I stand up for you constantly!"

"Not true. You look the other way and let things . . . play out."

"What are you talking—"

"Like, I dunno, when three masked thugs kidnapped me in the middle of the night?"

"Huh?" Talia said.

*Thwap.* We lurched forward, and I yelped.

"Did we clip a tree?" Talia asked, looking down.

"Looks like it," Brody said, following her gaze. "It happens sometimes. Hey. Reach out. See if you can grab a squirrel. Ha!"

"This is not funny!" I said.

"Don't worry. Your boy's got this." Brody blasted the propane, which I thought was supposed to make us rise, not descend, and I prayed our boy was locked in.

"You could've spoken up that night," Ozzie said. "What did you have to lose? No one was shipping you off to Utah, that was for damned sure."

"Is this about the boarding school?" Talia said.

"That whole thing was fucked up," I said. "I agree one thousand percent. But what could I have done? I was a kid. I was only sixteen!" I was also on Dad's shit list because a tree goat had arrived in the trash shoot two days before. Flare number four and yet another warning sign, given what would happen to Ozzie. "It's not like I thought you were truly kidnapped," I added. "Dad told me you were getting help and would be home soon, and I believed him. Obviously I had no idea that Canyonside wasn't a real boarding school and I didn't think you'd break any bones."

"Nice of someone to acknowledge it."

"What are you talking about? Dad *sued*. He got the place shut down."

Ozzie's face went white. "You knew about that?"

*Thwap.* We hit a telephone pole.

"Okay, guys, one more shot," Brody said, but none of us were listening.

"I'm not an idiot. I saw the cast and the sling," I said. "I noticed the hushed conversations. And yeah, maybe I wasn't at the top of my game, ready to step in and fight for you or whatever, but I had my own stuff going on. You might remember talk of a wolverine."

The day before Ozzie returned home, a wolverine scratched the shit out of the pantry. Flare number seven, the worst of the bunch. Honestly, how could dos Santos not buy my theory? It was a miracle this balloon basket wasn't infested with animals.

"I'm sorry, a wolverine?" Talia said.

"Yep! That pesky condition of mine. A wolverine in the kitchen, followed shortly thereafter by an emu."

"Hey, everyone, we gotta brace ourselves for a crash land-ing," Brody announced. "I'm gonna aim for a backyard. Hope-fully one without a pool."

"Oh God," I wailed.

"Holy shit," Talia said, grinning, oddly triumphant for some-one floating to her death. "This is all adding up. The cargo plane. The birds." She looked at Ozzie. "It's Gabby's fault you were cut off. She used Dad's credit card to charter a flight for a flock of flamingos."

"What the fuck!" Ozzie barked.

"Okay, guys, get ready," Brody said.

"A flamboyance," I clarified. "And you're making it sound like something it wasn't."

We smacked into a fence.

The basket hit the ground and skidded several yards.

We tilted to the side, and everything went black.

# Chapter Thirty-Nine

## Ozzie

The homeowner was shouting at the cop and pointing to Brody, saying he couldn't believe he'd been forced to meet this *motherfucker* three times. His backyard was not a balloon landing spot.

Talia and Gabby were on the other side of the lawn, inspecting Gabby's forearm, which honestly looked pretty jacked. Tears ran down Gabby's face, and she kept repeating something about a loud snap. Ozzie had heard it too, but everyone was alive so namaste, count your blessings, all that.

Ozzie unlocked his phone and clicked around, so angry he couldn't think straight. All this time, he'd given Gabby a pass. She'd been a teenage girl and probably hadn't understood the nuances of the situation. He'd even started to feel bad in the balloon for being so hard on her. But sixteen or twenty-four, Gabby was Gabby. She ignored things, picking and choosing what she allowed herself to see. Her chief objective in life was to protect her own damned self.

Now that Ozzie pondered it, of the two sisters, Talia was the one who gave a shit. It's why she was always in everyone's business. Unfortunately, he could never live up to the brother she expected or wanted him to be. No matter what he'd been through, Ozzie was a hopeless fuckup. These truths were kicking his ass.

"Oh my God!" somebody called out. "Is everyone okay?" Raj and the ground crew had arrived, and Raj made a bee-line for Talia, which was weird, because Ozzie thought he was Gabby's friend.

"We're lucky nothing caught fire," a crew member observed.

"No wonder they're banning this," said another, and Ozzie wanted to die. The others were right not to trust him. He *was* a freaking idiot. Some children were definitely left behind.

Ozzie's phone vibrated. The Lyft was outside. He glanced at Gabby, who had her head in her hand. "I just need to take a nap," she was saying, and Talia was yelling at her to get back on her feet.

"You might have a concussion. Don't close your eyes! You could die!"

Ozzie spun around. "Hey," he said to the other homeowner, who'd been observing all this through the screen door. "Can you call an ambulance? I think broken bones are involved."

"Yes. Of course," she said.

Ozzie smiled, thanked her, and left through the side gate.

# Chapter Forty

## Gabby

"Knock, knock," said a voice.

I looked up to find Ivan standing in the doorway. I'd been in the hospital twenty-four hours, and he was my first visitor. I knew Dad was busy, and Ozzie was mad, but you'd think they'd have a little compassion following an extremely harrowing balloon accident after which one of their own was hospitalized *overnight*. Also, who was taking care of my dog?

"I'm here to pick you up," he said, and wasn't that a kick in the pants. "So, what's the official diagnosis?" He lowered onto the end of my bed.

I brandished my arm, now in a cast. "Intra-articular fracture. They kept me overnight to monitor for a concussion, but it seems we're all clear. On the plus side, I got to learn more about the Gunn Hospital System." I gestured toward the brochure on my bedside table. "Fun fact. F.D. Gunn didn't do the giving in this state. It was his sister, Ellen Barlowe Gunn."

Ellen donated land for the hospitals, and multiple schools, and founded the marine biological institute. She provided the endowment for Gunn College in Pomona and throughout her life gave millions to promote democratic principles and women's education, all while living in an oceanside colony of unmarried ladies during the early decades of the twentieth century. Their dad lived on this property—no longer a colony—for two years as a teenager.

"I don't know why the Gunn men got all the credit for what the women actually did," I said.

"Tale as old as time. I'm glad you don't have a concussion, but how are you doing otherwise?" Ivan asked.

"I don't love the cast but am relieved the incident is behind us."

Although I wouldn't admit it to Ivan, I did see one bright side to the balloon crash. Flares preceded every bad thing that'd happened to me over the past eleven years, but there'd been no trace of an animal up there, not a single feather or tuft of fur, proving Raj was the answer. Now all I had to do was convince him to give me a toenail or strand of hair and all my problems would be solved. He'd receive his money, and I'd become the normal person I was meant to be. I'd already delivered the good news to dos Santos.

"Please stop asking Raj for his DNA," he said that morning on the phone. "I've been concerned this 'experiment' of yours is unethical, and your pressuring him for hair samples and skin grafts—"

"I never said skin grafts!"

"—feels like it's crossing a line. I don't care if he's being paid."

"Look, I'm not trying to make anyone uncomfortable," I said. "I want to *solve* this."

"Raj is not your answer," he said.

"He's stopped my flares twice," I said. "And I was in a major accident that landed me in the hospital. A flare always precedes something bad, and I didn't have a single symptom."

Dos Santos reminded me Raj wasn't in the balloon and while yes, this was true, Raj had ridden with us to the launch site, and he'd probably shed some of his essence onto me along the way. Gross, yes, but facts were facts.

"I'm going to share some data from the Campos study," dos Santos announced abruptly, and I was glad to be in a hospital, because the news almost made me fall over dead. I should've tried breaking an arm earlier. He sighed, mentally preparing to deal with me. "I've long believed there's a connection between the secretive, insular behavior of PBSers—"

"Okay, rude."

"—and the occurrence of flares. The data from the Campos sisters has borne this out."

Most recently, one of the sisters discovered she was pregnant. She'd been trying for a while, and this would be great news, but dos Santos asked her to wait before telling anyone. She agreed, and two days later flared an Afghan hound.

"The thing suppressed can be positive or negative," he said, "but of course we hide the negative more often."

"Hold on. You're mad because I politely asked Raj for a strand of hair when you're really out here experimenting on pregnant ladies?"

"There wasn't anything inherently dangerous about the request."

"Except for the possibility of a deadly animal?" I said, but dos Santos refused to concede, probably because he understood he'd been defeated by my rock-solid point.

According to dos Santos, once the young woman revealed her pregnancy, the symptoms disappeared, confirming his theory. The more a person afflicted with PBS suppressed their feelings and emotions, the more the disease reared its head.

"Hmm. Cute theory," I said lightly, I hoped. "First of all, I don't go around advertising my PBS, but everyone knows about it. Also, I've already pinpointed what causes mine. Impending disaster."

"I'm sure it seems as though your symptoms are linked to the disaster, but have you tried working backward? Perhaps you intuited or anticipated the problem and suppressed *these* emotions. And Raj *is* helping, but only because you're not as secretive with another PBSer around."

He then suggested I experiment by being more open about

my condition, and I suggested (in my head) he should try flying into the sun.

After I hung up, I thought back to the hot-air balloon ride and all the days leading up to it. *Had* I been more open about my condition? I did bring up the tree goat while we were in the process of crashing. And the wolverine and emu. Even the flamingos. *No*. I wasn't letting dos Santos put this on me.

"So, what did Dad have to say about all this?" I asked Ivan, speaking of impending disasters. "Or maybe you shouldn't tell him." *PBSers tend to be secretive*, rang dos Santos's voice in my brain. I shuddered, shaking him off.

"Too late," Ivan said. "I find it's good practice to be up-front with the candidate, even if it'll piss them off. You want everyone working from the same information, and he would've found out eventually. Kyle Sperber interviewed the homeowner about the crash."

I groaned. "Great. I suppose we can expect a story like 'Meet the Idiot Kennedys' or whatever."

Ivan chuckled and patted my leg. Or he tried to pat my leg but instead landed on a bunched-up part of the blanket. "Don't worry," he said. "Your father is just glad everyone's okay."

I had a hard time believing this.

"So, are you ready to go?" Ivan asked, standing up.

"Yeah. I guess." I swung my feet onto the floor. "Thanks for coming. I'm sorry you drew the short stick. Ozzie and Talia shouldn't have put that on you."

"There weren't any sticks involved. The HQ was kind of chaotic, and you texted you were ready, and I had a free moment and here I am."

"Yeah, but Talia or Ozzie could've insisted . . ."

He winced. "Truthfully? I think everyone's still shaken up about the balloon thing, and even the best siblings can be unreliable. In my experience, they tend to let you down with the little things but always show up when it matters."

"Huh. Guess I'm not injured enough," I said, slipping into my Birks. "So, how many kids were in the Ivan fam?" I could not for the life of me remember his last name.

"I'm the youngest of eight."

"Eight!" I coughed. "All from the same woman?"

"Same lady," he confirmed with a grin.

"Good Lord. That is too many children." Maybe that's why he was so pale. As the smallest, he probably couldn't wade through the crowd to reach the outside.

"Perhaps. But we had fun."

"Yuck. No offense. But I wouldn't survive the chaos. I prefer to be alone."

Ivan snorted. "Why would someone who likes to be alone start a theater company?"

"Oh, that has nothing to do with other people. It's purely chance, and a series of random events."

I'd been working in theater tech, I explained, when a friend's troupe lost their performance space. I didn't mention this friend was a girl named Bailey who I thought was cute. *You're buying a farm because of a girl?* Sydney griped at the time. *God, you're the worst at flirting.*

"Dad and Ustenya were harping on me to stop renting," I said. "A farm with a theater went up for sale, and I took the leap. Best thing I ever did. Got me out of the city, and got me away from . . ." I stopped myself, smiling meekly.

"Got you away from your family?" Ivan smirked.

I slipped into my jacket. "Listen, I love my family, but they have a way of appearing out of nowhere and causing problems. The farm is my way of maintaining some space. Believe me, it's better for everyone."

I thought of the Tasmanian devil I'd flared at Dad and Ustenya's engagement party. When I called the local zoo to check on him the next morning, they informed me the little guy had been put down. He had facial tumor disease, and the tumors prevented him from eating, so he would've died one way or another. It was humane and better for the species overall. The disease was so prevalent that there was a whole conservation movement to keep the endangered devils isolated from one another so they couldn't get or pass on the cancer.

"Like a Tasmanian devil with face cancer," I said to Ivan, "it's best I separate myself to ensure the survival of the species."

"That's a very specific analogy."

"I have a lot of specific references."

Ivan rolled his eyes. "Come on, you goof. Let's take off," he said, and opened the door. "We have a lot of work to do. The convention is in less than three weeks."

# Chapter Forty-One

## Ozzie

Ozzie sat in the middle of the meditation pavilion, on a yoga mat, legs tucked into a lotus position.

He tried not to think sister thoughts or about why he continued to shed followers like this was some kind of purge. One "fan" DMed him to ask when he'd become boring as fuck, and Ozzie didn't have an answer because losers could only hide their loser stripes for so long. He knew he shouldn't listen to the haters, but sometimes haters were right.

When Ozzie felt a sudden presence, he didn't open his eyes. The hesitant footsteps were giving Gabby. She grabbed a mat and sat beside him.

"How's your arm?" Ozzie mumbled, because he couldn't help himself. Yeah, she'd known about his broken collarbone, but these injuries were *his* fault.

"All good. I can't wait to make everyone sign my cast." She let out a puff of air. "Listen. I was thinking about what I said in the balloon—how I was only sixteen when you left." Her voice was getting very high, and she cleared her throat to bring it back down. "But I was sixteen! And that was old enough. I shouldn't have just watched you go."

Ozzie exhaled, a sense of relief washing over him. Finally she'd acknowledged that, yes, it was a tad "off" to stand in the hallway while three fat-ass linebacker types kidnapped your own brother out of his bed, shouting, *We can do this the easy way or the hard way.* Did she notice the zip ties? Maybe it didn't matter anymore.

"Whatevs. Like you said, you were a kid. I get it." He did get it, yet something still bothered him, something he couldn't put his finger on.

He hardly had a chance to ponder this, because here was Gabby yapping away about how Talia was correct, Gabby *had* used Dad's credit card to deal with a flare, and that's why they were cut off. She felt *horrible* and hoped this wasn't why he was here, too. Talia mentioned he was having cash flow problems? If there was any way she might help . . .

An idea pinged in Ozzie's brain. A miracle, right? Who knew anything happened up there. Could Gabby be the answer? She turned twenty-five in six weeks, which was more than thirty days, but close enough. Hell, maybe she had $400K already, given she lived on a farm, and dressed the way she did. Right now, she was wearing a T-shirt from a turkey trot they'd run in 2019.

"Actually," Ozzie said with a gulp. God, he hated to do this. He had a literal pain in his chest. It was one thing to ask Talia for money, what with her perpetual disappointment in him, but now Gabby would view him as a hopeless loser, too. Alas, he was out of options, and if Gabby wanted to hold herself out as the protective big sister—well, time to shine. "I do need your help."

He turned toward Gabby, debating which persona to don. Not @DegenerateOz, but one step back. The man behind the mask, who had swagger but could laugh about how he created a whole life out of an act. Ozzie wasn't used to going through personality math with Gabby, but things had changed. Or they were different than he thought. It was strange, how it made him sad and not angry now.

"I need money," Ozzie said. "And if I don't get it soon, I'm fucked."

Eyes wide and unblinking, Gabby asked how much. When he confessed the amount, she legit shrieked.

"I know! It's a lot!" Ozzie said, swearing it was temporary, only a loan. His assets weren't very liquid, and the art market was slow these days, but liquidation was in process!

"Ozzie . . ." Gabby said, her eyes now welling. "I don't have four hundred thousand dollars, or anything close to it. Why do you think I'm working on the campaign?"

Ozzie blinked. "Because you're agreeable?" And sneaky, he did not add.

"Because I need the money, too."

Ozzie was shocked, which was real rich (ha ha) since he didn't have it either. Apparently Gabby bought her farm at the height of the getting-out-of-the-city panic and had dumped a lot of cash into the theater, including for a new roof a couple weeks ago. As for the undetermined twenty-five-year gift, Gabby told him sheepishly that it was already spent.

Ozzie pulled a face. "On *what*?"

"I'm sorry. I can't say." Gabby squinted, furrowing her brow. "But listen. Let me noodle on your predicament a bit. Crunch some numbers."

"*You're* going to crunch numbers."

"Excuse you! I got a perfect score on the math portion of the SAT. Anyway . . ." She used her one good arm to push herself to her feet. "I'll see what I can do."

# Chapter Forty-Two

## Talia

"Heyyyyy, girl," said a voice. Gabby stood in the doorway, looking more like an elementary school kid than usual with her arm in a cast. God, why hadn't Talia vetted Ozzie's plans even the slightest bit? It was obviously going to end in disaster.

"Where have you been?" Talia asked her sister, hands shaking as she gathered her things. Mayor Robert Quinonez was scheduled to arrive in twelve minutes, and her Xanax hadn't kicked in. She was sure his endorsement was the key to pushing Dad past the "small, unexpected surge" in support, and Talia needed this meeting to go well.

"I'm supposed to take it easy," Gabby said. "And not stare at a computer screen. Do you have a minute?"

"Literally only a minute." If Talia shoved everything into her tote, she'd come across like a harried mom. Carrying her phone and notepad and lip gloss and mints seemed more laid-back but also potentially hazardous. She could easily drop any or all of these, probably into the pool. It'd be a whole scene.

"I know you're a real stickler for promises and rules and . . . mad respect." Gabby walked the rest of the way into the room. "But is there any way you could find it in your heart to tell me about the twenty-five-year gift?"

Talia's eyes narrowed. Right *now*? Before the most important meeting of the campaign? Gabby's timing was impeccable.

"The amount, specifically," Gabby blathered on. "And if you received it on your actual birthday, or is there paperwork to fill out, or . . . ?"

"I'm not telling you," Talia said. "A promise is a promise, and Ustenya has cameras and microphones all over the place."

"Wait. What?" Gabby said as Talia threw her junk into her bag.

"Your birthday is in a few weeks. It's not like you need the number right *now.*"

"No. I mean, *I* don't."

Talia froze. Everything clicked into place. "This is about Ozzie."

"Yes but don't get mad! He's in the lurch, and I want to help him. It's a timing thing. Most of his assets aren't liquid, and he's in a lockup period for some stock—"

"Do you even know what a lockup period is?"

"No, but it sounds tricky. Red-tape-ish."

"Do not fall for it," Talia warned. "God. This is so Ozzie. Expecting others to fix his problems but refusing to take personal accountability. At some point, everyone's going to have to ask themselves whether they're helping or hurting by giving him all these free passes."

Talia picked up her phone to check her reflection, more annoyed with Gabby than her brother. Of course Ozzie would ask for someone else's money. And of course Gabby would drop everything to help. Didn't she remember he'd *just* called her out for being fake?

"The worst part is . . ." Talia said, pulling her hair in front of her shoulders. She reconsidered and threw it back. "The worst part is, he could easily solve this. Like, tomorrow."

"It's four hundred thousand dollars," Gabby said.

"Yeah, I know." Talia put down her phone. "Someone offered to buy his *Winnie the Pooh* map," she said, and Gabby's eyebrows jumped. "The price was agreed to and everything, but he backed out at the last minute."

"Maybe he thought it wasn't market value—"

"Seven hundred fifty thousand," she said, and Gabby's eyes were now bulging out of her head. "And it's not like he had to recoup the sales price. He inherited it from Yvonne! The nicest thing she ever gave me was a thirty-piece silver set."

"I got the name of a plastic surgeon who could fix my nose," Gabby muttered. "But I talked to Ozzie yesterday. If someone had offered him seven fifty, he would've taken it."

"I don't know what to tell you, other than he didn't. The potential buyer is a partner at Spencer's firm. His wife wanted it for a nursery. Second wife, obviously." Talia studied the pair of wedges stashed under her desk, already doubting her ability to walk all the way to the main house in them. She thought of what Gabby had said, about her tendency to wear heavy shoes. She bent down to retrieve them. "We have to stop playing into this. We're all guilty of it. Hell, Spencer bought not one, not two, but *four* watches from his collection. Spent six figures even though he only ever wears an Apple Watch."

"Wow. That's really sweet."

"It is. Spencer is a great guy." Talia checked the time. She now had five minutes to get up to the house, and good luck with that.

"Who are you meeting?" Gabby said. "You look cute, by the way."

"Thanks," Talia said. She'd chosen a short-sleeved navy blue jumpsuit and heavy gold necklace in hopes it'd look appropriately *doing business in San Diego*, but she'd never been good at these things. Neither had Gabby, but it was nice to have one person's stamp of approval. "I didn't want to mention anything in case he canceled, but . . ." She flashed a grin. "I'm meeting the mayor of San Diego."

"Talia! That's amazing!" Gabby said. "Are you meeting him solo?"

"Yes!" Talia snapped. "Why? You don't think I'm up to the task?"

"What? No! Why would you say that?"

Talia closed her eyes, reminding herself not everyone was as hard on her as she was. "I asked Raj to join me," she said, looking at Gabby again. "But he declined for the oddest reason. Apparently he had a run-in with the mayor? I can't fathom. The entire conversation was strange."

He'd also invited her to the Padres game Saturday night to celebrate filing the lawsuit against the housing commission. A guy at BMWU had given him two tickets as a thanks for their work. Was it meant to be a date? Talia didn't think Raj would try to swipe someone else's woman, but also, she hadn't brought up Spencer much, only that he was so against California he'd threatened to break up with her. Talia let Raj draw conclusions from there, which was admittedly very questionable. Feeling awful for somewhat *wishing* it was a date, and apprehensive about returning to Petco Park, Talia put off the decision, saying she'd let him know.

"I need to go," Talia said to Gabby, cramming her feet into her shoes. "I'm a bundle of nerves. Will you walk me over?"

"Of course," Gabby said. "But don't be so stressed. You've got this." She grabbed Talia by the shoulders, holding her tight, as if trying to stop all the fidgeting. "You've got this," she repeated, staring her dead in the eyes. "You're Talia fucking Gunn."

Talia made a face because *Talia fucking Gunn* sounded like something she'd overheard in a high school bathroom, or during her brief inglorious attempt at sorority rush. "Is that a good thing?" she said, and Gabby laughed.

"It's a *great* thing. You've worked your ass off, and everything will go perfectly. Now let's get up to the main house so you can kick ass."

# Chapter Forty-Three

## Gabby

Talia was holding her meeting with the mayor out by the pool. Mindy had put out some snacks and a bottle of wine, and hallelujah, because my sister really needed a drink. As pretty as she looked, she seemed jittery, and notably thin, and her eyebrows were an unnatural shade of brown.

"Why am I so anxious?" Talia said, fanning herself. "I'm ninety percent sure I'll seal the deal. But. Gah! His endorsement could change everything for Dad's campaign."

I nodded, pretending to listen when my mind was on Ozzie. Since yesterday's chat in the yoga studio, I'd been reeling. It was an incomprehensible number of dollars, somehow both massive and distressingly small. An amount beyond most people's grasp, but for someone like Ozzie, it shouldn't have been a problem.

On the other hand, my brother's desperation pulled at my heart, but also? Four hundred thousand was an insane ask, especially now that I knew the truth. He'd turned down three quarters of a million dollars and I felt used.

"I don't recognize any of those people," Talia said, about the four staff members stamping across the lawn with their boxed lunches. "And they're my own volunteers! We're adding them so quickly I can barely keep track. It's amazing what the teeniest speck of good news can get a candidate. Die-hard political types are weird."

"For real," I said, though wasn't surprised Talia hadn't been fully locked in. With her housing commission lawsuit and related side quests, it sometimes felt like Talia was at LASD or the other place (BMW-something) more often than the Ranch.

"We have *five* new volunteers starting this week," Talia continued as we approached the brick stairs leading up to the pool. "They all need housing. Ustenya's beside herself, scrambling for somewhere to put them. She's actually building new space! Who knew we'd run out of room?" Talia let out a high, fluttery laugh. "Not sure what she'll do with the extra bedrooms when this is all over."

I blinked and mentally backed up several feet. "Hold on. You know about the construction?"

"I mean, sort of. Ustenya said—"

"Oh, thank God!" I released a long stream of air. I'd been wanting to mention it since Monday morning when I saw the first truck full of wood and asked Mindy what was going on. But Monday became Tuesday, and we crash-landed a balloon, and havoc had reigned ever since. "I was kind of freaked out," I said, "when I found out what was happening. It was like, uh, anyone tell Talia about this?"

Talia jerked her head toward me and narrowed her eyes. "What do you mean?"

"Um." I swallowed. "The renovation of Mom's art studio? That's what you were talking about, right?"

Talia stiffened. She opened her mouth for a second before letting go. "Yeah. Totally," she said, cheeks now red like cute little apples. "Anyway! Time to focus on securing this endorsement."

We stepped up onto the patio, where a charcuterie board was already laid out, alongside an open bottle of sauvignon blanc. Two chairs were under the table, and two chairs were pushed back as though someone had left in a hurry.

"It always takes longer to get around this place than I think,"

Talia said, consulting her watch. "Quinonez has obviously been here." She gestured to the chairs. "Where did he go?"

"Probably the restroom? Or Mindy gave him a tour of the house? It's fine." I placed a hand on her arm. "Remember. The vibe is casual. There is no 'late' here."

Talia nodded, but nervously, which I didn't know was possible. She circled the table, murmuring about how she had one job, and it was to arrive on time.

"You've got this. You understand what Quinonez is about, and you have your trusty notebook of facts and research." If I said it enough, maybe she'd believe me.

Talia sighed. "That does make me feel better," she said. "Raj should be here, though. God. What is his deal with the mayor?"

"Who knows," I said, guessing this was about the ribbon-cutting ceremony and Raj not wanting to be recognized as the skunk guy.

A clamor of voices interrupted my train of thought. It was my brother. And the mayor. Exiting from the back of the house. Ozzie was wearing his dress-up sunglasses, tight white pants, and an even tighter blue polo shirt. A hideous white jacket dangled from his left hand.

"Bobby Q., hear me out," Ozzie was saying as my stomach plummeted to center earth. "It's an *investment.*"

"I appreciate the uniqueness of the item," Quinonez said, "but I can't imagine what I'd do with it."

I squinted. Was that . . . *Oh my God.*

"OZZIE!" I barked, and both men looked up. The mayor seemed relieved to see me as I bolted over. "I'm sorry if my brother waylaid you, Mayor Quinonez. He's such a funny guy. Always eager to show off his one-of-a-kind treasures." My eyes skipped over to the jacket, landing on the blue circle patch with NASA stitched inside. Dear God. Ozzie tried to sell Buzz Aldrin's Apollo 11 jacket to the mayor of San Diego.

"I enjoyed checking it out," Quinonez said unconvincingly.

"But mayors don't make a ton of money, and I'd never be able to afford anything like that."

"Nobody's selling anything!" I grabbed Ozzie's arm, and his bicep flexed beneath my hold. Pretty impressive, actually. I'd have to give him some props later. "Sorry for any misunderstanding," I said to the mayor. "You have a meeting with Talia, yes? She's right over there." I pointed to where my sister remained by the cheese, eyes wide in horror.

"Oscar," I said, yanking on his arm. "You and I are supposed to be in our own meeting right now. Sheesh! The work never stops. Have a great afternoon, everyone! Ozzie and I will leave you to take care of business."

———

"This must be some kind of record," I hissed as I hauled Ozzie into the house. "In terms of getting into shit. Impressive, even for you." I wanted to strangle him, I really did. Talia complained no one was ever on her side and, *here you go, sis.* Ozzie had dealt with some tough stuff in his life, but it was time to grow the hell up.

"I was schmoozing," Ozzie said, squirming out of my hold. "You don't appreciate the value of charisma, but it goes a long way."

"Please." I tried not to gag.

"Wow. Okay." He rotated to face me. "I'm making things happen. I'm hustling, you feel?"

"First of all," I said, shoving him into the tasting room. With its medieval bricks and wrought-iron gate, it was giving "elegant jail." "Candidates are probably not allowed to enter into financial transactions with mayors. That could be seen as bribing."

"He would be paying me," Ozzie said and, honestly, a valid point.

"Or reverse bribing. Or something." A friend's dad got arrested for racketeering when we were in ninth grade. Maybe that's what this was? "Either way. It must be illegal."

"I told you about my situation. Maybe you think I'm full of shit, but this is serious, Bags." He somehow forced his brown Bambi eyes to flood with tears. "I'm desperate, and I need to get the money however I can."

"Not if it's going to mess up other people's lives." I laughed dryly. "That's the crux of everything, isn't it? You're never intentionally trying to hurt anyone, but you don't consider how your actions affect other people."

"You're one to talk!"

"If you're so desperate, how come you didn't sell your *Winnie the Pooh* map?"

Ozzie blanched, recoiling like I'd slapped him across the face. "How did you know about that?"

"Talia. It was Spencer's friend or something—"

"Coworker."

"You didn't even like Grandma!" *The nerve*, I thought. The nerve to act like I'd made an unthinkable suggestion when all I wanted was for him to do the thing that would cure his problem.

"I can't sell it," he insisted.

"Of course you can't. It's like you're determined to make life harder for yourself." I shook my head, wondering whether Ozzie had ever pushed me this far. "I love you, Oz, but I'm done. If you really want to help yourself, go back to New York and figure shit out. Stop making things worse for everyone here." I brushed past him, refusing to meet his eyes as I stomped out of the room.

# Chapter Forty-Four

## Talia

Standing on the edge of the putting green, Talia stayed quiet, waiting for Dad to sink his putt, which was taking way too long given how much time he invested in the sport.

"Yes!" he said when he finally did it. He retrieved the ball and whirled around, putter resting on his shoulder. "Hello, Talia. How can I help you?"

"Ustenya said you wanted to see me? I assume this is regarding Ozzie and the mayor?" Talia was speaking quickly, anxious to get this over with. "Again, I'm *so* sorry about what happened, but it's not as bad as it sounds. Gabby spirited Ozzie away immediately, and the meeting went quite well. I hoped to nail down the endorsement on the spot, but it's still very much in play, and—"

"Did you tell your brother to leave?"

Talia jiggled her head. Had her dad listened to a single word she'd just said? "No. I don't think so?" Talia racked her brain. She wanted him to leave of course but didn't remember ever saying it out loud. "Why? Did he say that I did?"

Dad studied her through one squinty eye. Out here in the bright San Diego sun, the silver streaks in his hair were actually see-through, and Talia again wondered when he'd gotten so old. Politics really took it out of you, like people always said. "Ozzie's exact words were, 'My own sister told me to get the hell out of town,'" he said.

"What? Dad! There's no way. I didn't even see him after the meeting."

"I'm not looking for a timeline or list of excuses. You need to make sure he doesn't go anywhere. And before you ask 'why me,' *you're* the one who's always against him. No one's leaving this campaign. Especially not him."

Talia gaped, confused. Why was she getting the blame? Also, she'd love to point out they were better off with him gone—hello? balloon crashes and moon jackets?—but it would definitely qualify as being "against him."

"Glad we've come to an understanding," Dad said. He pivoted and marched toward the house. "Now, let's discuss the real reason I wanted to meet."

"There's more?" Talia said, scrambling to catch up. She'd intended to use this impromptu meeting to ask about construction on the art studio, but that was out. Ustenya said early on that she planned to use the space. *If you need anything from it, now's your chance.* She'd told Talia to clean it out, and Talia had very specifically not done it. Did she even have a right to be upset?

"You *must* stop promising I'll get people off the Section 8 waitlist," Dad said.

"Oh. We're talking about that now." She paused to let her brain recalibrate. "Got it."

"I understand why you're so worked up. No one's gotten off the list for eighteen months and counting. Unconscionable."

"Wait. What?" Talia jogged after him again. "Eighteen months?" she repeated. Talia was rattled both by the math (seemed like the waiting list was fifty thousand years long, not fifteen) and the fact her dad knew something about the issue she didn't.

"Alas, a United States Senator can't change a city's Section 8 machinations," Dad went on. "Rules are set up locally. You know this. That's what your little lawsuit is about. It's why you're suing the San Diego Housing Commission and not some state or federal agency."

Talia smiled to herself. He'd been paying attention. "It's not a 'little' lawsuit," she said. "And I'm glad you brought it up! If federal laws were clearer, these things wouldn't happen. Cities couldn't skirt—"

Dad flipped around. "You need to stop." He slammed his putter onto the ground, and Talia jumped. "All the stuff with the housing commission and LASD . . . you can do that *after* the campaign. Right now, your focus should be on me. Name any other job where you'd be allowed to have so many side projects? Perhaps this is why you didn't get the mayor's endorsement."

Talia's mouth fell open. She was almost too discombobulated to speak. "I haven't gotten it *yet*," she said. If anything, she'd *saved* the endorsement after her brother nearly fucked it up. How come Dad couldn't see that?

"Since you have such a surplus of time, I'd like you to plan the cocktail party." The state Democratic Convention was coming up, and he wanted to hold a party beforehand. Dad swore they'd discussed this, but Talia was positive they had not. From what she'd read, the convention was a form-over-substance situation where people yammered and squabbled and ultimately decided nothing, and it struck her as quite silly to pre-game an event that did not seem like a big deal.

"But the work is for you—" she tried feebly.

"No more lawsuits," Dad reiterated. "No more side gigs. Are we on the same page?"

"Yes. Of course," Talia said, her eyes hot with frustration, although her dad wasn't entirely wrong. She *had* been distracted from the campaign, and the Section 8 waitlist *was* a local issue. Even if he were elected (ha!), he wouldn't be able to do much. Talia wondered when she'd get a clue and stop expecting a job to be more than it was.

*You're not Norma fucking Rae*, a partner she'd once worked for said. *You need to learn that sometimes our job is to help people get a little something and move on with their lives.*

"You'd better get cracking, kiddo," Dad said, and patted her on the head. "You only have two weeks until the party." With that, he strolled toward the house, whistling as he went, as if he didn't have a care in the world.

# Chapter Forty-Five

## Gabby

On Saturday morning, I realized I hadn't seen Ozzie in two days. He'd obviously been avoiding me, and enough was enough. We were there to campaign for Dad, and it was time to grow up. Plus, I refused to be estranged from my own brother.

First I checked his bedroom, only to find it empty, and his bed miraculously made. He wasn't near the pool, or on the putting green, or in the recreation pavilion. HQ was the last place to look and although I doubted he'd be working at eleven o'clock on a Saturday, the barn door was open, which meant someone was in there.

"Hello?" I called out, my voice echoing off all the brick. "Is anyone around?"

It took a second to receive an answer. Finally, from the last stall on the right, Bea called out, "Me."

I sidled up to her doorway. Bea waved but kept her eyes fixed on her screen as she explained they'd wanted to film some TikToks while the Ranch was relatively deserted. Montana just left. Some weather event was happening off western Mexico, and she planned to hit Suckouts, "the left-hand break off Cardiff Reef," whatever that meant.

"Cool," I said, like a dork. "So, um, have you seen Ozzie around?"

For the first time, Bea lifted her head. She stared at me,

cross-eyed. "Are you for real right now?" She took a hit of her vape. "Like, are you actually serious?"

I scrunched my brow, contemplating what he might've done this time. Ozzie wouldn't outright ask Bea or Montana to lend him money, but maybe he'd commandeered the TikTok account for financial gain?

"What happened?" I asked, heart thrumming. "Did my brother do something? God, it's like he's determined to break multiple campaign finance laws."

"He didn't *do* anything," Bea said with some disdain. "Aside from go home."

The news dropped swiftly, like someone had cut the lights. "You mean to New York?" I asked, and Bea nodded. My God, Dad was going to be pissed. Only Oscar Gunn could create as many problems in absentia as he did in person. It was truly a gift. I released a long, beleaguered wail toward the skylights.

"Okay, calm down," Bea said.

"You don't know the backstory. I get that he's super charming or whatever, but you have no idea the trouble he keeps getting into. It's fracas after fracas after—"

"You're the problem," Bea said.

For a second, I might've blacked out. *"Me?"*

Bea snorted. "Did you or did you not tell him to leave? That he should go back to New York and quote, 'figure his shit out.'"

Our fight existed as a hot blur in my mind. I didn't recall specifically saying this, but I'd felt it, so all bets were off. "It's possible?" I said, and Bea rolled her eyes almost all the way out of her head. "Look. We had an argument. He tried to sell an expensive jacket to the mayor, which might be a crime?"

Bea sucked on her vape again. "You're supposed to be the nice sister."

"No one believes that anymore!" I said. "With all due respect, there are multiple potential legality issues and *years* of context."

"Are you referring to his taxes?" Bea said.

Good Lord, was there anything he hadn't confessed? "Did you know he owes four *hundred thousand* dollars?" I tried.

Bea shrugged like it wasn't a big deal. "What?" she said. "You've never made a mistake and needed somebody's help? Or lied about something you're ashamed of?"

"He's not even attempting to fix it!" I said. "Ozzie has assets, including an extensive art collection. He could solve all his problems by selling one piece."

"All his problems? God. You guys are obsessed with money."

"I'm not the bad guy here. And I don't care about money! I live on a farm." Scowling, I crossed my arms. "Someone offered to give him seven hundred and fifty thousand dollars for *one* piece of art." I passed Bea a smug look, but she remained wholly unmoved. "He paid zero dollars for it, in case you're worried about him selling it at a loss or whatever."

"Right. Because the only value is what someone would pay for something."

"Oh my God!" Bea was pissing me off, and I was starting to appreciate why older people complained about Gen Z. We were so argumentative and difficult. "There's no reason for him to keep it. It was given to him by our grandmother. None of us were close to her. She was pretty mean." I stopped short of telling Bea that when Yvonne was on her deathbed, she asked where the chubby one was, meaning Ozzie, and told me I was smart to have bangs because they made me appear "less beaky."

"I know about the hundred-acre map," Bea said. "And that your grandmother was a raging bitch."

"Oh. Okay." I blinked, wishing we could go back to the conversation about left breaks and Suckouts. "Then what are we debating?"

"Do you understand how he sees the map?" Bea said, though it was obvious to both of us the answer was no. "Ozzie interpreted the gift as a message, an insult meant to sting. But instead of being bitter about it, he embraced the symbolism. Now, it's like, Winnie the Pooh is *him*."

"Ozzie is projecting," I said. Grandma Yvonne absolutely would've used her will to insult someone posthumously, but I doubted that was the case here. "He needs to get over the 'chubby' thing. It's not even accurate!"

"What do you know about Winnie the Pooh?"

"He's a bear? He doesn't wear pants?" I said. "Sorry. That's all I've got."

"Pooh is portrayed as naive and dim-witted, a bear of 'very little brain.' Imagine being told your whole life you're a stupid, self-involved fuckup. All you have going for you is your charisma and fortune. You're *that sort of bear*."

My breath caught. While I wasn't fully schooled in Pooh lore, some of Bea's words were familiar.

*Bear of very little brain.*

*"What sort of stories does he like?"*

*"About himself. Because he's* that *sort of bear."*

"Now he's lost his wealth and footing in the world and is having a motherfucking hard time of it. As for the offer on the map . . ." Bea stopped to level on me a hard, cold glare. "The buyer changed his mind. Turned out the baby wasn't his, and he's getting a divorce."

"WHAT!"

"There weren't a lot of other takers."

I wanted to melt into the floor. Ozzie *was* trying to fix his own problems. He just hadn't been able to. "What should I do?" I asked. "Call him? Beg him to come back?"

"I don't know what to tell you," Bea said, returning her eyes to her computer. "You're a big girl. Figure it out."

# Chapter Forty-Six

## Talia

Talia put off deciding about the Padres game, but when Saturday rolled around, Raj tracked her down. Richard from BMWU had given him *two* tickets to thank *both* of them. It was kind of rude if they let one go to waste?

Now Talia was at Petco Park, chugging a margarita while they sat through a weather delay. Staring out across the field, she struggled to recall how it felt to run around in foul territory in a pair of short shorts, launching swag into the stands with a T-shirt gun. Of course, it'd been eleven years, and the team and managers had probably turned over six or seven times. Even the colors were different. At some point, the Padres ditched their blue and beige, which they had the temerity to call "sand," and returned to their brown-and-gold roots.

Talia expected to be mildly traumatized to revisit the scene of the "crime," but in fact felt nothing, which was its own brand of remorse. She'd been so upset about a stupid boy whose face she could barely remember. Colt was his first name. His last name . . . Whittaker, or something? As far as Talia knew, he'd never done anything baseball-wise. A real nothing-burger all around. Why had Talia acted like he was the love of her life, hightailing it out of San Diego the minute another girl casually mentioned how he was into BDSM? Daphne pleaded with her to stay, but Talia refused, letting her mom down once again.

Couldn't bother sticking around because of a *boy*. Couldn't bother cleaning out Mom's art studio after she'd gone. In terms of daughters, Talia was a real prize. Everyone accepted Daphne wasn't the best mother, but maybe the problem lay in her shittier-than-average kids.

"I talked to Richard this morning," Raj said, yanking Talia out of her brain. On the field, the grounds crew was pulling back the tarp. "The head of a rural justice unit in Central California called to express their gratitude for giving them a model to create some accountability. No matter what happens with the lawsuit, it's already having the residual effect we hoped for."

Nodding, Talia took a sip of margarita.

"The fact a big city started the fight will give the smaller ones a chance," Raj said. "And it was *your* research with the smaller cities that helped drive the whole thing. If a tiny town like Encinitas can comply with the regulations, the eighth largest city in the US certainly can. For the next step, he's thinking we should—"

He paused, and looked at Talia, who couldn't seem to get her margarita cup back into its holder. "I'm sorry," he said. "Should I not have brought up the lawsuit? I told you I suck in social settings . . ."

Talia shook her head. "It's not you. I'm sorry but I can't really be involved in the lawsuit going forward. My dad lectured me yesterday about how I'm letting myself be distracted by the housing stuff. He says I'm taking my eyes off the prize."

And honestly? Fair enough. Talia did tend to fixate on the wrong thing. The Padre who liked ropes and chains. A lawsuit that would do nothing to fix a waitlist infinity years long and possibly even distract the Housing Commission from helping people find homes.

"Oh. Okay," Raj said and, God love him, he seemed disappointed. He started to say something else but his words were drowned out by a voice announcing the rain had stopped, and the game could finally begin.

A woman with long, curly hair stepped onto the field. The crowd stood as five men in uniforms marched out.

*"O say can you see, by the dawn's early light . . ."*

"Don't worry," Raj said after the national anthem ended and they trotted out some kid to throw the first pitch. "Richard will understand. You're a valuable resource, and I'm sure your dad needs your full attention."

Talia snorted, suddenly questioning whether she *was* the reason they'd failed to secure Quinonez's endorsement, after all. Ozzie could charm the pants (or NASA jacket) off anyone, and maybe she should've let him cook. Instead, Talia felt compelled to "fix" everything. *Her.* The least likeable of the three. No wonder she'd been demoted to party planner.

"Would you mind getting me another drink?" Talia said and waggled her cup. "And some of those street tacos you were telling me about?"

"Yes. Of course," Raj said, slowly rising to his feet, looking both physically and mentally discombobulated. "Be back in a few."

---

The thing about baseball was that it was boring.

Talia didn't mean to complain. She was glad to be here, and the margaritas (and tacos) were great, but she was a little bit drunk and moderately depressed about the state of her life. Plus it was chilly, and wet, even with the overhang.

The game had gone like this. The Dodgers scored two runs here, another run there, and the Padres accomplished not much. Raj grumbled about runners left on base and "that was so Padres coded." Die-hard sports fans were funny, always bitching about the teams they loved so much.

Now it was the bottom of the seventh. The Padres were down 0–3. Only two more innings, Talia thought, checking her watch. The first batter walked, and the crowd cheered, demonstrating how desperate people were for some action. The second batter roped it to center field, and the next guy hit an infield single, causing the runner to cross home plate.

"Now we're cooking with gas," Raj said. That he felt compelled to explain the game was heating up told a person all they needed to know about the sport. The score was 1–3, and the Dodgers called a time-out to yank the pitcher. *God*. They were really going to drag this out.

Talia's phone buzzed. She glanced down to see Spencer's face on the screen, briefly debating whether to take the call before sending him to voicemail instead.

The new pitcher finished his warmup, and her entire section stood. Oh, okay, so they were doing this. The Padres' leadoff batter approached the plate, and the stadium went wild chanting his name. *Ha-Seong Kim. Ha-Seong Kim. Ha-Seong Kim.* Out of nowhere, Talia found herself chanting, too.

Ha-Seong Kim ripped a double down the third base line. A runner scored. Everyone was jumping, and screeching. With the tying and go-ahead runs in scoring position, and no outs, the next batter's walk-up song erupted through the speakers. *Esa muchacha sí que baila bueno.* Talia and Raj danced, bumping hips. Problems? What problems? Talia felt them flutter away.

The batter took a ball. He took a second ball and swung at the next pitch, sending a line drive to deep right field. Another runner crossed home plate and Talia screamed, along with everyone else. The score was tied, with runners on first and third.

"Yikes," Talia said, checking the scoreboard as the next batter came up. "This guy is 0-fer tonight. Not lookin' good."

"Shhh!" Raj hissed, laughing. "Don't put that negativity into the universe."

The guy immediately fouled out, and Talia felt like maybe it was her fault. The Dodgers brought in another pitcher, which seemed weird with two outs, but maybe it was a matchup deal?

Twenty minutes ago, Talia barely knew the score and now she was contemplating pitching matchups. Nerves shot to hell, she chugged the rest of her third (fourth?) margarita.

The Jumbotron announced the next batter, and the cameras zeroed in on a section called the "Crone Zone," Crone being a play on his last name, and the Zone the place he hit home runs. After grinding his right foot into the dirt, Crone assumed his stance. On a two-two count he smacked a line drive to center field, scoring two runners, and making it to second base on the throw.

The crowd erupted. Talia and Raj jumped up and down, clutching each other, cheering like this was the best, most enthralling day of their lives. They were now winning 5–3. Had she actually called baseball *boring*?

At the top of the ninth inning, still up 5–3, panic began to set in. This game was taking too long, and Talia wanted it to be done, but not because she was bored. Now she wanted to lock in the win and clinch a spot in the NLCS. One step closer to the World Series.

The closing pitcher came out, and the stadium went dark. People waved the flashlights on their phones. The Dodgers were back to the top of the lineup, but the Padres' closer handled the leadoff no problem, getting him out in three pitches, and the next batter in four. *One more out to glory.* Talia consulted the Jumbotron and discovered that unfortunately this dude was three-for-three tonight. These were not good odds for the Padres, but streaks were made to be broken, right? That's something Spencer always said.

The three-hitter watched a strike go past. He swung and missed the next.

"Loser!" Talia called out, and then hated herself for talking trash. As the pitcher wound up, Talia held her breath. This wasn't exactly life-and-death, but in that moment, it felt that way.

The pitch left his hand. The batter lunged forward. He swung at a ball in the dirt. The catcher blocked it and tagged him. A bell rang and the stadium descended into chaos. They'd won. The Padres clinched the series against baseball's biggest assholes. No offense.

Fireworks erupted, and a song blared from the speakers. The entire crowd belted it out in unison.

*All the*
*Small things*

"They're a San Diego band," Raj said between verses, the fireworks reflecting in his glasses. Talia felt like she'd known that, or maybe not. Everything was too heady and exciting and hard to keep straight.

"Whoa," Raj said as Talia swayed. "Are you alright?" She nodded, though she was starting to feel woozy, but from joy, not booze, she was pretty sure. "Come on." He gestured toward . . . the aisle? The exit? Who could tell? "Let's go."

Raj grabbed her hand, and she squeezed back. He carved a path for them through the thick, pulsing crowd as Blink-182 sang them out.

*Say it ain't so, I will not go*
*Turn the lights off, carry me home*
*Na-na, na-na, na-na, na-na, na, na . . .*

# Chapter Forty-Seven

## Ozzie

Ozzie slumped through the front door. It was after ten o'clock and the apartment was empty and dark. Was Freja still working in Europe, or did she leave him? He wouldn't blame her if she did. She could do better.

After dropping his luggage beside the entryway table, Ozzie walked down the echoing hall, writing the inevitable real estate listing in his head. *Relax and indulge in this bespoke Park Avenue bachelor pad two blocks from Central Park! The interior is magazine-ready with moody neutrals, slate gray, and pops of money green. The foyer boasts stunning black-and-white inlay marble, making a perfect entryway to the exquisite gallery space. Herringbone hardwood floors throughout!*

A bar in the living room, a serene primary bedroom, and floor-to-ceiling white marble in the primary bath. So much white marble. White marble up the ass. This was how Ozzie should think about the place. Focus on the negative.

Ozzie entered the living room. He flopped onto the couch, pulling the handwoven Mongolian cashmere Hermès blanket up to his chin. Finally he turned on his phone. Unlike literally every other person on the plane, he hadn't reached for it the second he touched down, or stolen a glimpse in the cab. These days the news was mostly bad, and it was nice to be unplugged, even if while suffering the indignities of coach. Commercial air travel was a bitch. Nobody ever talked about it. Or maybe they did, and Ozzie hadn't listened.

Ozzie watched the missed texts filter in. The first was from Aunt Kathy. She'd visited Uncle Doug for his birthday, and he seemed fine, considering. Ozzie was the only Gunn who asked about him, including Tug, his own son, and it really meant a lot.

Spencer's name popped up. Ozzie didn't bother opening the message because he wasn't looking to get yelled at again. The dude had been *furious* but, sorry, asking whether the pregnant lady was still interested in the map was valid. Ozzie felt bad for Spencer's friend and everything, but the woman would still birth her baby, and had the requisite cash because she was heir to a pig breeding fortune. Baby daddy drama or not, Ozzie just needed the money. Regrettably, the mother-to-be didn't want to be reminded of being called "Pooh Bear" and fair enough.

Ballsack didn't have any updates on potential collabs. The landscape had changed and Ballsack suggested he pivot, though failed to explain which landscape, or why he was talking like that. No, Ozzie was not going to "pivot." He was who he was, and he'd made his bed and would lie in it, et cetera.

He'd reached the end of the list, deleting every missive from Gabby along the way. Ozzie wondered how long it'd taken her to notice he was gone. *Just as you wanted, sis. Enjoy!*

Tomorrow he'd list the apartment. Ozzie didn't know how much to expect, not even ballpark, because he'd never paid attention to real estate prices, or the price of anything, really. With any luck, the sale would cover the mortgage and the loan he took out to redecorate, with a chunk left over for the IRS. If worse came to worst, he'd take his lumps and bunk with Uncle Doug. Ozzie survived Canyonside, and honestly, Otisville seemed better. Their shoes probably weren't hidden. Inmates probably weren't thrown down concrete stairs.

After blindly scrolling through his phone, Ozzie opened Instagram. He bypassed the notifications (only five), went into Accounts Center, and clicked around to Deactivation and Deletion. Ozzie hovered, reconsidering for a moment before hitting Delete.

# Chapter Forty-Eight

## Gabby

A muffled yelp startled me awake. I sprang up in bed, heart thundering, a blanket held against my chest. Talia laughed, and I exhaled in relief. *Talking to Spencer*, I thought, checking the time. Or not. It was past four o'clock in the morning on the East Coast.

I wiggled back under the sheets, careful not to disturb the loudly snoring dog beside me. It'd taken me forever to fall asleep and here I was again, thinking about Ozzie, doing impossible math in my head. Maybe I could come up with the money. I owned my home free and clear, and Sydney had mentioned a home equity loan before. Dad was always pressuring me to "develop a banking relationship," and I wish I'd listened.

Talia cackled. I flipped onto my side with a huff. The problem with helping Ozzie get right with the Feds was that he wasn't responding to any of my calls or texts. He must've also blocked me on social media because I couldn't find any of his accounts.

Talia made another noise. I swung my feet onto the floor, ready to wake up that girl from her sleep-shrieking. As I stood, her voice crescendoed *and oh my God that's an orgasm*, I suddenly realized, hurling myself back onto my bed. "Gross," I cried, holding a pillow over my head. "Gross, gross, gross." She was awake, and doing phone sex, apparently.

Five minutes passed. Ten. Carefully I lifted the pillow. The frolicking had ended, replaced by a dull murmur. As I closed my eyes, a second laugh rang out. A male's, and I'd recognize that hesitant, Woody Woodpecker titter anywhere. *Oh, God*. It was Raj.

I scooted back under the sheets, as far as I could go, taking literal cover from this unnatural disaster. I'd suspected my sister harbored a small crush on Raj, but she was a flirt and got crushes on everybody because (sorry) she liked attention. When Talia had said they were going to the Padres game, I'd found it strange but said nothing because I was happy not to be asked. Did Talia get handsy after one too many beers? I hoped this wouldn't constitute sexual harassment.

I sat up again, certain I was about to throw up. This couldn't continue. I had to do *something*, though it was too late to do anything now. I lay back down and tried to sleep. Dawn could not come soon enough.

═══

It was nine o'clock in New York. Too early, perhaps, but I had to try. Spencer picked up on the first ring.

"Gabby! Did something happen?" he said, audibly panicked. "Talia hasn't responded to any of my texts. Don't tell me there was another hot-air balloon fiasco?"

"No. I mean, yes." I shook my head, angry at myself for not considering what it might feel like to look at your phone early on a Sunday morning and see the name of someone who'd never called you before. "Hot-air balloons are permanently off the table. And yes. Talia is okay. Everyone's fine."

Spencer exhaled. "Thank God. Sorry I was so freaked out. What's up?"

I hesitated, weighing my words. I wasn't going to rat out my sister but had to put a stop to this. Cheating was bad, and I knew Talia was in it for the wrong reasons. Attention, mostly. Meanwhile, Raj probably couldn't believe his luck.

*Raj and Talia*, I thought, mentally spitting. It was absolutely disgusting on both of their parts, but I was also confused by my own reaction. Why did I care so hard? It's not as though I liked Spencer. I usually made it a point not to judge other people's love interests—because who really knew?—but Spencer had the personality of a brick. All I'd gleaned about him over the past two years was that he adored a puffer vest and attended UVA. He referenced being "in Charlottesville" so often, I sometimes wondered if he meant at Charlottesville, as in the event, but there was no delicate way to ask one's sister if the man she loved was a white supremacist.

In sum, I wasn't a fan, so why *not* Raj and Talia? Probably because I viewed Raj as a brother figure, so obviously the idea of him hooking up with my sister was vile. Also, Talia loved Spencer. This much I knew. I would therefore step in for *her* benefit. Despite what Ozzie believed, I *did* want to help my siblings.

"This will seem random," I began, my voice cracking. "But the campaign has been a real stress pit—"

"Yeah, Talia's super grumpy."

"Mmm-hmm. Yes. Totally. And I want to do something nice for her. She's working so hard! I was thinking . . . Dad's hosting a party a week from Friday, and it might be a fun surprise if you came out."

Spencer coughed. He sputtered. "You're asking. Me. To go to California. In less than two weeks?" I could practically hear him scratching his head. "Why? Why would I do that when lately it's like she's fallen off the face of the earth? I've sent her . . ." He paused to check. "Eight texts over the past twenty-four hours, and she hasn't answered one of them."

"Yikes." I swallowed—hard—and cringed all the way to my bones. All the way to the marrow, in fact. *Friggin' Raj.* "She was at the Padres playoff game so maybe that explains it?" Thank God he couldn't see my face.

"Okay but it's deeper than that. She never picks up when I call and only answers one out of every five or six texts. Did you know we were supposed to be in Italy right now?"

"Um." I cleared my throat. The situation was worsening by the minute. "No. She didn't mention it? But don't worry! My dad will be out of the race any day. I'm sure you can get to Italy by the end of the year."

"I'd planned to propose," he said, and the admission sucked all the wind from my lungs. *God, Talia, what are you doing? You're supposed to be the reliable one.* "Had the ring and everything. Then she dropped the campaign on me and took off. I don't know what to think. I do want to see her but are you sure she even wants me in San Diego?"

"Yes! Totally!" I sensed his convictions were faltering and pumped my fist in victory. This must've been how Ustenya felt when I agreed to join the campaign. "I swear she misses you *so* much," I said. "Misses you like you wouldn't believe."

Spencer sighed. "Can I think about it?"

"Yes! Yes, of course. I'll send you a link to the invite," I said. "The dress code is California elegant. Whatever that means. And, again, not a word to my sister. It must be a surprise."

Surprise was the key. Talia wasn't thinking clearly and if Raj was a good fuck (*ew*), she might tell Spencer not to come and carry on this affair to its inevitable, catastrophic end. My sister found PBS irreparably repulsive, even when the animals were cute, and she'd never stomach a stink badger.

"Okay, I'll let you know," Spencer said and I hung up feeling confident. One down, one to go, in terms of getting grumpy, scorned men out to California. Unfortunately, Talia's hotness only registered with one of them, and Ozzie would definitely be the tougher sell.

# Chapter Forty-Nine

## Ozzie

Ozzie wasn't totally sure what he was doing here. He hated Connecticut, as a rule, but when he'd told Aunt Kathy the apartment was being shown all weekend and he planned to check in to a hotel—you gotta spend money to make money, ya feel?—she invited him to stay.

"Oh, yeah, I don't really do Greenwich," he'd said. She laughed and ordered him to get his ass over there.

Kathy's house was two-story, painted white with green shutters. Very Connecticut on the outside, but inside it looked like a '90s film set that'd been ravaged by raccoons. She was having trouble staying on top of things without a full staff and, honestly, same. Granted, he didn't have three small children, plus an oafish stepson named Tug, but Ozzie felt proud of himself for holding it together, on the surface anyway.

"Welcome to the jungle," Aunt Kathy said as he dropped his bag in the entryway and followed her down the hall. Ozzie didn't remember her hair being so frizzy and all over the place, but maybe she just needed a blowout.

They walked deeper into the house. *Geeeez* this place was a wreck. Ozzie tried to recall what Doug's previous house looked like, the one he shared with his first wife and Tug. Ozzie didn't want to judge. His aunt was going through some shit. But maybe not so many Uncrustables wrappers on the floor?

"How do you like the decor?" she asked, grinning over her shoulder. "Nothing like chintz and heavy, dusty drapes."

He smiled wanly. "I could give you the name of my interior decorator. She could totes zhuzh it up on the cheap."

Kathy chuckled. "You haven't seen the Tuscan-inspired kitchen! Thanks for the offer, but my parents are nice enough to let us stay here while I get my shit together. I don't think they'd appreciate coming back from Florida to find their place redone."

Ozzie grimaced, once again furious at his inability to hang on to the smallest detail. Maybe he'd never known this was her parents' house, but seriously, there were hints. For example, the giant portrait of a teenage Kathy, backlit and hands clasped together like she was being visited by angels.

"It's a take-what-you-can-get scenario," Aunt Kathy said, "especially since most people in both our families aren't talking to us."

Kathy paused outside a sunroom turned toy room, though who was she kidding? The toys were not confined to this space. Inside were three kids—two boys slouched in beanbags, tapping away on devices, and a little girl seated on the floor, sifting through items in a white-and-pink-striped box.

"Listen," she said, turning toward Ozzie. "I don't know what's going on with your branch of the tree, and far be it from me to intervene in other people's complicated relationships, but if you can change anything about the situation . . . you should try."

"Nothing I can do," Ozzie mumbled, glancing away.

Kathy smiled gently. "Whatever the case, you don't want to be me. You don't want to wake up one morning and find out your whole world has shrunk." She rotated back toward the playroom and rapped three times on the warped, scuffed doorframe. "Hey, munchkins," she said. "Please greet your cousin."

"Hey, rock stars," Ozzie said with a wave. Their *cousin*. It felt like the wrong word. Cousins were supposed to be peers and these guys were like three feet tall.

"Would you mind if I ducked into my office?" Kathy said. "I need to finish something by noon."

"But it's Saturday?"

She shrugged. "Saturday, Monday, it's all the same when you're a freelance graphic designer. Now, I'm not asking you to *babysit* them or anything. But can you sort of . . . hang around? Alert me if someone throws up or appears to be actively dying?"

"Er, okay?" Ozzie said with a swallow. Keeping kids alive seemed like a tall order, especially for a dope like him. Did Kathy know what she was doing?

"Not to worry," Kathy said, picking up on his angst. "They're not total degenerates." She squeezed his arm. "Promise."

Exhaling, Ozzie assessed the room. He could probably handle the iPad bros, and the girl seemed busy with whatever was in the box, so maybe he could stand there and exist.

"My office is right down the hall if you need anything," she said. "I'll be back in five, ten minutes tops."

As she darted away, Ozzie's phone buzzed. Another text from Gabby. After a week of ignoring her, she was finally starting to receive the message, and the communications were slowing down. At least he wouldn't have to block her, not yet. For now, he silenced the phone.

"Excuse me," said the girl, tapping on his shoe. She looked up at him with her big brown eyes. "What's your name again?" She pushed her wispy brown hair out of her face, reminding him so much of Gabby he almost burst into tears.

Ozzie cleared his throat. "Oscar," he said.

Her eyes popped. "Like the grouch."

"*Exactly* like the grouch."

She nodded, and Ozzie fished around for her name. Hadley or Hailey. Something with an *H*. "What do you like to be called?" he asked.

"Beautiful," she said.

"Same, girl."

Ozzie watched as she placed four miniature teacups—pink-and-white-striped like the box—on four miniature pink saucers. She pulled out a teapot—also pink and white, and adorned with ladybugs—and a little pouch from her hoodie. In the pouch were fresh pansies, which she artfully arranged around the plates.

"Wow," Ozzie said, legitimately impressed. "You have panache."

"Parties need themes."

"Period. Mind if I join you?"

"That would be great!" she said, beaming as Ozzie lowered himself to the floor. Leather pants didn't have a ton of give, but he'd make it work. "No one ever wants to join me, especially not my brothers." She glared. "They're so gross and annoying."

"Totally," Ozzie said, sneaking a glance. They honestly looked pretty unpleasant, which wasn't the nicest thing to say about kids who were in the single digits, but facts were facts. "You know, I've never been to a tea party, and I have *two* sisters." To be fair, they might not have had tea parties. Maybe Gabby, but definitely not Talia. She'd never sit still for that long.

"You're missing out." She poured from her teapot what appeared to be water. "Do you like anything else that's fun? Adults usually only do boring stuff."

"You're so real for that, H. By the way, if you ever meet a dude named Barclay, run."

H snorted. "Sounds like a dog."

"You might be the smartest person in the world."

"I'm the smartest one in this house," she said and sipped her "tea." "My mom always tells me that."

"I agree with your mom. Speaking of fun things," Ozzie said. Should he drink the water? Pretend to drink it? He was bad with protocol in general. "Are you familiar with *Winnie the Pooh?*"

"Yes! I love *Winnie the Pooh!*" Her eyes ballooned. "Do you know about the Pooh-seum?"

"I'm sorry, what? There's a *Pooh-seum?*"

"Yes! I've been there! It's at Pooh Corner!" With each word, she grew increasingly excited, practically lifting off the ground. "My daddy took me before he had to go to the time-out place."

"Oh. Right." Ozzie frowned. "I'm sorry, that must be—"

"The Pooh-seum was amazing. It's in England, right next to the Hundred Acre Wood."

"No shit!" Ozzie blurted, and H fell backward in a fit of giggles. It was a little dramatic but also kind of cute. "Sorry, Aunt Kathy!" he shouted down the hall, in the general direction Kathy had gone. "Please ignore my poor language," he told H. "I got excited because I have the original map of the Hundred Acre Wood. *In my house.*"

H stopped her flailing hysterics. "Really?"

"Yep. Maybe I'll show you sometime."

"Wow." She sat all the way up. "That would be great." She eyed him for a minute. "Are you really my cousin? You seem like a stranger."

"We've met a few times," he said. "But you were tiny."

"Hmm . . ." She remained skeptical. "I'd definitely remember. I like your pants, by the way."

"Yeah ya do," Ozzie said, nodding. "I love a kid who recognizes drip."

"You are the most interesting person in this entire family."

"Thanks, H." Ozzie flashed a grin. He at last took a sip of his tea. "You might be the only one who thinks so, but I'll take it."

# NOVEMBER

# Gunn still hanging on

BY KYLE SPERBER, *The North County Intelligencer*

SAN DIEGO—It's been an eventful few weeks for Marston Gunn's senatorial aspirations. Not only did all three of his children survive a hot-air balloon crash, but he's managed to cobble together five more union endorsements and, importantly, secure Mayor Robert Quinonez's stamp of approval.

"I admire what he stands for," says San Diego's chief. "We are aligned on many issues, and I believe Marston Gunn can serve this country as a member of congress while helping our community at the same time."

Next up, California Democrats will convene in Sacramento starting this Saturday to consider candidate endorsements ahead of the March primary. Candidates will get a chance to present their case before delegates cast their votes.

To receive a formal endorsement, a candidate must secure the support of 60% of the delegates. In the crowded senatorial race, it seems unlikely any one person will achieve this mark. While an endorsement from the state Democratic Party can boost a campaign, it doesn't necessarily signal how the wider electorate feels. There have been several instances of the party endorsing a candidate, only to have that candidate fail to make it to the general.

As of the end of October, Congressional representative David Slimp (16%) is the front-runner to fill California's vacated U.S. Senate seat, with Representative Angie Parker (15%) on his heels and Representative Sandra Grant holding steady at 10%. Gunn has moved from 0.2% to 4% in only a few months, an impressive jump, but his fundraising remains downright anemic compared to his opponents'. Slimp's coffers have climbed to $35 million, while Gunn's are dropping dangerously close to the sub-million mark.

Marston Gunn has been on an undeniable upswing, but the

grim truth is he remains an extreme long-shot, regardless of what does or does not happen at the convention. It's unlikely if not impossible he could catch up in terms of dollars, which doesn't afford him the time to catch up in terms of support. Absent an unexpected windfall, the question is, how much longer can Marston Gunn stay in the race?

# Chapter Fifty

## Talia

Everything was almost in place for the big send-off, and it hadn't been easy. Organizing a cocktail party was no joke, especially when it involved working alongside Mindy, who seemed at all times three seconds from beating Talia upside the head with a rattlesnake stick.

In truth, Talia enjoyed the planning. It was a nice distraction and also quite satisfying to have things to check off a list, as opposed to an infinite scroll of unachievable tasks. The affair would be top-notch, with the food and Paso cabernets and sauv blancs to prove it, and, at T-minus forty-eight hours until kick-off, Talia sat in the kitchen, reviewing the menus for the last time.

They'd have passed appetizers, obviously, as opposed to a sit-down snooze-fest or some dreadful buffet where everyone ate from the same trough of scalloped potatoes. As Talia debated whether it was too late to throw in smoked trout croquettes, she heard plodding footsteps and prepared herself for Mindy to reveal yet another of Talia's personal or professional deficiencies.

"Don't worry! We're a go on the steak frites bites!" Talia sang as the footsteps grew closer. "And I got Dad's friend to donate four cases of wine. He thinks he can write it off, which I guess makes us a charity. Ha!"

"Funny," said a voice. But it wasn't Mindy.

As Talia turned to find Raj, her insides went all wonky. This was another advantage to overseeing the event—she had to be in the main house and could therefore avoid everyone at HQ.

Raj had snuck out of her room shortly before dawn two Sundays ago, and they'd exchanged only bland pleasantries ever since. Talia didn't know how to feel about what happened. Guilty, yes, because of Spencer, but that wasn't all. Understanding Raj's take might clear things up, but Talia was too afraid to ask.

On a good day, Talia convinced herself it wasn't *really* cheating because they didn't have ordinary, could-produce-a-child sex. Of course, most people (including and especially Spencer) would beg to differ. *Oral sex* had the word right there in its name. And also? Raj claimed he hadn't dated much, but his skills told a different tale. Two full orgasms were had by Talia, which she'd thought was impossible without another woman involved, not that she'd personally pursued such a path.

"You've been hard to find lately," Raj said, sitting across from her.

Talia blushed, recalling the orgasms. "Yeah, totally," she said, looking away. "Busy with the party. A million things to do." Talia was speaking very quickly, and she took a beat to slow herself down. "Check it out. A sneak peek of the menu." She slid the paper toward him with a visibly jittery hand. "Thoughts?"

Talia watched as his eyes scanned the page. Could there ever be anything between them, or had she gotten caught up in the moment, and the tequila? She liked Raj as a person and was attracted to him. They cared about the same causes, and Talia briefly envisioned a world where they fell in love and spent their lives working together to solve various injustices. But that was a childish fantasy, right?

"Looks great," Raj said, bobbing his head. "It's nice of your dad to do this for the staff." He pushed the menu back.

"Yeah." Talia exhaled. "Especially in light of the numbers. I don't suppose you saw the latest finance report?"

"I did," he said with a wince.

The barely seven-figure number hit Talia hard, and it was the first time she realized, *Oh, we are definitely going to fail.* It was overwhelming to imagine that soon everyone would disperse and resume their lives, with nothing to show for it aside from money spent, balloons crashed, and art studios turned into housing for imaginary guests. "Not much runway left," she said, mournfully. "Guess we'll all have to come up with our plan Bs."

"Plan B is what I needed to talk to you about," Raj said. "Or rather my return to plan A. I'm leaving, Talia."

Her stomach plummeted. "Now?"

"The timing seems right?" he said, avoiding eye contact as he picked the plastic off a corner of her red planning binder. "Thanksgiving is coming up, and my family expects me to be in the Bay Area anyway."

"Of course," Talia muttered. Raj was close with his sister and parents and not for the first time she wondered how must it feel to have family who genuinely wanted you around and not merely to serve as an employee or campaign minion.

"When I spoke to them earlier, they hinted that they'd like me to come earlier, as soon as possible actually, so, yeah. I think I'm going to do that."

"Wow." Talia was unable to say much else. This was about *her*, she was sure of it. She'd endured a few bad hookups in her day but none that'd caused anyone to relocate, and now she wanted to die.

"It's not a referendum on your father," Raj added. "He could turn it around. Who knows? I certainly don't!" He laughed and Talia stared, dumbfounded. She didn't care about his views on her dad's long-term senatorial prospects. How did he not understand this? "As I said, the timing feels right," he prattled on. "I've become too caught up in the campaign. I'm acting like I'm on an extended vacation. It's time to get back to real life."

"So, that's it?" she finally managed. "You'll leave and we'll never talk again?"

"I didn't say that," Raj mumbled, picking harder at the binder.

"I don't need anything from you, okay? But I won't let you pretend nothing happened and run away. It's fucking rude, actually! I thought we both had fun the night of the Padres game."

Raj glanced up. "That night was amazing."

"Clearly," she scoffed.

He released a puff of air. "I've loved getting to know you. And you've been beyond helpful with the lawsuit—"

Talia glowered. *"Helpful,"* she said. "Exactly what every woman longs to hear." She didn't expect him to profess his undying love or anything, but *come on.* "It's fine, Raj. Just leave. Move on with your life and don't look back."

Raj groaned and ran his fingers over his head. *"Ugh!* I'm so bad at this. I warned you my romantic history is painfully brief. Truthfully? It's because of you I want to stay, which is a pretty solid indicator I should go."

"You're not making sense. If you want to stay, then *stay,*" Talia said. "Whatever happens. Whatever that . . ." She flapped a hand. "Whatever that was, or wasn't, I like having you around. Sometimes I think you're my only friend at the Ranch." Not until she said the words did Talia realize how true they were. "I need you."

Raj's cheeks burned. "Talia. You don't even know me. We've had an incredible time together—better than I knew possible—but, trust me, I have some significant bad traits. Even more reason to go, before the veil drops."

Talia rolled her eyes, seeing this for the excuse it was. "When you quit a job, you're supposed to give two weeks' notice."

"I don't believe I ever signed a formal employment agreement," Raj answered quite rationally, though Talia wanted to whomp him on the head with her binder. "And I *do* have to find a job."

"Please. Stay. Until Thanksgiving." Talia was begging now but she had no shame, apparently. He couldn't just leave her like this. "The campaign needs you. I'll help with your résumé."

"Talia—"

"I'll write you a recommendation, serve as a reference. My dad can make calls. If you feel awkward about us, don't worry. It's water under the bridge."

The relief that rippled across his face was a dagger to Talia's gut, though she supposed this was the way of things. The people Talia cared about never seemed to want all she was willing to give. Even Spencer seemed distant these days.

"I don't want you to find me a job," Raj said. "But I guess . . ." He paused for approximately five thousand years. "I guess I could hang around for a few more weeks."

"Really?" Talia's heart did a little leap.

"Sure. I'm not exactly roughing it, and there are a few benefits to staying." Raj pushed up his glasses and smiled, his dimples coming in strong. "Very compelling benefits. And I'm definitely not talking about letters of recommendation."

# Chapter Fifty-One

## Gabby

For a second, I thought he was dead.

"Dad!" I said, tapping his foot. Frosty sidled up beside me and gave his toes a sniff. "Dad!"

He jolted into a seated position, and Frosty jumped back. Gripping the sides of the napping couch, Dad looked around, wild-eyed and disoriented. "What? What's happening?"

I placed a hand on his leg. "Everything's fine. Ustenya wanted me to make sure you were awake. The party is in less than two hours. Are you going to be ready in time?"

"Please," he grumbled, rising to his feet. He passed Frosty a quick, confused look. "You'd be impressed how quickly I can apply a face. I'm a wiz with a makeup brush."

I chuckled—obligatorily—but honestly, he did need makeup. He'd seemed so pale and lifeless lying stretched out on the couch. Mistaking him for a dead man wasn't a joke.

As Dad staggered into the bathroom, it struck me this was the first time I'd been in any bedroom of his. In most homes we'd ever owned, my room was on one side, and his on the other, usually behind one if not two sets of double doors.

"Are you ready for the big convention?" I asked. "I lined up some interviews. The schedule is already in your inbox since you're leaving tonight."

"Thanks, Bags." He turned on the water. I heard him splash his face.

"Two pretty big newspapers," I said, proud of myself for the gets. "They appreciate how you're being very specific about solutions to the housing crisis. I really have to hand it to Talia for going so hard on that stuff because it seems to be paying off."

Dad poked his head through the door. "Listen, we're done with all that. It's pissing off too many people." He ducked back inside the bathroom, and it was like he'd slammed the door in my face.

"Dad!" I said, heart booming in my ears. "Didn't you hear what I just said? The housing stuff . . . people like that about you." It was just about the *only* thing they liked, I hastened to add.

"We're almost out of money, and a friend of mine said he'll kick in two million if I stop shit-talking private equity." Dad chortled. "For that I'm happy to oblige."

"Two mil, huh?" I said, my voice as dry as a Santa Ana wind. "As long as you're locking down such a vast sum." *Terrific*, I thought, *just what this campaign needs*. A few more bucks to limp along for another week or two. Talia was going to be crushed and maybe it was good that Spencer rebuffed my surprise visit idea. We were due for enough drama this weekend.

"Don't worry, Bagsy," Dad said, misreading my silence. "We'll find something new and fun to focus on."

"Great. Can't wait," I said through my teeth. "I'll let you finish freshening up." I began to walk away.

"Hold on." Dad peered out again, holding on to the door-jamb. He had a scab on the top of his hand, and it looked fresh. Why were old men always bleeding a little bit? "Your birthday is coming up. And. Well. There's no easy way to say this, but I'll need to use your twenty-five-year gift."

I felt the blood drain from my face. "But. That's . . . for me."

"Yeah, and I feel terrible, Bags. But I'll make it up later, I promise." He disappeared again. "Anyway. Good talk. Thanks for everything. I'll see you tonight."

Ivan stood at the bottom of the stairs, as though he'd been waiting for me all along. "Gabby? What's wrong?" he said, registering in one glance that I was about to lose my damned mind.

"What's not wrong?" I landed with a thump on the floor. "My brother. My dad. The fucking campaign. Have you heard? He's backing down on the housing stuff." *And stealing a million-plus dollars from me.* "Great timing, hours before he leaves for the convention."

"Shit," Ivan said, running a hand over his blue-black hair. "I was afraid of this. Whenever a candidate is suddenly stoked about his financial condition, they're about to sell out."

*You don't know the half of it, buddy.* There was a reason I'd created a hundred-mile barrier between me and the rest of the Gunns. I should've kept my distance.

"Let's not mention this to Talia, okay?" I said. Frosty whined, and I bent down to scratch his head. "Not yet anyway. She's put so much into the party—into the whole campaign—and I don't want to ruin her night."

Ivan bit his bottom lip and nodded once. "As you know, I prefer to be transparent," he said as we walked toward the back of the house, "but it's your family."

"Yeah. Lucky me. Sometimes I ask myself, what am I still doing here?"

No, but really. What *was* I doing? I'd received my monthly disbursement two days ago, and there'd be no twenty-five-year gift. My dad was acting like a spineless weasel who stood for nothing, and I saw no reason to stick around.

"Quite a career you've chosen for yourself," I said to Ivan as we stepped out onto the patio. Nearby hay bales and rotting pumpkins and fake fuzzy spiders were piled up—Halloween decorations collected but not yet discarded. In Ustenya's country, they only decorated for non-religious holidays, and for these she went all-out.

"How do you stand it?" I asked. "How can you work for these people?"

We stopped and Ivan pondered the question, his hands shoved deep into the pockets of his gray trousers. "When I first began in politics," he said, "a mentor warned me I wouldn't always be advocating for things I believed in. Any candidate I worked for would inevitably have positions I found less than ideal but it wasn't my job to push my beliefs on anyone else. My job was to fight for my boss using *their* platform, not mine."

"Bullshit job," I mumbled. "Or horse dick, as Ustenya would say."

Ivan snickered. "Yeah. It's not for everyone. The pay is crap, and the hours are worse, and if you can do anything else, you probably should. But I love a challenge. It's why I gravitate toward candidates like your dad."

"He is a challenge," I agreed. "Wish I'd talked to you before I moved to California."

"But then you never would've come." He smiled. "Between you and me, I suspect this campaign won't last much longer. Even with the cash infusion, I think Ustenya is fed up. She never expected it to be so grueling."

"And unglamorous," I said.

"And she keeps worrying about getting fat. At least she has her priorities in order." Ivan shook his head. "You know, for someone who never wanted to do this, you've been quite competent."

I grinned. "Thank you. All I've ever hoped for in life is to be perfectly middling," I said, not totally joking. "And it has been fun, occasionally."

Suddenly a high-pitched yodel erupted. Something flashed across my field of vision. I rattled my head.

"Um. Did Dad adopt another pet? Like a peacock or a . . . ?"

"I don't think so," Ivan said, brows pinched.

The animal flashed again, and my heart kerplunked. *No, please, not now*, I begged the universe, but the hives were already rolling across my skin like a tide.

"Ivan," I said, gripping his arm. "I need to check on something. Please. Don't ask any questions. Just walk away." Without waiting for his response, I took off, racing across the property, chasing God only knew what.

# Chapter Fifty-Two

"RAJ!" I screamed into the phone as I speed-walked toward the barn. "Meet me outside HQ. HURRY!"

The bird darted past. I startled, and my phone clattered to the ground. When I looked up, Raj was running toward me. The bird zoomed by again. "What the hell was that?" he said.

"How would I know." It yodeled again then took off. Now we were sprinting across the yard, officially giving chase. The creature was kind of fat and low to the ground, but the bastard was fast.

"I've never seen anything like it," Raj huffed as we wended through a rose garden. "It's very colorful. And muscular?"

I didn't realize a bird could be muscular, but Raj was right.

"Motherfucker!" I cursed, catching my hand on a thorn. "I guess you're not my antidote."

"Come on," Raj said, grabbing my elbow. "We're going to lose sight of him. Let's take that." He pointed to a golf cart.

"It's the landscaper's. We can't steal it."

"We're *borrowing*. And we have to. We'll never catch the guy on foot."

Before I could protest, Raj was behind the wheel. Such a man move, assuming he'd be the one to drive. Although, I'd never operated one and didn't want to be in charge, and so I kept my mouth shut and slid into the passenger seat. Raj hit the gas, and we pitched forward.

"What are we going to do?" I wailed. "The party starts in two hours. Should I call dos Santos? I'm calling dos Santos."

I went to unlock my phone, but in my frantic state, it didn't recognize my face.

"Here," Raj said, reaching into the front pocket of his flannel. "SD Wildlife Removal is one of my starred contacts. They usually give me a fifteen percent discount."

"Raj!" I smacked his arm. "A wildlife removal service? Do you know what that means? It's removal. *From existence.*"

We bumped over something, and Raj's glasses relocated to the end of his nose. "Well. Yeah." His cheeks flushed deep scarlet through his brown skin. "It's California law. Either they move the wildlife one hundred yards from where it was found—which, not helpful—or they exterminate."

I couldn't believe my ears. No, really. This was too much. I temporarily forgot about the extremely terrifying bird. "The badgers at the trolley station. You had them executed?"

"Not personally."

"Oh my God. Don't you see the irony? You're helping the unhoused in your spare time, but when some poor mustelid from the Sunda Strait loses his home and shows up at yours, you off him?"

"It's not the same."

The bird zipped past again, returning my brain to our present horror. But still! Raj killed all those badgers. They caused a lot of problems, I got it, but it wasn't their fault. They were doing their best! I couldn't believe my sister was cheating on her boyfriend with an animal killer.

"I'm calling dos Santos," I said, shoving Raj's phone back at him.

I finally managed to open mine and was rather stunned when dos Santos answered right away. "Gabby?" he said as I put him on speaker. "Did you hear the good news? Stuart's wife is out of the hospital, and with a clean bill of health."

"That's amazing," Raj said, and I looked at him. He reminded me this was Stuart from the message boards, the one with the fishy wife.

"Oh. Right. Yeah. Great news." I turned my attention back to the phone. "We need help. It's urgent."

Dos Santos made a noise, like sucking his teeth. "It's a Friday evening. We need to have a serious discussion about boundaries and respecting other people's time."

"This isn't about you!" We thumped over something, and my internal organs clanked. I told him about the flare and described the bird, or as much as I'd been able to take in. Squat, round body. Shaggy black feathers. A head that was turquoise, with a yellow neck and red wattle. "Basically, a cross between a turkey and a beefy, colorful emu," I concluded. "He also had this thing. Like a helmet situation?" I put my hand to my forehead in the shape of a ball.

"You mean a casque?"

"Sure. Okay."

"There he is!" Raj took a hard left toward a small to medium-sized cornfield.

"Oh my God, the cobs!" I said. The mystery was solved.

"Is the bird double-wattled?" dos Santos asked as Raj released his foot from the gas.

"It looks that way," he confirmed.

"Oh," dos Santos said. Or maybe it was *uh-oh*. "Any chance you can take a picture? Wait! Don't get too close. I'll send *you* one. Tell me if it matches what you're seeing."

This was going to take a minute. I was barely hanging on to one bar out here and had only twelve percent battery left. Meanwhile, Raj inched us forward, following the bird as he bounded through the corn.

"Yes! That's him!" I said when at last the pixels coalesced.

"Look," Raj said, pointing. "He's checking out the scarecrow."

"Aw. That's cute." I tilted my head and watched as the bird gently tapped the scarecrow with its beak, as if to ask, *Hello, are you real?* It made me a little teary, to be honest.

"GABBY!" dos Santos barked. "That is a cassowary. Do not go near it."

"He seems more rascally than mean," I said as Raj drove us closer. "Also lonely. He probably doesn't want to be here, and I don't blame him. When I tell you the vibes are off—"

"Gabby!" dos Santos snapped again. I was getting awfully sick of the sound of my name. "This is serious. You are in the presence of the only bird that's killed a human."

"Owls have killed humans. Haven't you seen *The Staircase?*"

"This is not a joke. Cassowaries are extremely dangerous."

"Calm down. He's not interested in us at all."

"They can run up to forty miles per hour and have been known to cut people open with their—"

I didn't hear dos Santos finish the sentence because the cassowary made a horrible gurgling sound. He craned his neck, then triple hopped. After releasing another gurgle, he leapt forward and proceeded to disembowel the scarecrow with his feet. Three seconds later, all that remained was a pile of hay and scraps.

"WHAT THE FUCK!" I yelled.

"What the fuck!" Raj agreed.

"They're related to the velociraptor," dos Santos said.

"THAT INFORMATION WOULD'VE BEEN HELP-FUL EARLIER."

"Shhhh," dos Santos hissed. "Keep your voice down. You claim he's not interested in you, and I'd like to keep it that way."

Raj pulled out his phone, and I began to spiral. Was I about to be gutted in a cornfield by a dinosaur? Right before Dad's cocktail party?

"They don't generally attack for no reason," dos Santos said, "usually only if they're defending their chicks—"

"Tell that to the scarecrow! He was doing literally nothing."

"Look!" Raj said, shoving his phone in my face. "This is what we're dealing with!" He jabbed at the screen, which displayed a list of cassowary facts.

- Gorgeous and colorful bird
- Has killed many humans
- Can chase you down with speeds up to 40 mph
- Will cut you open with its 4-inch claws!

That the list read like a first grader's school project made it no less terrifying, and now Raj was playing a YouTube video that started with a Florida Man pleading with 911 to send an ambulance because *I'm bleeding to death.* His pet cassowary had attacked him, and he did not survive.

"Stop," I said, practically knocking the phone out of Raj's hand. I rotated away from him. "Can you bring the van? And some kind of net, I guess?"

"This is what I meant by boundaries," dos Santos said.

"We're about to get murdered by a dinosaur and you're worried about boundaries?" I was glad I hadn't asked him to make it snappy because we had a cocktail party to attend.

"I work at a zoo. It's not a place for acquaintances to store their animals."

"If a cancer kid needed to use one of your enclosures, I bet it'd be no problem."

"You're not a kid and you don't have cancer, and I can't fathom why someone with cancer would need to be in a zoo. Anyway. I'll call around. I might be able to find someone willing to take him off your hands. But there's a huge accident at The Split, and I doubt anyone will make it up there tonight. In the meantime, can you lure him somewhere safe? Like a barn or an unused building?"

"We do have a lot of barns," I said. "And actually, tomorrow morning is probably better. We have . . . guests coming over."

"Oh, God," dos Santos groaned.

"You're not making me feel very assured!"

"Okay." He was out of breath, despite being safely ensconced in his office an hour or more away. "Find a way to corral him. If he does come at you, you have to be the aggressor. Look him dead in the eyes."

"Yeah, no," I said, thinking only a man would tell someone to make eye contact with a vicious predator.

"After you make eye contact, back away slowly," dos Santos said, "while holding something in front of you. Keep as much distance as possible, and don't let him near any children or pets."

"Obviously—" I started, and my heart lurched. *Frosty!* I clicked off the phone and turned toward Raj, tears running down my cheeks. "We need to get back to the house," I said. "I left the dog outside, and God knows where he is. Jindos are runners." I covered my face. "Fuck, fuck, fuck. I should've never tried to have a pet."

"It's going to be fine," Raj said, and I wanted to smack him because what the hell did he know, and also he was out here killing stink badgers on the regular. But he stepped on the gas and told me I was a great dog owner, and for a moment, I liked him again.

"Fuck, fuck, fuck," I repeated. As we crested the hill, I saw a figure in the distance. It was Ivan, running, carrying something white in his arms.

"Frosty!" I screamed. Before Raj had a chance to stop or even slow down, I was out of the cart, sliding across the dirt on my Birks. Within seconds, I'd toppled, head over ass, scraping my hands and cutting a hole in the knee of my sweatpants. "Is he okay?" I said as Frosty tried to writhe out of Ivan's arms.

"He's fine," Ivan said, his face bright red and drenched in sweat. "You took off, and Frosty was standing there, wondering what happened. Then I saw this weird creature?" He set down the dog and I reached out to grab hold of his collar. "This might sound absurd, but it reminded me of a dinosaur?"

"We are familiar with the dinosaur," I said, giving Frosty

a very thorough belly rub. Meanwhile, his eyes were bugged and his mouth hung open like he was happy, but also slightly insane.

"I probably didn't need to pick him up," Ivan said. "But it was my first instinct."

"Thank you," I said, starting to cry again. "I can't say it enough." I would've promised him Raj's million dollars if I still had it to give.

Ivan used his shoulder to wipe the sweat from his brow. "What the hell was that thing?"

"A cassowary," Raj said. "It's a long story, but hop in. We could use the help."

―――――

After locking Frosty in the music room with a bowl of water and pile of salami, we emptied the servants' kitchen of all its fruit. Thankfully, the party prep was being handled in the kitchen at HQ.

Next, we grabbed three buckets and filled them with freshly picked oranges, and I hoped like hell dos Santos was right about cassowaries liking citrus. Luring him into the recreation pavilion was our only plan, and if that failed, who the hell knew.

It took seven minutes to line the bowling alleys with oranges and peaches and piles of grapes, plus a few leftover Halloween pumpkins. After sprinkling the fruit with crushed-up Xanax (stolen from Talia), we created multiple fruit trails leading outside. As Raj laid down each piece, Ivan and I stood on either side, guarding him with patio chairs.

Next we attached several pieces of PVC together, leaving one end by the door, and climbing up into an old tree house with the other. Trap now set, we waited. And waited. I forbade anyone from checking their phones, especially if they intended to research whether cassowaries were good climbers. The HQ and ballroom weren't visible from here, and I prayed the cassowary stayed on our side of the property.

We waited some more, and it was unsettling to be simultaneously bored and worried about imminent death. Each second passed like an hour, but after twenty minutes, the cassowary finally took the bait, following one of the trails into the recreation pavilion. When he stepped inside, we used the PVC contraption to push the door closed.

"We did it!" Ivan said, scrambling down from the tree house, a set of keys in hand. He raced over to lock the door, the very definition of "taking one for the team." We'd previously pulled some kettlebells out of the gym, which he propped against the door to be extra safe.

"Wow," I said, looking around.

We were all pale-faced, sweaty, and visibly spooked, and none of us were sure what to do next. So far, it was quiet in the pavilion. The cassowary was either busy eating or already drowsy from the Xanax.

I snuck a glance at Ivan. "Um. You're probably wondering what that was all about . . ."

"Hey. No big deal. We all have our weird things," he said with a wink, and I snorted. "Your dad warned me that sometimes you show up with animals, and I should ignore it if it happened. He didn't mention ignoring might not be an option."

"Unfortunately, we will have to ignore it, for a while at least." I checked my phone and saw that dos Santos couldn't get anyone out here until morning. It was better, I assured myself, to take care of it after everyone left, including Ustenya and Dad. "Do we think he'll be safe in there?" I said, though what I meant was would *we* be safe. "All the main buildings are pretty far away, but . . ."

"Don't worry," Ivan said, landing a hand on my shoulder.

"I'll hang out . . ." He nodded toward the yoga studio. "And keep watch."

"But you'll miss the party."

Ivan sniggered. "Oh, I'm fine to miss the party. When else would I have the opportunity to add 'dinosaur watcher' to my résumé?"

# Chapter Fifty-Three

## Talia

Candles flickered. Music played from hidden speakers. Waiters stood with trays of champagne and Talia's carefully selected hors d'oeuvres. The "ballroom"—really, just another of the Ranch's repurposed white stucco, wood-beamed barns—was ready for its guests.

Talia glanced around, lightheaded thanks to the two glasses of champagne she'd guzzled in the kitchen. The question now was, where the hell was everyone else? She'd asked Gabby to come *early* and—quick check—she was certifiably late. Talia was stupid for expecting anything different.

Their days at the Ranch were winding down, and nothing she'd imagined had come to pass. For a second, Talia felt closer to Gabby, only to discover it was a mirage and, over the past few weeks, they hadn't been alone together for more than three minutes. It was partway Talia's fault—all that menu planning at the main house—but a simple query like "What are you wearing to the party?" caused Gabby to immediately bolt from the room. It was time to face the truth. They'd never have the relationship Talia wanted. That went for Gabby and every other Gunn.

People trickled in, and still no Gabby, or Dad, or Ustenya. Still no Raj, either, and Talia felt embarrassed she'd read so much into his "compelling benefits" comment. *I'm definitely not talking about letters of recommendation.* Classic Talia, seeing things that weren't there.

"Hey, Mindy!" Talia called out as the property manager whipped past in a two-piece lavender suit with big plastic buttons. It looked like something from an outlet mall, but who was Talia to criticize? She was grossly overdressed not to mention freezing to death in her skimpy, flashy dress. "Hold on! Mindy!"

Mindy hesitated, as if weighing the wisdom of full engagement.

"Have you seen Gabby? I'm kind of shocked she's not here yet . . ."

Mindy slowly pivoted, a hard smirk on her face. "Yes, I've seen Gabby," she said mysteriously. "A few hours ago, she and Raj were racing across the property in a stolen golf cart."

"I'm sorry, what? Gabby and *Raj*?" Talia said to Mindy's retreating back. The woman must've been confused. Talia could easily envision Gabby being party to a stolen golf cart, but the story sounded like Gabby and *Ozzie*, not Gabby and Raj.

Thirty seconds later, the front door swung open, and in walked Raj. Talia felt a small thump of relief that he wasn't off committing minor crimes with Gabby. She'd told him she was happy to be "just friends" and a friend was what Talia needed now, at this party she'd organized, to which zero Gunns had so far shown up. Talia snatched two champagne flutes from a roving waiter and bolted to his side.

"Raj! You're late!" Talia chirped, rushing up to him.

Raj startled. "Jesus," he said, clutching his chest. "Talia! You scared me."

Talia looked at him cross-eyed. She hadn't exactly snuck up on him. If anything, she could've been a bit more subtle, especially given the silver dress. "Sorry," she said, passing him a flute, which he accepted with a quivering hand. A line of sweat ran along his top lip.

"Is Gabby here?" Raj asked, casting his eyes about the room.

Talia scowled. "Not yet," she said—neutrally, she hoped—and stepped aside to let a pack of volunteers slide past. "Mindy had a crazy theory . . ." Suddenly Talia felt the weight of someone else's stare. She turned to see one of the volunteers studying her chain mail dress with great intensity. Talia had wanted to make a statement tonight, and congratulations, job well done. "Anyway," she said, exhaling, braiding her arms across her waist. "Mindy suggested *you* might know where my sister is."

"I haven't the faintest," Raj said, brow furrowed. Finally he looked at Talia, truly *looked* at her for the first time. She could practically see his train of thought screech to a halt.

"Yes, it's true, I'm a tad overdressed!" Talia squeaked. "Guess I was trying to get noticed. Ha!" *Oh, God.* She wanted to die.

"Uh. Yeah. You're noticed," Raj said, his eyes roaming up and down her body. "Wow. You look incredible."

Talia smiled as goose bumps ran along her skin. For a moment, Raj couldn't take his eyes off the dress, as if he was attempting to see all the way through it, to the almost nothing she wore underneath. No bra. Merely a very small flesh-colored thong.

"You're the only person who could pull that off," he said, and instead of die she thought she might melt. Talia was fine with her looks. Some or possibly many people considered her pretty even though her mouth was too wide, her nose too pointy, her features too sharp. Ozzie said she didn't eat enough so actually it wasn't sharp but *gaunt* but anyway fuck him. The point was, she couldn't remember anyone looking at her like this.

"Come on," she said, taking Raj's hand. "We both need another drink."

"I just started on this one—"

"We'll say hi to a few folks, punch the clock, and get the hell out of here. I don't want to be at this party any longer than necessary."

# Chapter Fifty-Four

## Gabby

After throwing on the only dress I owned, I trudged over to the ballroom, shoulders hiked up to my ears, in anticipation of that horrible yodel. No website on earth was able to tell me how many milligrams of Xanax were required to knock out a cassowary. Ivan was a damned hero, agreeing to keep watch.

The party was underway when I arrived and I looked around, wondering who I was supposed to hang out with. Having established myself as the world's worst sister, Montana and Bea were out. My tardiness would no doubt result in the silent treatment from Talia, which was fine on account of the Raj situation. Dad was off-limits, too, since I planned to leave the campaign in a matter of days, and was hiding a cassowary on the property.

Stomach churning, I ventured farther into the room. *Okay, universe, what new horror are you bringing tonight?* It had to be something—that cassowary was very intense—and honestly, dos Santos could get bent with his "suppression" theory. Raj was secretly sleeping with my sister and not a stink badger to be found. Lucky for the stink badgers, in light of Raj's tendency toward murder.

I bellied up to the bar. "Whatever's good," I said, leaving the bartender thoroughly befuddled. As he poured me a glass of white wine, I got the *feeling* of Talia hovering nearby. I checked and caught in my periphery a glimpse of my sister bopping around in . . . *chain mail*? Meanwhile, in my long flowing dress and thick pair of tights, I looked like I'd escaped a librarian speed dating event.

"Hello, Gabrielle," Mindy said, popping up out of nowhere like a gopher (or snake) from a hole. "Nice of you to make it."

"Yeah, sorry, I had some personal bus—"

She was already on her way to someone else. "Congratulations on getting your cast off!" she called over her shoulder.

I checked my phone. Nothing from Ivan, which was the best possible news. As I slid it into the pocket of my sweater, someone latched on to my arm and spun me around. And there Talia stood in her slinky, extremely reflective dress.

"Caught ya!" she said. "You're not ignoring me anymore!"

"Are you drunk?" I blurted.

She giggled and pinched her fingers together. "Teensy bit. I got an early start."

"Hey, Gabby," Raj said, appearing behind my sister. He wore a zesty floral print and smelled like he'd doused himself with half a bottle of his dad's cologne. "Cool outfit."

"Thanks," I muttered. "Well, I have to go. Have fun, everyone."

"You can't leave yet!" Talia reached for me but missed, stumbling forward, catching herself on a high-top table. Raj rushed to her side. "I'm okay, I'm okay . . ." she said, flapping a hand, brushing him off. "Gabby. Why are you avoiding me? Did I do something wrong? Am I in trouble?" She peered up at me, batting her watery blue eyes.

"Why would you be in trouble?" I asked archly, I hoped. "Do you feel guilty for some reason?"

Talia checked Raj, who shrugged haplessly. She flipped her attentions back to me. "I've barely seen you in weeks."

"You're the one who's been working in the main house."

"Because I had to plan this stupid party. Not stupid." She covered her mouth, but not before a burp slipped out. "Fucking *lit* party. You had the office almost all to yourself, but whenever I stepped foot in there, you'd leave to quote-unquote 'work from the library.'"

"The main house has better Wi-Fi—" I said.

Talia looked at Raj. They were standing ridiculously close together, touching almost. Didn't anyone appreciate the sanctity of a relationship around here?

"I told you," Talia said to Raj. "Wi-Fi is her favorite excuse for not being somewhere. She does it all the time. Even at her own Collective."

"I'm not making excuses," I lied. "I don't know what to tell you, other than if things seem 'off,' perhaps you need to look at yourself." With great flourish, I whirled around and beelined toward the bacon and parmesan baked oysters. Who needed friends or family when you had hors d'oeuvres.

# Chapter Fifty-Five

I was half-drunk standing alone in a corner when Dad stepped onto the stage in a bespoke dark blue suit and pink pocket square. As the mike crackled and whined, the din of conversation screeched to a halt. People exchanged looks, like, *Ugh, I guess we have to listen to a dumb speech by the boss.* I checked the time, wondering if I could leave soon. Talia, it seemed, was already gone.

"Let me begin by thanking everyone for being here to support my campaign," Dad said. His skin tone had changed, though not necessarily for the better. Instead of deathly pale, he looked like he'd had a mishap with Ustenya's bronzer. "I'd like to thank my wife specifically for putting up with the chaos." He smiled at Ustenya, who stood beside him in a metallic snake print jumpsuit. "Now, you've all seen the latest numbers, but—don't despair—I have some exciting news. We've lined up several new donors who want to help keep this train going."

Light applause filtered through the room, and I deeply rolled my eyes. Did that make me a "new donor," then?

"There's still a long road before us, but I'm ready for the trip . . ." He lifted his glass. "There's no one else I'd rather take the journey with than the people in this room. Cheers!" After taking a swig, Dad passed his glass to Ustenya.

"Now, you probably assumed this party was ALL about me, but I've assembled everyone here for another reason. Sweetheart?" He glanced back. "Will you summon our special guest?"

Ustenya hesitated before turning to peer behind a blue trifold screen.

"The bedrock of this campaign has been my oldest daughter, Talia. And tonight, she's in for a surprise. Talia?" Dad said, squinting, using his height to crane over the crowd. "Tal? You out there?"

"Um, I think she stepped out?" I said, my voice echoing off the stucco walls. I glanced over to where Ustenya was speaking to someone on the other side of the screen. First she shook her head no. Then she aggressively flapped a hand. A man in a tuxedo stepped out and around the screen. He strode confidently up to my dad.

"Oh, shit," I said, and five or six people turned to look.

"Everyone, I'd like to introduce you to a very important guest." Dad smacked the man hardily on the back. "Now, if we can locate your beautiful better half . . ."

I fumbled for my phone. Where the hell are you? I texted my sister. 911! 911!

"My friend Spencer here—" Dad said, gesturing "—has a speech prepared. Or a question, really. Where is my eldest daughter?" My father was now visibly sweating. "Um, Mindy? Would you mind finding Talia for us?"

"I saw her back by the main house," Mindy said, and a smile wiggled across her face.

*Shit*, I thought, every alarm bell inside me going off.

"According to the motion sensors . . ." Mindy consulted her wrist. "Someone's in the Jacuzzi? That's where I'd check, personally. Don't be shocked if she's not alone."

---

I'd remember the next several minutes only in fragments.

The word *Jacuzzi*.

Spencer fleeing the scene.

My feet on the ground as I chased after him.

The flop of his hair as he continued to outpace me. His speed was impressive. He wasn't even wearing his performance fleece.

Spencer crossed the road. He cut through a privet hedge and stopped on the patio. I ran up behind him, heaving and panting. To my left, a crumpled-up pair of khakis sat on the floor of the meditation loggia. Beside it, a puddle of chain mail. In front of us, in the Jacuzzi, were Talia and Raj, their shoulders touching, their faces illuminated by blue and purple lights.

"What. The fuck," Spencer said, clenching his fists.

"Spencer?" Talia gasped. She went to stand but reconsidered. I was pretty sure I could see her nipples from here. "What are you doing?"

"I was going to . . ." Spencer loosened his hand and slipped something into his pocket. A ring box, I recognized with a thud. "I thought we were . . ." He paused, pressing his lips together, his expression hardening as he zeroed in on Raj. "Who is this jack-off?"

"Raj is working on the campaign," Talia answered, as if this explained anything.

"I don't give a fuck what he does for a job—"

"He's my boyfriend," I blurted, and someone—Raj, probably—made a choking sound. It was possible I'd made things worse, but it was too late now. The horse, as they said, had left the barn.

"He's *your* boyfriend?" Spencer said. "Aren't you gay?"

"Jesus! I didn't realize you all spent so much time contemplating my sexuality." I rotated toward the Jacuzzi. "Rajeev! I've been looking for you all night. What are you doing in a hot tub with my sister?"

After swiping a navy-and-white-striped towel from the loggia, I scurried toward the Jacuzzi, defocusing my eyes so I wouldn't irreparably destroy them. Yep, those were my sister's nipples alright. I couldn't totally see what was going on beneath the water, but Raj appeared to have on boxer shorts. Thank God for small mercies.

"You know about my jealous streak," I added. "Please, stop

making moves on my sister. She has a serious boyfriend. Also, she told me you're unattractive and a loud chewer."

"Wait. What?" Raj said.

I crouched down and wrapped the towel around Talia, drenching the bottom third of it in the process. "Come on, let's get you into the house," I said, literally dragging her out as I decided Spencer might actually buy the charade. Talia was hot as hell, and why would she hop into bed with such a lanky, furry, unjacked man? No offense. "Goodness, that's a very revealing bikini. No wonder Raj was so taken by you. As if you'd ever date a big nerd like him."

"Hey!"

"Oh, Raj, I can't believe you'd do this to me." The more I wailed, the more convincing it seemed, in my own head anyway. I hurried my sister inside, shouting at Raj that I'd never forgive him, which was pretty damned close to the truth.

# Chapter Fifty-Six

## Ozzie

As the car pulled away from the curb, Ozzie questioned whether he was out of his goddamned mind. Or *out of his watermelons*, as Ustenya would say.

For two weeks, Gabby had been assaulting him with messages, voice and text. Even Dad left a voicemail—a real-life voicemail!—begging him to come back. Ozzie might've ignored them both forever if not for Aunt Kathy's words living rent-free in his brain.

*If you can change anything about the situation . . . you should try.*

Despite what everyone assumed, Ozzie wasn't afraid to make an effort. A fan base of millions didn't just *happen*, and surviving Canyonside was an active endeavor.

*You don't want to wake up one morning and find out your whole world has shrunk.*

Ozzie's world shrank once, when he dumped @DegenerateOz, and a second time when he told Freja she'd need to leave the apartment for more showings, and she said she was clearing out for good. Ozzie didn't blame her—the girl deserved a promotion—but he wasn't looking to downsize again, which explained why he was now in the back of a Lyft, on his way to catch a red-eye to the left coast.

It was the right move, Ozzie assured himself. Sure, he could stay in New York to sell his apartment and lick his wounds and complain about how his family treated him like trash. But family was a finite resource, same as money, and you couldn't ignore them and hope everything worked out. He did need every penny of the $50K, but more than that, these were Ozzie's people, and this time they'd invited him in instead of pushing him away.

# Chapter Fifty-Seven

## Gabby

"I'm sorry about calling you my boyfriend," I said to Raj, who was still in the Jacuzzi. "And the stuff about you being ugly and all that. Obviously, not true."

"What's that guy doing here?" Raj asked, eyes bulged and unblinking.

"Ummm . . ." I made a face, wondering how he couldn't put two and two together. Talia's boyfriend was here in a tuxedo and with a small square box in his pocket. My first inclination was to make an excuse, claim that Spencer was a lovesick, non-dangerous stalker, but maybe dos Santos was right. I was a filthy lying liar who was allergic to the truth.

I exhaled. "That's Talia's boyfriend. He was going to propose. Sorry if that's news to you. I know what's going on between you two. Not everything." I put up a hand. "So, no intimate details, thank you very much."

"He was going to propose?" Raj said. "I got the impression they were about to break up, and it was only a matter of time."

"They'll probably break up now?" I offered.

Raj nodded in a slow, circular manner. He had the countenance of a shell-shocked man.

Just as I was about to comment on the benefits of us all being on the same page, someone shouted my name, and I looked up to see Tony standing in an open doorway. His face was white, this man who once told me he'd seen and heard it all.

"It's wildest fucking thing," he said, stumble-walking outside.

"What?" Raj said, his voice so pitched and wobbly it made me do a double take. That's when I noticed Raj was very aggressively scratching his arm. *Oh, shit.*

"That guy in the tux was trying to leave," Tony said. "But couldn't get into his car." I clenched my eyes, my entire body. "He couldn't get in because the thing was filled with live skunks."

———

Dr. dos Santos stepped out of the official zoo van, to which a stink badger trailer was affixed. "I didn't know you were related to *those* Gunns," he said, right off the bat.

"Thanks for coming," I mumbled, hoping the grandeur of the Ranch didn't put him off. "We're really giving you a run for your money today." I hadn't wanted to drag him into a second PBS emergency, but Raj was right about California law. When it came to removing skunks, it was one hundred yards or death.

"I'm doing this for Raj," he said. "Not you."

"Cool. Also. The cassowary?" I whispered, eyes darting around. "You'll come back for him tomorrow, right?"

"I'm not fucking touching that thing," dos Santos barked, sounding awfully spicy for a veterinarian. "As I told your emissary—"

"Oh, his name is Ivan—"

"I'm working on a solution. I talked to some guys in Brawley . . ."

"As long as there's a plan. I don't want the nitty-gritty. Now. Back to the badgers. That's the car." I pointed to Spencer's rental. "There are seven inside. Two got out and are wandering the grounds."

"The grounds," dos Santos repeated with a snort. "Welp. Off I go. Wish me luck."

As I watched him circle the vehicle, debating how the hell to get inside, I felt someone step up behind me. The waft of white wine gave her away.

"Care to explain what happened?" Talia said. She was back from checking on Spencer, who'd vomited from the stink badger scent. He'd also slipped and hit his head and was now going through a concussion protocol with Dad's personal physician. "A dozen *skunks*?"

"There are nine, actually. And they're stink badgers, not skunks," I said, crossing my arms, thinking my sister should be grateful the animals showed up to pull attention from the proposal fiasco.

"Gabby the math wiz. Pretty rude to make Raj find the missing ones."

"Yes. Poor Raj. I pray he knows what he's looking for, given he's never been acquainted with a stink badger before. It must be very confusing!"

Talia sighed deeply. "That was a flare, wasn't it?"

"It wasn't me," I said, as I started to panic about what Raj's stink badgers might mean for all of us, given the cassowary. We'd doubled down on PBS out here, and the realization sent shivers along my spine.

"You expect me to believe you had nothing to do with it?" Talia said. "The zoo guy seemed awfully familiar with you . . ."

He was also familiar with Raj, I did not point out. *Think about it*, I imagined saying. *I met Raj on a message board. You never asked what kind.* But Raj's PBS was Raj's business, and I wasn't going to out him now.

"Ya got me. The stink badgers were PBS-induced," I said, proud of myself for not totally lying.

"I knew it." As Talia cursed and complained, I took the opportunity to sneak a glimpse of dos Santos. He'd placed the trailer flush against a car door and was trying to open it without touching any badgers.

"I wasn't aware you were still doing the PBS thing," Talia said.

I cranked my head in her direction. "Yeah. I'm still 'doing' my incurable disease. Thanks for your concern, though."

"What's with the attitude? You can't be mad at me for not knowing. You never talk about your PBS. I can't remember the last time it came up."

"Can you blame me?" I said. "Everyone gets so annoyed, saying it's all in my head, while accepting flimsy excuses about flamingos in ponds in upstate New York. It's best to keep you all out of it. You're welcome."

"I did think the flamingos were strange," Talia said. "I was going to ask but didn't want to make you mad. I never meant to give you the impression I don't care. It's just . . ."

"It's easier to look away," I said. "I get it. We're all guilty of ignoring things, pretending problems don't exist. Gunn family trait."

"Um, not sure I'd agree. Aside from PBS on occasion . . ."

"Oh my God!" I tossed up my hands. "Be for real! Everything gets swept under the rug around here. My PBS. Uncle Doug. Ozzie and the Troubled Teen Industrial Complex. Heck, even Mom's mental state, if you want a deep cut." I was seconds from mentioning the eating disorder Talia did or didn't have—seriously, what was up with the fork dip in salad dressing routine?—but couldn't bring myself to say it out loud.

"Mom's mental state?" Talia repeated, looking at me like my hair was on fire.

"Her depression. Whatever." No one ever told me her official diagnosis, and what little information I'd gleaned over the years was strictly from Grandma Yvonne's snide remarks about Mom's *nervous temperament*, plus a few crumbs left by Diane here and there.

"Mom had incurable *cancer*," Talia said.

"Yeah. Okay," I said with a quick roll of the eyes. Sighing, I glanced back at the car. Dos Santos was now inside, wrestling with the stink badgers. This did not seem to be going well, and I briefly wondered whether I should step in.

"You said you believed me." Her cheeks flamed.

"Yeah, I did." She was right. I'd said I believed her, but maybe that wasn't true. "So, while we're on the topic of long-festering problems," I said, eager to move on. "What will we be doing about the tuxedoed visitor? A botched engagement. Awkward!"

Talia paused. A look of horror passed over her face, the reality of what happened hitting her at once. Stink badgers weren't even the top issue around here. "Oh, God. Oh my God! What did I do?" she wailed. "Spencer will never forgive me. I fucked things up, didn't I?"

"Probably," I said. "But do you even want to be with Spencer? It sort of seems . . ."

"Spencer is great," she said, with force, like Tony the Tiger talking about Frosted Flakes. "The absolute best."

"Hmmm. To each her own, I guess."

"But I'm so confused." Talia's shoulders dropped, and her gaze followed. She stared at the ground, eyes glistening in the zoo van's headlights. "Sometimes when I look at him, I think this is not it. Then the next minute it's like, who am I to dump this man?"

I blinked, pondering where to begin, when a metal door slammed. Seven stink badgers had been successfully moved into the trailer. The other two would have to figure out life on their own.

"My feelings are complicated," Talia continued, and I watched as Mindy offered dos Santos use of a shower. Sometimes she wasn't the worst. Who knew. "Spencer is a catch. And he loves me. I forgot, being so far away."

I shook my head. This was half her problem. Unless something was right in front of her face, Talia had a hard time buying into it.

"Him loving *you* isn't a reason to stay together," I said, despite being wildly unqualified to offer romantic advice. "I mean, it's a start. It's necessary. But shouldn't it go both ways?"

"You don't like him. I get it."

"It doesn't matter whether I like him. The real question is, do you?"

# Chapter Fifty-Eight

## Talia

Raj sat on the edge of the Jacuzzi, his legs dangling in the water, the lights reflecting in his glasses. The faint scent of skunk—sorry, *stink badger*—lingered in the air.

"Sooooo . . ." Talia said, sitting beside him. She pulled up her sweats and dipped her feet into the spa. "How's your night going? Pretty uneventful, huh?"

"I told you 'going for a swim' was a bad idea."

Talia winced, recalling how she'd begged him to leave the party. *Don't be a stick in the mud! Let's take a dip!* He'd refused because it wasn't swimming weather, and anyway he hadn't brought a swimsuit to the Ranch. Talia laughed and said no swimsuits required. *Oh, calm down! Wear your boxers!* No one would be around the main house tonight. They were all at the party, and guests had been instructed to park by HQ.

*Come on, Raj. Do you want to make the most of the night or not?* Talia was trying to sound sexy and fun but suspected she came across as impossibly awkward. But Raj ultimately relented, and now this. The most humiliating night of their lives.

"I'm sorry. For everything. There's no need for you to be embarrassed," Talia said, speaking so quickly she might've skipped a few words. "This is on me. And you probably don't care one way or another, but my relationship is officially over."

The breakup was easy, as far as breakups went. Spencer was

the wronged party, and Talia needed to grovel to win him back but couldn't bring herself to do it. Gabby's question hit hard—*did* she like him? Talia's inability to readily access the answer told the story. Spencer booked a flight out for tomorrow.

"Anyway. Chapter closed!" Talia's voice was thin, her brain scrambled. "Soooo . . . feel free to chime in."

"I'm still trying to . . . work out what happened," Raj said haltingly. "It was a . . ."

"Shit show. Yeah." Talia flicked her hair behind her shoulders. "Listen. I want you to stay. But I also understand if you need to go. Either way, I'm sorry. I never expected Spencer to show up, but I should've been more forthright. There's something about being here. You said it yourself. It's like some kind of alternate reality."

Talia studied Raj. He appeared calm, thoughtful even, and she felt momentarily hopeful he didn't hate her guts.

"As for the skunks," Talia went on. "Stink badgers. It was sweet of you to try and help catch the runaways. You almost got the one!"

"Hmm," Raj said, and his eyes slid away. She couldn't fathom what was going through his mind.

"Who knew that animal existed? And God, the smell. Spencer is puking his guts out as we speak." When she checked Raj again, his expression had turned serious. "Raj . . . ?"

"We need to talk about the stink badgers."

Talia groaned, covering her face. "Ugghhhh. There's an explanation. You're not going to believe me, but I swear to God it's true." She dropped her hands. "It's Gabby. She has a condition. It's extremely rare."

"PBS," Raj said.

All air briefly left Talia's lungs. "She told you?"

"First time we met."

"Um. Okay." Talia swallowed and puzzled through this, wondering if she could take it as anything less than a personal insult. "Good for her. Not sure what it means when some escape, but I guess we'll find out . . ."

"So you believe her," Raj said.

Talia blinked. "About the PBS? Yes. Obviously."

Raj smiled, and now she wondered what the hell was going on. "I think Gabby has at times questioned whether you truly accepted it as a real syndrome."

"Of course I do," Talia said emphatically, for Raj's benefit and for hers. "I just wish she'd be more open about it. Yes, it took time to come to terms with the diagnosis. Because—sorry—it's so bizarre. But, like, she has it? So admit what's going on? I'm her sister. It's so annoying. You have no idea."

"Don't be too hard on her. I'm sure it's difficult for her to discuss."

"Didn't hesitate to tell you, though!" Talia tossed her hands into the air. "You probably think I'm being mean but she's so weird and sneaky about it. She even tried to claim she had nothing to do with the stink badgers."

"Maybe she didn't?" Raj suggested.

"Come on. They wouldn't just magically appear, and she admitted—"

"Stop." Raj grabbed both her hands, which she'd previously been flailing around. "Gabby didn't cause the problem," he said, and Talia froze. "Not this one, at least."

"There are more?!"

"Talia. The stink badgers *are* because of PBS. But they belong to me."

# Chapter Fifty-Nine

Talia peered outside. Inhaling, she stepped onto the landing and looked around. The Ranch seemed normal, its usual self, making Raj's barrage of texts seem even stranger.

> Stay in the apartment.
> Keep the door locked.
> Whatever you do, don't go near the recreation pavilion.

Raj was very serious but these warnings might as well have been an open invitation. Talia was helpless against her own curiosity. Nosiness, some called it.

Gingerly Talia crept down the stairs. The apartment was way out in the sticks, by Mom's art studio—incidentally, now missing its roof—but it was Raj's place, and she'd stayed overnight. It didn't matter that they'd merely talked, and nothing physical happened. It was a bad look, especially with Spencer still somewhere on the property. Luckily this part of the Ranch was empty and, after a quick scan of her surroundings, Talia sprinted to the dirt road.

She took a circuitous route toward the recreation pavilion, to make it appear to anyone watching as though she'd come from another direction. As she passed the family barn, Talia noticed how quiet it was. Almost too quiet. Until she reached the horse trail and heard a faint yelling.

Talia picked up her pace. As the basketball court came into view, two landscapers blew past in a golf cart, followed by an ambulance. Talia broke into a full jog and soon spotted a familiar figure in the distance. Was that . . . ? Ozzie? *Oh, shit.* Well, that probably explained the sirens.

# Chapter Sixty

## Ozzie

His oldest sister was not blessed with athletic prowess, which she demonstrated by running at him like a drunk, red-faced puppet. Ozzie was low-key worried she might need an ambulance, too.

"Where did you come from?" she asked, huffing and puffing and blowing the little pigs' houses down.

"New York?" Ozzie said.

"Yes. Obviously." Talia's eyes darted toward the recreation pavilion, and it dawned on Ozzie that she'd already chalked the melee up to *him*.

"I literally just got here," Ozzie said before Talia had the chance to sneak in a comment. He couldn't believe he'd traveled all this way, only to be blamed for something the moment he walked onto the premises. "I have no idea what's going on," he added. "That guy—" Ozzie gestured to a fireman blocking the door "—won't let me in. I'm guessing it's some sort of electrical fire?"

"Fire," Talia repeated, scoffing. "Do you even smell smoke? Somebody's clearly hurt. There's an ambulance. Right." She pointed. "There."

Ozzie started to suggest that perhaps the fire was out, and the ambulance one of those "just in case" situations, when Ustenya came flying around the corner in a sports bra and a pair of bike shorts. *Hottie with a body for real*, Ozzie thought. *Good for her.*

"Surprise!" Ozzie said. "Guess who's back!"

Their stepmother sprinted at them, screaming their names, using some new idiom about beasts in a gym.

"Ustenya," Talia said, "why are you here? You were supposed to leave last night."

"The beast in the gym! The beast in the gym!" Ustenya said. She hurled her body into Talia's, burying her face in her chest. Meanwhile, Talia stood frozen, stiff-armed, seemingly unsure how to respond.

"Hey, U-ten," Ozzie said, rubbing her back. "Slow down. Tell us what's wrong. Whatever it is, we'll deal with it—"

Ustenya glanced up. Trails of mascara tears streaked her cheeks. "No, Oscar. It won't be okay." She snuffled, and heaved, and when she finally got ahold of herself said, "Something has happened to your dad. Nothing will be okay ever again."

# Chapter Sixty-One

## Gabby

We barreled down the back roads in Ozzie's rental car, Talia gripping the wheel, her mouth in a tight, angry line. Nobody had any details about the incident other than the fact Dad and Spencer went to work out, saw "a beast in the gym," and were *both* hospitalized.

"I thought the gym was abandoned," I said for the tenth or twelfth time. "We all saw it, remember? Tarps covered everything?"

Talia punched the gas, and I closed my eyes, my heart beating a million miles per hour. It'd been pounding since the sound of sirens woke me up and I checked my phone to find a thousand missed calls and texts. By the time I'd hauled ass to the recreation pavilion in bare feet, the ambulance was gone. None of the people still around had seen Dad, and his physical state remained unclear.

"One of you said it looked like it hadn't been touched in years," I added.

"But, like, you put a dinosaur in there and didn't tell anyone?" Ozzie said, and at least one sibling was speaking to me.

"It showed up right before Dad's party," I said. "And we planned to deal with it in the morning. How was I supposed to know Spencer would convince Dad to work out for the first time since we arrived?"

And Ivan—poor Ivan. He felt like hell, but none of this was his fault. He'd guarded the pavilion's entrance all night, but unfortunately Dad and Spencer went in through the back.

"When are you going to realize you don't exist in a vacuum?" Talia said. She was furious but had acknowledged my existence, which was a step in the right direction. "What you do affects other people."

"For real, Bags," Ozzie said. "You done fucked up." He was right, and watching him and Talia band together against me threw another hurt on top of the pile.

After driving the rest of the way in frantic silence, we staggered into the tan and brown and beige waiting room of the Gunn Hospital Critical Care Pavilion. They refused to update us, as per Ustenya's request. All the nurse could say was Dad was stable and would be in surgery for another three to four hours.

*Three to four hours?* I flinched against this punch. What if Dad was permanently injured or died? I'd never be able to live with myself. As for Spencer, he strutted out not five minutes after we arrived, the only hint of a scuffle his slightly ripped T-shirt and the medium-sized bandage on his forearm.

"Anyone else get mauled by a dinosaur?" he said. "Check it out." Spencer lifted his bandage to reveal a single red mark. It was neither particularly long nor especially deep. I scowled. Some guys had all the luck.

"Wow," Talia said, running her finger along the mark. "I'm so glad you're okay."

Spencer looked at Ozzie. "Hey, man. What's up? You're the last person I expected to be here."

"Same," Ozzie said.

Spencer pressed the bandage back onto his skin. "Jesus Christ, that bird goes hard. I can't believe we made it out alive."

"How *did* you escape?" I asked, and Spencer couldn't have missed the tone in my voice. It's not that I wanted him disemboweled or anything, but why wasn't *he* the one in surgery?

"Well, some gut instinct told me to stare the motherfucker dead in the eyes and use a pool cue at him to fend him off."

"Unbelievable," I muttered. It was exactly what dos Santos had advised.

According to Spencer, by the time he grabbed the pool cue, Dad was on the ground. It wasn't possible to repel the cassowary while also calling for help, and so he screamed and screamed until a landscaper appeared. He alerted the security team, and they dialed 911.

"Don't worry, guys," Spencer said, "Your dad's gonna be fine. He's a tough old man."

"Thanks, Spence," Talia said, and threw her arms around his neck.

After they parted, she stepped back. Spencer glanced away and blushed. "I should head to the airport," he said.

Talia nodded. "I'll walk you out," she said, placing a hand on his back. They disappeared through the automatic doors, and Ozzie and I were left to stew and—separately—imagine the worst.

# Chapter Sixty-Two

## Ozzie

Even though he'd deleted his social media, Ozzie was happy to fake-scroll if it meant ignoring Gabby. Talia was outside, walking Spencer to his car for twenty freaking minutes, apparently.

"So, the *Winnie the Pooh* map," Gabby piped in, and Ozzie almost lost his damned mind. Oh, if she was gonna make him talk, they'd *talk*.

Ozzie straightened out of his previously slouched position. "Are you deadass harassing me about my assets right now? When our dad is in surgery?"

"No! Not at all!" Her face flamed. "I heard your buyer fell through, so I wanted to apologize."

"You already did," Ozzie said and slumped back in his chair. "Do you know how annoying it is to pick up your phone and see a thousand voicemails?"

"Okay, it wasn't a *thousand*," Gabby muttered, and Ozzie rolled his eyes.

"Go play with a dinosaur," he said.

"Just hear me out for a second. You haven't been around, so you can't grasp how important the party was to Dad."

Ozzie glowered. *You haven't been here.* What a swipe.

"I had a plan, which involved locking him up while we got help. Not an easy task, by the way!" Gabby blathered about how she'd never dreamed Dad would use the gym, and he wasn't even supposed to still be in town. Plus, Ivan was keeping watch, et cetera.

"Oh my God!" Ozzie chucked his phone onto the table and sat all the way up again. "You have no self-awareness. None. Your excuse is the whole fucking problem. You do all kinds of shit to avoid the fray, and in the process create more . . ." He fished around for the word. "More fray!" It wasn't the perfect way to put it, but close enough.

"Fine! Message received! I suck. For the record, you don't need to be so pissed off." She sniffled. "No one could hate me more than I do at this moment."

Ozzie shook his head, almost feeling sorry for her. But *no*. He refused to fall for her watery-brown-eyes nice girl act. "The bird is the fucking least of it," he grumbled, and Gabby took a second to process this.

"Are you, um, uh . . ." she stammered. "Are you still upset about Canyonside? I thought we were on the same pa—"

"Yes, I'm still upset about Canyonside!"

Gabby blinked. "But I agree with you? It was shitty of me to watch while those men . . ." She let her words trail off.

"What happened nine months later?" Ozzie said. "When I came home *literally* broken? You said nothing. You didn't even ask where I'd gone." *This is it*, Ozzie realized. This was the rock in a shoe that'd niggled him for weeks. Gabby knew about the lawsuit, which meant she knew everything else, and she never said, *Hey, what happened?* Or even, *That sucks.*

"I was gone for nine months," Ozzie continued, "and you expected us to pick up where we left off. As though we were the same old Oz and Bags. Since you didn't ask then, I'm going to tell you everything now, because you need to hear it."

Nine months. Nine grueling months of physical and mental abuse at a "therapeutic boarding school" that had jack shit in terms of therapy or school. The so-called students spent most days digging pointless ditches (usually in bare feet), and the only "therapy" involved daily group sessions during which kids sat in a circle and verbally ripped one another to shreds. Every few weeks Ozzie met with a "counselor," who was some dipshit from the nearby town paid eight dollars an hour to list all the things he didn't like about him.

And then there were the punishments. One ill-timed eye roll could result in carrying a rock-filled backpack for days. Failure to complete an arbitrary number of pull-ups meant a week spent wearing a shirt that read "LOSER."

Ozzie was often deprived of food—not a punishment, more like the status quo—and thrown against walls and down the stairs. One of the "teachers" loved to knuckle him in the forehead as though knocking on a door. Weirdly, he found the physical abuse easiest to take, probably because it was unquestionably wrong, and definitely illegal, and it was nice to realize you weren't the problem here.

In the one call allowed per week, Ozzie told Dad what was going on, but, presumably, parents were coached not to listen to a word their manipulative little demons said. But Dad was no idiot and the accumulating bruises and cuts made him suspicious, likewise the multiple foot infections and wounds that refused to heal. When explanations about a fractured collarbone didn't add up, Dad hopped on the PJ and brought Ozzie home.

Once he comprehended the full scope of Ozzie's injuries—two to three concussions in addition to the broken bones—Dad unleashed the lawyers. Ozzie got his settlement, and Canyonside was shut down. Mostly Ozzie forgave their father because he likely thought he was doing the right thing. But trusting him was another matter. Having your kid abducted and shipped off without notice was some depraved shit. Ozzie didn't know if he'd ever get over it, but he'd been trying to for almost nine years.

"God. Ozzie," Gabby said, when he finished. All blood had

drained from her face. "I had no idea. Well, I had some idea but not the extent of it. I can't believe you still speak to Dad. Or me . . ."

"Come on, now . . ."

"I should've asked."

Ozzie nodded. "Asked, yes. Also, it would've been nice if you'd acknowledged I was home?"

Ozzie remembered it so clearly. Standing beside Dad in the elevator, a green duffel bag at his feet, expecting to see Gabby any minute. But when the elevator door slid open, the gray marble foyer was empty. As he shuffled down the hall, Gabby poked her head out of her bedroom and gave him a quick, hurried hug before slamming the door shut again.

"You didn't even bring your whole body out of your room," he said.

"Oh, God," Gabby groaned. "I *did* do that. There was a reason. I'm not making excuses. I was an asshole. But the day before you came home . . ." She cleared her throat, and a funny look wiggled across her face.

"Jesus. Was there an animal?"

"An emu?" she said, her voice cracking at a very high register. "I found him in my bathroom, guzzling water from my toilet for five minutes straight. They tend to fill up, an adaptation to Australia's harsh climate."

"Fascinating," Ozzie said flatly.

"Anyway. I didn't tell anyone. Long story short—and this is going to sound stupid—but I decided to keep him? Dad is so uptight about indoor animals, and I'd always wanted a pet."

"And you figured an emu would be chill?"

"I wasn't thinking, okay? But he was so cute, and I liked having him around. He sat there quietly, staring at me with his beady orange eyes, a dopey look on his face." She sighed. "I didn't know he was breaking into other people's apartments while I was at school."

"Hold on," Ozzie said, a new memory popping into his brain. "Was this why a cop came to our door the day after I got home?"

Gabby nodded. "To ask about our pet 'ostrich.' Which, like, *rude*. It's an emu."

"You little jerk!" Ozzie said, giving her a light shove. He was surprised to find himself smiling, and about forty percent less mad. "That scared the shit out of me."

"But I fessed up! Right away!"

"Wow. Thanks for not letting me take the fall for an *ostrich*," Ozzie said playfully. "So, what happened next?"

"The officer accused me of training it to break into our neighbors' apartments," Gabby said, "but I explained I wasn't interested in Mrs. Bianco's tacky-ass jewelry—no offense—and it was an innocent mistake. Emus eat household stuff. He was just being himself!" Because the cop couldn't prove she'd broken any laws, he let it drop. So when Ozzie sensed she was hiding out in her bedroom, he was correct.

"That's me," Gabby said, "causing more fray. And for the record, I *was* worried about you, especially when I saw your arm in the sling. I wanted to know what happened." Biting the inside of her cheek, she seemed to consider this. "Or maybe I didn't?" she said, and hallelujah, some actual learning could be done. "I convinced myself Dad wouldn't have sent you anywhere too awful, and now you were home, so why rehash the past." Her expression soured. "Good Lord, I sound like Dad. *Onward and upward*. Focus on the positive. Blech."

Ozzie chuckled. "And I got that sweet, sweet payout."

"Right," she said, her face darkening. "You *did* deserve all that money, but not the suffering that preceded it."

"I deserved it a little," Ozzie said. "I was being kind of a shit."

"Gee! I wonder why! Our mom died suddenly, and nobody talked about it."

"Yeah, because nothing changed. Right?" He gave an exaggerated wink. "It was no big deal, life goes on, blah blah blah. In your version of events, anyway."

Gabby blinked. "Huh?"

"That's what you said in the recreation pavilion," he reminded her. "I agreed with you at the time. On some level it's true, but also, not? Our day-to-day routines might've stayed the same, but our lives *were* different from then on. And you completely changed."

Gabby had the nerve to feign shock. "No, I didn't!"

"You did. You used to be so open and free and game for anything. After she died, you were secretive and closed off and, honestly, a lot less fun. We no longer had our little adventures."

"We were older," she said. "And that's when my PBS started."

PBS. Her excuse for everything. "Whatever you say," Ozzie said, shaking his head, now feeling more worn down than angry. He rose to his feet. "If you ask me, it's a bit of a chicken-and-egg scenario, but whatevs."

"Chicken-and-egg," Gabby repeated, narrowing her eyes. "Have you been talking to dos Santos?"

"The fuck? Two *Santas*? Why are you attempting to speak Spanish?"

Gabby stared at him—glared, even—but then her expression shifted, like a light had turned on. One could dream. "Ozzie—"

"Anyhow. Good chat," Ozzie said, grabbing his phone. "I'm gonna go fuck up some cafeteria fries. Stay here and watch Talia's stuff."

# Chapter Sixty-Three

## Gabby

I found Talia outside, sitting on a concrete bench.

"Well, three votes have been cast, and we've come to a unanimous decision," I said, plunking down. I placed her water bottle and purse on the ground near her feet. "I'm the asshole. If I'd texted you or Dad, everybody could've avoided the pavilion."

It was exactly what Diane said months ago when I was contemplating the flamingos in my pond. *Your good intentions always spiral out of control.*

"And in case you're wondering," I continued, "the cassowary should be gone soon. There's some guy in East County who agreed to take it. He has a farm or something." A farm with no other animals, I hoped. This was one flare I would not be checking up on.

"What's done is done," Talia said, her eyes fixed on a white Tesla pulling into the parking lot. "You weren't trying to hurt anyone, and Spencer really thinks Dad will be okay. There wasn't much blood."

"I noticed the same thing!" I blurted, then promptly covered my mouth. But Talia didn't react. Instead, she let out a long, sad sigh. I did not like this resigned side of her. I preferred quick-to-anger Talia, the gal with the short fuse. The *reasonably* short fuse, I recognized. The rest of us didn't make it easy for her.

"Just so we're clear, I agree with the theory that I'm not actually nice."

"Gabby—"

"And, also? Things did change for me after Mom died," I said and Talia jerked her head toward me. "I chalked it up to the onset of my PBS, but now I think maybe it was only an excuse." My instinct was to brush off Ozzie's words, dismiss him as full of shit, but he understood human nature better than anyone. "We were *all* in a state of shock. You'd dropped out of school—"

*"Temporarily."*

"And Ozzie dialed up his shenanigans one thousand percent. I was initially kind of numb, and Dad kept praising my strength, saying he felt lucky he didn't have to worry about me. And I thought, yeah, true, I'm totally fine. I barely saw Mom and still had Diane. That same old line."

I paused to check Talia, but she simply stared, mouth slightly open, as she absorbed all this.

"You've always pressured me to talk about her," I continued, "and I didn't want to. One, because we had such wildly different memories. And second . . ." I batted this around in my mind. "Honestly, I was pissed!" The forcefulness of the words surprised me. Maybe Talia wasn't the only person dragging Mom along wherever she went. She was just capable of admitting it.

"I shouldn't have been angry," I said. "What happened was awful and tragic and not her fault, but when we were there that summer, she was openly bragging about not taking her meds."

It wasn't the first time. Mom believed antidepressants made her foggy, less attuned to her work, and if it was a choice between art and mental stability, she chose art every time. She'd joke that her mind was "natural speed," and if she could bottle it up, she'd be richer than Dad.

"I hated how she treated her mental illness like an extremely helpful drug she could consume as needed," I admitted. "She was our mother. Didn't she have an obligation to take care of herself? Put her oxygen mask on first, et cetera. Not a fair assessment, but here we are."

I shook my head, reminding myself I was no longer thirteen years old, and now I knew better. Mom wasn't selfish. She must have believed she was in control of the chaos. We'd all done it to some degree or another. "One last thing . . ." I said and eyed Talia again. She was awfully quiet, and I wasn't sure how to take it. "I'm sorry for questioning the cancer narrative. It wasn't fair."

Talia lowered her chin. I watched as a single tear dropped onto her clasped hands. A second tear, onto one of her platinum Cartier LOVE bracelets.

"The cancer thing," Talia said, and my heart boomed in my ears. "You thought it was an excuse, a way to make her death more acceptable. The truth is . . ." She swallowed, a big lump that seemed to stick on the way down. "You might be right. I don't know if her cancer came back. I only heard about it after the fact, same as you."

# Chapter Sixty-Four

## Talia

"There weren't any signs of cancer," Talia said, zipping her diamond *T* pendant up and down its chain. "None that I saw, but we never discussed health stuff. I left in August, and she died in October, so it might've come back in between. I had my doubts but accepted Dad's explanation."

"Why didn't you tell us?" Gabby asked. Talia couldn't look at her. She couldn't bear to see her expression.

"I'm not sure," Talia admitted, and it was the truest thing she could've said. "Probably because it was only a suspicion. Also, I really needed to believe the cancer narrative? Otherwise, I would've been consumed by guilt. I was already worried you and Ozzie blamed me for not preventing what happened."

Gabby didn't say anything, and Talia's body tensed. She'd been right all along.

"Your silence tells me everything," Talia said, jaw quivering. "We all agree. I should've stopped it."

"Talia! The silence is because I'm literally speechless. How could you have stopped anything? You weren't even there!"

"But I knew she'd gone off her meds."

"We *all* did. It wasn't exactly a secret."

"Still. I was older," she said, "and didn't intervene. I figured she wasn't hurting anyone, and she wasn't visibly *depressed*."

If anything, it was the opposite. That summer, their mom

had never been more vibrant, more interested in the world. Never more interested in Talia, she was only realizing now.

"But what could you have done?" Gabby asked. "If Mom wasn't listening to her doctor, she wouldn't have listened to you, and definitely not Dad." As Gabby spoke, Talia's heart swelled with gratitude. She hadn't understood how badly she'd needed to hear someone else say these things. "Mom was the adult—"

"Technically, so was I."

"Okay, but barely. And if you somehow managed to talk her into going back on her meds, how long would it have lasted? You couldn't stay at the Ranch forever."

"But I left," Talia said, wondering why the hell she seemed so intent on proving she deserved to be hated. "I went to school and stayed there, even when it became clear something was seriously off." As each week passed, Daphne got harder and harder to reach, or she'd call at odd hours and jabber away. Mindy said she was working a lot, hardly leaving the barn.

"What were you going to do, fly all the way back?"

Talia finally looked at her. "Mom begged me not to leave. She wanted me to stay until the end of the year."

Talia watched a jolt of shock run through her sister. Gabby would blame her after all, and fair enough. But just as quickly, Gabby composed herself. She grabbed both of Talia's hands.

"Listen to me. You couldn't have changed anything. Not if you stayed another month, a year, two years. It wasn't your job."

"If not me, who? Mom and Aunt Dee weren't speaking, and her lifestyle wasn't conducive to forming lasting close friendships."

Gabby smirked. "Nor her tendency to ask friends if she could paint their children nude. I'm sorry!" she said, laughing when she clocked Talia's wide, alarmed eyes. "But you have to admit, most people would find that off-putting."

"You're not wrong," Talia said, and a smile snuck out. "I

hope you don't think I'm being weird, implying I was her *only* friend, or the one thing she had to live for."

"I don't think you're being weird. Not about this, anyway." Gabby playfully bumped Talia's knee with hers. "And you *were* her closest friend. Closest everything."

With these words, Talia was swamped by a sudden and overwhelming sadness. She was supposed to be Daphne's favorite and had been trying to prove she was a good daughter, the *best* daughter, for decades now, and to what end? If something happened to Dad—God forbid—she'd technically be an orphan stuck with siblings she'd alienated most of her life.

"It's kind of insulting, actually," Gabby said, yanking Talia out of her own head. "To listen to you blame yourself for what happened to Mom when I directly caused an injury to our dad." Gabby laughed, but concern was written all over her face.

"I'll repeat your wise words. Dad's the adult and you're the child. It's not your fault."

"I'm not a child, and it literally is my fault."

"Maybe he shouldn't have been working out in an abandoned recreation pavilion."

Gabby chuckled, obligatory, pretending she believed this. "Come on," she said as she stood. "Let's find Ozzie. See if there's any update."

"Oh. Um. Thanks, but you go ahead. Text me if—"

"Nuh-uh," Gabby said, reaching out, pulling Talia to her feet. "No more doing this family bullshit alone." She put an arm around Talia's shoulders and led her back inside.

# Chapter Sixty-Five

## Gabby

At two o'clock, the doctor came out to announce Dad was in recovery. The surgery had gone well, and he didn't expect any lasting damage. With these words, I almost collapsed in relief. Perhaps if Dad could fully recover from what happened, so would I.

"I knew he'd kick ass," Ozzie said and shoved a french fry into his mouth. He hopped to his feet. "It's Marston fucking Gunn. He's goated."

"So goated," Talia agreed.

"When can we see him?" Ustenya asked, materializing out of nowhere. Aside from a text asking whether anyone wanted tacos, she'd kept her distance. "How is he feeling? Is he normal?"

"She means is he okay," I clarified.

"Uh. Yes." The doctor adjusted his fingerprint-smudged glasses. "He still has a breathing tube and will be in the ICU a bit longer for monitoring. Standard for this type of procedure. But everything's been textbook, start to finish."

"Textbook?" I repeated.

"You've done this before?" Talia asked.

The doctor laughed haltingly. "I'll take that to mean I appear impossibly young. Yes. I've performed the surgery many times." He turned to address Ustenya. "Now, young lady, if you'd like to avoid a return trip, your husband must follow instructions more carefully this time."

I glanced at Talia. Her features were pinched together in confusion. Ozzie was leaning forward, squinting, as if reading something on TV.

"We'll send Mr. Gunn home with several prescriptions," the doctor continued, "and a list of instructions, which will include lifestyle adjustments."

*Lifestyle adjustments.* Was Dad missing a limb? Would he be forced to wear a colostomy bag? Was he permanently unable to walk? All because of *me*? Dread landed like a boulder in my gut.

"Yes, of course, we'll do whatever you advise," Ustenya said, and thanked him again, using some idiom from the old country about a pot of stew.

"What will we need to do to the house?" I said, my mind going wild as it conjured ramps and elevators and widened doorways. "We'll probably have to do some kind of remodel to accommodate him?"

"Before you jump to conclusions, or God forbid involve contractors, maybe read the instructions first?" the doctor said. "Most of the recommendations are very basic and don't require extra equipment. Better stress management, for example. Eating a low-fat, low-salt diet that's rich in fruits, vegetables, and whole grains. Being more diligent about taking heart meds."

I cocked my head. "Managing stress?" I repeated.

"Heart meds?" Talia said, as Ozzie asked, "What the hell?"

"These might sound like minor suggestions, but they can have a tremendous cumulative effect."

"Yes, yes, message received." Ustenya rushed toward the doctor and physically turned him around. "Thank you so much for the update. Glad all is fine! Let's pray it continues." She spit over her shoulder twice for good luck. "Now get back in there and finish taking care of my husband!"

"He must take it seriously this time," the doctor said, stepping out of Ustenya's reach. He pivoted to face us. "I spoke to the team at Mount Sinai. They told me when they first diagnosed Mr. Gunn with CAD, they'd warned him that a complete blockage could result in a major cardiac event. From what I've gathered, he followed none of the instructions, and the heart attack came to pass. We're fortunate his son-in-law had the foresight to call an ambulance right away."

"Not his son-in-law," Talia said unnecessarily.

"What the fuck," Ozzie said.

"Ozzie! Language!" Ustenya barked, even though she said *fuck* all the damned time.

"Wait." I blinked. "Dad wasn't disemboweled by a bird?"

"A pterodactyl, basically," Ozzie clarified.

The doctor blanched. He hurriedly flipped through the chart, no doubt panicked he'd shared medical information with the wrong family. "Marston Gunn," he said, and peered up. When no one corrected him, the doctor lowered the clipboard. "I don't know what you're referring to, but your father has coronary artery disease. He chose to roll the dice and not do anything surgical. But he didn't follow treatment protocol, resulting in the heart attack he suffered today."

---

The story went like this. Last summer, after repeated bouts of chest pain and frequent shortness of breath, Ustenya forced Dad to see a doctor, where they discovered a buildup of plaque in the wall of an artery, which affected the flow of blood to the heart. Their father was presented with three options.

On the most extreme end, he could undergo a bypass to create an alternate path around the blockage. A second, less invasive choice was to use a balloon to widen the artery and insert a stent. Open-heart surgery wasn't exactly risk-free, and both the surgery and the stent merely reduced symptoms but didn't solve CAD. Dad picked the third option: cardiac rehabilitation, but didn't really do this, either.

"Your father was impossible!" Ustenya said. "Sauerkraut for

brains. He told me no to everything under the sun. No surgery, no balloon, and his diet was horse dick. I thought it was going to kill him. I'd be a widow, and he'd be smelling worms from below."

"Yet . . . he decided to run for office?" Talia said. "And you were fine with it?"

"I was not fine! When he mentioned it, I almost divorced him on the spot."

Alas, Ustenya loved him too much to follow through, and with her back against the wall, she supported the politics thing, hiring a personal physician and dragging his children along for the ride. If things went sideways, at least the whole family would be there when he *paid the priest.*

"I figured he'd enjoy having you around," Ustenya said. I looked at my siblings, and we all silently agreed that the notion Dad enjoyed our presence was a wild assumption to make. "And maybe a new adventure would be a stress reliever. He could forget about losing the old business and focus on something new." Ustenya's brow darkened. "But I did not anticipate he might be the loser in last place."

"Why didn't you tell us?" Talia crossed her arms. "It makes us look like idiots, being kept in the dark."

"Parents should not shackle children with their problems," Ustenya said.

"We're adults," Talia said. "And if our dad drops dead, it's our problem, too. We've been shielded from a lot of stuff over the years, and I'm not sure whether you've noticed, but we're all a bit screwed up."

Ozzie cackled. "Heard that," he said.

Ustenya sighed and closed her eyes. "You're right, of course. All these things you're saying. But we are humans. And humans take a long time to learn from our mistakes."

# California Democrats cancel convention among norovirus surge

BY DAMIEN PATTERSON, *The Sacramento Bee*

SACRAMENTO—A violent stomach flu caused California Democratic Party officials to cancel the remainder of their state convention on Saturday night, "for the health and safety of our delegates."

California Democrats had been meeting in Sacramento this weekend to consider candidate endorsements ahead of the March primary, including for the competitive U.S. Senate race that features three sitting U.S. House members.

"It was horrific," one delegate told *The Sacramento Bee*. "People were vomiting right there in the convention hall."

According to several independently verified reports, by three o'clock, most of the toilets were backed up, and every trash can was full to overflowing with underwear and soiled khakis.

"The things I've seen," another delegate said, shaking her head. "I don't think I'll ever recover."

By six o'clock, the chaos reached its peak, with all but two toilets declared officially out of service, and one third of the delegation lying on the floor. Democratic Party spokesperson Keisha Finch was forced to announce the evening's events had been canceled.

"For the health and safety of our delegates and convention participants, we are canceling tonight's caucus meetings, hospitality suites, and VoteFest," Finch said.

Voting for the U.S. Senate endorsement finished minutes prior to the cancellation, but no candidate reached the 60% of votes required to earn the party's formal nod. Given the crowded and well-funded field, this was not a surprising result.

U.S. Rep. David Slimp has been widely deemed the favorite due to name recognition and his $35 million war chest, but in this first round of voting, he was second to U.S. Rep. Sandra

Grant. U.S. Rep. Angie Parker came in third. The full breakdown was as follows:

Rep. Sandra Grant: 934 (40.2%)

Rep. David Slimp: 870 (37.5%)

Rep. Angie Parker: 436 (18.8%)

Marston Gunn: 47 (2.0%)

35 delegates did not cast votes for any candidate.

Marston Gunn, a businessman best known as the former chief of For Real TV and brother to disgraced financier Douglas Gunn, of the notorious Granny Gate scandal, has seen his support increase in recent weeks. Based on polling results, his "gravitas" appeals to voters, likewise his ideas to tackle the California housing crisis. His more popular stances include banning hedge funds from buying residential units, stricter restrictions around flipping homes, and raising taxes on billionaires to fund the voucher program.

Although these plans have resonated with voters, insiders say Gunn intends to back off on housing and instead focus on Congress's ineptitude. It's a significant change in tack and one wonders whether he's shooting himself in the foot. Notably, Gunn was a no-show at the weekend's events.

"He got a bit over his skis," says independent Democratic strategist Theo Lemke. "Gunn put a stake in the ground without thinking through the repercussions and now he needs money from the very people who profit from an unjust system. It's an odd choice to skip the convention, which would've given him the opportunity to reframe his change in position. I guess he got lucky with the norovirus outbreak."

Gunn could not be reached for comment, though his spokesperson notably didn't refute the rumored change in position. Whether this is a fatal mistake remains to be seen.

# Chapter Sixty-Six

## Talia

Talia sat in the rental car, staring at the hospital. Gabby and Ozzie waited near the entrance. Dad was out of the ICU, and Talia needed a moment to collect herself before going inside.

The past forty-eight hours had been a blur as they processed their new reality while attempting to rid themselves of a violent dinosaur-bird. Talia gave her sister a ton of credit for dealing with her PBS alone for so many years. Gabby showed her the tattoos, and there were a lot of them. Talia hadn't been aware of any screaming hairy armadillos or swamp rabbits.

After dispatching the cassowary, the three Gunns combed through the doctor's instructions, stocking the kitchen with the right food and briefing Dad's traveling physician on the new protocol. Honestly, what had he been doing all these months if not making sure Dad stayed healthy?

"He'd visibly lost a step lately," Gabby said as they broke it all down.

"Yeah, and he was super wheezy at the volleyball game," Ozzie agreed.

Talia thought he definitely seemed older—paler, thinner, worn out—but had chalked it up to the campaign, and losing FDG. They'd all sensed something was off but no one spoke it out loud and now it made Talia wonder whether maybe, just *maybe*, Mom's downward spiral was obvious only in hindsight.

Would Dad stay in the race? The answer remained TBD, and Ustenya threatened to poison anyone who asked him directly. If he did keep going, they'd need to devise entirely new messaging. Talia couldn't believe he'd jettisoned the housing angle without telling her. Then again, this was also a man who'd harbored a secret heart condition, so who really knew. She worked hard to tamp down her anger about his change of position because you weren't supposed to be mad at an old man in an ICU.

"There go my plans to change the world," she'd half joked to Raj last night, as they sat beside the outdoor fireplace, sharing a bottle of wine. She didn't know what they meant to each other, or what would happen in the future, and maybe that was okay.

"He wasn't going to change the world," Raj said because he understood her joking was something less than "half."

"Yeah, my expectations were high, but if changes don't come from above, how will anything get fixed? It's quite demoralizing. Even Gabby's packing it up and going home!"

"If you're expecting a politician to save you, you're screwed. You'll only ever be let down. You need to start smaller, and accept that if you can make things a little easier for one person, then it's a win."

"But is it a win? You can't move anyone higher up on the list," Talia said. "You've personally put hundreds of hours into LASD, and you'll put in hundreds more, but every problem you run up against is ultimately unsolvable."

"True, but I can give them hope, and the knowledge someone out there gives a shit. Sometimes it's enough. You have to remember who you're doing this for. And the answer isn't, you know, society."

"I didn't say *society*," Talia grumbled as his words began to soak in. *Remember who you're doing this for.* Raj was right, of course. Talia came to California to help Dad, not help other people through him. That she'd have to do on her own.

Suddenly, somebody rapped on the car window. Talia almost

jumped out of her clogs. It was Ozzie, motioning for her to hurry up. They'd driven all the way to the hospital, and she should exit the car at some point. Gabby was already inside.

Talia kicked open the door. "Sorry," she said, stepping out. "Just pondering some stuff. Also, procrastinating. I'm nervous to see him. I'm not even sure why." She weighed this for a beat. "Maybe I'm afraid of how he'll look, or what he'll say. Maybe I'm afraid of what *I'll* say. Like, what the fuck, Dad?"

Ozzie chuckled. "In reference to . . . ?"

"I dunno, take your pick!" she said as they stepped up onto the curb. "This campaign. His platform. The heart disease."

"And he'll be like, counterpoint, 'the fuck happened with Spencer?'" Ozzie said, a devilish glint in his eyes. Talia groaned. "Did I hear correctly? Were you caught fucking Raj in the Jacuzzi?"

"Oscar!" Talia shrieked, slapping him with the back of her hand. "I was not *fucking* Raj in the Jacuzzi."

"Somewhere else, then?" Ozzie said, and Talia punched him this time. "JK, JK. I do *not* want to know the details. But God, what a way for the guy to find out. Sorry, sis, I love ya." He rumpled her hair. "But I've gotta be Team Spencer."

"Yeah, no, I get it." They walked through the hospital's sliding doors. "But in a month, he'll be thanking me. Probably earlier. It was the best result for everyone. Not the way it happened, obviously."

Talia didn't feel particularly sad, which was a weird thing to say after two years with someone, but her heart was never fully in it, she realized now. Had it ever been, in any relationship? Talia was a serial monogamist, starting the summer after her mom died, when a guy she met at Columbia invited her to spend June and July trotting the globe. New Zealand and Mallorca and his family's cabin in Maine. *Why not?* Talia had thought. Better than thinking about how she wasn't at the Ranch.

The travel was fun but not life-changing, yet they stayed together for eighteen months. Her next relationship wasn't any shorter or deeper, and this pattern repeated. Boyfriend after boyfriend, Talia always held back, as though she feared giving her all but not getting enough in return.

They walked into the waiting room, where Gabby was chatting up a nurse. "What about you?" Talia asked Ozzie. "Are you nervous to see him at all?"

"Nah. It's Dad. He's just a person, like the rest of us."

Talia snorted. "So casual. So chill. Explains why you're the favorite."

Ozzie looked at her. "Literally the first time anyone's ever said that."

"Because no one has to say it out loud. It'd be like pointing out, hey, there's oxygen in this room."

"I'm oxygen." He bobbed his head. "Nice."

"The worst part is, you come by it naturally. You don't even have to try." Talia flashed a grin. "And you're lucky I don't hate you for it." Not anymore.

# Chapter Sixty-Seven

## Gabby

"Remind me," Ozzie said as we approached Dad's door. "Are we mad? Or are we saving our big feelings for later?"

"I'm not in a position to be mad at anyone," I pointed out.

Ozzie shrugged. "Personally? I'd rather have a dinosaur-induced heart attack than contract norovirus in a packed convention center."

"Here's an idea," Talia said. "Maybe we should try being . . . normal?"

Ozzie snorted. "Yeah. Good luck with that."

"And please, no one pressure Dad about the race. For those of us leaving the campaign . . ." She locked her eyes on mine. "Let's keep that info for later." Talia whipped back around and threw open the door to reveal Dad, propped up in bed, reading *The Wall Street Journal*. Old habits died hard.

"Nice crib," Ozzie said, sauntering in. "The decor is fire. Did you notice the nurses' stations are shaped like surfboards?"

Dad smiled in a tired, half-drunk way. "It's so good to see you all," he said. His voice was raspy and thin.

"How do you feel?" Talia said, pulling a chair up beside his bed. "You look fantastic!"

Fantastic was a stretch, but he didn't look terrible, especially for someone who'd undergone open-heart surgery. His skin was a little gray—not yellow, at least—and his hair was more salt than pepper, wavy and unkempt without the gel holding it in place.

"Bullshit," he said. "So. Who's going to explain the bird?"

"It was a flare," I said, stepping in front of my brother.

"Wow," Ozzie said. "Get it."

"You're welcome to speak to my doctor if you want reassurance that it's not migration or whatever," I added. The fact dos Santos worked for the zoo would not likely help my case, but he was all I had. "Also. Fun fact. The only 'expert' in the field thinks PBS is triggered when the person who has it suppresses important things."

*PBS.* I couldn't recall ever speaking those letters to Dad. When I was first diagnosed, Diane delivered the news while I sat beside her, mortified, picking at the hole in my jeans. To his credit, this time he didn't even flinch.

"Suppressing things seems to be a pattern around here." I took a step closer. "Seriously, Dad. What the hell? How could you keep a potentially fatal heart condition from us?"

"It's my health, not yours. And I didn't think you needed to know . . ."

"I appreciate your hesitancy," I said evenly, I hoped. "But, like, as a family, we have experience hiding medical stuff? And it hasn't really worked before?"

"Gabby. That's not fair. *You've* hidden your disease, not the rest of—" Talia began.

"I'm not talking about me," I said, and Dad startled. "I'm talking about Mom."

"Oh, shit," Ozzie said. He lowered onto the end of the bed, putting a hand on Dad's leg, as if anchoring him down.

"Did she have cancer? Or is that what you told people because it's more socially acceptable than suicide?"

"So much for acting normal," Talia groused.

"I'm sorry. My timing is shit," I added hastily. "But. Here we are."

A pained expression washed over Dad's face. *Great*, I'd probably just given him another jolt to the heart. I fought the urge to take it back, but no one was demonstrably angry, so I stood in this truth while we waited, exchanging anxious looks.

Finally Dad sighed. "To be perfectly honest," he said, "I'm not sure."

"What!" Talia chirped.

"We were separated, and she didn't keep me apprised about her illness day-to-day. She *was* in very poor health that fall and briefly hospitalized. With bits and pieces, I drew my own conclusions, and no one gave me a reason to believe otherwise. Not even her sister, her next of kin."

I nodded, silent, because I'd suspected this all along. Admittedly, her semi-estranged sister wasn't the most reliable narrator, but did it matter? Mom had been in pain either way, and we'd never really understand what happened, just like we'd never really understand her. We all sat on this, ruminating for what felt like ten minutes until Dad softly cleared his throat.

"Probably handled it poorly," he said. "Handled most things poorly. I was a bad parent. Guess I don't need to tell you that." We protested as he laughed grimly. "I never imagined I'd be completely in charge of you guys. Then your mom left, and I was fixated on keeping you safe and in New York. I never questioned whether you were getting your emotional needs met."

I tilted my head. "What do you mean, keeping us in New York?"

"The custody battle," Dad said. "With you and Ozzie. You remember."

My heart stopped. A bad analogy, seeing as how we were in the cardiac unit, but it was the only way to describe the quick, sharp tug in my chest. "I absolutely do not recall a custody battle."

"Definitely fresh information," Ozzie concurred.

I glanced at Talia, but she stared down at her lap, refusing to meet my eyes. Was this what she meant when she said we could've spent more time at the Ranch, but Dad always got in the way?

The fight over custody, Dad explained, was why they never formally divorced. Talia was seventeen and allowed to decide for herself, but Mom demanded primary custody of Ozzie and me. Dad was willing to give her everything else she asked for—the Ranch, half his ownership in FDG—literally anything but that. Daphne loved us but was too unpredictable, and he didn't like the idea of us living so far away. He fought like hell, but they never came to an agreement. Then she died, settling the matter once and for all.

*I could've lived at the Ranch full-time?* Between this and Dad "fighting like hell," my mind was quietly blown. I'd always assumed we ended up with him because we were already in New York and it was easier for everyone.

"Maybe I should've given her what she wanted," Dad said. "I didn't really knock it out of the park in terms of parenting."

"Ah. It's fine." Ozzie slapped the air. "Doing the best you could."

"But why," I pressed. Unlike Ozzie, I couldn't so easily let it go. "If you wanted us, why didn't you say anything? Or explain what was happening? You let Mom leave and kept up the 'it's temporary' charade until it wasn't temporary anymore. Then we simply . . . carried on."

"You were young," Dad said as tears pooled in his blue, veiny eyes. "And you had Diane and seemed so happy, and it felt cruel to force you to dredge up old wounds."

"Diane was great," I said. "And I tried to be fine because everything was in turmoil, and I was afraid of causing more problems."

"Me," Ozzie said, raising a hand. "The turmoil is me."

"Meanwhile I had animals coming out my ass?"

"I know." Dad rubbed his face. "But I wasn't in my right

mind. Even though we were separated, I loved your mother. I just couldn't live with her. Her death left me devastated, and furious, and every other thing. It took me years to . . ." He rattled his head. "I'm not sure I'll *ever* get over it."

Just like that, the ice around my heart started to crack. "God, Dad," I said, lowering onto the bed, too. "I never thought about it that way." I never considered he might be grieving, too.

"I loved your mom," he said as a faraway look passed over his face. "When Daphne was doing well, she was *dazzling*. It's a tragedy she couldn't find help or accept help or give herself a chance to improve. Maybe she wasn't meant to live long. Who the hell knows." Sighing, Dad closed his eyes and sank back into his pillows. "I don't have the answers, and I'm sorry for all I did or didn't do. But I love you guys. And your being here, right now, in spite of everything, is one of the best things that's ever happened to me."

Ozzie smirked, though only Talia and I could see it. "All you needed was an ill-conceived senate run and a heart attack," he said.

Dad chuckled through his nose. "This campaign hasn't always been smooth," he said, speaking with his eyes shut. "But whatever happens, I don't regret it. My old life wasn't working, and I had to try something different. I'm glad I did while there was still time left on the clock."

# Chapter Sixty-Eight

## Ozzie

They tiptoed out of the hospital room, Ozzie bringing up the rear. As Talia and Gabby strode ahead, arms locked, Ozzie glanced back.

"Hey, Pops," he said quietly. His dad opened one eye. "I wanna say . . . you did a good job, like, overall. Big picture. Don't beat yourself up."

Dad pressed his lips together. Not a smile, exactly. "I'm sorry," he said. "For everything. But especially . . ." He swallowed. "Sending you to Utah was the biggest mistake of my life."

"Oh. Yeah. We're chill." Ozzie's stomach low-key churned for reasons not even he understood. Maybe he was afraid of what Dad would say, or what he'd leave out. When it came to Canyonside Academy, there were no right words.

"No. Seriously, son." *Son.* One brush with the word and Ozzie's shoulders hiked up to his ears. "I need to explain where I was coming from. You were . . . acting out."

"Setting fires for funsies, you mean." Ozzie was teasing, but also telling the truth, and it was one of those moments where he had to stop and think, *Wait, maybe I did deserve to spend some time in the teenage prison experiment.*

"Funsies. Yes. Very fun," Dad grumbled. "It wasn't the fire, per se, or the fact you were suspended. It felt like an escalation, and I was terrified of what might come next."

Dad was in this state of mind when the headmaster at Ozzie's school pushed a brochure across the table. Canyonside Academy. When good kids went south, they could turn them back around. And look at this place! A top-notch facility with beautiful dorms (barracks, really), an indoor pool (stock photo), a restaurant-quality kitchen (garbage food), and a cutting-edge education (Ozzie never set foot in a classroom).

"It seemed like the answer," Dad said, his eyes watering again. "And I wanted so badly to *fix* whatever was going on with you."

"Of course you did," Ozzie said. "Preying on parental desperation was their business. Thousands of parents fell for it, but unlike most, you actually listened when I told you the school was run by sadistic motherfuckers. They probably swore I was a manipulative, lying little shit and not to believe a word out of my mouth."

"Yes." Dad glowered. "They did."

"But you saw through it and said . . ." He raised a hand. "Not today, assholes. So you're the number one dad, and that's just math."

"The worst part is, I had a bad feeling long before the broken collarbone, but I couldn't admit I'd made a mistake. God, I was so angry," he said, face reddening.

"Uh, Dad. Deep breath, 'kay?" Ozzie checked the machine next to his bed, half expecting it to start wildly beeping.

"I was mad at myself, furious with them. I thought the settlement would somehow make it better. Right some wrongs."

"You did get the place shut down. So that's something."

"I guess. But it felt so hollow. And now I know declaring victory allowed me to move on, when I should've spent time looking back." Dad exhaled. "I'm sorry. For everything. And I'm proud to be your dad. You've built a life for yourself *in spite* of me. You play Degenerate Oz, but you're not that person at all."

Ozzie smiled thinly, thinking, *The Internal Revenue Service might beg to differ.* "Aw, thanks. We're all out here doing our best." Hopefully his best would be enough. "And don't worry, Dad. I forgive you," he added, grinning now, because he meant it. "Period."

# DECEMBER

# Chapter Sixty-Nine

## Gabby

I'd never viewed birthdays as a big deal, but Sydney considered twenty-five a milestone, million-dollar check or not, and thought it deserved celebration. We could also make the event a quasi–welcome home party, she decided, even though I was only gone for two months.

"Go home, Bags," Dad had said from his hospital bed when I told him I was leaving the campaign. My heart wasn't in it, I explained, and he nodded, his expression full of understanding. "Go," he said. "Get out there and do good things."

Now, three weeks later, at seven o'clock on a Friday night, I was walking into the theater barn, which Sydney decked out with pink-and-gold streamers and handcrafted bronze butterflies attached to the walls. Finger foods were set out on long tables, and the actor who played Daddy Pig manned the bar.

"Sydney!" I said, a smile spilling across my face. "This place was a regular barn this morning. It looks incredible."

"I love shit like this. I hope you're not offended by the theme."

I peered up at the animal garlands crisscrossed overhead—monkeys and gators and lions. Flamingos, of course. "No cassowary, no problem," I said.

Scanning the room, I saw there were thirty or forty people at this party, more guests than years I'd lived. Bailey, the girl who gave me the idea to create the Collective, looked over and gave a small wave. My heart quickened. Sydney called this a welcome back, but it felt more like starting over.

"Here you go," Sydney said, handing me a Shirley Temple. "Thought it'd be fun. Whimsical."

"It's perfect," I said, and we clinked glasses. As I took a sip, something caught my attention near the door. A pair of identical figures walked through. My heart—all of my organs, maybe—leapt up into my throat.

"Diane!" I yelled, flying at her for one chaotic moment before stopping short. In front of me stood a set of twins, identical, right down to their clipped brown bobs. I knew about Diane's sister, but she lived in Canada and we'd never met, so this was freaking me out. After looking back and forth between them, I hugged the twin on the left.

"It's so good to see you," Diane said, squeezing me tight, confirming I'd guessed correctly. This woman smelled like *Diane*, like a wool sweater and Herbal Essences and a hint of that morning's perfume. "Wow. I don't think I've ever seen you so effusive."

"New year, new me," I said, stepping back. "I can't believe this is the first time I'm meeting your sister. It's so weird to see another Diane." The two even dressed alike—dark jeans, boots, and a silky "going out top," as Diane would've called it. Diane's was blue and purple, and her sister's was green, and they both had camel-colored coats. The sister was wearing hers, while Diane's was slung over an arm.

"Dawn was at your high school graduation party," Diane informed me. "But she didn't stay long."

"Oh, right! Silly me!" This explained why halfway through, I'd pulled Ozzie aside to report Diane was "trying to fuck with me" by changing clothes. We'd had a teensy bit of weed before the ceremony, so I'd chalked it up to that.

"Bill wanted me to tell you happy birthday," Diane said.

"He's sorry he couldn't be here." He was in Florida, on a golf trip, with his college buddies. "So. Do tell." She put a hand on her hip. "What's this 'new year, new me' business? What's changed?"

"Everything? Nothing?" I laughed. "Who the hell knows? Oh! I have a dog now. He's at the house. Jindos are runners, so I'm not taking any chances."

"Yes, I'm familiar with the dog. I want to hear about *you*. You've been quite MIA, my friend. Did you move to California and memory hole your past life?"

She said this jokingly, and with a smile, but her eyes hadn't come along for the ride. I glanced at Dawn, who stood there listening. They were identical, but Diane was obviously the better twin. I couldn't explain how I knew. I just did.

"I'm sorry," I said. "I wanted to call you a million times but was giving you space. It felt wrong to bother you since you didn't work for us anymore."

"It's kind of insulting that you deem our relationship nothing more than an employment arrangement," Diane said, crossing her arms. "For the record, I could've left at any time, but I stayed, even as your dad kept ratcheting down my pay."

This caught me by surprise. "He did?"

Diane nodded. "And rightly so. Who was I nannying?" She frowned. "I'm sorry about his heart attack, by the way. I'm glad he's on the mend."

As it turned out, Diane had known about the heart condition all along, which was why she'd pushed me to go to California, not because she considered meeting dos Santos so important. "I knew you wouldn't find an antidote or anything," she'd said, laughing, when she told me last week over the phone. *Oh, boy*, I thought, *wait until she hears about the Raj saga.*

"Anyway, no more ghosting, okay?" Diane said now, pulling me into a hug. "Let's keep in touch like regular friends."

It was all I wanted this whole time.

As Diane began to ask about the PBS and what dos Santos was like, a small woman walked in carrying a very large . . . poster? Whatever it was, it bonked every person within a one-foot radius.

"Is that . . ." Diane said as we all squinted. "I didn't know your sister was flying all the way out from California. What a surprise!"

# Chapter Seventy

## Talia

Maybe the prop was a bad idea. The party guests certainly thought so, given all the dirty looks. *Here's a tip . . . maybe move out of the way?* Sorry to Gabby, but theater nerds were weird. Speaking of Gabby, where was . . . ?

"I can't believe you came," Gabby said, swooping in out of nowhere, trying to hug her around the awkwardly sized gift. "For one dumb birthday. There has to be a better use of your time and money."

"It seemed like a great use of both to me."

Things had been quiet at the Ranch, with Dad's surgery, and Thanksgiving, and orders to curtail his schedule. Talia wasn't sure what would happen next. His polling numbers hadn't improved, and the coffers were draining, but he remained in it. Marston Gunn was never great at admitting defeat.

"Is that for me?" Gabby said, inspecting the present, which Talia had wrapped in shiny white paper and tied with a red bow. "So mysterious! Gimme." She put out a hand.

"Um . . ." Talia's eyes flicked around the room. In her excitement, she hadn't thought this through. "It's probably better if you open it in private?"

"Ugh! You're so difficult!" Gabby said, dragging Talia toward the door. "I'm stumped about what this could be. You're not really an arts and crafts girlie. Oh!" Her brown eyes went wide.

"Are these the HR posters you're always harassing me about? Now everyone at SHCC will be fully informed of our veterans' benefits and services, or lack thereof. Only you would give me compliance for my birthday, and I love you for it."

"Hilarious," Talia said as they stepped into the crisp December air. "I did not get you HR posters, though FYI, you are legally required to post them."

"You're the one who says this isn't a legit place of employment." Gabby spun around. "So! Can I open it now?"

Talia sighed. Part of her wanted to trash the whole plan—not the present but the *presentation*—but it was too late now. "Yeah. Go ahead," she said, cringing as Gabby untied the ribbon. "It's sort of hokey." Gabby gently picked at the corner but was taking too damn long. Talia reached over and tore off the rest in one big sheath.

With the wrapping paper now covering her feet, Gabby stared at the gift. It was one of those prop checks, made out to Oscar Gunn in the amount of four hundred thousand dollars.

"This is insane."

"The fake check was Raj's idea. So stupid!" Talia slapped a hand over her face. "Obviously I gave him actual money. This is symbolic. And I'm aware it's not really a gift for you, but when you left, you were so worried about what would happen if he didn't sell his apartment."

"Yeah," Gabby said, wincing, scratching the back of her neck. "Him telling me it'd all work out wasn't the most reassuring thing in the world."

"I know I made a big production about responsibility and lying in the bed he made, et cetera. But I had the money, and it felt so stupid. Like I was hoarding it or something."

"I can't believe it," Gabby said, her eyes a little glassy. "This is beyond generous. And you're wrong. It *is* a gift for me. But, I mean, if you're looking for something else . . ." She leveled her gaze on Talia, an impish spark in her eyes. "You could spill the tea and tell me the amount of the twenty-five-year gift."

Talia threw back her head and laughed. "Oh my God, let it go!"

"You might as well tell me since I'm not going to receive it."

"Fine." She exhaled. "One million dollars, exactly."

"I knew it!" Gabby said with a small jump. "I just knew it." She pondered this. "Not sure why I'm so excited to have made the correct wild guess about a sum of money I'll never touch, but it's extremely satisfying."

Talia smirked. "It's nice to be right. Sorry for this," she said, gesturing to the check. "Raj tried to convince me I should send one to Ozzie along with the money, but I was nervous he'd post it online. Given he's back on social media and all."

"But would the newly minted @RegenerateOz do such a thing?" Gabby lightly rolled her eyes. "He never RSVP'd for tonight. Not that regenerative after all. So, Raj. Is he mad I promised him all that money and skipped town?"

"Oh, Jesus. That was so idiotic I completely forgot. Luckily he's a rational person and was never going to take it."

"Wow. You must be really good in bed."

"GABBY!" Talia said, giving her sister a swift backhand.

"Thank you for your sacrifice," Gabby said with a bow.

"He's sorry he couldn't come, but last-minute tickets were expensive, and one of his clients had a hearing with the housing authority." *Raj.* Talia felt a flutter in her stomach saying his name. They weren't in a relationship, and he'd moved back into his apartment, but they were working together, and spending time together, and who knew what would happen down the road. For once Talia was going to sit back and see how life played out instead of worrying about every little move she did or didn't make, or the attention she was or wasn't getting from the people who were meant to love her. "Dad wanted to come, but he's not supposed to fly yet. And Ustenya stayed to make sure he's following doctor's orders."

Ustenya. Another name that made her heart swell. "You can stop the construction," Talia told her shortly after Dad returned from the hospital. There was no reason to shell out for new living quarters when volunteers were dropping left and right. Ustenya stared blankly as Talia said these things, until Talia blurted out, "I'm talking about the art studio."

"You jizz!" Ustenya barked, then laughed maniacally. "You ruined the surprise!" She wasn't building housing for volunteers. As far as Ustenya was concerned, the barn belonged to Talia, but "the next person who walked in there was going to die from a beam to the brain," and so she'd embarked upon a project to spruce up the building, and install proper lighting, and a desk. She'd also framed and hung several of Daphne's sketches and finished pieces, including one she'd literally pried out of some woman's "cold, almost dead hands." This was not a metaphor, Ustenya assured her. The old hag had since "sailed into eternal rest."

"It's a portrait of little Talia," Ustenya explained. "I knew as soon as I saw it online. You'd just done finger painting, which I find so joyful!" This was an incredibly positive way to look at it, especially coming from Ustenya, and because Talia knew the piece and always assumed it was a medieval boy toddler who'd murdered someone with his bare hands.

"Use the space for work, creativity, sleeping, whatever you want!" Ustenya had said. "But you must show some respect for the place." In the end, the art studio was both transformed and left intact. The same yet different. Exactly what Talia needed.

"Um, guys?" Sydney said, poking her head outside. "People are kind of wondering where the guest of honor is?"

"Sorry, my fault." Talia propped the fake check against the barn. "I'll bring her back to her fans." She grabbed Gabby's hand. "Where can a gal get a drink around here?" she said as they walked inside.

As she turned to find a bartender, something caught her attention on the far side of the room. It was a commotion. A bright light. A man in a white turtleneck and black pants. Loafers, no socks.

"Yo, bitches! What up?" Ozzie called out when he saw them. "Regenerate Oz is here."

Talia shook her head. "It's true what they say. The Gunn family. Charming but dysfunctional."

"*One* person," Gabby reminded her. "One person said that. And honestly?" She looked at Talia and grinned. "When it comes to personal slogans, we've definitely seen worse."

*GUNNING FOR YOU!*

# Marston Gunn ends long-shot bid for U.S. Senate seat in California

BY KYLE SPERBER, *The North County Intelligencer*

SAN DIEGO—A former media executive is ending his long-shot campaign for the vacated U.S. Senate seat in California, he announced Tuesday.

Democrat Marston Gunn said in a statement that he has been unable to raise sufficient funds to compete in the nation's most populous state against three sitting congresspeople with strong name recognition. He has also recently faced some health problems.

The former F.D. Gunn Company executive joined the contest in August, at first positioning himself as fresh blood, and later the man to solve the housing crisis. During the final weeks of his campaign, Gunn had backed off on the issue of housing affordability, specifically his vow to keep Wall Street out of the residential market.

Through the end of November, Gunn had raised approximately $4.2 million for the race. After an expected $1 million from an unspecified donor did not materialize, he ended the month with about $600,000 in the bank.

"Marston Gunn left a mark on this city and the people working for his campaign," says spokesperson Talia Gunn. "His candidacy is over, but he's inspired others to continue seeking ways to improve California and serve the public."

Ms. Gunn is referring to Rajeev Khan, the former Gunn campaign worker who recently filed paperwork to run for the open San Diego City Council seat in District 4. The seat was vacated when the prior council member, Lottie Bartholomew, assumed her new role on the San Diego Board of Supervisors. A special election to fill the seat will be held alongside the California primary on Tuesday, March 5.

Khan entered the race to actualize Gunn's abandoned plans to fix California's housing crisis, with a focus on San Diego. His approach will be "multi-pronged," starting with restrictions on permits for renovations and new build projects.

"Ideally, no new permit will be granted for construction of a single-family home until a defined number of citizens are moved off the Section 8 waiting list and placed in acceptable housing," Khan says.

He also intends to pressure Sacramento into changing single-family zoning laws.

To make it onto the March 5 ballot, Khan will need to collect 120 signatures in the district before December 14.

"That is not a problem," says Ms. Gunn, who will be working as Khan's communications director. "District 4 is ready for someone like Rajeev Khan."

As for Marston Gunn, he won't spend much time agonizing over his failed campaign.

"Someone might look at the year I've had and think, *poor bastard*," Gunn says. "I lost my company and most of my money. I ran for office but was barely part of the race. My health deteriorated. It was hard, excruciating at times, but I'm a better person, and it was worth it. It's never too late to change."

Mr. Gunn was coy about what comes next. "A new adventure," he says, though he refuses to disclose more. When asked about the potential of another family business, he grins. "I'm percolating on some ideas. Stay tuned."

★ ★ ★ ★ ★

# Acknowledgments

Unlike with my previous books, I don't need to include several pages parsing out "fact versus fiction" for the real-life characters in the novel because this time . . . there aren't any! The Gunn family's history is very loosely based on the Scripps family, but all embezzling, wild animals, and ill-fated senatorial campaigns are entirely fictional.

Because it takes over a year to write a book, compiling acknowledgments can be daunting, and never feel complete, but I'd like to specifically thank the following for all they did to bring *Darling Beasts* to the page:

My agent, Barbara, for encouraging me to write something different (and reading drafts same day!).

My amazing editor, Melanie Fried, for *letting* me write something different, and for helping to shape the narrative and characters, with never a stone left unturned.

The entire Graydon House team, including my copy editor Jennifer Stimson, publicists Justine Sha and Diana Franco, and, of course, Tara Scarcello for creating the perfect cover. The fact it includes a Jindo is a dream come true (no exaggeration).

The Gable family for providing endless inspiration. My father never oversaw a media conglomerate or ran for office, both of my parents are alive and well, and my siblings are successful, kind, and not problematic. Our dysfunction has never escalated to crimes or live animals, but being raised in a "colorful" family definitely informed this book. Thanks to Brian and Lisa for the BB gun and other stories—I love being the much older sister to a thick-as-thieves pair. Hopefully I'm not as insufferable as Talia. I love you guys!

My youngest daughter, Georgia, for acting as a second copy editor during her winter break. Thanks, Georgie Bear (sorry!), for your eagle eye and Gen Z knowledge. Go Big Green! (And Go Hokies for Paige).

My husband who *still* treats writing a book as a huge accomplishment. Thanks for being such a phenomenal dad, husband, and overall person, and for making our empty nest a million times better than I ever expected it to be.

My writer friends—especially Shilpi Gowda, Liz Fenton, Lisa Steinke, Kristina McMorris, Allison Winn Scotch, and Kim Hooper—who all keep me sane.

My friend of forty years Karen Landers for inspiring Raj's career. (Alas, no stink badgers for you!)

The bookstores and influencers who champion authors' work—you are the backbone of this industry.

Finally, thank you to the readers. Writing can be lonely and overwhelming and scary but when someone connects with a character it's everything.

# Discussion Questions

1. Gabby Gunn suffers from the fictional "Portum Bestiae Syndrome," which results in the manifestation of live animals. What do you think this syndrome represents? Why do you think the author chose to give her a fictional condition? Did your perception of PBS change throughout the book?

2. How do you think PBS shaped Gabby's personality, aside from her desire to keep "flares" from her family?

3. Many of the Gunns' problems arise from keeping secrets from one another. Which secret do you think did the most harm or caused the most hurt and confusion? Have any secrets been uncovered in your own family?

4. How does wealth and privilege shape *Darling Beasts*? Which characters most feel the impact of this? How does each one experience it differently?

5. Gabby's point of view is told in the first person, while Ozzie's and Talia's are told in third. How did this affect your reading of the novel? Why do you think the author did this?

6. What aspects to the siblings' relationship(s) could you relate to? Have you ever had a "block" or misunderstanding with a sibling that you ultimately broke through?

7. Did you gravitate toward any particular Gunn sibling? Why?

8. By the end of the novel, the inter-sibling relationships have transformed. How did each pairing (Gabby-Talia, Gabby-Ozzie, Talia–Ozzie) evolve over the course of the novel? Was there a defining catalyst that allowed them to come together, other than what happens at the end of the book, after the cocktail party?

9. What do each of Gabby, Talia, and Ozzie value in a relationship in general, and a sibling relationship in particular? Do you think the Gunns' relationships will continue to evolve when they're no longer working together under the same roof?

10. What did you think of Ustenya? How did your view of her change over the course of the novel?

11. What do you think really happened with Daphne Carter Gunn? We do not see her point of view, but what was your opinion of her? How does her story affect the overall narrative?

12. What purpose did Raj serve in the novel? What do you expect will happen to this character long-term?